MW01272975

ON A WEDNESDAY IN SEPTEMBER

Journalist und psychotherapist Stephan Niederwieser became known as an author in Germany, his home country, because of this very novel. *On a Wednesday in September* was voted Best Gay Fiction of the Year in 1998. Four novels followed, which made Niederwieser one of Germany's most-read authors in this genre. Beyond fiction, he has written many guides on gay sex, including the audience favorite *Bend Over. The Complete Guide to Anal Sex*; all have recently been translated into English.

Born in Southern Germany, he lived in Manhattan in the mid-80s and now calls Berlin his home.

More about the author: www.stephan-niederwieser.de.

Stephan Niederwieser

On a Wednesday in September

A Novel

Translated from the German by Nicholas Andrews

BRUNO GMÜNDER

1st edition

© 2012 Bruno Gmünder Verlag GmbH

Kleiststraße 23-26, D-10787 Berlin

info@brunogmuender.com

© Stephan Niederwieser

Translation from the German: Nicholas Andrews

Translation of the poem (page 317): Mitch Cohen

Cover art: Steffen Kawelke

Cover montage: © Steffen Kawelke (large photo);

© collection Albrecht Becker, Schwules Museum Berlin

(small photo on the left and back cover: soldier, around 1940)

Printed in South Korea

ISBN 978-3-86787-444-1

More about our books and authors:

www.brunogmuender.com

For my father

PROLOGUE

He marches through a gate stretched menacingly against the sky like a fist defying the enemy. Flags blaze like eternal flames; swastikas whirl gloomily in the wind. Comrades look up, wrenching their hands into Hitler salutes—blinded by his shining insignia, they squint. Above his head, squadrons of fighter jets zip past. Playfully, they form triangles and enormous circles, effortlessly melting into figures of eight, virtuous and proud as the men who fly them.

Though he's marching on gravel, he can't hear his own steps. Even later, cowering in the field, hiding his face in the dew-soaked grass, he cannot feel the tickling blades. He watches the enemy as they advance over the hill like a dark green wave. His finger decides over life and death. A single rehearsed motion and he will save them all: his comrades, his family, his fatherland. He needs only to focus, breathe calmly and wait for the right moment. Wait, breathe and focus.

"Philipp! Philipp!" His pulse raced; his muscles tensed. Terrified, his eyes widened as he caught sight of the pale, gleaming face. He wanted to jump up, stand at attention, and reach for his weapon, as they had trained him to do at the academy. There, in the glow of the flickering lamp, was his mother.

"Your father told me not to worry," she whispered agitatedly, lowering her head. She had always been tall and large, but that night she had withered away to a shadow of herself.

"You needn't be afraid," Philipp said woodenly, grasping the bedspread. It was warm and heavy; he felt safe beneath it.

They had made it clear to him that he needed to be strong. They had explained why it was necessary to defend Germany from evil forces, to regain the honor his fatherland had lost during the Great

War. And they had made it clear that everyone who was afraid was a coward, a worthless good-for-nothing.

"I'll take care of myself," he said, his stomach heaving. His hands and feet felt icier than the dream-soaked breath freezing on the window into finely veined crystals.

Snowflakes drifted down gently outside, covering the footprints of all the sons who had left in these last days. Philipp's mother set the lamp down on the night table. A piece of the wick flared up and went out. In a few hours, the rising sun would warm the cool walls of this room. Its light would break into crystals, casting playful dabs of color onto the worn floorboards. It would melt a few icicles that were clinging to the gutter, causing them to fall and split the snow, pushing into the earth like a draft notice into the heart of a mother. No, the greatest pain in a woman's life was not to give birth to a child. It was much more painful to let the child go, to see him taken by a war from which hardly anyone returned.

"This is for you!" she said, pressing a piece of flesh-warmed metal into his hand. She looked into the blue pools of his eyes, through which she had once been able to see straight into his mind. But tonight they were as veiled and gray as all the lies of this time.

Philipp studied the ring as it caught and reflected the light, penetrating the oppressive darkness of the room. Wide-eyed, he let the blanket fall, uncovering his pale torso, the deep cavity in the middle of his chest.

"It is the Ring of Lovers," his mother said, staring at Philipp as if trying to engrave his image into her memory. "I wanted to keep it until you had found the right girl. But I'm giving it to you now because..." She hesitated. Hardship and loneliness would fill the place where Philipp had once built castles out of pieces of rock, where he had once carved reeds into shrill whistling flutes. Soon his bed would be as empty as her heart. "...because it will protect you."

His eyebrows were as delicate as lines drawn in charcoal; his long lashes reflected the light, capturing it in an aureole around his eyelids.

With a warm finger, she drew three crosses on his flat brow. A tear ran down her cheek, and Philipp understood that his mother would not be standing in the door the next morning to see him off.

The floor creaked beneath her feet, the door shut with a dull thud. Philipp couldn't take his eyes off the ring, its gold bands wound like ribbons or hands clasped together. Two stones were embedded in it: a ruby and a diamond. The gold was polished, as if no one had worn it before.

He turned down the flame and put his mother's gift on his finger. It carried him away into his dreams as softly as a stone sinking into a pond: bombs falling noiselessly, tanks reducing enormous trees to sawdust beneath them, machine guns rattling in slow motion, as slow as a heart's beat. Lead raining down hotly while smiling soldiers melt into the steaming ground and Philipp crosses an open field towards a far light. An altar—and behind it, in the pews of a chapel, people whispering happily. At the end of the aisle, a bride.

"I'm getting married! I'm getting married!" his heart rejoices.

"...by the power vested in me, I now pronounce you man and wife."

Air raid sirens drone harmoniously above the ceremony, only drowned out by the priest's voice: "You may now kiss the bride" the words echo like church bells in his head and fade away. Philipp lifts the veil and kisses the firm, strong lips of a handsome soldier.

1.

By swaying a few inches to the right or left, he could make the trees seem to move: imperfections in the glass window transformed sturdy branches into breathing diaphragms. Behind him a murmur welled up.

Bernhard Moll turned to face his students. He often paused in this manner, having learned that imparting facts alone was not enough to inspire understanding. Repose was necessary, the depth of silence; this alone allowed knowledge to grow. A lesson is like an infusion of black tea, leaf fragments swirling excitedly about. It must be allowed to sit a while until the leaves coalesce, in the bottom of the pot, into images and ideas.

There were girls who had tears in their eyes when they saw their teacher standing like this. For them, these were not moments to process what they had heard, but their only opportunity to catch a glimpse behind the outer façade of this man, who often seemed far too mature.

"Good, then let's summarize. Which factors contributed to the breakdown of the Weimar Republic?" He looked around at their pale faces.

"Yes?" He pointed to a young man in the last row.

"The fear of a revolution."

"Right. What else?"

"Inflation."

"Good. Germany was suffering under enormous inflation: one dollar to four billion Marks. What else?" Bernhard Moll slowly went up to the board.

"Extreme unemployment rates. In 1930 it was more than 20 percent, with 30.000 bankruptcy proceedings on top of that."

"Exactly, and what else—very important!" He raised his index finger above his head, a caricature of himself: tall and thin, with a slight kink in his neck, like a bendable straw. Sometimes it seemed as if he would just break down, but he never did, at least not in school.

"Racist paramilitary groups and the influence of the growing national socialist party, whose member lists grew proportionally with the rise in unemployment."

It made the faculty uncomfortable that students learned more in Bernhard Moll's class than from any of his colleagues. It couldn't be because of his appearance, the conspirators all agreed on that. What was attractive about a man in his mid-thirties who still dressed, in the 90s, the way he had in his youth? His face looked creased and tired; dark curls raged on his slim head. There was no elegance to his awkward movements, his long limbs that flapped around as if they didn't belong together, his bony, much too white hands that knocked against the desks as he walked around the room or made the chalk screech across the blackboard.

His colleagues viewed these pauses as a waste of time, a breeding ground for inattentiveness, the seeds of disobedience. They didn't understand that in those moments, time stood still—time, and the world itself. They couldn't see with the eyes of fifteen-year-old girls.

Yet they had never found an opening to take a shot at him. Bernhard Moll was much too friendly and courteous, far too obliging. Besides, he seemed to carry a shield of compassion around with him, a constant pain in his eyes, a pain he himself could not name. This something pulled at the corners of his mouth, made his eyebrows slope off suddenly at the sides, and impressed a helpless dimple no bigger than the tip of a tongue above his nose. His appearance made people want to protect him, not attack him.

It was simply impossible not to like him, even if—or perhaps because—one didn't try to get to know him. And, for his students, there was another reason: there was something fundamentally *good* about him. "It's a shame that he's a teacher," a girl once said in the schoolyard, and the others had sighed in agreement.

"Is that all clear?" He turned around, looking for questions in his students' eyes. Nothing.

The sound of a scribbling pencil reached his ears. It sounded excited, purposeful, defiant. Bernhard turned to the source of the noise. "Are you filling our reflective pauses with art?"

The student shrugged as Bernhard suddenly grabbed the sheet from him, a sketch of a handsome young man with wild hair, much-too-narrow pants, and a seductive expression. Bernhard folded it and hid it behind his back without commentary.

"Or are you not interested in what we are doing?"

The student looked at him wide-eyed and turned red. "I mean, this is total garbage, isn't it?"

"Garbage?" Bernhard went to the board. "An important comment! Much obliged. So—is there any point in still thinking about all this after sixty years have gone by?" He let the caricature fall onto his own desk, watching it glide over his papers.

"No," piped up a dry voice from the third row. The students laughed. The boy beamed at him defiantly.

"Stand up!" he said. "Come on, stand up!"

The student followed his command hesitantly.

"Close your eyes!"

The boy didn't understand. Bernhard went up to him and placed his hand over his eyes.

"Take a few steps, and tell me what you notice."

The student took two steps. "Nothing. What am I supposed to notice?"

"What do you feel under your feet? What do you hear?"

"Linoleum."

"Okay. Now come up to the blackboard."

Bernhard looked for something on the evenly green surface. "Here, right here." He pointed to a particular spot. "What do you see here?"

"A blackboard." He turned proudly around to his fellow students, who laughed.

"Clever, really clever." Bernhard drew a circle with chalk. "What do you see inside this circle?"

"Green."

"Good, very good."

He soaked the sponge with water and pressed it against the board for a moment, then took it away again.

"What do you see now?"

"A wet blackboard."

Bernhard grabbed him by the neck and pushed his face up closer to the blackboard.

"And now?"

The student hesitated for a moment, the color draining from his face. He saw that Bernhard was serious.

"I see…I see…the wood bulging out underneath the surface."

"Thank you." Bernhard pushed him back to his seat. Then he wandered, deep in thought, between desks defaced with inky scribbles and chairs stuck with chewing gum. His thoughtful steps echoed under the high ceiling.

"Linoleum doesn't yield. It doesn't creak either, unless…?"

"There's a layer of wood underneath it."

"Bingo! What we see is an unwashed linoleum floor, but something very different is hidden beneath it. It's the same with the blackboard. We see a consistently green surface. A little bit of water, and the wood beneath it becomes visible. Understand?"

A few heads nodded back at him, but there were still question marks on most of the faces.

"What I want to say is that the past is often much closer to us than we perceive it to be."

He went slowly around the room. Another one of those timeless pauses arose. The entire classroom seemed to sink into stillness; the floor creaked beneath his feet.

"Consider our economic situation. Some circumstances that we're coping with today were also present before the war: growing unemployment, cutbacks to the welfare state, racism, conservative influences, very,

very conservative influences even. Does that mean we're heading towards a Fourth Reich?" He stood still and looked out over the entire class.

"Just say what you think. What is your opinion on this?"

The students looked down at their books, embarrassed; a few girls turned to face him expectantly. It was an unreasonable question; that became clear to him as his eyes ranged through the classroom, lingering on the posters advertising jeans, on the close-up photos of stars with seductively distant expressions. What did a fifteen-year old care if the Third Reich returned, if his favorite actor was lovesick, or is his favorite soccer player had just missed a penalty shot?

"No," one of the boys said, just to break the silence.

A glimmer of hope flashed over Bernhard's face. "Now explain to me why not."

"No idea. Maybe because people don't even trust our chancellor. Who could become as powerful as Hitler?"

"Okay. Who has another idea?"

"I mean, maybe it hasn't gotten bad enough yet. In a few years, if things just keep getting worse, and the issue of political asylum seekers becomes correspondingly more heated…"

"Yeah, and then all it would take is for a minority to be seemingly better off than the majority…" the girl sitting next to him finished.

"…and there would be quite a lot of fuel. Well reasoned." Bernhard took a long pause.

"Is that really going to happen?" one of the students asked, his eyes opened wide in fear.

"Is it?" Bernhard took a few steps. "I wasn't trying to predict the future with that question, I'm not a prophet. But I wanted to show you that it's necessary to understand the past in order to get an idea of where we are heading. Only when we know where we're coming from can we know where we're going."

"And what about the war in Yugoslavia?" someone answered defiantly. "We knew that thousands of Muslims were executed. That was no different from how it was with Jews back then. But nevertheless nobody cared about it."

"Your objection only seems to be correct," Bernhard answered, "but when it comes to understanding the past, the question is always who is using the information and how. For example, if you explain how robberies are committed, people can protect themselves better. At the same time you're giving potential crooks tried and tested instructions. Does that mean that it's better to keep quiet about the truth?" Bernhard looked questioningly at his students. Some of them murmured, some of them shrugged their shoulders, and some had already closed their books.

"Do you understand what I'm trying to say?" He looked at the clock: thirteen minutes to one. This discussion was not going to be wrapped up in three minutes.

"I just wanted to say one thing: if you don't concern yourself with the past, you are robbing yourself of the chance to understand the present." He looked around. Frowns.

"When we have the chance, we should follow up on this," he said. "Those are my closing words before vacation. I hope you'll get lots of presents, a good chance to relax, and that no one comes back from a ski trip with broken bones!"

The students jumped up, a few crumpled balls of paper flew through the room, a girl fell into her boyfriend's arms, then the room emptied quickly.

Two girls approached Bernhard hesitantly. One of them held a lavishly wrapped package in her hands. Bernhard looked up, saw the girl, saw the gift, and turned his head back to his desk.

"For you," she said, turning red, and held out the present to him.

"That is very nice—and entirely unnecessary." Bernhard smiled, but he was uncomfortable. The two girls stood stock still in front of him. "Have a nice vacation," he said and turned to his desk again. But their yearning eyes stayed fixed on him. He looked at them again and nodded. "Don't forget the assignments for January. Now be on your way."

They sauntered off; Bernhard watched them go. As soon as he was alone, he sat down on his desk and picked up the drawing. An echo of his past overtook him, filling him with memories that he had long since repressed. Pain caused a shiver to run through his skin. He hoped this young man would be spared all that.

Bernhard raised his eyebrows high, deepening the dimple above his nose. Then he stuffed his papers in a battered leather satchel, stuck the present under his arm and plunged into the chaos of students in the corridor.

"You ready for the Christmas party in the faculty lounge tonight?" The question caught him on his way into the main building. It sounded familiar, friendly and inviting, but Bernhard grew stiff. He turned around and looked into the perky eyes of a small, dainty woman. Her fire-red hair lay curled up like a sleeping cat on her too-small head. She was carrying a pile of books in her arms. To balance herself, she was leaning back from the hips.

"Ruth!" He looked around and whispered. "I...um...I won't be able to make it."

They had known each other since they were students. There was a time when people had referred to them as inseparable, and their friends back then had assumed they would end up getting married. But that was long ago.

"Now why do I have the feeling you don't want to tell me why you're not coming?"

She lowered her long lashes against the harsh sunlight.

Bernhard looked down at the ground.

"Whatever it is," she said, "At some point I'll discover your secret."

He lifted his head; his injured smile awoke her protective instincts. She leaned over and held out her cheek.

"Maybe you'll have time for a cup of tea over vacation."

"Of course," he said much too quickly. "I'm going to see my family in Frankfurt tomorrow, but I'll be back by Monday at the latest."

"Call me!"

Bernhard gave her a brief kiss. Then Ruth moved away. Her pointed boots clacked off down the hallway, then she disappeared in the shadows of the classroom doors.

An aroma of citrus reached his nostrils. A young man sitting across from Bernhard in the tram was peeling an orange. His eyes were large and alert, his face smooth and shockingly pale. He was perhaps twenty or twenty-two, in any case much too erotic for his age. An aura of warm physicality surrounded him, an aura of bodies wrestling in twisted sheets. His lips were dangerously moist. And when he lifted his lips from the sweet fruit and saw Bernhard, he opened his mouth—only a small gap wide, but Bernhard was afraid it would swallow him up. He grasped his briefcase, but he needed more support, so he stood up and grabbed one of the poles. He started to sweat. A baby in a stroller saw his face and frowned. Bernhard started laughing; the child chuckled and clapped its hands. Then it contorted its face, as if it were trying to imitate Bernhard's expression. Now it was Bernhard's turn to chuckle.

"Next stop, Karlsplatz Stachus." He went down the steps into the cold, then turned around and helped the young woman struggling with her stroller. A quick pull, a smile, a nod. The older woman, who must have been her mother, said: "Now isn't that man friendly? Look how helpful he is." And then, to him: "Thank you, sir. Nowadays, one seldom encounters men like you." Bernhard lowered his head and moved away quickly.

Pulling his bordeaux-red knitted cap with its earflaps and pompom down over his face, he walked along the crowded pedestrian mall towards Marienplatz. The air was heavy with cinnamon and cloves; it promised so much, and contained so little.

Reaching the Christkindl market, Bernhard roamed among stalls selling porcelain replicas of half-timbered houses: made in China, of course. There were thick Bavarian stockings from Taiwan, mulled wine without the wine, and small hand-made reverse glass paintings, winter scenes of Filipino craftsmanship.

Bernhard looked up at the hundreds of branches covered with lamps spread around the broad trunk of the Christmas tree like a skirt. He saw that the figurines and the tips of the city hall's towers were covered with snow like a gingerbread house caked with icing and for the first time this year, Bernhard felt like it was actually Christmas. He could sense it, he could smell it, he could taste it. Comfortable evenings by the fire, good food, heavy aromas and a stillness that contained far more than the mere absence of noise. For a short moment his work slipped away from him, peace spread through his head like an impenetrable blanket of snow, a white vastness settled in place of the raging din of students. Freedom.

He stood still, his boots sunk deep in the snow. He looked up on the statue of the Virgin Mary, which glimmered strangely. People jostled against him constantly in passing, but he felt the tension of the past few days fall away nevertheless. He breathed in peace.

Then he heard a scream. A man lay on the ground, twitching, while a woman kneeled next to him, crying, and everything was suddenly changed. The sweet air became heavy and thick, much too thick to fill the tiny sacs of a lung. The vastness of Bernhard's thoughts shrank into a space scarcely wider than a needle's eye. Panic mingled with the Christmas carols, immobile observers breathed deep as if their own hearts were threatening to stop.

"Everything can change so quickly," he heard a voice say. He turned around. An old woman with a bent back, carrying heavy plastic bags, chewed the words from her toothless mouth. "No one knows what the Lord has in mind for us."

Bernhard didn't notice how cold it had become until he arrived home. His apartment was damp; thick drops of condensation on the windows muddied the waning daylight. He laid his hand on the radiator: cold. He must have forgotten to turn it on. The thermostat said 56 degrees. He put down the present, placed his briefcase on the chair, since there was no more room on his desk, fished out his student's drawing and pinned it to the corkboard already overflowing with pieces of paper. Then he swept the small snowflakes, which had melted to drops of water, from his coat and hung it on the door to the living room.

He set the teakettle on the gas stove and turned it on. In the cupboard, he found a cup of instant soup; on the back of an envelope from the IRS he put together a small list of things not to forget when he went to visit his family: toothbrush, underwear, sleeping bag. Where was it, actually? Bernhard looked in the storeroom, in his dresser, behind his books. By his coat rack he found his suitcase, but not the sleeping bag. He looked in the dresser.

No sleeping bag, but the teakettle was whistling. He poured out his soup and scribbled more things on his list: aspirin, gifts, book: *The Thirty Years' War.*

He sipped his soup. Bernhard had always intended to write up a packing list on his computer. Then he remembered. He turned on the computer and entered the keyword "sleeping bag" in the search field. The database window opened, and there it was: *On the shelf above the door.* He retrieved it and laid it down next to his travelling bag, then turned back to his lunch. By the time he sat down at his desk around three o'clock, the thermostat had risen to 76, and the windowpanes were still covered, though now with fat drops of water.

Books about World War II were piled against the walls: teaching materials for the months to come. He had been meaning to prepare for weeks, but kept putting it off. He turned the books with their backs facing the wall, so their titles wouldn't be staring at him any longer, pushed some materials to the side and took down the math assignments for 11A from the shelf. He switched on the lamp on the writing desk and looked over the first exercises.

Bernhard loved math. He loved numbers, their indisputable clarity. They weren't susceptible to influence; rather, they were subject to exact laws, and above all they were predictable. They could be added and subtracted, multiplied, or their wonderful roots could be extracted, and everywhere, whether in the thin air over the summits of the Himalayas or in the humid, steaming heat of the jungle, whether on a bullet train or two miles below sea level, the result would always be the same. One and one were two, that was the way it was. At least most of the time.

History was similar, or at least that was what he had assumed when he began studying. It was in the past, it couldn't be altered anymore, so it must be predictable. However, as he had learned over the years, a diary or a new statement from a witness could change everything, and history books had to be rewritten—or at least, they should be. This threw the whole idea of predictability out the window. If, as had often happened, a single typo could turn history upside down, how did history react to conscious manipulation, to the suppression of information? Entire generations lived believing in false realities. They assumed events to be factual that had never happened the way they thought. And based on these false representations, they made decisions for the future. If they were ever to find out the truth, worlds would collide.

Weariness overcame him, and Bernhard stood up and went to lie down on the couch of his 180-square feet study-living-dining-guest-room. He wanted to calm down for a while before he plunged into the evening's adventures.

He reached for the catalog for the Rubens retrospective. He had used to study history books in every moment of his free time. But when it became clear to him that what was written in them was only one view of reality, he wanted to read everything and learn everything: the more one knew, the more one understood—or so he believed back then. As time went by, he had learned that it was sometimes better to just forget the past.

2.

The sky was clear and cloudless, full of stars, as if someone had attempted to paint over wax wallpaper with black paint. Slowly, Bernhard's eyes became accustomed to the dark. A shooting star burst across the sky, then another, and another one farther to the left. For a moment it seemed to him as if the whole Milky Way were about to collapse.

Two arms slipped around Bernhard's stomach, and hot breath swirled around his ear.

"What are you pondering about, my little professor?"

"About the void," Bernhard whispered, leaning his head back on the other man's shoulder. "And what it means when you see three shooting stars in a row."

"Three? That means you have to think hard what to wish for. Because it will definitely come true."

They stood for a while listening to the stillness, the floorboards creaking beneath their swaying bodies.

"So what did you wish for?" Edvard asked softly.

"I'm not allowed to say, otherwise it won't come true."

Bernhard turned around. The night cast a blue glow on Edvard's face, which was clean, radiant and summery, as if it were full of colorful blossoms and the delicate smell of roses. A man much too beautiful to be real.

Bernhard stroked his short blond hair and held him by the neck. Edvard pressed against him. Every time they embraced, Bernhard had the feeling of merging with him a bit more.

"We've still got a few things to do." Edvard gave him a quick kiss. "Our guests are coming soon." Then he went back into the kitchen.

Bernhard watched as his lover strode into the hall: black, skin-tight jeans, thick-soled boots, a white satin shirt that hung out a bit on the left side over his studded belt. Bernhard was always touched when Edvard tried to seem casual for him, because it never really worked. His jeans were ironed; not a wrinkle in his shirt.

Although Edvard was rather petite, Bernhard often compared him to Obelix, who, having drunk a magic potion, couldn't judge his own powers, or rather: who assumed everyone else possessed the same energy as he did. On the other hand, Bernhard often seemed like Obelix' little dog Idefix: much too small, constantly afraid of being trampled. Who could keep up with so much imagination, euphoria, ecstasy, desire, sadness, compassion and love?

"Are you dreaming?"

Edvard stood like a silhouette in the brightly lit doorframe. Only the thin halo of light around his hair outlined him. His hand reached into the room and flipped the light switch.

"I never dream!" Bernhard responded, and pushed himself away from the windowsill.

At the clearance sale of the old airport Edvard had won a big neon sign in an auction. It said *Riem* in large black letters, with an arrow pointing towards the sky. After having an acrylic sheet mounted on it, he used it as a bar. Bernhard pushed the bar against the wall and plugged it in. The neon tubes flickered, then yellow light streamed out, offset by a harsh green glare that transformed the room into a Martian landscape.

"Can I put the *magic* dresser in the bedroom?" Bernhard began to lift the piece of former child's furniture, but Edvard pushed him to away with dishwater-soaked hands.

"No!" he called. "Don't touch it!"

The drawers were bursting with tarot cards, incense sticks, lotus seeds, perfumed oils, Indian medicine cards and other spiritual crap, as Bernhard called it. For Edvard it was holy.

"But if you keep it there, everyone will mess around with it."

Edvard laid his hand on it protectively. "You think so? All right. But be careful."

They lifted it and brought it into the bedroom. There, Edvard straightened the Celtic runes on the silk handkerchief that lay on top of it.

"Thank you!" He gave Bernhard a kiss, then looked around the living room. "Take the lamp from the bedroom and put it near the window so it's not so gloomy when you turn off the ceiling light." Then he disappeared into the kitchen. "And when you've got that taken care of, you could put these lilies on the bar."

Bernhard stepped out into the long hall. Seven doors led to the bedroom, study, guest room, living room, kitchen, bathroom and stairwell. 3.750 square feet, if you counted the terrace as well. Bernhard still got lost in these rooms, he even had trouble in his own 650 square feet. Edvard might have been a head shorter than him but he needed five times as much space—for his aura, as he said. But it was probably more for his expansive emotional world, which would have felt restricted in the Sahara Desert.

Edvard rinsed champagne glasses with hot water, cleaning off the dreaded water stains with a towel made of Irish silk. Bernhard leaned against the doorframe, observing how meticulously he worked. This tidiness, this urge for perfection, for a superficial luster, was entirely foreign to him. But deep down Edvard was a wild bird, greedy as a predator, with cat's paws. Perhaps it was this tidiness itself that kept him fenced in. It gave him a frame, a cage to run wild in.

He often thought about his lover, who lived in an entirely different word. For Bernhard he was a freely floating hot air balloon, and his love was the anchor Edvard could use to bind himself to him. But sometimes he escaped him, as he did now. Bernhard was standing less than three feet from him; he would only have had to reach out his hand to feel his warmth, his pulse, the storm of life that whirled around him like a cyclone. Nonetheless, Bernhard felt nothing but incredible desire.

The doorbell rang.

Birgit was sturdy and round. A black cape lay on her shoulders like an eagle's wings, her gray, brown and black streaked hair was strewn with snowflakes, dripping down onto her warm face.

"Well, my darlings!" she greeted both of them, handing Edvard a mysterious package. "For both of you," she said, pressing him tightly to her generous bosom.

She was almost seventy-five, but her face radiated the curiosity and alertness of a twenty-year old. Bernhard stretched out his hand to Edvard's private oracle, whose deliberate nods were a necessary part of all Edvard's major decisions.

"Well, well, well now. Surely you can give your old friend a kiss." She held her cheek out to him, clapping him on the shoulder. "That's better." Then she looked at him with her deep, still eyes. "Congratulations. Two hundred and twenty-two days with this powder keg. Not easy." She made a tragic pause and drew breath. "But don't think you're in the clear. You still have some things to learn. And if you're not careful…" She tapped his chest with a gnarled finger and left him standing.

Bernhard understood little of what she said. But that was nothing new. Unlike Edvard, he had little use for this esoteric drivel. He didn't believe in reincarnation, UFOs or unredeemed souls. Tarot cards, pendulums and astrology were nothing but hocus pocus to him, with a good splash of escapism mixed in.

"You're early, Birgit. And everything else is late," Edvard explained, pointing to the empty table. "The catering team is stuck in traffic."

She took his head and pressed it against her cushioned shoulder to comfort him. Then the doorbell rang again; Bernhard opened the door.

"We're terribly sorry, Mr. Bornheimer," said a charming young man in a white suit, holding out a bottle of champagne to Bernhard. "The streets are smooth as glass, traffic is at a standstill. This bottle is on us, of course. I hope we're not too late."

"Much too late," bleated Birgit. "I'm already starving to death."

The young man looked deflated.

Edvard escaped from Brigit's grasp: "Just joking."

Bernhard gave him the bottle. Then large silver platters with pastries, salad and various bread-rolls were brought past him, covered by a fog of cold winter air. They placed the dishes on the long dinner table, one of the many pièces de resistance in Edvard's private collection of unusual antiques: a breakfast table from an English monastery, dating back to the 14th century.

"You promised to get something simple. This must have cost a fortune."

"Don't worry about it." Edvard squeezed his lover's arm. "I'll take care of it."

"But Edvard. This was supposed to be *our* party."

"Of course!" He stroked Bernhard's forehead and opened the door, which had just rung again.

A whole flood of guests surged in; Edvard covered their frosty foreheads with kisses.

"You didn't need to do this," he said, holding a large packet up high.

"Open it and you'll see how badly you needed it!" Some of Edvard's former lovers enjoyed embarrassing him with their irreverence. Alfred was one of them. Bernhard preferred to avoid him, so he slipped out into the kitchen.

Excitedly, Edvard tore off the wrapping paper: a photograph of a young sailor in the bushes, and an enviable erection covering his face in semen.

"Oooooh!" Edvard squealed, laying a hand flat on his chest. "A real Pierre et Gilles! I can't believe it. What have you done? This needs to go in a special place." He looked around the walls. "There, above the dinner table. That would be wonderful," he giggled.

Bernhard, drawn by the laughter, came from the kitchen carrying a tray. "Or maybe not," Edvard said and put the picture down facing the wall.

Bernhard passed champagne around, the first glasses rang.

"Music. Where is the music?" Seconds later, Barbra's voice was resounding from the speakers.

Bernhard opened the door for more guests. Jeans, striped shirts and light brown Doc Marten's. As if cut from a mold, Bernhard thought, interchangeable, like thousands of others in this city. He hugged both of them, friendly but cool.

They filled the apartment slowly, and it grew warm. The floor sighed under so many feet. Edvard had invited a mishmash of people, lots of the kind that heteros typically branded as gay: the owner of a nail salon, whom they called Lipstick, the *asparagus queen*, who delivered asparagus to the markets in the spring, florists, dancers, actors, kindergarten teachers and the like.

Bernhard retreated between two tall bookshelves and observed them all. He had known many of them for months. He knew what films made them cry, what excited them, the way their apartments were decorated and what party they would vote for in the next election. Nevertheless, they remained foreign to him.

Edvard jumped among them like a bee from one bloom to the next; parties were the honey of his life.

"That face over there, is that an ex too?" He looked at the young man who wore his shirt open down to his pierced belly button.

But before he could open his mouth, another man answered for him. "You expect him to remember faces? Edvard only knows most of the guys here by their dicks."

"Good thing for me. He definitely won't forget mine," the first one said.

"Right. Weren't you the one who couldn't get it up?" Edvard asked with a frown, and all three of them laughed.

"But come on, you're not serious about Bernhard, are you?"

"Why not?" asked Edvard. His voice sounded annoyed.

"Well, you've never slept with the same guy twice. And now someone like *her*?"

"You're exaggerating," the other one clarified. "He did it three times with me."

"Only because you had tied me to your bed," Edvard joked.

"I can't imagine it otherwise. Anyone would sleep with him more than once has either never seen a real dick, is homeless, or already dead," one of them said to the other. Edvard laughed.

"Oh, how very witty. I didn't know an old frump like you could even form a sentence you haven't read on a bathroom wall somewhere."

"Come on, girls. Don't start squabbling about Bernhard. I'm very serious about him and there's nothing to be done about that. So that's that!"

"Congratulations." Gerhard shook Bernhard's hand.

"Thank you." Bernhard clinked his glass against his.

"You should consider yourself fortunate. Other than you guys, every relationship I know is in crisis. Most of them haven't even been together as long as you two."

"How does it feel to be the lucky one?" Gabi clinked his glass as well.

She was expecting something like "happy," "content," or "fantastic," but Bernhard answered: "two hundred and twenty-two days aren't exactly eternity, are they?"

"I'm ready for another round!" She waved her empty glass and entered the party again with Gerhard on her arm.

"Awesome vibe," said Florian.

"Yeah, I guess."

"I think it's great that you're sticking together like that."

Bernhard looked past him at his lover. Their glances met. Edvard paused briefly on the way to his next conversation partner, holding Bernhard's eyes captive. They were shy, open, but like a camera lens they were ready to close up any moment. No one, not even Bernhard himself, knew what would happen then.

"You're really a dream couple, you know?"

"There's no such thing as dream couples, Florian. If a relationship works, it's only because you want it to. Dreams are random, unpredictable. And if you try to grasp them, they slip away. You can only find footing in reality."

"I guess you're not a born romantic," Florian said, disappointed.

"Don't be so sure." Edvard had joined them. "Bernhard is unbelievably romantic. He just doesn't like to admit it."

"No, I'm not. I'm a realist. I don't think anything of dreams."

"Yes, Mr. Einstein," Gabi joked, returning with a full glass.

"Einstein was the purest dreamer. He came up with his theory of relativity while he was sitting in front of a blazing fire in the hearth. What's more romantic than that?"

"I never claimed I was Einstein." Bernhard's pupils contracted. "I just don't think much of dreams. I don't dream, I've never dreamed, and I don't want to either."

Edvard hung on his boyfriend's neck, marveling at him. If he weren't already his, he would have fallen in love that very moment.

"Look at those lovebirds," Gabi chirped.

Bernhard pulled his head from his lover's clutches. "I'll go open another bottle."

"He still gets a bit embarrassed when other people are around," Edvard whispered, looking after him yearningly.

"You don't find him a bit aloof?" Gabi asked. Edvard's face showed that he did not like the question at all.

"He's so wonderful, my little professor."

"He doesn't have much imagination," Florian asserted.

The music broke off, and Heiner's voice rang out for attention. "Time for presents!"

Ursl dragged a big silver package down off the coat rack.

"How did you smuggle that into my apartment?" Edvard wanted to know.

She lifted her finger to her lips and pointed to the pink ribbon holding it together. "It's from all of us. May your love last forever."

Edvard's eyes grew moist. He threw himself about her neck and blew kisses to the others. Then he set about opening the package. As soon as he had taken off the ribbon and pushed the paper aside, an over six-foot tall rubber man was catapulted out of the box. He was equipped with every male attribute, truly every one, and nothing done by half measures.

"Big Jim, large as life! I can't believe it. You're so sweet. But where…?"

"He made it." Ursl pulled Harald by the hand up to the front.

"Custom-built," he said, and blinked shyly, though radiating pride.

"A true masterpiece," Edvard felt the doll's smooth skin. "Who was the model for him?"

"His name is Georg," Harald admitted, growing red.

Bernhard bent over the box and tried to figure out how to inflate the doll. "The mechanism is really simple," Harald boasted. "Very simple."

Edvard was overwhelmed. "I'm so grateful. You are my darlings." He lifted the glass.

"To the two of you," his friends answered in chorus, while their glasses clinked hollowly. "To long, intense love." "To lots of children." "To a happy life."

"Sweet," Edvard said. "I'm glad you all took the time so close to Christmas. You're just wonderful."

Bernhard sunk his head. Now it was his turn to say something, but what? "To you all!" he said drily.

All eyes were on the two of them. Edvard, visibly moved, reached for Bernhard's hand.

"My dears," he began with a broken voice. He flourished his champagne glass to ensure everyone's attention. "My dears. I would like to seize this opportunity to tell you all something. Today Jupiter, Ruler of Happiness, reached his highest point in our relationship horoscope. That's why I'd like you all to be here, our family gathered together…" he put down his glass and pulled a small black box from his pants pocket, "…when I propose to my lover," and put a ring on Bernhard's finger.

Suddenly it was very quiet, so quiet that Bernhard heard the blood rush in his ears. He looked at the piece of jewelry: a diamond and a ruby, held in two golden hands. The ring shone brightly, but there was something dark and magical about it. Heat radiated from it, as if all the light in the city were concentrated within it.

Bernhard vibrated. Suddenly there was something light in his chest, an unknown warmth. His eyes burned. As he rubbed them, he noticed they had grown moist. He would have liked to hug someone, but at the same time he wanted to disappear.

Their friends' faces looked at him expectantly. He needed to react somehow, but he couldn't think of anything. So he gave Edvard a shy kiss.

A tear rolled down Willi's cheek, Uli and Dieter reached for each other's hands and Florian began to rummage around for his handkerchief. Within this impassioned atmosphere, Birgit stood still, holding her hands clasped in front of her chest. Her eyes were large and deep.

The glasses clinked again, somewhat more lightly this time. Andreas demanded: "A waltz! A waltz!" and the guests clapped encouragingly. Ursl put on a wedding waltz, and groom and groom began to dance.

"Say something," Edvard begged, but Bernhard shook his head. "Do you like it?" Bernhard nodded.

Edvard spun him around, Bernhard missed a step and stumbled.

"You're really pale. Are you all right?"

"I'm dizzy. Maybe I drank too much."

Edvard lead his lover past dancing couples and giggling guests into the bedroom. Bernhard felt as if they were staring at him.

"What's wrong?"

Bernhard's stomach cramped, his throat felt tight, something tugged at his chest. And that ring. It glowed so warmly that he was afraid it would burn him. His knees gave out; he sat on the edge of the bed. Edvard stood before him and drew Bernhard's head to his narrow, bony thighs.

"I'm afraid," whispered Bernhard.

"Afraid? Of what?"

"I don't know." He clasped Edvard's thighs, pulling him closer. What were these feelings? Where did they come from? "Hold me!"

"Don't be afraid. I'm here with you," Edvard whispered, giving him a kiss.

Bernhard wrapped himself closer around his boyfriend, clasping him tightly, as if he were in danger of losing Edvard forever.

Edvard snuggled up against him. His breath quickened. He pulled his lover's sweater over his head. On the surface, Bernhard always seemed so stiff and hard, as if he were surrounded by a wall. No one would have believed what he was hiding under his old-fashioned clothes: a chest as gentle and fragile as dragonfly wings and skin as soft and smooth as a calm ocean, overgrown with fine, light hair.

They fell back on the bed. Edvard lay on his boyfriend; his heart began to gallop. Blood streamed through his body, and within seconds his pants began to tent. He wanted Bernhard, he wanted him here and now.

Swiftly and eagerly, he opened Bernhard's belt; Bernhard submitted, and was naked in no time. While Bernhard's eyes stared at the ceiling, Edvard grasped greedily at his flesh. Then Bernhard held his breath.

"Bernhard? Bernhard!"

A black cloud formed in the room. It smelled musty. Bernhard's hair stood on end, his eyes opened wide. Horror rose up inside him. An icy shudder made him jump up and look for his clothes.

"Hey, what's wrong?"

Frantically, he put on his pants and sweater, not answering. Edvard leapt after him, embraced him, looking into his distraught face. Bernhard's eyes were full of panic—and something else, something unrelenting… like hatred.

"Bernhard!" called Edvard. These eyes made him afraid. He let go of him, terrified.

Bernhard ran out; the door to the living room slammed, and Edvard heard the guests grow quiet. He stood there, beaten down. Since the day that strange man had sold him the ring, he had been convinced it would seal their relationship more tightly. And Jupiter reigned over this party, he brought happiness, not discord and fear. Something was going wrong here. But what?

"He has a bad headache. He needs a little peace and quiet," Edvard explained, smiling as much as he could, when Birgit popped her head around the door.

"Trouble in the air?" Andreas asked over her shoulder. Someone pulled him on the arm and hissed: "Just shut up, you awful gossip!"

"The young couple just needs to sow a few wild oats," another guy said.

Birgit laid a fleshy hand on Edvard's arm. Heiner sat next to him on the bed, and Birgit retreated. "Must be a really bad headache?"

"You want to say you told me so. You can spare yourself the trouble," Edvard said resignedly.

"Would I ever do such a thing to you, darling?" Heiner fluttered his eyelids and lowered his head to his chest in shame.

Edvard lifted his head wearily. His eyes were dull, the gleam of his white-blond hair was extinguished. He couldn't even laugh anymore.

"Come on, have a drink, then explain to me again what you see in this guy." He poured out a large glass of vodka and held it under Edvard's nose.

Edvard took the glass and placed it on the nightstand. "You've never tried to see the person behind the disheveled hair."

"That's not what I'm talking about at all. It just seems to me that at some point or other, your math teacher got rid of his emotions. Or do you not find him a bit stiff?"

"He's not stiff. He just doesn't feel the need to rub other people's noses in his feelings."

"Would it be rubbing anyone's nose in them to smile at his friends every now and then?"

Edvard looked into the eyes of the man across from him.

"He doesn't even go out to bars."

"There are other reasons for that."

"Yeah? What then?"

"Bernhard doesn't care for organized identity."

"Oh, that sounds lovely! Like organized crime."

"Nonsense! He just doesn't like queens, that's understandable."

"Look who's talking now! Do I need to remind you of your performances as Sister Edith?"

"Oh come on, that was something else."

"Yeah, your nun striptease set off what may very well be the biggest orgy in the history of Munich."

"That was just a bit of fun." Edvard took a sip of vodka. His eyes grew wide, he swallowed loudly and sat down.

"In my day, this sort of thing wouldn't have happened," Heiner said, looking out the window. "Today anyone can turn gay. That's the one thing that liberation has brought us." He shook his head.

Edvard ignored his friend's ironic commentary. "When I was a kid I always felt that I had a brother my parents were hiding from me. I was quite certain of it. Then when I saw Bernhard for the first time, I was convinced it was him. We searched for one another for thirty-five years. Suddenly my life was complete. There was nothing missing anymore, do you understand?"

"You're not exactly identical twins!"

"Bernhard has very special qualities: he is intelligent, he doesn't value all that insincere consumer-speak. He knows what's going on in the world."

"You're not trying to say he's got both feet on the ground?"

"All right. He's an absent-minded professor. But if you really want to know, that makes him more loveable to me."

Heiner lifted his eyebrows.

"After all, we've been together seven months. Who in our group can match that?"

"It's not about setting records."

Edvard looked Heiner in the eyes for a long time before saying: "I want a serious relationship. I'm sick of waking up in a new bed every morning."

"The question is, have you picked the right one?" Heiner asked.

Edvard stared at him. "What are you trying to say?"

"I'm trying to say that there are people who split up after thirty years of marriage, after fifty even. Seven months, what's that?"

"Seven months are nothing. You're right about that. But the fact that we met is no coincidence, I know it. That's why I won't give up."

"What are you going to do?"

Edvard didn't answer.

"Hello? Is anyone in there?" Heiner tapped him on the forehead.

Edvard turned to him: "I'm going to woo my prince back."

3.

Roswitha hardly dared to breathe. In sleep, his angular lower jaw relaxed, his narrow lips swelling to fleshy hills beneath his black mustache. Her hand moved, trembling, over to his chest again and again, but each time she felt the wiry hair on his body, her hand pulled back. Then she would lie on her back and stare at the dark ceiling, hoping to finally find sleep. But every time she shut her eyes, she would open them again right away, turning her head towards him to make sure he was still there. This was how it had been for weeks.

Four fifty-two. Eight minutes to five. Her feet groped for her pink slippers. She got up, her dressing gown trailing behind her like a cloud of perfume. Fred remained in bed, lying as if tossed there. He had been tossing and turning under the blanket. His ass lay free, round and hard, tugging at her desire. If she covered him up, she would be able to touch him again. But she hesitated, and didn't do it in the end. Instead she steered herself into the kitchen, where she carried out her morning rituals, almost without a sound: putting water in the coffee machine, a filter, coffee powder. It had all been rehearsed a thousand times. She didn't need to think about it at all. Wipe off the yellow tablecloth, put out the brown earthenware plates, take knives and coffee spoons out of the drawer: but for the past four weeks she had been doing this for two, not just for herself alone. It was a ceremony she conducted as if in a trance.

Then she turned on the shower, hung her nightshirt on the door next to his bathrobe, brushed her hair and put a shower cap over it. The neon light shining off the bright green tiles made her face look pale, casting a black shadow on her deep eye sockets. She looked in the mirror: a few more wrinkles.

In the shower she lathered herself up with musk gel, picked up the loofah, which hung from a hook in the shape of a splayed foot, and scrubbed her body. Routines made life simpler; she had learned this from her mother. She rarely deviated from them, not even on weekends. But today she desperately needed something new. Something absolutely had to change. She dried herself off and slipped into her underwear. She hesitated with her sweater. A winter pattern of silver beads on black angora? No!

The machine had stopped bubbling. Roswitha set the sweater down on the table, poured some of the coffee into a mug, and the rest into a beige thermos patterned with flowers. With a dash of condensed milk, she lightened the liquid up, pulled the wool curtain aside and looked out. Snow. Snow again. Flakes as large as playing cards pranced towards the ground, where unrelenting car tires pressed them together into hard sheets. Today, it would take her longer to get to the other end of the city.

This early in the morning, it was usually still quiet in their building. A drain gurgled, a flushing toilet sent water gushing through the pipes. Heels clacked down the dark-grey marble stairs, the door to the building fell shut.

Roswitha rinsed and dried the mug in the sink, then paused. Something was missing. She folded a red napkin into a heart and placed it in his mug. Finished!

Then she took the sweater and went into the bedroom. Fred was tossing in bed, mumbling and sighing deeply. He had slid over to her side. If she were still lying there, his arm would be around her now. Blood rushed to her lower body, her pulse throbbed in her throat to imagine it, but there was no time for that now. She went to the dresser and pulled out a red blouse and a cardigan of the same color. When she turned around, his clothes caught her eye: a leather jacket, worn-out jeans and cowboy boots with spurs lay next to the bed. What if she hid them? Then she could be certain he would still be there in the evening when she came back from work.

In the kitchen, she left the light on; in the bathroom she turned it off. Then she slipped her keys into her pocket, reached for her scarf and left.

Her small Fiat was waiting at the end of the street. When the weather was damp, it would hardly start at all. Fred claimed it was because it was so old. And he would know: he was a mechanic after all. But Roswitha couldn't afford to buy a new car right now. She had just invested a lot of money in the French bed, and she had opened up an account for Fred so he wouldn't have to ask her for money.

Before she turned the key in the ignition, she hit the starter with a hammer. The high-pitched, penetrating clink echoed through the street still heavy with night. In response to this attempt to start it, the motor wheezed. Once more she hit the oil-smeared metal drum behind the radiator, her fingers already stiff with the cold, looking imploringly up to the fourth floor, where Fred was struggling with fitful dreams. In the spring, as soon as it was warmer, he would surely repair the car. Until then, it would have to be this way.

After the fifth attempt, the car finally sprang to life. Slowly, she stuttered down the empty street. Her breath froze on the windshield into tiny crystals, blocking her vision.

If only she could be lying next to him now! Every morning it was the same thought: if she could only stop time, shut it off like the light in the bathroom or the coffee machine. By the time she came home, Fred would already be done sleeping. She would bring him breakfast in bed and snuggle up against his hard, angular muscles while he swallowed croissants and coffee down into his deep throat.

How could she keep him? Another thought that occupied her at least a hundred times a day. But what could a twenty-five year old man see in a thirty-eight year old woman, in the long run? Roswitha would not have believed she would ever have to ask herself that question, but ever since she had met Fred, four weeks ago, anything was possible.

It was a Saturday, and Roswitha had earned herself a Kreutzkamm day. As a child, her grandmother had taken her to this fancy café several times. To this day it gave her a feeling of security to drink coffee among these old women adorned with their heavy jewelry

Suddenly, Fred sat next to her at the table. "What is a young lady like you doing here with all these old bags?" he asked her quietly.

Roswitha was so surprised that it took her a while to even understand the compliment.

"I could ask the same of you," she answered, blushing slightly.

His face fell as he said: "It reminds me of my grandmother. Sometimes I come here when I feel lonely."

Roswitha was speechless for a minute. She knew all too well how he felt, and it made her oddly uneasy that he shared her emotion.

"Imagine that, me too," she said, her voice sounding conspiratorial.

Thinking about that moment, even today, made her heart beat faster. She had been surprised at how well Fred had expressed himself. He was so chivalrous, almost sophisticated. Why hadn't he made more of himself than an auto mechanic?

Two cappuccinos and a paper-thin, beautifully decorated piece of cake later, he told her his story:

His father had died in a car crash. No one in his family ever talked about it. Since then, his sister had gained weight every day, six months afterwards his brother jumped out of a window, breaking both ankles and his shins. Child protective services had offered therapy for his mother and her children, but she refused. And Fred soon found out why: she had secretly begun drinking, and lost her job, not even two months later. The household's only income now consisted of Fred's earnings. But he had just been given notice. The company couldn't afford him any longer, was the reason given. The orders had been dropping off.

Fred was so young. Roswitha didn't have anything else in mind when she took him home. She just wanted to get a proper meal inside him, since his mother most likely wasn't taking care of him.

And he was hungrier than she had expected. But it was not just his stomach that was hungry: it was also his heart. She laid her hand on his head while he packed away roast potatoes and schnitzel. When she stroked his face, his fork stopped in mid-air. He kissed her fingers, her arms, her chest. She was surprised at this sudden outburst of emotion, and before she could react he stood up and tried to leave. It wasn't right, he said, he couldn't expect that of her, and slunk out of the kitchen. They ended up in bed.

Roswitha left the highway, making a wide turn towards the east. She left the city behind her; the snow-covered fields broken off from the morning sky. As the car slowly warmed up, the ice melted off of the windows, but a bracing wind came in through the dent in her door.

In the last few weeks she had often asked herself what she liked so much about Fred. Was it the touch of his soft, innocent hands on her skin? Was it his cool thighs or the heat that made her body blaze when he entered her? No matter how much she thought about it, there was only one truly good reason, which she called out into the morning atmosphere: "I'm thirty-eight! I can't expect many more offers at my age."

She slowly began to put on the brakes, and turned into the company lot.

Her office was overheated. She opened the window, hung her coat in the closet and turned on her computer. Within seconds, the room cooled down, then she felt around for moisture in the soil of her jade plant and set to work.

Hour by hour, the pile of files on her desk grew smaller. Since her colleague had called in sick, she could barely keep up. A few short phone calls interrupted her workflow, startling her out of the mechanics of flurrying fingers, the monotonous clicking of the keyboard, the black letters forming long chains on the screen.

At ten, the personnel manager burst in. "Mrs. Wengenmayer, I'm at the end of my rope!"

"Good morning, Mr. Gaus."

"I'm sorry. Of course. Good morning! Good morning. I don't know how it can go on like this. Four sorters have called in sick, and we have twenty-seven dumpsters down there to be recycled. After Christmas we'll be suffocating in used glass!"

He leaned on her desk and regaled her with his famous hangdog look. This must be how he became personnel manager, Roswitha thought, and smiled. He smiled back, and ten minutes later she was standing at the conveyor belt.

"Only till this afternoon. Then you'll get backup," he promised. Roswitha didn't care either way. This is where she had started, with heavy plastic bags, thick latex gloves, boots and protective goggles. Every now and then she had to fill in for someone down here, and she sometimes preferred it to her flickering computer screen.

Endless miles of champagne and wine bottles, jam jars and glass shards filed by her, and above all loads of trash: champagne corks, toilet paper rolls, condoms packages, orange peel, cookie boxes, model tanks, badminton rackets, dashboards, envelopes and chicken bones. They told of other people's lives.

To pass the time, she thought about the fate of some of the objects, while her hands picked out everything that didn't belong in the furnace.

Jam jars made her think of a large garden in summer, ripe strawberries and thick aromatic apple trees. Jam boiling in pans, children running wild outside the kitchen window, and a grandmother watching them as they play. Applesauce jars made her think of a child, maybe five or six years old, and a party with streamers and shrill noise. The table was groaning under its load of gifts, and in the middle of it was a layer cake with plump cherries.

With many objects, she could think of a wide range of possibilities. But with champagne bottles, she could only ever think of one thing: a wedding party and a bride, overcome with joy and dressed in white, filing out of a church. Friends and relatives formed a lane, all of them pressing towards her, because kissing the newlyweds brings luck. Flowers, a car with empty cans tied to the fender and a huge sign on the back: JUST MARRIED!

Hour after hour passed in this fashion. Roswitha leaned against the metal paneling, her ears humming with the grinding of the conveyor belt and her colleagues' chatter. The huge vats began to fill up, and then she reached out her hand for something small and shiny. And in that moment, she believed all her dreams had come true, once and for all.

4.

Bernhard leaned his head against the vibrating windowpane. The wheels whirred along the tracks towards Frankfurt, towards his family. Clackclack, clackclack, clackclack. Hypnotizing. Images were pinned roughly to the events of the last few days, intermingled with the feeling of being carried, of weightlessness and distance. Snowflakes danced like dervishes; the evening atmosphere in front of Edvard's house, as soft as St. Nick's castle; Birgit's deep, night-black eyes, the otherworldly images reflected in them.

Now and then he emerged from this semi-conscious state, only to sink back into it again. This half-reality was comfortable for him—to take part, yet not to be touched. All he needed to do was open his eyes, and everything would be over.

He hovered from one dream world to the next: glasses clinked, bread rolls floated on a bubbly sea, gave way under his bare feet. A large yellow sign flickered, with a black arrow pointing towards the past.

Bernhard arrived at a wall of party guests. They parted like the Red Sea. Friends crowded against strangers, students, neighbors, and new faces, frightened faces, dark and dirty faces. And they all were staring at him. Something dangerous was creeping up on him. It was unknown, and yet familiar to him. Sharp and cold, it shoved against his chest, clutched his stomach, stretched its poisonous tentacles out towards his genitals. Slowly it squeezed the air out of him. Malicious laughter rushed to his ears. The people pointed at him, spit at him.

Beads of sweat formed on Bernhard's forehead. He pushed himself deeper in his seat. Open your eyes, said an agitated voice. Open your eyes, quickly, and he obeyed it.

An old woman sat across from him knitting. The slow, constant clicking of the needles filtered through to him; she smiled suspiciously. Next to her sat a thin man in purple boots, a purple jacket and purple pants. A gray, over-long strand of hair was combed over to cover his bald spot, and he acted as if he were deeply involved in the book on his lap, but Bernhard felt as if he were watching him. The punk girl next to him bobbed her booted feet up and down, deep in thought. Sound droned from her headphones, her eyes were closed. What were they up to?

They acted so innocent, but he felt certain of a threat. Bernhard pushed himself further down into his seat and hid his face behind the coat hanging next to him. His breath became faster, he could feel his heartbeat throughout his whole body. It was so unreasonable. But no matter how wide he opened his eyes to prove he wasn't dreaming, the fear wouldn't go away: on the contrary, it grew stronger.

He had felt the same way the night before. The musty smell, the cold, as if death were near. An indefinable horror, disgust and despair.

Bernhard rubbed his eyes and pressed his fingertips to his temples. Where did these irrational feelings come from? He hadn't felt them until putting on the ring. But they couldn't have anything to do with it.

He wanted to look at it in the light of day, but he noticed he wasn't wearing it on his finger anymore. Where was the ring? Frantically, he shoved his hands in the cracks of his seat cushion, digging among crumbs and candy wrappers for his lover's gift. He rummaged around in his pants and jacket pockets. Again, nothing. Maybe it had fallen to the ground. He leaned forward and pushed a newspaper page aside. Then he got on his knees and felt around on the ground. No ring.

The knitting woman looked at him inquisitively, but he didn't want to explain himself. Distrustfully, he avoided her glance. Maybe one of them had stolen the ring? His eyes wandered from one of his fellow travelers to the next. But it immediately became clear to him how absurd that thought was. While he was sleeping, his hands had been folded tightly under his arms. Besides, how could one of them steal the ring without the others noticing? Unless they were all working together…

Bernhard grabbed his coat and pushed past the others into the corridor. Thick clouds of smoke hung in the hot air. He pulled down a window. The biting cold hissed over his arm, numbing the tip of his nose in seconds. The sweat on his forehead cooled rapidly, leaving him freezing. He pushed the window shut again: the noise of the train was muffled, and his stomach slowly relaxed. He exhaled.

Exhausted, he sat down on a folding seat. Next to him an elderly man was removing sunflower seeds from their shells, spitting the shells into his hand. Further off, a longhaired girl in overalls was busily attacking a box of Christmas cookies.

What had gotten into him since yesterday? For the hundredth time in the last few hours, he went over what had happened in his mind, step by step: the last day of school, relaxing with the Rubens catalog, the preparations, the party, the guests, Birgit's observation, all the words of congratulation. He simply could not find a single indication of what had caused his uneasiness. He had put on the ring, then tripped while dancing and gone into the bedroom with Edvard. Then he felt sick, and fear crept into him. And when Edvard came close to him, the horror spread into his life like oil—and it wouldn't let him go.

Bernhard wished he could have told Edvard about his panic, about the feeling that everything was about to be ruined, finished, destroyed and annihilated; but he had felt paralyzed. He couldn't even look him in the eye. Instead, he had packed up his things like a crazy person and run out into the cold. Wandering through the streets, he sank into the intoxication of strangers. Friendly bars are the best hiding place for intrusive feelings. There, they can be covered in a fog, drowned in meaningless conversations with lonely people. But the ring on his finger had always pulled him back, back to that feeling of foreboding. Its bizarre shimmer, such heaviness and confusion. The ring. Where could he have left it?

He still had it when he went home on the subway at five o'clock in the morning. It had hung loosely on his finger, he remembered that much for sure.

He should call Edvard and explain everything so he didn't jump to false conclusions. Was there a phone on the train? Bernhard looked up and down the corridor. No sign. The conductor approached him. "Your ticket, please!"

"I already showed it to you." In response to the conductor's skeptical look, he said amiably, "I was sitting in there."

"Right," said the uniformed man.

"Is there a telephone on this train?"

"In the dining cart."

"And where is that?"

"Between first and second class. About four cars from here."

Bernhard looked out the window at a gleaming sea of white snow. The golden light of the morning sun cast long shadows. Where could the ring be? Statistically, the chances were around one in twenty thousand of losing an important object, Bernhard knew that exactly. But if Edvard heard that Bernhard had already lost the ring, he would interpret it as a bad omen. He was superstitious enough. Edvard was never guided by reality. He preferred to follow Birgit's flights of fancy. Or he might even think Bernhard had intentionally lost the ring to avoid all that talk of marriage.

Maybe it would be better not to say anything to Edvard about it right away. The ring was probably next to the sink or on the kitchen table, he would only worry unnecessarily if he knew.

The purple man from his compartment opened the door. Bernhard followed his movements distrustfully out of the corner of his eye. Then he returned to his seat. As soon as he sat down, he felt as though his bones were made of lead.

Or did I lose it at the train station? If only I knew whether it was still on my finger when I brought the bottles to the dumpster?

The utility poles cast their shadows on his fellow travelers as they rushed by, darkening their faces for hundredths of a second. Bernhard leaned his head against the wall; it was cool and vibrated. The wheels of the train hummed a rapid, sleep-inducing lullaby. His exhaustion flooded out of him down to the railroad tracks, and melted into the snow. In a few days, Bernhard would return along this exact path. Only a couple of days of rest, rest and nostalgia, before his fear returned to him on his way back.

His eyelids pressed down heavily on his pupils. He couldn't hold them open any longer. He wanted to sleep, he wanted to drift away, far away, to a place without rings or dark faces. He burrowed into the headrest, and his horror crept back into the compartment, under the doorframe, clinging to his boots. It was cold and toxic; it was as old as death.

5.

He opened the door. A wave of heat, steam and excited chatter clouded his view. Shocked, his fleshy hands felt around his round, rosy-cheeked face, and only then did he become aware that he was still wearing his gold-framed reading glasses.

Lamps from various eras, picture frames on the smoke-yellowed walls, diner tables and wobbly wooden chairs. His eyes took some time to get accustomed to it, and so did his ears. It was loud, the café was full, but no one turned towards him. This was not the kind of place where anyone would crane their neck for a portly sixty-five year old in a dark-brown loden coat and hand-knit scarf. Mansonis was a place of youth, full of life, fraught with the oxygen of love and the prickling aura of sex.

Cakes stood in the glass display case. Small yellow ones with delicate leaves on top, one with fat cherries leaking their sweet juice into the cream, one covered in marzipan and strewn with small pieces of walnuts, two varieties of layer cake, pound cake imbedded with fruit, apricots perhaps, or apples. Behind the counter, a young man was standing.

Raimondo lowered his eyes when he met the man's friendly, radiant gaze.

"Kim, darling. Nice to see you!" Raimondo took the delicate, ivory-white hand of a young woman who had up until now been leafing absent-mindedly through a fashion magazine. His red mustache, sprinkled with grey, wet from condensed breath, tickled the back of her hand. "New haircut?"

"Do you think it's too short? Be honest! Do you like the color?"

She always had a different "latest style," as Kim called it. As a kind of surrogate father (and mother), he had seen many facets of his foster daughter in the past few years, all the way from purple-haired hippie girl to killer blond. She was twenty-five now, and he was still waiting for this small, fragile being to become calmer, more balanced and maybe even a little grown-up.

"Like a pot of delicious vanilla pudding," he gushed, knowing that she took any sort of criticism very hard.

"Oh, Raimondo, you'll be the death of me with all this fuss." Kim made room for him.

And what was her look today? Thick black leggings, light brown hiking boots, a silver miniskirt and a skin-tight orange top, with a green fur-collared bomber jacket to top it off. Young people astonished him.

"I've been waiting five whole minutes already. Punctuality must not be your strong point anymore."

"I'm sorry, dearest. But it wasn't so easy to find this…establishment." He laid his coat down over the back of the chair and concealed his rough elbows with his hat.

"Greta Garbo in a golden frame. And on purple wallpaper! I mean, really."

A young man with a jet-black mustache and a red flannel shirt observed him, then smiled at Kim.

"Sorry, I'm already taken," she whispered to him jokingly. "But this one," she pointed to Raimondo, "he's available."

The guy in the flannel shirt laughed and turned away.

Raimondo watched this interaction carefully, then squeezed his flanks between the armrests of his chair. Everything here was a bit narrow. Kim poked him in the belly and giggled excitedly. "I thought it was about time for you to see some men again." She raised her narrow, plucked eyebrows sassily.

"You know I don't feel very comfortable in this kind of place," he said moodily.

"Judging by your mood, you spent last night alone." Kim stroked her mother's childhood lover affectionately across his raw, ice-cold cheek.

Raimondo snarled at her with a muted voice: "Would you please!"

"I can't believe I never noticed it before," said one of the two older ladies at the table next to them.

"Finally, our sort of café," the other lady agreed. "And it's nice that so many young men come here."

"And so well-groomed," the other one praised further.

Kim and Raimondo smirked at one another.

"Do you know what you'd like?" a young man asked them. He was enormously tall and lanky, with prominent cheekbones.

Kim leapt up. "You must have milkshakes, right?" she said and continued before the man could answer: "Well I'd like a strawberry milkshake, no, walnut. Or lemon? You have lemon shakes too, right? And then a piece of whatever that is, with lots of cream. And could you please bring me a pack of cigarettes."

He swaggered away, somewhat confused, and Kim called after him: "And matches! And an ashtray!" Just like her mother, thought Raimondo. So completely full of herself.

Kim turned to him reproachfully: "But you haven't ordered anything!"

"He'll come back," he said, "and it's not as if I'm going to starve in the meantime." He laid a hand softly on his stomach.

Raimondo loved Kim as if she were his own daughter. She had been only three when her mother had sent her off to a home - for one of her lovers. Although this one hadn't stuck around for long either, she had never taken her daughter back. Kim's mother's countless love affairs had always been more important to her than her daughter's needs.

Raimondo had often visited Kim in the home; someone needed to look after her. In the grey courtyard she had danced pirouettes for him and told him her dream of becoming a ballerina. He would never forget her face as it clung sadly to the windowpane each time he left her.

"Tell me, dear Ms. Stewardess. Now you finally get to fly abroad. Are you excited?"

"It's all right."

Raimondo wasn't surprised. After many years in which Kim had never held down a job for longer than two months, the stewardess job was her first professional ray of hope; finally she had found something that totally matched her fickleness. He had hoped it would be a perfect job for her, always hopping around the world: but he had figured it wouldn't take long before she got sick of it.

"I thought you had had enough of Bremen, Berlin, Düsseldorf, Frankfurt? Aren't you excited about America's wide-open country, the perpetual bloom of the Canary Islands, the scuba diving paradise of the Maldives?"

"You know, all that stuff about going abroad, that was under different conditions."

"Which conditions?"

"I've met a man," she said, trying to give her voice a casual touch.

"Another one?"

"Please." The waiter brought the cake covered with whipped cream. Apricot, Raimondo decided. Kim grabbed the pack of cigarettes and tore it open.

"Hey, what about you?" The young man addressed Raimondo. He held his breath. Being talked to so informally made him uncomfortable.

"Do you have tea?"

"What would you like?"

"Well, Earl Grey maybe?"

"No, we only have fruit teas or black tea."

Raimondo looked at him with contempt: "Then I'll have the black tea, please."

"With lemon or milk?"

"Without, thank you. But would you happen to have a few pieces of rock sugar?"

A wordless smile passed over the waiter's thin, delicate face.

"It's fine," Raimondo said. "And a piece of the marzipan cake, please."

The young man was still smiling. Raimondo turned away.

"With whipped cream please," he added, and the waiter disappeared.

"What do you mean, another one?" Kim asked heatedly, lighting a cigarette. "You act as if I always have a new one."

He lifted his hands up in apology. There was no sense in arguing with her.

"He's just wonderful. Raimondo. I'm telling you. He's generous, funny, bursting with ideas. He's the first man who values me as a partner, and doesn't just use me as a sex object." Kim drew herself up, her eyes grew wide. "You know, he's so…human. He's considerate of me. He asks how I'm doing, he's interested in me. It's a totally new feeling."

She was so young, so open and so innocent. The only thing that protected her was her hyperactivity. It hurt him deeply to see her fall into the same trap again and again. He couldn't help saying: "You told me the same thing about Richard and Stefan and what was that handsome guy's name, from last year?"

"Marcus?" She puffed out a thick cloud of smoke that slowly spread out and hovered in the room. "No, they were all very different. They didn't want a woman to be their equal, they wanted a wife! If I had married one of them, I would be darning socks today. I want a man who treats me well. Like Fred."

"That's his name?" His voice was glum. He saw that she had already made her decision. "Does the young man have a last name as well?"

"It's funny, I haven't even asked him," she laughed coquettishly and puffed smoke in his direction. Raimondo waved it away, annoyed.

"But hopefully you've thought of a few things. You know what I mean."

"Condoms?"

"Kim!"

The waiter brought a glass of steaming water in which a tea bag lay soaking forlornly. But the sight of the marzipan comforted Raimondo's upset sense of taste.

"What? Is 'condom' a dirty word now?"

The young man smiled and went away. The two elderly women at the table next to them went quiet.

"And what is it that your…Fred…does?" Raimondo spit out the name and stabbed into his cake with annoyance. Much too sweet, he thought, marmalade, marzipan, crust and a layer of almond slivers, something about it was not quite right.

"He's a rock star."

"Ah. And you snuck into his hotel room as a groupie, I understand." He shoved a second forkful of cake into his mouth. The nuts weren't very fresh, that was it. That's why it tasted so stale.

"You're so wonderfully old-fashioned, Raimondo. Musicians aren't always on tour. I met him in a bar. He's totally sweet, as tall as me, with a black mustache. He's muscular, and he's got thick hair everywhere. His chest is just like a fluffy carpet."

She put out her cigarette and observed Raimondo's reaction as he pushed together the last crumbs on his plate. He took a deep breath, scratched his nose, and pretended not to have heard the details about Fred's manliness.

"His band is called *The United Steaks*, you get it? Like the United States. All of the band members have steak names: there's Pepper, Rump, T-Bone, Rib, and Fred's stage name is Sir Loin. Isn't that funny?" She stuck her straw into the thick shake and stirred it in the glass, lost in thought.

"He's a real big deal. Fred was friends with Kurt Cobain."

Raimondo frowned.

"Kurt was a star from Seattle. He's the one who really got grunge started. Shot himself in '94. With a shotgun…you know that already."

"Well, at least he has money," Raimondo said. She had always been on the lookout for that.

Kim hesitated and smeared the whipped cream around on her cake. "Not quite. He left the band. Stress, you know. He always had to give so many interviews and travel around the world. He had no time for his private life. Just business, schmoozing. He's much too sensitive for that. He had to leave it. Now he's suing the record label for compensation. He needs to raise the money for a lawyer. They froze his accounts, you know."

"You are not going to lend him any money." Raimondo stared at her with concern.

"Why not?"

"Kim, you're making a mistake. My advice to you: stay away from him!"

"But he's the one, that's something a woman can just tell."

"Maybe that's so, but building a relationship on financial debt is the wrong way. Believe me."

Raimondo leaned back and crossed his arms. He didn't even want to think how this was going to end. He looked into her dark, stubborn eyes. "All I want to say is that maybe you should give it a little time."

Kim leaned into him, too close. "But this time I'm completely certain. Everything's just…right."

She was so fixed, so determined.

"Do I hear wedding bells?" he asked, and there was something hopeful in his voice.

Kim lowered her eyes and grabbed a strand of hair to chew on. Her leg started to wobble dangerously.

"So there's a problem?"

"What kind of problem could there be?" she asked sharply.

Raimondo fished the tea bag out of the glass and looked for a place to put it.

"So he's married, all right, so what?"

"Married?" Raimondo's spoon fell out of his hand, tea splashed over the table. "Bankrupt and married, that's a new variation."

"I knew I shouldn't have told you." Kim crossed her arms over her chest, pouting.

"But my darling, how can this ever turn out well?"

"He's going to get divorced," she explained, and her voice rose dangerously. "He just wants to wait until the lawsuit is over with. Two break-ups at once are too much. I can understand that. I'm not as cold and emotionless as you are."

"So he's going to get a divorce? He's probably already been married fifteen years, and then some twenty-five year old kid comes along and he's going to get divorced. How long have you even known him? Two days? Two weeks?" Raimondo pushed his tea away. It was bitter and flavorless.

"I just want a man I can actually count on," she said defiantly.

If Raimondo could only make her learn from her mother's life. What was it about these women, who alternated between blind love and deep hatred for the opposite sex? Why couldn't Kim find a middle path? When she was in love she tore herself up, and at the first sign of disagreement she ran away. "You're right. You can only try. I hope for your sake that he's really the right one."

"Don't worry, Pop."

"Well, sometimes I do worry."

"I think that's wonderful, but it's not necessary. I can take care of myself."

Her sharp eyes rested on Raimondo. Then she reached across the table for his liver-spotted hand, which had never touched a woman with desire. "I should have married you."

"Kim, my love. You know how much I care for you, but…" he said, winking secretively.

"But what? You think I couldn't convert you?" She threw her head back and giggled.

Raimondo was disarmed for a moment. "There are things in heaven and earth that just are the way they are. And that, my dearest, is one of them."

"Like the sweet looks that handsome baker keeps throwing your way from behind the counter, trying to catch your attention?"

"Kim!" Raimondo acted heated. "One notices such things, but one does not speak about them." He made an angry face, but his chest inflated victoriously.

"Which reminds me: how's Serge?"

Raimondo slumped again. "Well, I think. I haven't seen him for three weeks. He's on vacation."

"Vacation? From what? Mooching?"

Raimondo slumped even more. It was like someone had pulled the stopper from a beach ball.

"Ah, I see, vacation from you." Kim was visibly upset by her friend's suffering. In her eyes, Raimondo was the manifestation of love in human form. He was always there for others, full of concern, generosity and dedication. Many people exploited this; few gave him what he deserved. She knew he longed for someone he could shower with all his love, bathe him in it and bond with him. But somehow it had never worked out—except with Serge, that menace. She called him "parasite" whenever she was forced to spend more than two seconds alone with him, and she had always tried to drive a wedge between the two of them. Raimondo deserved better. She became furious. "Tell him to go to hell! How long is this supposed to go on for?" Raimondo deserved a geisha boy, someone who would lie at his feet and give him back what he gave to others. If only she could find someone for him. "Take the cake baker home with you. He looks so sweet," she said full of promise. "He's got a real sweet tooth. How does it go: true love is a piece of cake?"

It was uncomfortable for him when his foster daughter tried to set him up; Raimondo turned red. "Please, don't say things like that," he said, trying to get away from the subject. He didn't want to admit that he stayed with Serge because he was the only one who kept coming back.

"I know exactly what you're thinking," she said when she noticed that he had withdrawn far within himself. "But if you think it's better to be exploited, then you're nuts." Raimondo gave her an injured look. "You're much too good for him. I just want to see you happy for once." He chewed at his lips. "What Serge is doing to you, you can't allow that. It's a question of self-respect."

Kim saw that she wasn't getting through to him. So she stood up and adjusted her leggings. Then she threw the bomber jacket over her shoulders and snuggled into the fur collar. "I've got a visitor coming. Kiss!" She smacked her lips loudly in the air.

"Take care."

"I'll be back on Monday. I'll call you."

"Where are you living now?"

"In Ortrud's apartment, she's in L.A. I can stay there for two months." She bent down to Raimondo and pressed him tightly against her. "I love you." Then she stroked his cheek and strutted out on her high heels.

So she ended up a ballerina after all, thought Raimondo. He followed her footsteps to the door and noticed that even the gay men in this place were turning their heads for her. With so many offers, it wasn't surprising she ended up with a new man so often. If only she wouldn't take it all so seriously.

Kim hadn't even touched her cake. Raimondo piled the rest of the whipped cream on it, cut it with his fork and shoveled the two halves into his mouth one after the other. Too little vanilla, he thought, and a tad too much sugar. Then he put 40 Marks down on the table and threw on his coat.

As he left, his met the baker's gaze. Raimondo hesitated, then lingered at the counter and asked in a subdued voice: "Do you also do home deliveries?"

"Of course, sir. I make sure to do them in person."

"Could you make it tonight, around eight?" Raimondo pulled an old business card from his vest pocket and laid it on the glass surface.

"Certainly." The baker grinned broadly. "Which would you like?"

"Well, which one do you like the best?"

6.

Roswitha had read that, at the moment of death, people saw their lives flash past them like a film. She had never been able to imagine that—until today, until it had seemed to her as if the conveyor belt had decelerated, workers were suddenly walking through the hall in slow-motion, the violent noise of machines grew still, forklifts stopped in mid-drive: and for a moment scarcely longer than the blink of an eye, Roswitha believed she could see her future.

Roswitha held up what she had found against the light. The ring blurred before her eyes. In the harsh neon light, the gold had looked like worn brass, but now that she turned it around two stones gleamed back at her: a diamond and a ruby. She had often heard from her colleagues that they had found coins, or particularly beautiful bottles, which could be made into flower vases, but something like this?

It was unbelievably beautiful. Roswitha had only seen jewelry like this in the display cases of expensive jewelers, or in the movies. She had never held something like it in her hand. It must be very valuable, maybe a month's salary or more. If she sold it, she could afford a lot for herself: payments for a new car, a nook for the kitchen, the tableware she'd been wanting to buy for ages. But she didn't think of selling the ring for an instant. It was her ticket to the future. It would make dreams come true, dreams she had given up on fifteen years ago.

Marriage—that was the answer. Why hadn't she thought of it earlier? Then Fred wouldn't be able to run away.

"Hey, no fall asleep!" A colleague nudged her back into reality with her elbows. Roswitha looked into her gold-toothed grin, and everything came back: the crunching of glass, the grinding of the conveyor belt, the din of the forklift motors. As she looked around, the world creaked along in its tracks again.

Roswitha shoved the ring under the large cuff of her glove: "I thought I saw a ghost."

"No good," answered the woman next to her on the conveyer belt, and fished a broken hairbrush out of the fragments. Roswitha grabbed faint-heartedly for a Coke can and threw it into the vat with a clank. A rusted jam jar cover swam past her in the endless stream, followed by the tattered remains of a map, a can of sardines, and again and again the golden foil from around the necks of champagne and wine bottles.

"Ghosts no good," her colleague said again emphatically.

Roswitha could only think of the party. The image of a bride, all in white, thrust itself before her inner eye again. Radiant wedding guests congratulated her on the prince at her side.

"I will get married in the Asam church," she whispered, "And for coffee, we'll go to the Chinese tower."

She would invite Aunt Sigrid and Uncle Ludwig, her cousins, her school friends and Frida, Hiltraud, Gerda, Toni and Paula, all her neighbors, Mrs. Semmelweiss from the vegetable shop, and—a tear ran down her cheek—her colleagues had to come as well, of course.

Roswitha looked up and turned to them. "You all need to come!" she called out in the wide hall, but her invitation was swallowed up by the noise. A few heads lifted and then lowered again to the infinite glass kaleidoscope.

"Keep dreaming," the forewoman called to her, "But don't forget to sort." She pointed to a crushed plastic bottle, and Roswitha nabbed it quickly from the belt. Roswitha Wolf. Wolf, she liked that name much better than Wengenmayer.

"What changes when you get married?" She asked her colleague excitedly.

"Don't know. I marry already in Turkey. Husband do everything."

Your I.D. certainly, driver's license, bank accounts, rental lease. Oh God, the whole world would change.

Roswitha tried to concentrate, but her imagination was unbelievably strong. The first glass of cherries she saw, she relocated to a dining room table full of friendly married couples. The room was filled with laughter, hospitable warmth and a feeling of belonging. In their midst, a cake piled with cherries. Were there children running wild around the table? Of course! How many would they have?

The coffee party became a Caribbean vacation, long walks on secluded beaches. She imagined a new, much larger apartment, evenings spent cuddling in front of the TV and celebrating Christmas under the tree.

It had grown dark again by the time she left the factory. She scraped the window clear and set out on her way home, her heart beating rapidly. The ring had opened up a wellspring of desire within her that would not run dry. Images flowed out in such a way that she wondered, in a lucid moment, whether it was even necessary to experience it all. Her imaginings were as clear and palpable as pages in a photo album, her desires for the future almost as real as memories.

She parked the car in front of the door to the house. Could she just ask him to marry her? No, that was impossible. She had to orchestrate it somehow so it seemed like his idea. But what would she do if it didn't occur to him? After all, they didn't know each other very well. Fred hadn't even introduced her to his mother. Would she accept Roswitha? She was probably barely older than her. But as an alcoholic, she most likely didn't care at all. That was probably the reason he didn't want to take her home with him.

She turned off the car and went into the house. When she got to the stairs she leaned on the rail for a bit. Maybe she should wait until the next time he took her into his arms and told her he loved her. Then she would give him the ring, and the idea would come into his head all by itself. Or she would lay it on Fred's pillow, or on his plate before he sat down at the table. And what if she just asked him? No way! A man with no work and no income—he would feel humiliated. That wouldn't be a good way to start.

Pulling her way along the railing, she climbed the steps slowly, and came to the decision to say nothing for the moment. She wanted to wait for the right opportunity. It would come on its own. If it didn't she could bring it up during a romantic movie as a joke and see how he reacted. The worst thing she could do right now, would be to rush into it.

Roswitha rummaged around in her coat pocket. For a second she was afraid she had forgotten the ring in her work gloves. She breathed on it and polished it on the inside of her shirt. The diamond scattered the light in the stairwell and cast a rainbow over her nameplate above the doorbell; the ruby was almost black, and secretively dark.

I will give Fred the ring and wait, she told herself. I will restrain myself and wait.

She was so nervous that she barely managed to get the key in the lock. In a rush she took off her coat, put her purse down on the hall-stand, and was about to walk into the room when she remembered her decision again. She closed her eyes and told herself with a firm voice: you will restrain yourself.

"Darling. You're home early." Fred came up to her with open arms. She pressed herself against his chest, submerged her face in his aura of leathery cologne, nicotine and that inexplicable aroma of motor oil. Her knees felt weak.

"Are you all right?" He lifted her away from him in order to see her better. Roswitha shook her head.

"You look as if you've seen a ghost." Fred led her into the living room and sat her down on the couch. "Give me your feet. I'll massage them for you."

She shook her head faint-heartedly again, then opened her hand and held out the ring: "Fred, will you marry me?"

He took the ring, slipped it on his finger and played with his hand beneath the standing lamp. It was a perfect fit.

"Of course we can get married," he said, his eyes still fixed on the ring. His voice was dull, as if he were speaking in a trance.

Roswitha shivered. She leaned forward and grabbed his hand. It was as cold as her own hand, as cold as his eyes.

"I've got to head out for a while," he said after a pause, and pinched her cheek. "You don't need to wait up for me for dinner." Then he walked out the door.

He just left. She asked him if he wanted to marry her, and he went away.

What have I done, she asked herself.

Kim dashed about her apartment. Her lover had said he was coming, and she wanted everything to be perfect.

After her coffee date with Raimondo, she had bought another bouquet of tulips and a papaya for dinner and had picked up a few dresses from the drycleaner's. Then she hurried back home, where she turned on Bon Jovi, listened to her messages and thrust her dirty laundry under the bed. She didn't have time to take a bath, so she jumped under the shower quickly, blow-dried her hair and tried on several dresses. In the end, she decided on the outfit she had worn in the café, making several adjustments in front of the long wall mirror: she took off the thick stockings, and her panties as well. Now it was fresh and airy between her legs.

"Like Sharon Stone in *Basic Instinct*," she giggled to her mirror image. What was love without thrills?

She was powdering her face when he rang the doorbell. He had barely walked in the door before she jumped into his arms.

"Oh, my sweet, sweet darling! I'm so glad you're here. I could hardly wait to see you. I've been longing for you so much. Since I woke up this morning I've thought of nothing but you. I even dreamed about you, about us. And all day all I wanted was one thing: to feel your warm hands on my naked skin."

The words sputtered out of her, mixing with hundreds of hot-lipped kisses into a barely understandable gibberish.

"I have a little surprise for you," she whispered and led his hand underneath her skirt. His hand was icy and stiff, which made it even more of a turn-on. She wanted him now, in the hallway, right now. No time to go even a step further, to close the curtains, to turn on romantic music. She stroked his shaggy hair, tugged at the leather band adorning his chest, pulling him down. And before he could fight back, they were both kneeling half-naked in the corridor.

"You're the best. I love you. You're my lover, my rescuer. You're more than a lover, you're my advisor, my worshiper, my teacher. Through you, I've gotten to know my body for the first time, my desires, my lust, my needs."

She covered him with wet kisses and swore she never wanted to live without him. And while he sent cold showers of arousal down her back with his icy hands and snow-moist mustache, she wished she could melt into his hard, unyielding body.

She pushed Fred down on the floor and sat on him, trapping him between her knees. Her back bent far back behind her, her hands searched between his cold thighs for the hot object of her desire. Then she paused abruptly: "Did you talk to her yet?"

"Yes, I told her. We're going to split up, but give me some time. She's been really affected by the lawsuit." His lips were so soft, so sweet, his smile was like a perfumed bed of straw.

"But I promise you, as soon as I have the money…Have you thought about how much you can lend me?"

She hesitated and was uncertain for a moment. Raimondo's voice echoed in her head: you don't want to lend money to a stranger. But Fred wasn't a stranger.

He pulled her towards him by the shoulders, his strong arms embraced her thin, fragile torso.

"Think quickly, or else I'll have problems. If they lock me up, you won't be able to see me for a long time."

He rubbed his hard member on her soft thighs. The thought of losing him scared Kim. She embraced him, threw herself on his chest. Then she felt something really cold on her back, something very, very cold.

"Who is that from?" She held the hand with the ring up against the light.

Fred answered with a helpless look.

Another disappointment. She wasn't going to put up with it. Not again.

"It's from her, isn't it?" The way he lay there helplessly in front of her made everything clear. His wife gave him a ring, and he wore it. That could only mean one thing: he would never leave her. He was just another scumbag like the rest.

She pounded furiously at his bare chest and jumped up. "You pig! Raimondo was right, and all I did was defend you!"

She threw open the door to the apartment and tossed out his jacket, his shirt, his tank top.

"Get out!" she screamed and pointed to the door. "Out, you cheat, you swine, you, you miserable rat!" She pulled him into the stairwell by the arm. "I never want to see you again." Then she slammed the door behind him.

The woman next door poked her head out of her apartment. When she saw Fred sitting on the ground, she shook her head uncomprehendingly.

Fred shrugged his shoulders, remained sitting, and lit a cigarette. Then he began to turn the ring slowly in the hallway light.

7.

The door opened. First Bernhard saw the face of his oldest sister Sieglinde, red from exertion, then a wave of domestic warmth washed over him, bringing the sharp odor of cinnamon and the pleasant smell of potato soup to his nostrils.

"Hey, little brother. I thought you were avoiding the preparations." Sieglinde ushered him in. "You can set up the Christmas tree with Karl. I've been working on it for a while already." She swung a cleaning bucket and disappeared into the guest bathroom.

Bernhard set down his bag and hung up his coat.

Gudrun, his second-oldest sister, greeted him through the open door to the kitchen, where she was slicing apples.

"Well, did you have a good trip?"

"It's over, at least."

Gudrun was more than a head shorter than him, so he kissed her on the forehead. Her lips glowed deep red, and her eyes seemed much bigger due to the eye shadow she wore. Bernhard noticed how much she tried to emphasize her femininity recently. Earlier, she had believed she could only get her own way with men by fighting. But since that women's seminar earlier in the year she had been practicing another tactic: men were much easier to manipulate when you duped them with feminine charms.

"Sieglinde looks a bit exhausted."

"A bit?" asked Gudrun, rolling her pretty brown eyes. "She's been sweeping around the house since she got up this morning. And all I've been doing the last week is cleaning."

"Isn't she getting on your nerves?"

Gudrun sighed and let her arms fall exhaustedly. "Yes, but…" She looked towards the door and continued in a low voice: "Eberhard moved out two weeks ago. I think if Sieglinde doesn't clean she'll go crazy."

Bernhard scratched his neck. His sister's marriage crises were a common topic in the Moll house.

"Why don't you go and say hello to the others?" suggested Gudrun, starting to slice the apples again.

"I'll finish up with this, then there will be coffee."

Bernhard nodded and went into the living room. His youngest sister Barbara was lying in her lover's lap. He had been baptized under the name Thadeus, but the family had started calling him by his nickname "Mausi" a long time ago.

"Hi," she greeted him drily. She gave Bernhard a brief, bored look, then turned back to Mausi's prickly mustache.

Out of his four siblings—Ludwig, Sieglinde, Gudrun and Barbara—she was the one he had the least in common with. In his view, she was an emotional catastrophe, a box of fireworks that were always going off. And her behavior had stayed stuck at the level of a nine-year old's.

He couldn't take Mausi seriously, a man trotting along behind his girlfriend like a dachshund. Every irregular breath she took made him panic. Bernhard was just waiting for the day his future brother-in-law would supply her with babies on demand.

Karl, Gudrun's husband, sat on the couch studying the sports section of the newspaper. He was the image of manhood: large and stocky, radiating calm and equilibrium. Years ago, when Gudrun had brought him back to the house for the first time, Bernhard had dreamed of lying in his arms.

"So, you're taking a break from corrupting the children?" Karl asked, lifting his head from the newspaper.

"You know how it is: torture is more effective if you don't give them the chance to get used to it." Bernhard shook his hand. It was firm, warm and dry. "And you?" He asked the architect. "How many of your houses have collapsed since I asked you last?"

"Oh, only two I think," he answered with a grin.

"Great! Maybe you'll make something of yourself yet." They laughed.

Teasing one another had been their form of greeting for years. It was hollow, but it was secure, and it gave both of them the distance they needed.

"What are you doing?" Sieglinde's penetrating voice echoed down the hallway.

Bernhard and Karl looked at one another in surprise, then opened the living room door, and Sieglinde pushed her daughter into the room. "She was going through your bag, Bernhard. I'm sorry. At the moment there's nothing but nonsense in that head of hers."

Bernhard didn't see the blonde Pippi-Longstocking pigtails, he didn't even notice Manuela's glare. But he noticed right away that his niece had gained a lot of weight since summer. Gudrun had already mentioned it. Manuela was very rebellious in school and provoked her fellow students into stupid fights. But could she be blamed? A father whose constantly-changing secretaries were more important than his own daughter, and a mother who was either wallowing in tears or lost in a cleaning frenzy.

"No problem." He kneeled down and opened his arms wide.

"Hello, Uncle Bernie. My ball fell into your bag, I really didn't mean to…"

"It's all right. Just forget about it, okay?"

Biggy and Sissy, Gudrun's daughters, appeared at the door, standing there until Bernhard's arms were free again. Then they charged towards him and threw him to the ground.

"Uncle Bernie, Uncle Bernie! It's so nice that you're finally here."

He acted overwhelmed, kissed them, and made the kind of compliments he had always hated when he was a kid. "Hey, my sweet girls. My goodness, don't you look grown-up!"

Then the two girls' brother, who was not yet a year old, wobbled in. Bernhard lifted the little man, held him above his head and spun him through the air. That was Flo's favorite game. He squealed and concentrated frantically on not losing his pacifier.

"Play with us! Come up with us! I have something to show you!" the three girls called excitedly.

"Give him time, he just got here," said Karl and flipped through the newspaper without looking up.

"I'll be up in a second," said Bernhard, putting Flo back up on his short legs. "You go back up."

The girls stormed away hooting. Sieglinde scolded after them: "Don't make such a din!" But it was swallowed up by their din.

Bernhard sat down. Flo stretched his arms up as a sign that he wanted to be spun around again. Bernhard laid his hand on Flo's white-blond hair. It was fine, crinkling into delicate curls around his round face. His light-blue eyes seemed transparent. They radiated so much love that tears came to Bernhard's eyes.

Flo nudged Bernhard. "Up! Up!" he seemed to want to say, but Bernhard couldn't. He was dizzy all of a sudden. He heard the blood rushing in his ears, his chest felt tight. He knelt down as his breath became faster and shallower.

"Are you all right?" asked Karl.

"It's okay. I just slept badly." Bernhard sat up straight and staggered shakily into the kitchen. It was awfully hot, the air was rubbery as chewing gum.

With a shaking hand he took a glass from the cupboard and went to the sink. When he tried to turn on the water, the glass fell out of his hand and shattered. He braced himself.

"Bernhard. You look all pale!" said Gudrun. "What's wrong?"

As soon as she came over to him she saw that his whole body was shivering. She took another glass, filled it with water and held it out to him, but he pushed her hand away. His forehead was cold and covered with beads of sweat. He shook his head and shut his eyes.

"You're scaring me. Should I call a doctor?"

"No, no. It's all right. Just give me a sec."

Slowly and carefully he opened his eyes again: brown-speckled floorboards, granola, milk bottles, coffee machine—as suburban and stuffy as it was here, he had always felt at home in his sister's house before. But in this moment, between the refrigerator and the simmering soup, he felt like a stranger, he felt lost.

Gudrun laid her hand on his arm. He felt her warmth flowing into him and took a deep breath. Slowly, color returned to his face, and when he looked Gudrun in the face he felt as if he was returning from a long journey.

"Does this happen to you often?" she asked in a muted voice.

Bernhard shook his head. "The third time since last night."

"Maybe I should call a doctor after all?"

He hesitated. It was plain to see that it cost him a great effort to speak. "Can I talk to you?"

Now Gudrun was the one turning pale. "Is it something terrible?"

"No, I just need to talk to somebody. Alone."

"Yeah, wait a second." She took off her apron, turned off the stove and put a plate over the apples strewn with sugar and cinnamon. "Let's go for a short walk. That way we won't be bothered."

Hurriedly, she slipped into her boots and jacket, pulled the key out of the lock and opened the door. Bernhard took his coat and went out into the snow.

Gudrun looked at her brother. "Are you feeling better now?"

"Yeah, it's all right."

They walked quietly down the street, past houses with gardens the size of tablecloths. Stars glimmered behind windows, where mothers baked Christmas cookies with their excited children. Ravens hopped over the neighboring fields; the farther they walked out of town, the louder their boots creaked in the snow.

Bernhard slowed his steps and observed his sister. As a child, she had often comforted him when he had scraped his knee or when his father forbade him to take part in a science competition because he had gotten a D in gym class. That was long ago, twenty-five years or more. Would she understand what he was trying to say now?

"Do I need to be worried about you?" she asked, breaking into his thoughts.

He searched for the right words. He couldn't just say he was gay.

Admitting this to himself was enough to give him stomach cramps, how would his sister react? "I love men!" What does that mean? A man can also love his father or his job. "I sleep with men?" "I have sex with men?" "I have a boyfriend!" He just couldn't find the words to properly describe his feelings. But it was so important to be precise.

"I'm not going to get married," he said finally, and realized in the same breath that this was dumber than all the rest.

"What?"

"I…don't like women," he burst out with an aggressive undertone.

"Oh!"

Oh? Was that all she could think of? Bernhard's heart thudded, and he felt his pulse in his throat. But what was she supposed to say? Awesome? Congratulations? Fantastic?

They went down a hill; the noise of the town went mute, leaving them alone with their thoughts, with themselves.

"And you're quite certain of this?"

Bernhard nodded and looked out into the distance. "Very certain."

"Do you think you might change your mind at some point?"

He looked over at his sister; in this wide field, with her red nose and that furrow in her brow she looked much smaller than she had in the kitchen.

Was being gay somehow an opinion? Is it possible to change something about it, the way it's possible to be against nuclear power today and for it tomorrow?

Gudrun stopped abruptly and looked at him fearfully: "Do you have…? I mean, are you…sick?"

"No, for God's sake," Bernhard affirmed, turning pale. He hadn't thought about AIDS. These fits of dizziness, breaking out in sweat, this fear of death. No, it had nothing to do with AIDS. They had gotten tested after all.

"I assure you, there isn't even the slightest possibility."

Gudrun was relieved.

"No, I just…it's since last night. Very strange." Bernhard fought with the words. "I've been together with a man for the past seven months."

He noticed that Gudrun winced, and he knew exactly what she was thinking: seven months, a damn long time to keep his siblings out of the loop.

"His name is Edvard, he's an antique dealer. He has a small shop in Munich." Bernhard's face became tender and red, and his steps became as light as the flakes that were beginning to fall around them.

"We had a little party yesterday, and he gave me a ring." Gudrun looked at Bernhard's hands, which were hanging out of his coat sleeves, red with cold. "And suddenly I felt dizzy. This morning on the train again. I always have the feeling something horrible is about to happen. Maybe I'm just overworked."

"Or you've got what 50 percent of all couples get when a ring comes into play: fear of commitment. It was no different with me and Karl."

Bernhard let her words sink in. A raven took off, and began pecking at another in its black, purple-gleaming coat of feathers.

"Really?"

Gudrun nodded, smiling. Or was it just the cold crinkling her face? Bernhard wasn't sure.

"Do you think the others can live with that news?"

"It doesn't matter," she said, and there she was again, his big sister, who had rocked him in her lap when he was a child. "All that's important is that you can live with it." Her eyes became anxious. "But I would maybe avoid talking about it with Papa."

Bernhard stopped.

"I think the old soldier would have a bit of a problem with a…, you know, …with a son like you." Apologetically she added: "Now, after his third heart attack. He's not even allowed to drive a car anymore. Imagine, you tell him, and he has another attack. You would never forgive yourself."

Bernhard shivered.

"Listen. Can we talk about this later?" asked Gudrun, who saw how he was thinking it over. "I absolutely need to take care of dinner. Papa and Mama are coming at six, everything should be ready by then."

"Of course." Bernhard nodded. "I'm going to stay out in the fresh air a little while longer.

"Ok, see you in a minute." Gudrun squeezed his arm awkwardly and trudged back.

The sun was already low, lending the snow an orangey-golden light. His sister grew quickly distant, soon she was just a shapeless dark spot, and then he was alone.

Snow was a deceptive phenomenon. Even as a child, Bernhard had had an ambivalent relationship with it. He liked it, but while his friends had frolicked around it, he had stood idly by. He always asked himself what this white, harmless-seeming product of nature concealed beneath it. The seeds of beautiful flowers or deep puddles, a coin perhaps or a corpse.

Snow could freeze to ice, melt into streams or tear down an entire village in an avalanche. This made it something uncontrollably large, which frightened Bernhard and yet at the same time filled him with wonder. He always had the impulse to turn away and flee its power. But every time he ended up on his knees, as if he had no choice but to bow down before it.

With closed eyes, he kneeled down and laid his hand flat against the surface blown smooth by the wind. It was cool and raw, but slippery; carefully, his hand glided across it. After a while, he felt the cold stabbing his hands.

When he opened his eyes, he saw a thick, blood-black stain, and nausea overcame him.

8.

As a child, Lydia Moll occasionally left Heidelberg to visit her grandmother in Vienna—on her bicycle. Back then, she thought nothing of walking an hour to school every morning, and it went without saying that she helped her mother break up stones after the war. She had never complained about physical exertion, had never wasted a moment's thought about it.

These days she couldn't go to Vienna anymore, even if she were carried there on a litter. There were days now when she didn't even go to the bakery on the corner or the supermarket at the end of the street. Lydia didn't have the strength to carry shopping bags anymore, and she was only sixty-three.

It had nothing to do with the five children, Ludwig, Sieglinde, Gudrun, Bernhard and Barbara. Nor was it from all the diapers she had washed, or the floorboards she had scrubbed and polished. What exhausted Lydia were a handful of confused cells in her breasts that had decided to stop following the rules. They grew however they liked; they ran rampant, robbed Lydia of her breath, and lately even took away her belief in a future.

She was tired of fighting for every breath, she was tired of waiting for nightfall every morning, and waiting for the next morning when nighttime came, always hoping she would improve a little, that she would experience more joy in life, that the swelling at her throat and under her armpits would go down.

She still remembers the young medical assistant: "Essentially these cells are just programmed wrong, misinformed," he explained with his finger on the cauliflower-shaped lump on her X-ray, visibly fascinated by what the human body was capable of.

"Misinformed?" she asked. Like a misunderstanding?

No, it wasn't a misunderstanding. She knew this. The cells had been properly informed—by her soul. Lydia had burdened herself with guilt and carried it around with her for decades. At first she refused to believe it, but then when she could deny it no longer, she tried to ignore her guilt. Now it was pushing out of her like a mole out of the ground, leaving behind a steadily growing pile.

Because of this, an operation would do no good. Even if she rinsed out her arteries with bleach, it would not clean her soul. She had to repair the injustice, she had to atone, she had to find forgiveness. But how?

After the diagnosis she went home, and for weeks she told neither her husband nor her children about it. Not about the cancer, and not about her guilt. That was something she had to work out for herself.

Since then, she hadn't gone to church as a service to God. She had gone to that holy place to find answers to her questions, to have conversations with the blessed Mary. She was the only one who could help her now, Lydia was convinced of this, if only the Mother of God would find the time.

Lydia had been right. Neither the operations nor the chemotherapy had alleviated her gnawing guilt. That was why she was taking it upon herself now to travel in this overheated, overcrowded train: to see her children again.

For the family, this weekend was a pre-celebration for Christmas; for Lydia it was a farewell. For a while now she had felt certain that everything was going to change completely very soon, so she wanted to sit at the table with everyone one more time, to eat and drink with them, to say a prayer together. She would go through with it as long as her legs would still carry her emaciated body and as long as her thoughts were clear enough to form full sentences. She wanted to hug everyone one more time, as long as she had the strength to hold another person.

The door of the open coach retracted with a loud hiss, giving way to the conductor's heavy footsteps. "Shift change, tickets please!" he called out in a nasal voice.

She held her tickets out to him. With silver tongs he made two indentations in them and handed them back to her. Lydia put them under the velvet gift bag in her purse. These were for the children: earrings her grandmother had given her on her first day of school, an armlet of her mother's, the pearl necklace she had received for her wedding, and various rings. She wanted to give away the jewelry on this trip, since she wouldn't need it anymore.

Giving away possessions made it easier to let go. She had given up so much in the last months: her sharp eyesight, hearing, the feeling in her fingertips, her lust for life, hope. Giving made it easier to give up: she was just learning this now. Years ago, when Lydia was not yet fifty, she had altered her wedding dress for Sieglinde.

"You're not going to get married again," her daughter had told her then, without noticing that to do something for the last time is like a little death, a foretaste of the one true end. Lydia had just swallowed and kept on sewing.

She rummaged for her glasses in her stiff, dark-brown purse and tried to make out the time on her wristwatch. It was a quarter to six. Twenty-eight minutes to go.

Siegi was much younger, and still needed to learn her first lessons in yielding: her husband Eberhard had cheated on her more than once, and Lydia was afraid that her daughter wouldn't be able to put up with it much longer. Siegi still had to learn that life is sometimes very different from the way we hope it will be.

Even her boys made her worry. Her oldest, Ludwig, was a house painter like his father. He had an income, he had a roof over his head, a car and a pension fund, but at forty-one he still lived like a vagrant. She wasn't concerned about his life, she was worried about his heart.

And Bernhard had always been her problem child. He always got things wrong in his head. At twelve, while the neighbors' kids were scuffling on the soccer field, he was sitting in his room learning Greek epics by heart. Then he studied Nietzsche and got into higher mathematics. At seventeen, his classmates went out to find the girls of their dreams and plan their futures, while Bernhard set about poring over thick historical volumes. Bernhard, Ludwig and Theo, they were all so closed-off. Sometimes it seemed to her as if her men were carrying a huge secret.

Tears flowed down her cheeks. This made her uncomfortable in public, but she had started to get used to it. A profound sadness came over her frequently these days; she did not know why. She plucked a small handkerchief from the sleeve of her flower-patterned wool dress. It rubbed roughly at her cheek—her skin had become so sensitive.

But she worried about her husband the most. What would he do without her? Over the years, he had become more and more peculiar. Theo had never been a communicative person, but in the last few months he had become even more separate from her. Sometimes it seemed to her as if he was having inward conversations with someone else. When she spoke to him at those times, he often had no idea what she had asked him.

Would one of the children take him in? She looked over at him. His head rocked softly in time to the train. He had been bald for a long time now.

He wore a light-blue striped shirt whose buttons stretched over his shapeless belly, gray pants with suspenders, and on his feet (which did not even reach the ground) he wore dark grey fur boots. His lightly yellowed face was distorted with rage even in sleep, but Lydia still saw him as the most beautiful man in the world.

The older he got, the grumpier he became. The last odd thing he had asked of her was to fly to Miami with him. Suddenly, after more than 40 years of marriage, after heart attacks and breast cancer, he wanted to go on a second honeymoon. And to Miami? Why not Mallorca or Tenerife? When she barely had the strength to get into a taxi, how was she supposed to make it through a flight like that? But there had been a pain in his eyes, something so wretched that Lydia couldn't shake it out of him. He had set down two airplane tickets and a hotel reservation next to her jam-smeared plate, and Lydia had stood up and packed her suitcase.

She stared out the window. Snow covered meadows rushed past her, small sheep pressing against their mothers with crossed hooves. This winter was dark and much colder than the previous years.

A train pulled past the window, throwing her reflection back at her without warning. Lydia started back. She still hadn't gotten used to her new face: emaciated, bony, everything seemingly hanging off her cheeks. Only her gray-tinged curls sat perfectly, as if she had just come from the hairdresser—while beneath the artificial hair she had lost everything, a constant preparation for her approaching death.

She pulled a mirror out of her pocket, fidgeted with the wig and adjusted her artificial breasts. Her green eyes were dull; a grey veil hung over her pupils. Then she leaned back. If only she could sleep. But that had been difficult for weeks. Since her last chemotherapy, a dark fire was burning in her, not leaving her any peace. Did the fires of purgatory feel this way as well, she asked herself.

Her heart beat carefully against the inside of her chest. Thump-thump, thump-thump. It answered, but Lydia didn't understand its language.

She pulled a cross on a neck-chain out from under her blouse and held it fast in her hand. Then she closed her eyes: "Holy Mary, Mother of God, pray for us sinners…"

9.

"They're here!" called Gudrun, hearing Sieglinde's car approaching. Barbara jumped up from Mausi's lap and ran to the mirror to fix her ponytail. Karl folded the newspaper and laid it on top of the other half-read weekend editions. Then he gave Ludwig, the oldest in the clan of Moll siblings, a poke in the ribs, and stood up.

Ludwig had arrived an hour ago and fallen asleep on the floor within minutes. He had red-blond hair and a golden beard. Over his dark brown eyes there was an odd shadow. It was never clear whether he was looking at you or through you. When he spoke, he spoke softly, but that was rare.

Ludwig mumbled, turned on his side sedately, and raised himself up on one arm. Through the open door he saw Barbara, Gudrun and the children streaming out into the icy twilight, followed by Karl and scrawny Mausi. Slowly he climbed to his feet, pulled his sweater over his open belt and tucked it into his pants.

When he came outside, Sieglinde was already dragging the luggage from the trunk; Karl was at her side. Gudrun had opened the rear door and was helping their mother out. The lantern in the garden threw a green glow onto her face; her legs seemed so thin, it looked as if they would break at any moment.

"You look good," Gudrun said over the screaming of the children who were pushing to get at their grandmother.

"Thank you, I'm doing very well," Lydia answered with a shaky voice. Then she took the children one after another into her arms.

Their father had stayed motionless in the passenger seat, as if he had fallen asleep. But his eyes were open.

Barbara opened the door. "Papa, aren't you going to get out?"

He looked at her briefly and pushed himself wordlessly out of the seat; the family stepped aside to make way for him.

"The ride was very strenuous," said Lydia into the sudden stillness.

Theo placed his fur boots onto the ground and sank into the snow up to his ankles.

When he straightened up, his face screwed up painfully, and the family held their breath. For a moment he looked down at his boots as if they had sunken in shit, then he lifted his pants high and trudged silently towards the house.

His children looked at him, shrugging their shoulders. Barbara whispered in Sieglinde's ear: "I was right after all. I was just telling Mausi that Father was always grossed out by snow, and for a minute I wasn't sure if I had imagined it."

Sieglinde glared at her sister, and she fell silent.

Bernhard walked out of the door and suddenly found himself face to face with his father. His back straightened, his eyes pulled back.

Like two soldiers at the change of the guard, Gudrun thought. Somehow they were incredibly similar, although Bernhard was a good head taller than his father and his chest was only half as broad. And while Bernhard's face seemed soft and vulnerable, their father's face seemed as dangerous as a powder keg surrounded by fire. Maybe it was the way they held themselves, the cricks in their necks that caught the eye. Or maybe it was the scars on their chins, which were now glowing angrily. Bernhard had scraped himself in a bike accident, Gudrun still remembers it well, because she had to rock him on her lap for hours back then. But where did Father get his scar from?

Bernhard stepped aside mutely, and Theo passed by him without a word.

"Ah, my boy." Lydia pulled her son down to her. "It makes me so happy to see you all together again."

Bernhard hugged her, then slipped quickly out of her embrace.

"We'd better all head in now," said Karl, herding the family towards the door.

Theo had already sat down on the couch and was clicking on the remote. His grey winter coat lay next to him.

"Karl, could you please turn on the TV?" asked Gudrun, taking Theo's coat and hanging it on the coat rack.

"Are you hungry?" Sieglinde asked her mother.

"No, Papa always wants to watch the news before we eat," Lydia answered, sitting down next to her husband. The children came into the living room with coloring books and laid siege to the grandparents.

Ludwig sat down at the dinner table. After turning the television on, Karl went over to him; they grinned at each other silently.

"Would you at least like a cup of tea? Gudrun bought *Chimney Fire*, your favorite tea."

"Papa, would you like tea?" Lydia asked her husband.

"No!" He flipped through the channels.

"All right. Gudrun and I have a bit more cooking to do. We'll eat after the news." Sieglinde led Manuela by the hand. "And you, my dear little daughter, can set the table."

"But I don't want to," she moaned, tearing herself away from her mother.

"Leave her," Karl said soothingly. "I'll do it."

Sieglinde glared at her daughter, then disappeared into the kitchen.

"Am I imagining it, or has he gotten more impossible?" asked Gudrun in a low voice as soon as Sieglinde had closed the door behind her.

"He's a sick man. What do you expect?" Sieglinde stirred the soup, then tasted it.

"Respect maybe. Treating his family like human beings, and not like his subordinates." Gudrun poured milk over the strudel, and the sweet scent of apples spread through the kitchen.

"Gudrun, you're exaggerating. He's just not particularly talkative. He was never that way."

"I'm not expecting an entertainer. But is it too much to expect a friendly smile when you haven't seen each other for half a year?

I mean, why am I doing all this work? For myself?" She slammed the oven door shut and stood up straight again.

"We did the work for Mama—and for ourselves. Who knows how many more times we'll all get to be together."

"Which is why I think he should make a bit of an effort. After all, it's his wife who's dying."

"Shhhh!" hissed Sieglinde at her sister.

"You want to know why Papa is so upset about the *Wehrmacht* exhibition? Because the people who put it together weren't there themselves. That's why," said Lydia, playing with her handkerchief. Bernhard sat next to her. Theo had fallen asleep on the other couch; his head lay tilted back on the armrest, his throat was exposed and horribly vulnerable.

"Mama, those are documents of the times. He wouldn't claim the pictures are faked, would he?"

"I don't know. But the exhibition is one-sided. Anyone who sees it might assume that all the soldiers were criminals. No one shows how hard it was for them." She laid her head to the side thoughtfully.

"But that's nonsense, Mama. We can't remain silent about some men's crimes just because others might fall into disrepute because of them." Bernhard watched his father's carotid artery swell and subside.

Lydia lifted her head. Her eyes were soft and a little damp. "You know, I don't think any of us can imagine what those men lived through back then."

Theo's chest didn't move anymore. It looked as if he had stopped breathing. Gudrun's words went through Bernhard's head again: "Just imagine you tell him and he has another heart attack. You would never be able to forgive yourself." Sweat formed on Bernhard's brow.

"Isn't it understandable, after all they've gone through, that when it's over they don't want to lose their reputations as well?" Lydia stressed again.

His father could drop dead, thought Bernhard. He could drop

dead at the dinner table if he found out that he had a gay son. And everyone would think it was Bernhard's fault.

"We should eat now," Gudrun said briskly, setting placemats on the table. "The kids should get to bed. Normally we eat a lot earlier."

Lydia laid her hand on her husband's knee. He twitched, rubbed his eyes, looked around and grabbed the remote to turn the sound back up.

"Just start," said Lydia. "We'll be there in a minute."

Gudrun sighed and went back into the kitchen.

Flo slipped down from Ludwig's lap and wobbled towards Bernhard. His lips sucked attentively at his thumb, while his other hand reached out for his uncle's pants leg.

The news report continued. A good time to call Edvard, thought Bernhard. "Is it all right if I use the telephone?" he asked his brother-in-law.

"It's out there," he answered, his eyes glued to the screen.

Bernhard picked up his little nephew and held him close. He made his way to the phone and dialed, but the line was busy. Meanwhile, Flo picked at his uncle's hair. Then he looked into Bernhard's eyes, clapped his hands and giggled.

Bernhard dialed again. Still busy.

Biggy, Sissy and Manuela were fighting over who got to sit next to their grandparents. In a sharp voice Gudrun threatened that all three of them would be sent off to bed without any dinner if they didn't quiet down. Sieglinde served apple strudel, Karl poured out milk and Bernhard passed around the vanilla sauce. Theo sat still over his plate while hot steam swirled around his immobile features. He was like a big magnet: all attention was drawn into the aura of his silence.

"Who would like to say grace?" asked Lydia. She turned to her grandchildren, but all three of them shrugged their shoulders in a daze.

"I'll say grace," cut in Sieglinde, prompting the girls to fold their hands with a sharp look.

"Dear God, thank you for these delicious gifts. May we feast upon them…"

"Come, Lord Jesus, be our guest, and bless what you have bestowed upon us," Lydia added with a painful smile.

Sissy grinned across the table at her sister and giggled. Gudrun glared at her. Ludwig was about to dig into his meal, but their mother jumped in again: "I have something else to say to you. It makes me glad with all my heart to be sitting here with you. This is something I really wanted. After all one can't know how many more times we'll be able to do this."

"But mother!"

Lydia waved it off. "It's all right. I'm just so thankful that I have you all." She turned past her husband towards Gudrun and Sieglinde. "My hands won't reach any further," she said. There was a tear in her eye. She lowered her head and grabbed her fork.

Quietly, the family stuck their forks into the soft baked apples, which melted on the tongue with their mild taste. Bernhard stared at his own plate, but his attention was focused on the others. Why did they do this every time? No one had anything to say to the others. The whole family was a motley pile of miserable fates, connected only by a name: Moll.

"It tastes fantastic," said Barbara, smilingly sweetly across to Gudrun.

"It's strange. The rest of the year it doesn't taste this good. It only works when Mother comes."

"It's really quite wonderful," their mother confirmed. "But when Gundi makes it, it always is."

Gudrun smiled sheepishly.

They were all so quiet, so restrained. This feigned politeness. Bernhard would have given quite a bit to know what was going through his siblings' heads.

Lydia wiped her lips, folded her napkin elaborately and set it next to her plate. When all eyes were on her, she gave an account of their travel plans.

"When are you heading out?"

"The day after tomorrow at twelve."

"Why are you going to Miami, actually?"

"The sun will do us good."

The girls poked around on their plates, piled mushy apples into little mountains, made canals in them with vanilla sauce.

"But why so far? Wouldn't Mallorca have been enough, or Tenerife?"

Lydia smiled and brought another piece of strudel to her lips. Her eyes swiveled shyly over to Theo; he didn't even lift his head. He stayed quiet, as if he had had nothing to do with it.

Gudrun set her elbows down on the table and held her head up hopefully; Lydia sank her fork into the soft dough. She pierced a steaming piece of apple and put it on her tongue, chewing on it as if she could taste the answer. Why Florida? Why anything? Had anyone ever understood what went on in that man's head?

"A real success, that's all I can say," Barbara gushed in order to break the silence.

The three girls had stopped playing with their plates and showcasing the architectural wonders of piled apple slices to one another.

"Grandpa?" Sissy's legs shifted back and forth. She couldn't take the suspense anymore. "Are you going to eat your strudel?"

"He'll eat it," Lydia answered for him and smiled at her granddaughter. "Grandpa is just tired from the trip, you know."

"What is your favorite part of the strudel?" she pressed him further, tugging at her grandfather's sleeve. "I like the crust best. I don't really like the apples at all."

"Do I have to remind you not to talk while you're eating, or would you rather go straight to bed?" Sieglinde hissed.

"Why Miami, Mama?" Gudrun asked again, this time much more insistently, and her siblings held their breath.

Then Theo lifted his head and stared at them one by one. His gaze was cold, his lips tight.

"Yeah, well, why not?" said Barbara and took a sip of milk.

10.

His hands were soft, strong and determined. They ignited small fires on his skin, and cooled them before the flames grew too high; they pinched and stroked, even slapped at just the right amount, only to caress and calm a moment later, until his body quaked and shuddered, until he was so excited that only screams would release him, until he unloaded with an rush of convulsions and sank down exhausted.

After that night, Raimondo had thought of the baker often. But it was his hands above all, and what they had done to him, that he couldn't get out of his head.

Something moist slapped against Raimondo's neck.

"You're not even listening to me!" Kim nagged, lifting her hand to throw another a tear-soaked tissue at his head.

"Of course, my darling," he said in a collected voice, turning towards her. She was huddled in a white wicker chair, her legs pulled tight against her chest. Her thin nightshirt hung down over her knees. The table was covered with crumpled-up tissues in pastel blue, pink and yellow.

"I heard every word. Men are all pigs, you never want anything to do with them again."

Raimondo placed the chopped-up garlic in the press. The scent of warm olive oil spread through Kim's apartment—food, he believed, was the best medicine.

Of course he hadn't been listening; he wasn't able to. His attention was far too focused on the events of the night before, his thoughts occupied with a future he yearned for. But he knew Kim's rants by heart, they were always the same after all.

She had called him right after throwing Fred out. Raimondo rushed over to her, knowing that if she was left alone with a disappointment like this she would hole up in bed and eat nothing but chocolates all day long until fat zits popped up on her soft skin, at which point she would truly see no point in living.

"That pig! That pig! That pig! He lied to me. I feel used, abused, mistreated, robbed. I could kill him! I'll never trust a man again. They're not worth loving. I should never even speak to one again."

He threw a skeptical glance over his shoulder and chopped the soft dried mushrooms into small pieces.

"I don't mean you. I'm talking about real men."

"Thanks."

"No, I didn't mean it that way. You know what I'm trying to say." She hurled another damp ball in his direction. A light blue one this time. "I hate them! I hate them!"

Raimondo was used to this. In the past two years she had gotten into this state six times; he was keeping track. In fact, Kim had been overdue. Thank God, it normally didn't take her long to work through her disappointment. In a few weeks, maybe even days, she would fall in love again, and her old pain would be forgotten.

Raimondo opened the refrigerator; the sight dismayed him; a gaping emptiness. He shook his head and pulled butter out of one of the three shopping bags he wisely had brought with him. "Oh! Did you bring me chocolates?" she begged.

"My dear, I'm cooking us a risotto funghi porcini, maybe you'll feel a bit better after that."

"But I don't want risotto." Kim twisted a tissue into the shape of a little man. "I want chocolates," she moaned stubbornly. She curled up more deeply in her chair.

Raimondo didn't answer. He knew that contradicting her would only make her more stubborn and pig-headed. The best thing to do was to let it go quietly.

"I should have told him to go to hell from the start."

"Yes, my little one."

"Of course, you saw it coming. But I have news for you. This time, I was unsure about it from the beginning."

"Of course, I know that, darling dear."

"*United Steaks!* Who calls themselves *United Steaks*? It was too smooth, too perfect. It could only be a lie."

And his lips, thought Raimondo. Only a confectioner could taste so sweet…

"Fucking men! How do you stand it?"

…sweet and deep, like black cherries…he could still feel those small, nimble hands on his skin.

"You could try women."

Kim reached back and hurled the wet tissue-man in his direction, but it fell flatly to the ground.

Raimondo tossed onions and mushrooms into the pot, where olive oil was already sizzling.

"Maybe you should pack your suitcase at some point."

"No, I don't want to."

"But Florida is a beautiful place."

"But I can't. I'm sick."

"Do you want to put your job on the line too, all because of this liar?"

Kim was tearing little shreds from her tissue, rolling them in little balls and flicking them across the kitchen.

"I won't let you ruin your life because of this affair. If you don't pack yourself, I'll do it for you. Either way—tomorrow you'll be sitting on that airplane." He stirred energetically with a wooden spoon.

"What if Fred calls tomorrow?" she whispered to him, barely audible.

"Excuse me?"

Kim was silent.

"You're a few cards short of a full deck, aren't you?"

Raimondo turned back to the pots, poured a splash of white wine into the broth and tasted it. Then he turned back the flame and set next to Kim at the table. As he sipped from the blue cup of the long-stemmed glass, it was plain to see he didn't think much of the new-fangled design.

"Maybe I was just overreacting. What could a ring like that even mean?"

"If you were my daughter, I'd put you across my knee right now."

He stood up, poured a ladleful of broth onto the frying rice and started stirring carefully. Slowness was the secret to a tasty risotto. Good ingredients alone meant nothing if you didn't have the patience necessary to prepare them properly. Heating them up too quickly could ruin everything; you had to estimate the right point in time to stir, when to pour in broth and when to just wait. Cooking risottos was like a night of love.

Kim howled bitterly. If only she could get her emotions under control, thought Raimondo, but it pained him to see her suffer.

To think all of the guys she'd fallen in love with: one of her flight attendant trainers, a fairly dirty vagrant she wanted to travel the world with, a farmer with all his cows and tractors, the manager of the store she used to work for, and…he couldn't remember any more. And every time, she glorified the men to a point where they could only leave her disappointed in the end. It got worse and worse. This Fred really seemed to have promised her the earth.

Raimondo spread a spoonful of risotto smoothly onto the plate and decorated it with a large serrated piece of carrot and a sprig of parsley. To top it off, he drizzled truffle oil over it, and a whiff of old sneakers penetrated the warm air. Then he set next to her at the table.

"The essence of most Italian dishes is parmesan," he began to explain. "Fine, young, violet-scented parmesan for truffle spaghetti, spicy, lightly sour parmesan reminiscent of licorice with red wine, and strong, full-bodied parmesan for risotto." He grated the cheese onto the dishes, then saw Kim's face grow pale.

"I'm so confused, Raimondo," she said, poking around the plate with her fork.

"I just don't know how to go on. Why does this always happen to me?"

It nearly broke his heart. "It's only natural after an experience like this. You need to digest the disappointment a bit first."

"I'm not talking about Fred."

Raimondo laid the parmesan aside and propped his head up on his wrinkled hands.

"When I meet men, sometimes it feels as if another soul is taking possession of me. I lose all sense of reality. I can't see what's really going on out there. I hear things as if through a filter. And the worst thing about: I don't notice it until it's too late."

Raimondo grasped for her delicate white hand. Kim lifted her head and looked him deep in the eyes. "You knew him, right?"

"Who?"

"My father."

Raimondo dropped her hand in surprise: she hadn't asked about him for a long time.

"My mother always acted as if he didn't exist. But there must have been some way he looked, he must have breathed and thought like everyone else."

This was a side of Kim that Raimondo didn't know. "Why do you want to know this all of a sudden?"

Kim took her fork and maneuvered the carrot piece like a submarine through the semi-liquid rice. "Sometimes it feels as though I'm missing something, like an organ or something."

Raimondo couldn't resist the aroma any longer, and shoveled a forkful of risotto into his mouth. It melted smoothly on his tongue, the perfectly cooked grains of rice still retaining the necessary bite. But perhaps it could use just bit more truffle oil.

"You know those big plastic cubes people give to small children to play with," Kim continued. She set down her fork again; her eyes wandered towards the ceiling of her snow-white kitchen. "On each side, there are different-shaped holes cut out. And then there are colored blocks you have to put into the right holes. Sometimes I feel like one of those cubes. For years I've been trying to find a man that fits me. But the problem is, I don't have any idea what shape I'm supposed to be looking for."

"But my dear, it's like that for everyone."

"No, you don't understand…"

"Of course I understand you. Think of who you're talking to."

Kim looked so vulnerable. Raimondo had rarely seen his little doll so upset. As a child maybe, when she found a dead hedgehog in the garden or when her cat chased that excitedly flapping sparrow through her parents' house.

"You're a good person," she whispered, stroking his stubbly cheeks.

After dinner, he sent Kim to her bedroom to pack, while he put on plastic gloves and started on the dishes.

"How long are you staying in Miami actually?"

"Two days," she answered with an effort. She was in the process of pulling her dark blue stewardess suitcase out of her closet and throwing it onto her bed. It was already half full: with underwear, tights, a few T-shirts.

"You should travel out to Key Largo and swim with the dolphins. It's magnificent."

"You think so?" she asked skeptically, looking for her bikini.

"You won't regret it. I thought it would be something for children, but Serge enjoyed it a lot."

Kim went into the bathroom and pulled her cosmetics bag from the cupboard. A quick look informed her that everything she needed was inside it. The packet of pills was still lying on the counter. She hesitated a minute and then put it back. I won't need these anymore, she thought. I'm not going to let myself get involved with another man so quickly!"

"Kim!"

"Yeah?"

"You lucky girl. Don't forget to think of your old uncle Raimondo, sitting here at home waiting for you. Have a cocktail at sunset for me. Ah, how I love Florida."

Mushroom-brown foam flowed from his glove, which he had just pulled out of the water. Maybe he should just surprise his baker with airplane tickets. Or was that premature? But when he left he said he would like to see Raimondo again, and he had no choice but to believe those sweet lips. After all, he was the one who had been looking at Raimondo in the café, not the other way around. And after a night like that!

"Kim?" Raimondo felt the heat of Florida on his hands, the smell of moist, salty air came to his nostrils, and he saw lots of young bodies glistening with sweat pass by his inner eye. Holding hands, they would walk together down the beach. In little restaurants on the ocean, he would show him all the gourmet cuisine of Florida. Which hotel should he book?

"Kimmy!"

Raimondo took the gloves off his hands. Kim was curled up next to the open suitcase. A few pieces of clothing lay scattered around her.

"Get up! Finish your packing! There's no point in wallowing in self-pity."

He bent down for the pink bikini, folded her light-blue jeans and placed them in the suitcase next to her other clothes. Then he heard Kim sobbing lightly.

Raimondo sat down on the bed and stroked her back slowly. God didn't give me the option of having my own children, he thought, but he certainly made sure I would have to take care of one.

"Will you stay with me tonight?" she asked in an imploring voice.

Raimondo shrugged. His bed was still full of the baker's horny sweat. He had left behind an aura of vanilla and cinnamon. Raimondo had been planning to talk to him. He was certainly waiting for him to call. He needed to kiss those lips again that tasted like Christmas, feel those hands that made his body quake just to remember their touch. And if he didn't come again, he wanted to at least wrap himself in those still fragrant sheets and dream of him, to soak it all up down to the last molecule and live off it.

Kim laid her head down in his lap. "Please!" she begged.

Raimondo gave her a kiss on the forehead. "Of course I'll stay with you. Of course."

11.

Bernhard awoke with a start, shivering. In his nose, there was an odor of gunpowder and burning flesh, and he had the distinct sensation of mud smeared all over his skin. The images in his dream wouldn't go away: it's night, he's huddled with fellow soldiers in a trench. Bombs fall all around them, the constant hum of tanks and propellers drone in his ears, and his bones have grown weak with all the tremors.

A cigarette is passed around, a last glimmering spark. They don't speak, they just stare outwards with widened eyes. The little red end flares up again and again, then wanders a few inches in the icy darkness. It's like eenie-meenie-minie-mo, but no one knows whether the one who took the last puff will be the next one to die or the only one to survive. One of his comrades starts laughing resoundingly, and Bernhard can see the madness in his eyes.

Flo waddled into the room and gave Bernhard a soft kiss between his lips and cheek. To do this, he even took his dripping pacifier out of his mouth, then held it out to his Uncle: "Eeerni!" was all his little sweet lips were able to squeak.

"Good morning, little thing." Bernhard pulled him in to return the kiss, but Flo held the pacifier out to him stubbornly. The child squealed gleefully and wobbled away unsteadily.

Noise pressed at his ears. It sounded like the girls playing tag in the living room; between those sounds he could hear plates clattering.

He looked at the clock; it was eight. Edvard would be leaving the house about now. Edvard! He still hadn't given him a call.

Bernhard jumped up, slipped into his shirt and pants and hurried down the stairs.

"Is it all right if I…" he asked Karl and pointed to the telephone. Karl nodded.

Bernhard took it into the hall and closed the door to the living room. He dialed Edvard's number. "You've dialed the right number at the wrong time," the answering machine chimed at him.

Sieglinde called for breakfast, and Bernhard heard Barbara and Mausi on the stairs. He hung up again.

"Would you like some bread?"

"No thanks."

"Can I pour anyone some tea?"

"Yeah, that would be nice."

Friendliness spread around the breakfast table, as if this could make the family hide the fact that their father's chair was empty. It stood there like a ghost, and no one dared even look at it.

The girls ran around the living room. Again and again one of them would come into view with flying pigtails, red in the face, running past the open door. Stirred-up clouds of dust played in the sunlight.

"What's the plan for today?" Sieglinde held Flo in her lap, who was digging into her honey roll with both hands and giggling happily.

"I'm all for a walk," said Barbara, pinching Mausi's cheek.

Bernhard caught his brother's disgusted look.

"Mother, what would you like to do today?"

"Oh, you know, make your own plans. I'll join in afterwards."

"I assume it's too strenuous for you to go for a walk?" Barbara was trying to act concerned, but she only sounded didactic.

"That's not a problem," said Sieglinde. "I brought a wheelchair. We'll get you into it and bring you along."

In an instant, all eyes were on Sieglinde, even Ludwig looked up. Wheelchair! They felt the word deep in their bones.

"I thought it would be more pleasant for you to spend some time in the fresh air."

"I don't mind." Lydia plucked lint from her dress.

"So everything's settled?"

"Yes, let me just bring Papa his breakfast."

"Where is he?" asked Gudrun.

"He's not doing very well. He's going to stay in bed for a while."

"Aha," said Gudrun much too snappily. Barbara stared at her.

Lydia pulled her handkerchief from her sleeve, folded it, and, after a moment of hesitation, spoke. "I know he's difficult," she said, blotting tears from her eyes. "I wish he was different as well, but what am I supposed to do? He's my husband."

Gudrun exhaled angrily, Sieglinde looked over at her coldly.

"Do you really need to start bickering at breakfast?" Ludwig grumbled, reaching into the breadbasket. Bernhard understood why his brother tended to stay away from the family.

"He's really not doing well," said Lydia, looking over at her daughter imploringly.

"It's all right, Mama." Barbara stroked her mother's shoulders. Karl laid his hand soothingly on Gudrun's knee.

"I wasn't trying to get at you. It's just…"

"I know, I know. But…" Lydia sniffled. "You can't be mad at him. He's had a hard life, and he's always been there for you all." She hesitated and swallowed. "Without him…" Her upper lip trembled. Gudrun waited with wide eyes, but her mother just took the plate on which her roll was wobbling back and forth, and disappeared from the room.

"Was that necessary?" Barbara aimed the words at Gudrun like a pistol, but she didn't react.

If their mother couldn't handle him, how were any of them supposed to manage?

Gudrun had always believed there were logical reasons for his behavior. At some point, someone would explain it to her, and she would finally understand why she had felt rejected her entire life.

Gudrun went into the kitchen and shut the door behind her. Karl followed her, rocking her head between his warm hands, whispering as he often did with the girls when they cried: "What is it, my little butterfly? Did the bees chase you away?"

But this pain was different from a bump on the head or a forgotten invitation to a friend's birthday party. This pain had destroyed Gudrun's last hope.

Sieglinde maneuvered the wheelchair leisurely around the neighborhood. Lydia was well wrapped up in a cap, scarf and extra layer of socks; the tires squeaked in the snow and left narrow, deep trails. The siblings followed her at a distance.

"Gudrun lives in such a beautiful area, don't you think?" said Lydia, pointing to the wide forest surrounding the village.

Winter swallowed up the noise of the city.

"Yes, well, she's always been a bit luckier than the rest of us." Sieglinde paused. That came out more bitterly than she had intended.

"You have no idea how much I'm enjoying this air. It's only when you look death in the eye…"

"Mother, please."

"…that life really becomes precious. I hope you don't have to deal with illness, but you won't be able to avoid growing old."

Sieglinde watched the girls climbing around on the mounds of snow on the roadside, as if she could avoid the conversation this way.

"When you get older, you see things with different eyes. Years ago I was convinced it would have been better to leave your father. Now I'm certain I made the right decision."

"Definitely, mother."

"I still don't understand your father, but I've come to believe it's possible to love without understanding. Do you know what I mean?"

"Yes," sighed Sieglinde. She was prepared to agree with anything as long as her mother kept Eberhard out of it.

Gudrun carried Flo on her shoulders. His cheeks glowed; a long clear string dripped from his nose, thin as a spider web. Biggy and Sissy pulled at Bernhard's hands, trying to get him to run races with them.

"Sieglinde is always so awfully organized," said Barbara quietly as she strolled next to them, hanging from her Mausi. "I think it's how she compensates for her unhappy relationship with Eberhard. I don't understand why she's gone through with it for so long."

"Well she's not setting the best example." Gudrun pointed to their mother, who was wobbling from side to side in her wheelchair.

"Maybe neither of their relationships is that bad," said Barbara sharply. "We only see them for a short period of time, we can't really judge how they interact with one another when they're alone."

"Isn't it obvious how he is controlling her? Mom's completely subservient to him."

"He's sick. Have you forgotten? She loves him and wants to spare him. I find it rather understandable."

Bernhard didn't like the tone the sisters' conversation was taking. Why did they always have to take sides when it came to their father?

"Since his heart attack. Since his heart attack! That's been the excuse for his messed-up behavior for years. Just ask Ludwig. He's known him ten years longer than you have. The truth is, Father was never any different, even before the heart attack. He's just completely dysfunctional when it comes to relationships."

"Maybe you're dysfunctional about relationships. You have a problem with men! That's the point here."

Bernhard saw Gudrun's eyes blaze resentfully. "Maybe the problem is somewhere else entirely," she answered sharply. "Maybe the problem is that your eyes are so fixed on your little sweetheart that you've become blind to everything going on around you."

Barbara stood still: "And now you're nagging me about Mausi too. You don't have to take your problems with Karl out on me!"

"My problems with Karl? What problems? The only problem I have right now is that your I'm-the-good-daughter performance is getting on my nerves!"

Bernhard took a step ahead. He had heard enough.

"Should I take over for you?" he asked Sieglinde.

"Please." She was visibly relieved. Bernhard gave Sissy and Biggy to her, but Manuela scampered away, and they wanted to follow.

"See you soon." Sieglinde gave her mother a kiss on her cold red cheek and then stood still waiting for her sisters.

"Are you warm enough?" Bernhard asked his mother.

"Mmm, it's wonderful." She shut her eyes and soaked up the little bit of sun shining down on her.

"You know what made your father so bitter?" she asked. "He never learned to talk. Since I've known him, he has always worked things out on his own. That's not good."

Bernhard shrugged. "Ah, really?"

"Who would have thought our little brother was carrying a secret like that around with him?" asked Sieglinde.

"You really can't tell by looking at him," said Barbara. "I mean, by his clothes or something." All four of them looked forward at their gangly brother, whose coat was flapping around at his knees; the baggy elbows shone like warning lights. There was nothing feminine about him, no affected movements. He wasn't overly groomed, nor was he fashionably dressed, the way it usually was with gay men.

"I'm just wondering why? I mean other than him there's no other…" Barbara lowered her voice. "…homosexual in our family."

"There's one thing you can't forget," explained Sieglinde to her sisters, shooing the girls away who had crept up with wide-open ears. "Bernhard was the first one Mother told about her cancer. And if I remember correctly, he went to the doctor with her a lot."

"What are you trying to say with that?" asked Gudrun. Manuela stalked up to her again.

"It's obvious. An old woman's breasts aren't exactly eye candy, particularly not when she has cancer! That can't have had an encouraging effect on his sexual desires," finished Barbara with satisfaction.

"Oh, so you're now an expert on sex too?"

"Why are you being so snotty?" Barbara sneered back. "We're just trying to find an explanation. Our brother is a homosexual and we're worried about him."

"Manuela, let us talk alone for a few minutes. Is that all right?" Sieglinde's daughter stalked off with an injured expression.

"You're not worried about him, you're looking for excuses. That's all. You just can't accept that he's gay," Gudrun reproached them. She was furious, and had to restrain herself from bursting.

"Well I'm glad you know exactly what's going on in my head," countered Barbara. Her voice became very shrill. "Next time I have a problem I'll come right to you." She turned away and clung to Mausi.

Gudrun stood still and scolded them: "All you ever do is bad-mouth each other. This family makes me sick!"

Then she ran forward to Bernhard and their mother.

"Mother was just telling me about the article she was reading this morning," said Bernhard, faltering as he saw Gudrun's angry face. He looked at her questioningly; she laid a finger on her lips and shook her head.

"Yeah? What kind of article?"

"There was a mother with five children who all died one after the other supposedly of sudden infant death syndrome. When the neighbors were building an addition to their house they found the corpses."

"That's terrible!"

"The woman claimed she couldn't stand hearing the children cry." Lydia told the story in a monotonous voice.

"Only a mother can understand that," said Gudrun.

"What did her husband say about it?" asked Bernhard.

"He stood by her. In court, he held her hand," said Lydia. "She killed all five of his children, and he stands by her just the same."

"That's a great story." Gudrun pointed to the left. "Let's head this way, it's shorter."

"Don't we want to keep going a bit longer…?"

Gudrun rolled her eyes and made it clear to him that she had had enough. She turned left and followed the bridge over the stream.

Karl opened the door and let them into the house. He, Ludwig and Theo were playing cards in the kitchen.

"I don't understand men." Gudrun shook her head.

Theo tilted back his beer, Ludwig nodded briefly to the walkers, then popped a card down on the table.

"It's like magic!" he grumbled.

Lydia confirmed knowingly. "Men amongst themselves, now there's a sight to see."

Bernhard shrugged.

Sieglinde and Barbara went single file through the kitchen into the dining room. When Karl saw their faces, he whispered to the other two: "Just glad I didn't have to be there," and all three of them laughed.

Whenever more than two of the Molls met, there was tension. Bernhard christened this the Mollian constant; since the walk, it had been growing steadily. On the family's own open-ended Richter scale, they had reached approximately a six, and a strange feeling was setting in. It was like a carnival ride: you're strapped in and you know nothing can actually happen to you, but even if you've ridden it a thousand times you never dare to let go, because you're still afraid to come flying out of it.

The only way the Moll family could keep the tension in check was by splitting up, forming smaller, harmless groups, sleeping, concentrating their eyes on the flickering TV screen, or sitting quietly in a corner and watching.

And this how it went today as well. Gudrun flipped through knitting magazines with her mother. They looked for patterns, planned to knit socks, sweaters and gloves for all the children in the family. Neither of them really believed that Lydia would complete any of them in her remaining months, but it reminded them of those winter months when Gudrun was still small and the word 'cancer' was not yet integrated into the family's vocabulary. It had a calming effect to act as if life went on forever.

Sieglinde advised the children as to what colors they should use to color in the Santas and Bible scenes in the Christian coloring books their grandmother had brought with her.

Barbara lay in Mausi's lap—where else? Aside from the constant whispering and repeated smacking of lips, little more was heard from her.

The men only left the table when nature called. Bernhard was positioned at the corner. He spent several hours staring into the open fire and enjoying the fact that those strange panic attacks weren't affecting him anymore. It must just have been over-exertion, nothing more.

But the children wouldn't follow the rules for balancing out the Mollian constant, and kept acting out. Biggy was watching *Mouse TV* excitedly when Manuela decided she wanted to watch another program, changed the channel and waited for Biggy's reaction. It came quickly, and for minutes afterwards they were pulling each other's hair and screeching. Then Sissy sat next to her uncle and wanted him to admire her little painting. Bernhard nodded in agreement, but he didn't want to say anything. He was afraid of drawing attention to himself. Then Manuela pushed herself between them and asked him to color in a manger scene with her. Bernhard refused, which turned out to be an even bigger mistake.

"But I want you to color with me."

"Manu, I'm tired. Just let me lie here a bit, please."

"But you've been lying around all day. Did you not get enough sleep?"

"Manu, I don't want to color right now." He looked around nervously. The atmosphere in the room was that of earthquake survivors waiting for an aftershock, always ready to jump up and run to safety.

"You never want to color with me," she said, and there was trouble in the air.

"Manuela!" Sieglinde flashed. "If Bernhard doesn't want to, then leave him alone. Stop getting on everyone's nerves. That's enough."

"These stupid family reunions," moaned the child resentfully. "No one pays attention to us. Why are we even here? I want to go home! Right now."

Sieglinde gave her daughter a slap and dragged by her the arm out of the living room.

Blubbering, Manu turned around to Bernhard, her eyes narrowed to spears, and Bernhard knew: the hour had not yet struck.

The poltergeist made itself evident at first in the fallen beer bottle whose contents splashed over their father's pants and soaked into the new carpet. Then an ember leaped out of the fire onto Karl's chest, burning a big hole in his sand-colored cashmere vest. At six, the age-weakened television set gave out. The image collapsed into a single glowing point, then went still.

As the unrest grew, so did the necessity to split up further. Gudrun and Sieglinde disappeared into the kitchen, Lydia retreated to the bedroom to rest, and Bernhard ran to the pay phone on the corner. The earpiece was ice cold, the dial tone irregular and distorted. He had scrounged up a handful of coins, but none of them would stick. One after the other, they fell out of the machine. He hung up and went back home.

At dinner, they all sat down together again. Plates full of tomato slices were passed around wordlessly, onions, breadbaskets, butter, cold cuts and pickles. They avoided eye contact. If it occurred, they interrupted it with a friendly smile. Movements were mechanical, everyone wary of the erupting volcano.

Bernhard occupied himself solely with his father. He sat stiffly in front of his family at the head of the table, his plate orderly, everything on it arranged by color and shape like a storage facility. Gudrun often called him "the soldier" as a joke. But she wasn't wrong. All those rules in his life. Towards police and other authorities, he behaved downright submissively, while he expected full compliance from his family. The embarrassing orderliness in his house, the constant arguments back then, because it was impossible for anyone else to follow his laws. Maybe, Bernhard thought, maybe he never stopped being a soldier deep down. In any case, there was something there that had always connected him with the war. Just as this question went through his head, Bernhard smelled mud again, and he saw his father as a young man in uniform.

Manuela had the whole family in her crosshairs. Her eyes jumped furiously from one to the next. She awaited her entrance. Now that everyone had served themselves and were all turned to their plates, now was the best opportunity.

"Mama, what does 'gay' mean?"

"Now what kind of expressions have you been learning?"

"Me?" She asked and rolled her eyes innocently. "Aunt Gudrun said earlier that Uncle Bernie is gay."

Silence. Everyone stopped moving. Theo lifted his head and looked at his son from across the table. His eyes drilled into Bernhard like a bayonet. Then he went pale, and his eyes widened. But there was no disgust in them, no hatred, not even rage, just pure panic. The fear of death was visible, thickly, beneath his skin, where his racing pulse made the sides of his throat flutter.

"Oh, I'm sure you misheard." Barbara tried to rescue the situation.

Bernhard wanted to say something, but it was as there were a stone weighing down on his chest, cutting off his breath. "Just imagine you tell him and he has an attack. You would never forgive yourself," Gudrun had said. Terrified, he looked over at his father, who was visibly processing the information.

The others stayed stock-still as before; only Manu leaned back contentedly in her chair.

Theo stood up and left the room; a heaviness set in.

"Where's Grandpa going?" asked Biggy softly.

They heard his heavy, slow footsteps going up the stairs.

"Maybe he's just going to the bathroom," Sieglinde spoke carefully.

"...or to get his pills?" Lydia suggested. But his standing up had something final to it, and they all knew right away that he wasn't going to come back.

"Keep on eating, children. Don't wait for me." Lydia pushed back her chair and drew the door shut behind her. Then they could hear her steps on the stairs as well, timid, hesitant, fragile.

Theo had locked himself in the bathroom. Lydia knocked at the door.

"Open up, Theo. Let me in." But she got no answer. This was so emblematic of their relationship. There was always a door he closed in front of her. And all the knocking and pleading in this world wouldn't help her get behind it.

"Well tell me! Are you all right?" It stayed quiet. She wanted to say: "Don't be so pig-headed!" but she didn't dare. Lydia was helpless, the way she often was with this man.

With great effort, she sat down on the stair landing and decided to wait. It would pass by itself, as always. He came out of these moods, sat down in front of the TV, and everything returned to the way it was before. Patience was the magic word.

While she kept thinking about it, she heard a soft whimpering coming from underneath the door. And she understood that this was about more than having a gay son.

"Anyone else want cheese?" asked Ludwig, holding a piece of Emmenthaler up in the air.

Barbara looked at him disdainfully. "How can you eat now?"

"He's hungry," explained Biggy with a grin, dangling her legs.

"Don't get smart with me."

"All right, you're going to bed," Sieglinde determined. "Off you go."

"It's only seven o'clock!" Sissy rebelled, pushing her lower lip forward. Gudrun grabbed her daughters, whispered something in their ears, and they shuffled off looking hurt.

"Of course it had to turn out this way," said Barbara reproachfully, looking around.

"What?" asked Gudrun.

"You know what I mean."

"That Father ruined another family celebration?"

Ludwig poured out beer. "Do you want any?" he asked Bernhard, though his glass was still full. He shook his head.

"This time he has every reason to!" said Barbara.

"What my daughter said was certainly not the reason," Sieglinde defended herself, and as the others looked at her questioningly, she added: "And if it was, then it had much more to do with our brother's particular preferences, which he has managed to keep from us for so long."

Bernhard twitched; his eyes narrowed. Now it was out. He knew he couldn't count on his siblings.

"I'd like a bit more bread," said Ludwig, reaching his hand across the table.

Gudrun knocked on the door to the study, where Bernhard was lying rolled up in his sleeping bag.

"Listen," she said through the crack in the door, not daring to go any further. "I hope you don't think it was intentional. The girls must have overheard us when we were walking. I didn't tell them anything."

Bernhard didn't answer. He felt naked. Worse: exposed. Like an animal in a cage, and people were standing outside it staring at him. What did his sexuality matter to them? What did Sieglinde's accusation mean, that he had kept quiet about it?

"I know this situation sucks," she tried to persuade him. "I can imagine what it feels like for you. Probably you'd prefer to just run. But that would be the wrong thing to do."

Of course he wanted to leave. Preferably right away.

"It might be the last time we're all together. You've got to stay here for Mama." Gudrun came into the room and shut the door behind her. Sinking her voice she continued: "Besides, it would seem like an admission of guilt."

"It's okay," he whispered from his sleeping bag.

"Will you promise to stay?"

"Yeah, I'll stay."

Gudrun looked at her brother, who had buried his head deep in the sleeping bag. Sometimes it seemed as if they were kids again.

"Don't you want to talk?" she asked after some hesitation.

Bernhard had trusted her. She had disappointed him. That was the way it always was in this family.

"No, I'm tired. I want to sleep."

"All right," she said resignedly. Then she stood up and left the room.

A little while later Lydia knocked on the door, and Bernhard turned towards the wall. He didn't want her to see his face, the tears of disappointment in his eyes, and the shame.

"Do you not want to talk to me?" she asked, her voice full of love.

"No, Mama. I have a headache."

There was nothing more to say. Through their behavior, the family had turned his love for Edvard into something common. They didn't understand at all. And why should they? For the past forty years his mother had been with a husband who only tormented her. Sieglinde let her husband constantly go behind her back. Gudrun spent more time in women's seminars than with her own family. It wasn't even worth thinking about Barbara. And Ludwig had never had a real relationship. Edvard's love was better than his entire family put together. Bernhard could depend on him, that much was certain.

With horror, he thought of the ring again. How would Edvard react if he had really lost it? No, it wouldn't become a problem, he thought. He and Edvard loved one another. They trusted each other, they were faithful to one another. What did a ring matter?

And then he heard his mother close the door behind her.

12.

It had gotten colder. During the day, the landlord had shoveled the snow into large piles, but already by evening the sidewalks were covered with a thick layer of snow. Anyone with deferrable business stayed at home, cranked up the heat, watched soap operas or eyed the snowflakes dancing to and fro in front of the windows, skipping around in the warmth rising from houses as if led by puppeteers.

Fred rode the tram down Bayerstrasse, past the main train station, into the middle of the already dark, abandoned city. Even around there, it was quiet. A few mummified pedestrians made their way carefully along the sides of buildings in order not to slip. Taxis stood in a long line, some of them with their engines running, thick white shrouds of exhaust fumes hanging over their fenders.

Fred felt trapped with Roswitha. Before, he had never given a second thought to the people he used. It's only money, he had argued. But Roswitha was so dumb. She was so incredibly dumb. He knew he could have asked her to undress in the middle of the street and she would have done it. He could have run away with everything she had, and she wouldn't have moved a muscle. There was something about her that was so fragile it hurt him.

At Café Kreutzkamm, Fred got off. The cold was relentless. When he had first hit on Roswitha here, he had just wanted to relieve her of a thousand Marks. He had no way of knowing she would take everything so seriously, that she would even want to marry him now. At times he was fed up with mooching off her. People who trusted him blindly made his work difficult. Then he had to find justifications for himself. Not to mention that it wasn't so easy to compliment older women, to settle into their insular worlds, to please their worn-out bodies.

Fred could feel the heavy ring on his hand, which even in the dark night spat out glowing signals like tinder. Stupid cow!

Kim, on the other hand, had fit the bill. He hadn't had any scruples with her. She was overqualified. Too bad it hadn't worked out with her. He needed to find somebody new, he wasn't going to be able to stand it much longer with Roswitha.

He walked across Marienplatz. A violinist played Mozart, accompanied by a cassette recorder. Classical music had never interested Fred, but it lent a melancholy tone to the winter atmosphere, and it fit his mood. So he stood for a while and listened. Then he strolled past Dallmayer, past the National Theater, past the royal palace, into the empty courtyard. With every step it grew quieter around him, until all he heard was the silky crunch of snow beneath his boots and the unceasing murmur of his thoughts: today is Saturday, in three days it will be Christmas. If I haven't found a solution by then, I will have to celebrate with Roswitha. I won't be able to stand it. I can't do that to her, nor to myself.

"Why is your name actually Edvard, Edvard?" Karli von Hohenschlossburg asked pointedly. He emphasized the D so affectedly that it hissed.

Edvard could have answered that his mother had named him after King Edward, because he was just as beautiful and successful. He could have said that his godfather was Prince Edward of Scottsdale, and that he had been given the name because of that, but he didn't want to be drawn in by Karli's taunts, so he had left it at the truth: "My parents were living in America when the Kennedys were in fashion there, and my mother took it into her head to name her next son Edvard, though with a V, not with a W. She found the V more German."

Karli gave a superior look around; he had been expecting something this banal. But no one took any notice of his triumph. His friends were bending their heads over the lavishly decorated plates, reveling in the aroma of delicate duck breast, suckling pig, or St. Peter's fish.

This pre-Christmas exchange of ideas among business friends in Käfer's baroque restaurant had become a tradition. Every year they sat down together, told one another of their successes, gossiped about their competitors, and planned joint projects for the coming year.

Bernhard hadn't wanted to take part in this meeting at all. He called it "the boys of the dueling fraternity," which Edvard found pretty down-putting. Sure, they all came from well-off circumstances, and of course they helped one another, but you couldn't call it "dueling"—at least not in a traditional sense. Despite the recession, they had all made a profit. This certainly was related to the fact that they all had been ensuring business for one another for years. It helped to maintain intimate connections with management, city councilors, contractors, timber merchants, publishing directors and other people in leadership positions.

"How's Christmas looking?" Edvard asked around, before Karli could take aim for the next shot.

"I'm meeting Jeff at my chalet in St. Moritz."

"You mean the general?"

"Ssshhh!" hissed Gerhard, looking around to see if anyone had heard. "That could cost him his head!"

"Ooh, a mysterious man, how romantic! Is he really a grenade in bed?"

"Not a grenade! They call him Kalashnikov. No explanations are necessary."

"He's blushing," Karli hissed, pointing to Gerhard.

"You're just jealous," Gerhard snapped back, and Karli pursed his lips.

"We're going to fly to the Caribbean," said Günther. "Hartmut heard of an island there that's for sale for a good price. We want to take a look at it."

"And then what? Play castaways?"

"We'll take a Friday off and jump around the island naked," Günther teased. The others laughed.

"What are you doing?" Karli asked Herbert.

"Wolfgang has been begging me for weeks to visit his parents. They live in Kiel and are fairly lonely. At least that's what he says. I personally have the impression he wants to introduce me. I'm probably the first showpiece lover he's had."

"Showpiece lover? If he only knew!" joked Heiner.

"We could tell him a few stories, that's for sure," said Gerhard, and everyone laughed.

"You remember that time on the island of Sylt?"

"Oh, don't start with that again."

"Why? It was fun, the hottest orgy south of the North Pole. And the look in your eyes when you found out he was the prime minister of…"

"That's quite enough!"

Gerhard placed two fingers on his lips and looked bashful.

"Are you going to go along with him?" asked Edvard.

"I don't know."

"If you love him, you have to."

"Well, that's how it is."

"I'm going to Morocco for Christmas," Karli burst in. "I absolutely *must* soak up a bit of sun." He laid the back of his hand on his forehead, threw his head back and rolled his eyes skywards.

"Poor, exhausted Ms. Thing." Herbert stroked his head. Karli pawed at his hands. "You always think I just live off my large inheritance. But I have to work hard."

"It must be really strenuous, staying still for so long." Heiner slapped his thigh, Günther snorted into his napkin. "His knees must have grown an inch of calluses."

Now Karli was really stung, and Edvard tried to change the subject before things escalated.

"And how are the shopping-mad spending Christmas?"

"We're staying home. We traveled so much this year. I just need a bit of a rest. Turn on the answering machine, start a fire in the hearth and then go through the whole video collection in one fell swoop," said Heiner. "And you guys?" he asked Edvard.

"Bernhard is coming back from his parents' tomorrow. I booked us a little hotel room in Vienna, with a Jacuzzi and so on. He doesn't know about it yet."

"Vienna? Isn't that a bit cold?"

"For sure. But the Christmas Mass in St. Steven's Cathedral is supposed to be something special. And it's only for Christmas after all. Anyway, I'll have someone at my side to keep me warm."

"How did things end up with you guys anyway?"

"Right. The way I hear it, there was a little scene between you. Did Bernhard really run out on you?" That was Karli again, who had converted his disappointment at not being invited to the party into a dig at Edvard. Heiner threw him a nasty look.

"A little trouble in their domestic paradise, I believe," Herbert added.

Edvard didn't answer, trying to cover up his displeasure by grabbing for the water bottle. When he reached for it he knocked over the saltshaker. A few grains rolled onto the tabletop.

"Bad luck! Bad luck!" called Karli. Edvard gathered up the grains and threw them over his left shoulder.

The waiter came around with a wine bottle and filled the glasses. Heiner made use of the distraction to ask Edvard on the quiet: "What did actually happen?"

"He wasn't home," whispered Edvard, his face growing dark.

"Not home?" Heiner set down his fork, which he had just stuck through a piece of delicate suckling-pig.

"Maybe he was out for a walk. I don't know."

"How long did you wait?"

"Until two o'clock."

"A three-hour walk? In the cold? With a headache?" Heiner stroked his chin reflectively. "What did he say when you asked him about it the next morning?"

"I haven't spoken to him since then," he said glumly, holding out his glass rudely to the waiter.

Gerhard offered to drive him home, but Edvard wanted to walk.

"I think I ate too much."

"Hey, Edvard. Don't take it so hard," said Gerhard from the rolled-down window of his new BMW. "You know we're all just awful bitches. The next time it'll be someone else's turn." Then he stepped on the gas.

"It's all right."

Edvard pulled the collar of his coat over his ears and walked down Prinzregentenstrasse toward the middle of the city. The angel of peace towered in the night sky. Carefully, Edvard climbed down the slippery steps and crossed the little square. A few cars creaked past him at a walking pace. He had never experienced so much snow in this city before.

He felt sick after the meal, but it wasn't because of the duck. His friends' wisecracks had upset his stomach. Who knows, maybe they were right. Recently, Bernhard had been acting truly strangely, and his thoughts were always somewhere else. Now, when he thought back on it, his actions seemed even dismissive and cold. Why did he run away when Edvard tried to take off his pants? How could Bernhard do something like that to him in front of all the others? But what troubled him most of all: why hadn't Bernhard been home? And why hadn't he called since then? Was it a mistake to ambush him with a ring like that? They had never spoken about the future of their relationship. Edvard was simply not used to being in one, and it didn't seem to be an issue for Bernhard. But after seven months, it was time for a decision. Right? Edvard had given up screwing around. Not from any sort of conviction, but because he hadn't felt the need for it since Bernhard. He had been so certain that Bernhard felt the same. Didn't he? In any case, it was time for Bernhard come out. Being half gay was like being half pregnant—impossible!

Edvard was sunk so deep in thought that he passed by one of his favorite streets without thinking: Reitmorstrasse. He had always admired it. Nor did he notice how the Bavarian National Museum, with its arches and battlements, towered next to him like a knight's castle.

Somber, ghostly, unapproachable. So he also didn't notice that he was turning automatically into the English Garden, like he used to do on warm nights when he didn't want anything to do with relationships.

A strange light lay over the park. The moon shimmered flatly over his head; out of the thick covering of snow, the silhouettes of trees reared up. He crossed the thicket and headed towards the Ice Brook, which was living up to its name now. On the armrest of a bench, he saw the shadow of a man, barely distinguishable from the dark background.

"Looking for something this late?"

The other man shook his head quietly.

"It's pretty cold. I don't think there's much use waiting."

"Oh really? How do you know what I'm waiting for?"

"You're either a tourist or you've got a few screws loose," Edvard railed.

"Do you hit on everyone you cross paths with?"

Edvard recoiled. Hitting on him? He was not in the mood for that at all, so he got moving again.

"Hey, I didn't mean you should go. Cigarette?" He held a packet out for Edvard, but he refused.

In the next moment, a match flared up, lighting two hands, a pointed nose and bushy eyebrows. But before Edvard could commit the face to memory, the penetrating glare of a once-familiar ring jumped out at him.

"Wait a minute, I know that!"

"No, we don't know one another," the other guy said.

"Not you, the ring. Where did you get it from?"

"From my sweetheart, where else?" he whispered.

Edvard staggered, suddenly overwhelmed by this reality. At once it was clear, the pieces of the puzzle revealed an image, and he understood why Bernhard had been acting so strangely the last few days, why he had been so withdrawn, why he had suddenly run away from the party but not been at home, and why he hadn't even called: Bernhard had a lover. That was why he reacted so strangely to the ring.

It was serious with this new guy, Edvard could see that: Bernhard had even given him his ring!

A flaming sword pierced through Edvard's chest. He was finally ready to open up to another person, and right away he was betrayed.

Thick white smoke puffed out into the black sky. The brook murmured in the background, the moon played on the waves.

Edvard was close to tears, but that was the last thing he wanted to show this man.

"What's wrong? Cat got your tongue?"

Edvard jumped on the other man, grabbed him by the collar and pushed him over the bench into the icy snow. If he had to let Bernhard go, he at least wanted his ring back. "You pig! I'll kill you! And you can tell your little sweetheart that he had better not show his face in front of me. I never want to see him again, you got that?" He tore the ring off his finger. "And this, you hear me, this belongs to me!"

The other man was so surprised that he didn't even defend himself. He only thought one thing: that's the third time that ring has brought me trouble. I never want a ring again.

Edvard felt his eyes beginning to fill with tears, then he punched the helpless man on the nose. There was a crack, and Edvard felt appalled with himself. Then he disappeared into the night.

13.

Lydia woke up shortly before six. Theo set on the corner of the bed wheezing. She had tossed and turned all night, trying to be quiet in order to not bother him; but this time he had woken up anyway. She wanted to get up, but she felt like lead. The air was much too warm for her; her head was pounding.

Theo pushed himself off the bed and trudged off towards the bathroom. He splashed water on his face and stared into the mirror for a minute, as if he were afraid of his own image. He was pale, and Lydia saw how his hand lay on his chest. Was he in pain?

Theo came back into the room and stood at the window. Maybe he just had gas again? He looked off into the distance, past the roofs of the neighboring houses, towards a point far beyond the city. For Lydia, the horizon was a distant, unreachable place. Yet Theo was closer to it than he was to his own family.

She coughed slightly. Her throat was dry with the warm air, but Theo didn't react. What had she done to him?

After the war, when he had taken her in, Lydia believed she could pay him back with love. Out of gratitude she had given him a family. But with each child, he had drifted away a bit further. For forty years she had made an effort to fish for him with outstretched fingers as he bobbed around like a cork in a pond, but with every one of her movements, with every attempt to grasp him, he had only drawn further away from her.

She observed him standing there in his white tank top and light-blue pajama pants. Since she had known him, that terror had been in his eyes. Back then, she had believed that in her arms he would be able to forget everything. But she was wrong. The more she attempted to draw him away from his memories, the more they seemed to haunt him. If only he would talk about it.

She could still clearly remember the day when she found out she was going to bear his child. She was so happy, so convinced that this news would bring the first smile to his face. But he only shrugged his shoulders, no more, then looked past her. Maybe it was the surprise, Lydia thought then, maybe he just needs more time.

Theo was breathing heavily. He leaned against the window frame and bent forward. He did this whenever pain shot through his chest like a bullet. He had learned to hold his breath for a few seconds. It usually got better with that. But he had also learned that the pain would come back. What was locked up in his chest? And when would it ever let him breathe in peace again?

His gaze was still directed off into the distance, far out into nothingness, as stiff as a man about to go to war. He went into the bathroom and shut the door behind him. She heard the soft, muffled hum of his razor, its sandy scratching at his face, and nodded off again.

"Wake up!"

She turned around. "Theo?" Her voice complied laboriously.

"I'm going to the airport. If you want to come with me, hurry up. The taxi will be here in ten minutes."

"But…" Lydia reached for her watch. It was only half past six. They still had four hours before their departure. Why the hurry?

"But Theo, we still have time." He buttoned his shirt and grabbed for the suitcases. Lydia pushed herself up and slid to the side of the bed. "The children wanted to celebrate Christmas with us this morning. We can't just…" but Theo shut the door without even turning around.

Lydia slipped out of her nightshirt. She bent down for her tights and straightened up again. She had never seen him like this. What had gotten into him now?

She pulled the tights up over her knee. Then she heard a car drive up, looked out the window and saw a taxi. He had actually done it.

She slipped her dress on, took the wig from the nightstand and straightened it in the mirror. Then she hobbled down the steps; her bones were still stiff. She wanted to convince Theo to come back inside, so she went out and opened the door to the car. Warm air rushed out at her.

"Theo!"

Theo stared adamantly forward and said without moving: "Get in!"

"But Theo, you can't just…"

He grabbed her hand and pulled her into the back seat before she knew what was happening.

"Drive!" he ordered, and the taxi set into motion.

She hadn't even closed the door behind her. Speechlessly she pointed towards the house. She saw Gudrun standing there with a questioning look on the landing; Manuela was pressed against her leg. Lydia felt hot tears run down her cheek.

14.

"Papa was just worried we wouldn't get to the airport in time," Lydia said, clinging to the receiver.

"Mama," Gudrun's voice drilled into Lydia's ear. "We wanted to celebrate Christmas this morning. Did he forget about that?" She was disappointed, and furious. "The kids were so excited about it. We would have brought you there in time."

"But you know how he is," she tried to calm her daughter. She was used to apologizing for her husband's behavior. "He didn't want to cause you any trouble."

Gudrun gave up. She knew her mother would defend Theo no matter what arguments she could think of. An old game, the rules never changed.

"Did you at least get there all right?"

"But of course." The tension resolved. Someone let out a breath on the receiver, and each of them thought it came from the other end of the line. "Papa sends his regards to you all, by the way."

Gudrun swallowed. "At least the weather is cooperating." She couldn't bring herself to say hello to him.

"Take care of yourself, Gudrun. And don't forget to extend Papa's greetings to the others."

"Have a good vacation, Mama."

Theo stood at one of the large windows that bordered the ticket hall, staring out. The landing field was visible, covered with brake tracks, lamps and lines of aircrafts waiting for approval for take-off. Maldives, Geneva, Berlin, Hamburg, Dresden, New York. One machine after the next roared off and disappeared.

Theo stood there without moving, his face turned towards the starting planes. To Lydia, he seemed like a lion in a cage, waiting for the right moment to escape forever.

Anxiously, she approached him. Though she was standing a mere arm's length away from him, she felt as though if she were to reach out her hand towards him, she would grasp at nothing. It was as if he had already vanished above the clouds.

She sat down on a bench and waited.

At 11:30 Theo picked up the small bag from Lydia's lap and placed it over her shoulder. She had nodded off.

"It's time to go."

She startled up, fidgeted with her wig and looked at his face. All of a sudden, he seemed so relaxed, there was almost a smile on his lips.

"We need to board."

He seemed relieved—and he carried her bag for her. When was the last time he had done that? Lydia couldn't remember. She slid forward in her seat until her feet touched the floor, then stretched upwards with difficulty. Theo grabbed her under the arms. She looked at him again. His eyes were soft. Something had happened within him, and Lydia had slept through it all.

She hooked her arm through his; together, they went down the walkway to the plane. Hot air streamed from the vents, but it was so cool nonetheless that Lydia had to wrap herself tightly in her coat.

Theo studied the mechanism of the airplane door. Thick bolts protruded from the fuselage, and small sharp hooks. It looked as stable as the door to a bank vault; after all, it needed to remain on its hinges at a height of thirty thousand feet. But as soon as it was closed, the airplane was a bit like a coffin. Once you entered it, you could never leave.

Kim had already greeted thousands of air travelers in her short career. Standing up straight, smiling professionally, radiating trustworthiness, so the passengers wouldn't think about the dangers of flying, not even about the discomforts undoubtedly caused by being holed up in such a narrow cabin for hours at a time.

Lydia felt relieved when she caught sight of Kim's delicate face. Her slender fingers playing with the buttons of her dark blue uniform, her left foot tapping as if she were trying to slip out of her ankle boots.

There was a softness to Kim's appearance, insecurity paired with a good dose of courage, an ability to face life in spite of everything. And that gave Lydia hope.

As soon as the first passengers boarded in Munich, Kim noticed how different people were when they were going on vacation. No suits, no ties, no briefcases: instead, there were Hawaiian shirts, baseball caps and sneakers. One man had even worn shorts. Kim had looked at him with such surprise that he had shrugged his shoulders and explained: "Why should I bother with long pants? I won't need them over there—at least I hope not." His freckled face turned slightly red as he said this.

Kim's large, round eyes roamed among the boarding passengers, up and down the aisle. Passengers blocked the entrance as they chatted, full luggage compartments started arguments and a particularly nervous traveler sat down in the wrong seat, causing confusion.

As soon as the door was closed, the airplane rolled backwards onto the landing strip. Kim went up the rows one more time, closing the overhead compartments and checked to make sure everyone was buckled in.

She was excited: it was her first time flying over the Atlantic. And Fred was still floating around in her thoughts. As more time passed, she found it harder to believe what had happened. She barely noticed as she slipped on the life vest while the passengers were expecting a demonstration of the seat belt, and then showed them how to use the oxygen masks as the steward was talking about the emergency exits.

Perhaps Fred had meant to give her the ring? But then why had he worn it himself? Why hadn't he protested when she threw him out? There must be an easy explanation for their misunderstanding.

If only she hadn't tossed him out the door, she wouldn't be asking herself all these questions now.

By now they had reached the take-off strip. Kim sat next to her colleague Margret on a foldout chair and strapped herself in, while Lydia Moll looked out at the landing field. Small lights flashed; large signs with numbers stood in the white fields of snow. Her first take-off, her first time in the air, her first time with neither water nor earth beneath her feet. It was a little bit like just after the cancer diagnosis. She opened the top button of her blouse, fished out the cross and clasped it tight.

The turbines began to wail, and the thrust pushed the passengers deep into their seats. After a few lurches they were lifted up into the air. Outside the plane it was grey, but a few minutes later they broke through the layer of clouds, and Lydia looked out on a beautiful landscape of white hills. The cross slid from her hand.

Kim folded down a screen on which passengers could follow the altitude, speed and flight path. *Ground speed: 553 mph/890 km. Altitude 31000 feet/9400 m. Time to destination 10:40.* A small yellow airplane inched forward on the map: Amsterdam, Birmingham, Newcastle Upon Tyne, then out onto the open seas.

The seat-belt sign switched off. Headphones were handed out, passengers played with the buttons on their armrests. A few children started moving around in the aisles.

It was warm inside the plane. Theo opened the collar of his shirt, turned the nozzle above his head and let cold air stream over his sweating face.

"Everything all right?" Lydia looked over at him.

Instead of answering, Theo pressed her hand and tried to smile; he looked cramped. Lydia leaned back anxiously in her seat.

Kim pushed the drink cart out of the kitchen and starting opening juice cartons. Endlessly rehashed thoughts filled her head: she should never have gotten involved with Fred! How could she have believed it would end well? And why did she always have the bad luck to end up with the wrong guys?

A few cups fell to the floor; Kim hated turbulence. Would she ever meet Fred again? And how would she feel then? Would she scratch out his eyes or beg for forgiveness? Or would she manage to act cool and distanced?

"Kim." Margret nudged her with her elbows. "Can you go check? Someone's sounded the buzzer in row 40."

Kim slipped past her cart and went forward.

"Miss, could you bring my husband a glass of water, please?" asked Lydia.

"We'll be there with the cart in a minute. Would it be possible for you to wait till then?" Kim put on her broadest smile.

"It's just…he's not feeling well."

Kim turned to Theo. He was pale. Large round beads of sweat stood on his forehead, his eyes were closed, his breath shallow.

"This must be your first time flying?"

"Yes."

"I'll bring you something."

Kim went back to the kitchen. An elegantly dressed man, around fifty, winked conspicuously at her. She had noticed him during boarding.

"Someone's not feeling well," she said to Margret, who was currently juggling hot foil trays.

"I love those men who pee their pants at the first turbulence."

Kim brought a cup and a pill forward.

"It'll be better with this."

Lydia prodded Theo: "Drink this!" He took the pill and washed it down. Then he looked his wife in the eyes. They were watery and wide as the ocean beneath them.

"Don't be afraid," he said and grabbed her hand. "Everything will be all right!"

He was actually concerned about her. That alone made her afraid. He was so different all of a sudden.

Lydia took the little bag out of the pocket of the seat in front of her, then leaned back in her seat.

As Kim distributed the meals, the elegant man winked at her again. She smiled back and looked to the ground. Was he trying to hit on her?

Lydia didn't want anything to eat.

"And your husband?"

He just raised his hand loosely and declined.

"But maybe you have a damp towel. He's sweating so much."

Kim grabbed a couple moistened paper napkins, then pushed the cart further and continued handing out meals. When she reached the front, she pulled the cart back down the aisle. She saw fear in Lydia's eyes, and smiled at her encouragingly.

But Theo's breath kept getting shallower, and Lydia was getting more anxious. She opened her seat belt and went back into the kitchen.

"I just wanted to tell you that my husband has serious heart problems." Kim looked at her questioningly. "I'm concerned."

"It will be all right. Don't worry about it. If you've never flown before, it's no wonder you're anxious."

"You don't know…he's never looked this bad."

"If you'd like, I'll come up and look after him again."

"Please."

Kim followed her up the aisle and leaned over to Theo. He was greenish pale. "Can you hear me?"

Theo opened his eyes.

"Is everything all right?"

He nodded slowly and let his head fall back again.

"Your wife is concerned about your heart. We could call for a doctor if you'd like."

"That won't be necessary." Theo tried to smile.

Kim spoke with the steward: "I think we have a problem. The man in row forty is deathly pale. His wife says he has a heart condition."

"I'll take care of it." Ritchie patted her hand, throwing an extremely fatherly glance at her as he rushed off. Tanned brown, with nearly white hair, white eyebrows and a white mustache, he looked thirty, though he was at least forty-five. Definitely gay! She thought. Then she cleared out her cart and started collecting trays.

Halfway along the way she passed Ritchie, his stiffly gelled hair bobbing up and down at every step.

"Everything's all right. You can relax." He pushed past her; a self-satisfied 'nice steward' grin flashed on his face.

Kim had arrived at the elegant man. "Is everything to your satisfaction?"

"It tasted wonderful," he said. The woman next to him placed her jewel-ringed hand conspicuously on her forehead and gave Kim a nasty look. He must have a lot of dough, thought Kim, he's probably a doctor. And his wife is definitely super-jealous.

"Is there anything else you'd like?" Kim took the tray from his hand and placed it on her cart.

"Nothing that could be taken care of right away," she heard him say, and tore one of her nails.

Margret and Ritchie were chatting about some of the stewards that Kim didn't know. She filed away at her nail and started thinking.

Total embargo on relationships. She needed a break. Then she would look for a man who wasn't married and who didn't have problems. She would talk to him about everything, she wouldn't tolerate any unclear circumstances or secrets. She wanted to finally do it right.

Setting down the nail file, she stared through the little window into nothingness.

If only Raimondo weren't so terribly controlling. She knew what she was doing. He always used her old lovers as examples, but it was different every time.

Markus had been a total chicken. He had always talked about great love, but then over Christmas, when his mother had criticized Kim non-stop, he hadn't opened his mouth. It would hardly be possible to live with someone like that. And Stefan? He was addicted to work. You can forgive someone for coming late, but she couldn't accept the fact that his meetings were always more important than she was. And Richard couldn't bring himself to say he loved her after two weeks. What was she supposed to do with that?

Two hours had passed since the meal. They had flown south past Iceland, and were now approaching Greenland, rushing past icy cities with fascinating names like Godhaven, Godthab, or Angmagssalik.

Lydia prayed. If the Virgin Mary wouldn't take care of Lydia, maybe she'd at least stand by Theo. He needed to stop sweating; he needed to breathe regularly again and not be struggling for every breath. A little more color in his face would calm her down.

"Holy Mary, Mother of God..." her thoughts became hazy. The excitement made Lydia grow weak, ultimately closing her eyes. She fell asleep.

Theo lifted his head: a stewardess was offering him aspirin. He felt cold, freezing even, but sweat was nevertheless running down his face. He pushed the pills away without a word. It was light outside; harsh light reflected from the clouds, blinding him. Theo bent forward and looked out. The snow, winter, the cold, everything had disappeared. What remained was warmth, the secure feeling of not having to encounter the snow ever again.

The wing glinted. *Do not step beyond this line* was written there in black letters, and at the end of the wing there was a light, so comfortable and soft that Theo stretched his hand out to it. When he touched the cold window, a flash shot through his left arm down to the tip of his little finger. The flash was quick, as if it had no time to lose, and a spasm ran through Theo's body. His chest felt tight as a hose, his breath galloped away from him.

"I was afraid!" Lydia heard him cry, and for the second time that day she was torn from sleep.

"Theo! For God's sake, what's wrong?" Her husband crumpled over in her lap. She grabbed his hand and stretched out for the call button. Theo whimpered incomprehensible things.

Kim saw the passenger gasping for air and held the call button down until Ritchie leaped to her side. He pulled Theo onto the floor, Margret made an announcement asking for a doctor. Seconds later a married couple bent down over Theo: the elegant man and his wife. Kim passed them their emergency equipment: the Ambu breathing bag for artificial respiration, and a small case with medication.

He opened Theo's shirt and listened to his chest. They whispered to one another, pushed small orange pills under his dry tongue and injected something into his arm.

"If I hadn't done it, they would have killed me…" stammered Theo. His voice became more and more incomprehensible.

Lydia hung in her seat as if paralyzed. The stewardess had demonstrated to her how to put on a life vest in an emergency, how to strap on an oxygen mask and how to follow lit-up strips towards the exit, but no one had explained to her how she should behave if she lost her husband at thirty thousand feet.

"You have this under control, right?" she heard the steward ask the doctors. They looked up at him, and Kim could see in their eyes that Ritchie was wrong. Then they sent Kim to the pilot.

The female doctor gave Theo's chest a muffled thump, his heart beat again, his hands twitched and thick oily tears ran down his cheeks.

"I was so afraid," he said barely audibly. His lips moved imperceptibly.

When Kim climbed back out of the cockpit, she saw a female passenger looking at her imploringly. Kim went past her, and another held her by the arm. "What happened? Was the food bad?"

Kim trembled. "No, nothing to worry," she answered and walked on.

"The pilot says there's no hospital nearby, nothing for miles. We're in the middle of the water."

"There's nothing we can do for him up here. If he doesn't get to a hospital soon, he'll die."

Lydia heard the doctors' words. She felt tears roll down her cheeks. They weren't tears of mourning for his death, they were tears of fear for her impending loneliness. They were tears of guilt. She would have liked to take Theo into her arms, but she couldn't even reach him.

The doctors pushed down on his chest again; it wouldn't lift on its own. They put the plastic bag over his dry lips and pumped air into his already dead body.

I shouldn't have taken him with me! Thought Lydia. He had fought against the family reunion tooth and nail. For weeks, he had been making cutting remarks, and every time they had talked about it he had just left the room or turned on the TV.

He had wanted a two-week honeymoon, and she had seen her chance there. She simply blackmailed him. Either he came with her to see the children, or she wouldn't fly to Miami. They had made a deal on it, a deal he was now paying for with his life. If only she hadn't begged him. All she had wanted was to have everyone together one last time.

"He's not breathing anymore," said the doctor's wife. Her husband shrugged his shoulders. The color faded from Ritchie's face. Deathly pale, he kneeled down on the ground.

"For God's sake, keep going!" he whispered, wiped his face and then ran forward to the cockpit.

The doctor stared at Kim, his wife pumped Theo's chest, he twitched, and his lungs filled again with air.

Hope sprang up within Lydia. Her husband was breathing again, he opened his eyes, and his face relaxed into a nearly peaceful, loving smile. What had she done to him? She asked herself again, reaching out to him, but he didn't see her anymore.

"Forgive me," he gasped, and he was convulsed by something once more, as if he had been hit by a bullet. Then it was very, very quiet in the cabin.

The steward came back, kneeled down next to the doctors and whispered: "The pilot says you should keep resuscitating him."

Kim felt very hot, then ice cold. A shivering feeling rumbled in her stomach.

"Have you lost your mind?" the doctor's wife whispered. "What are you thinking? We're still four hours away from Miami. We'll put him in some free seat."

"Unfortunately, we can't do that. The flight is completely booked."

"But rigor mortis is going to set in. We need to close his eyes and seal his mouth."

"I don't like to say this, but the pilot isn't asking you. This is an order. He's afraid panic will break out when the others find out that someone has died."

The married couple stared at each other with wide eyes. The woman buttoned up the dead man's shirt and laid her hand on the stiff chest.

Kim felt nausea rising within her. She jumped over the dead man and rushed into the kitchen. Her skirt flapped open, and the doctor's eyes widened. With lustful eyes he watched Kim flee, then stood up and went after her determinedly.

When he came into the kitchen, Kim was hanging over the trash bag gagging. "Everything okay?" he asked compassionately, laying a hand caringly on her back.

She just shook her head and gagged again.

"Is this your first...death?"

She nodded.

He poured apple juice into a cup and passed it to her. And while she tossed it down her throat, the doctor pulled her sweaty hair out of her face. Kim's knees grew weaker; she felt dizzy. And because she was afraid to lose her balance at any minute, she grabbed for his shoulder.

Shortly afterwards, a young woman's muffled cry passed through the rear passengers seats. But before they could determine the source, the steward was on the spot, directing them back to their seats. As he slipped behind the curtain, he saw Kim sitting pale and trembling on the drink cart, her eyes pointed in fear at her naked, sprawled legs. The doctor leaned back against the wall, panting exhaustedly, with a satisfied smile.

As he noticed Ritchie, he turned around and buttoned his pants. Then he rubbed a stain off his shoe onto the rug and went forward without a word. His wife saw the wet spot slowly spreading on the front of his pants. Enraged, she struck at the dead man's chest.

Forgive me, Theo had said. Lydia was completely confused. When she was about to ask him for forgiveness, he asked her to forgive him?

15.

Bernhard opened the blinds. A bluish-gray sheen lay over the village. He felt around for his watch. Ten twenty-two! Last night they had agreed to get up early in order to celebrate Christmas with their parents before they went to the airport. A lit-up tree, *Silent Night*, presents for the kids and then goodbye.

Bernhard listened at the door. Silence. He slipped into his clothes quickly and went down the stairs into the living room. With every step, the atmosphere became more uneasy.

Karl was laying a few logs on the fire. His siblings sat mutely around the Christmas tree, whose lights were flickering. His nieces, surrounded by torn wrapping paper, made long faces.

"Why did you let me sleep in? I thought we wanted to celebrate Christmas with our parents?"

Sieglinde stood up, took Bernhard with her into the kitchen and shut the door behind them.

"Mama and Papa went away early this morning. We won't be celebrating with them," she said almost casually while she took butter and jam from the refrigerator.

"Went away?" asked Bernhard. There was rage in his voice. It was immediately clear to him why they'd done that. They hated their son. They couldn't accept that he loved men.

Gudrun came into the kitchen and saw his injured look. "They thought it would be simpler for us if they took a taxi. They didn't want us to go to any trouble."

She acted so natural, but Bernhard could tell by her bustling that she was lying.

Gudrun wouldn't even look him in the eye. But he didn't say anything; this mendacity robbed him of his strength. He couldn't even walk upstairs and pack his things, though he wished for nothing more at that moment than to flee into Edvard's arms.

Sieglinde carried the tray loaded with jam, sweetbread, butter and coffee into the dining room, Gudrun shut the door behind her.

"Bernhard. If you want to live that way, you've got to learn to deal with situations like this. The last thing you can do now is leave."

She tried to meet his eyes, but he stared past her onto the street that would take him home. "If our parents can't handle it, they need to go. Now that they've done it, there's no reason for you to go as well."

He turned to her. The Molls were a family of separations, he thought, over time he had gotten used to this—the way you get used to toothaches if they show up on a Friday afternoon, knowing you have to put up with them until Monday.

Gudrun was right. How much longer did he want to run away?

In the next few hours, the tension of the previous days transformed into its opposite: Ludwig followed the overacted emotions of second-class soap opera actors on TV, Gudrun read, Karl listened to classical music through his headphones and Barbara lay motionless in Mausi's lap, who stared ahead of him silently.

Ludwig left after lunch. Handshakes, pats on the back, a kiss on the cheek, smiling faces. Bernhard wanted to prove that he could stand his ground. He had expected they would ask all the questions hanging in the air, the usual ones that floated around in straight peoples' minds: what made you gay? What's different about loving someone of the same sex? Are gay people really the way people say they are?

He would have told them how Edvard had made chamomile tea for him after an extravagant dinner had made Bernhard feel queasy, and how Edvard would often just lie in his arms for hours and stare at him. But they didn't want to hear about that. Apparently they would rather stick to their bizarre projections of what it meant to be gay, Bernhard said to himself. Instead of talking about it, they brought out Christmas cookies and boiled a deep-red tea that smelled of cinnamon, of oranges and Christmas trees, open fires and blissful peace.

Bernhard's uneasiness had curled up like a fox in its cave. He felt it the way you feel headaches after taking aspirin: the pain went away, but the pressure remained.

Flo climbed up to him on the sofa and snuggled up against him. He sucked on his pacifier, making soft chirping noises. His nose was crusty, which meant that every breath was accompanied by a barely audible whistling sound. Bernhard's bones grew heavier. If only the panic would stay away. Bernhard sought refuge in sleep, and slid instead into a dream that would change his life forever.

Shortly before dinner, Bernhard woke with a start. His mouth was dry, his heart racing, his chest felt tight and painful, he could hardly breathe. Images danced in front of his eyes and his whole body trembled. In his mouth, a metallic taste of fear lingered.

"Bernhard, do you feel alright?"

When he saw the shock in his sister's face, he realized he was no longer dreaming. He tried to answer her, and fainted.

The ceiling light blinded him as he came to. Everyone was standing around him; his shirt was unbuttoned and his forehead felt icy from the cold compress.

"Bernhard, do you hear me? Bernhard!" Karl shook him.

He squinted around at them; his breath was shallow. His left arm hurt from his ribcage down to his little finger. It kept twitching in flashes, but it barely hurt.

As if through a mist, he heard the church bells ringing. Excited voices filled the hallway, then he saw an unfamiliar face, a black bag and a stethoscope. Shortly afterwards he felt cold metal on his chest.

"Has your brother had problems with his heart in the past? Episodes in the last few days, you say. Aha! You say it runs in the family. No, it doesn't seem like a heart attack. Did something happen that could have agitated him? I doubt it's a heart attack. But we'll only know that for sure if he goes to the hospital."

For the first time, the doctor turned to Bernhard. "Better now?"

Bernhard felt another sting run through his arm. He nodded.

"They should be able to clear it up in the hospital. Shall I have you admitted?"

Bernhard shook his head.

"It would just be to have some blood taken, and an ECG. It wouldn't take long."

"It's all right. I just…" He shook his head again, his eyes filled up with tears. "I just need some air." Bernhard pushed himself up and stood on his wobbly legs. "I'm better now, really!"

Unsteadily, he went into the guest bathroom, all eyes following him. In the mirror he saw how pale he was. Terror was visible in his eyes. He sat on the toilet and waited until the door to the house shut and the voices outside faded away, then he went up into the study and curled up on his sleeping bag.

Gudrun knocked on the door. "Is everything all right?" Bernhard shrugged. "What happened to you? I'm really worried."

"It was just a terrible dream!" he said, sounding distant.

Gudrun sat down next to him. "A dream?"

"I had the worst nightmare of my life." His voice broke.

Gudrun laid her hand on his shoulder and felt how he was shaking. "What kind of nightmare?"

"There was a pain in my chest, as hard and sharp as an exploding grenade," he began, his eyes transfigured, his gaze disconnected, as if he were far off in his own thoughts.

"But it was just a dream," she tried to calm him, as she saw tears rising in his eyes.

"At first I thought what I was hearing was my own pulse, a racing, frantic, panicked pulse. But that's not what it was." Bernhard laid his head back. "It was the rattling of machine guns."

"What?"

"It must have been raining for days," he explained. "The ground was soft, there were puddles everywhere. I was standing among a company of soldiers in file. The barracks were behind us, fighter jets over our heads. Then men in black uniforms came up to us. They were so…clean, like models. Silver insignia gleaming on their collars…" he concentrated. "Skulls…yes, they were skulls."

"My God." Gudrun pulled her hand back in horror.

"There was a man. He was a naked, tied hand and foot like an animal. They dragged him through the mud and trod on him with their boots. They wanted to know something from him, but I couldn't hear what."

Bernhard wrinkled his brow, tears dripped from his chin.

"He was handsome. Blond with thin temples, as if you could see right through them into his thoughts. His eyes were deep blue and determined. He didn't even flinch as they beat him nearly to death." Bernhard's voice grew quieter, as if he was telling a secret. "His lips were sealed—with forbidden kisses. His eyes stared off into the distance, beyond the horizon, out where memories are kept."

Gudrun stroked a few hairs from her brother's face. She had never seen him so emotional.

"There was blood on their boots, blood on their hands." Bernhard's chin trembled. His eyes burned; they saw more than they could bear. "Every soldier had to come up to him individually and spit in his face. There were hundreds of us." He hid his face in his hands. "I wanted to help him," he affirmed. "I wanted to run up and take him into my arms, to save him from these murderers. But I couldn't, I felt paralyzed. I prayed someone would throw a grenade that would tear us all to pieces. I hoped for an air raid that would put an end to this horror. I felt so guilty. I was so ashamed to stand there, to witness all of that. I was ashamed of being human, do you understand?" He lifted his head from his arms and turned to his sister. "What are we capable of?" His face was old and grim, his eyes full of bitterness. "My heart raced, and my chest grew tighter and tighter. Then they cut his throat…and then…finally…my heart stopped."

The shrill ringing of the telephone interrupted his words. It was already a little after ten. Who would call so late? Gudrun asked.

"I want to! I want to!" she heard Biggy's excited voice, then Gudrun laid her head on Bernhard's, whose body was still pulled tightly in on itself in desperation.

"Hello?" Her daughter's squeaky voice echoed up the stairwell. "Hi Grandma!" she called excitedly. "I just colored in a bunny. He has green eyes and long blue ears." Then she went quiet. "It's Grandma," she heard Biggy say softly, and there was an undertone to her voice that made Gudrun uneasy. "I can't understand her. She's crying."

Gudrun jumped up and ran to the stairs. Then she heard Sieglinde's officious voice. "What? I can hardly hear you. Could you speak up a bit…?"

Gudrun ran down to her.

"Oh God! No! Oh God!" Sieglinde sank to the cold stone floor, her sister paused on the stairs.

"Don't be afraid, Mama."

Biggy started crying and clung to her father: "I think Grandpa is dead."

And Gudrun froze.

16.

Monday! Bernhard had promised to be home today at the latest. But he wasn't there. And he hadn't even called. Edvard dashed down another shot of whiskey. Since he had caught that man with Bernhard's ring, his life had been turned upside down, and it got worse every day.

The light brown liquid burned in his throat. He hated whiskey, but what else was he to do besides drink when his life was breaking into pieces? Alcohol numbed him, covered the corners and edges of his painful thoughts with a thin layer of indifference.

Edvard was still trying to think of a plausible explanation. Every possible scenario ran through his head, but each was worse than the next: if the man had robbed Bernhard, he would have called. And if he had lost the ring he would have stayed around to look for it, or at least told Edvard so he could look for it himself. Unless the ring meant nothing to him. And then what did that mean?

No matter how he spun it, when he added it all up, he could only come to one conclusion: things were not looking good for his relationship with Bernhard. Sometimes, life was like a game of Othello. One false move and all the white pieces were turned to black.

"One more!" Edvard pounded the glass against the bar.

"Take it easy, young man."

Edvard looked through the cigarette smoke at the face of a small, well-built man. He was wearing a leather jacket, worn-out jeans and cowboy boots. An Indian string tie swung at his throat. With his thick, long tongue he licked beer foam from his mustache. "Problems?"

"You could put it that way." Edvard lifted his full glass and tossed its contents down in one go.

"That was number four. Anyone who's in such a hurry to get that infernal stuff down their throat can't be doing well." There was something strong and stabilizing in his voice. For Edvard, it was like an anchor in this ocean of impenetrable thoughts.

"You must be an expert?" His face seemed familiar to Edvard, but he couldn't connect a face or memory to the gleefully mischievous gleam in his eyes, nor to the blue-colored tip of his nose.

"I'm a psychotherapist."

Edvard didn't need a second glance to know that he was much too young for that profession. But why shouldn't he play along with this game, he had to do something after all.

"Well then…to a successful diagnosis?" He tilted back the next whiskey. Slowly, the longed-for, pleasant indifference set in.

"So where does the problem lie?" The other man offered a pack of cigarettes to him, Edvard declined.

"Well, where do you think?"

"In love. What would be worth drinking for, if not love?"

Edvard saw his conversation partner as if through a veil. "What are you supposed to do if you fall in love with someone who fundamentally doesn't fit with you?" Suddenly, Edvard heard Heiner speaking out of his mouth: Bernhard's clothes, his way of life, his inability to just enjoy himself and this reluctance to own up to being gay. Essentially, they lived in two different worlds.

"If you see it so clearly, I would say: split up! Anything else would be masochism," the young man said, pulling on his cigarette.

"But if you also have the feeling you're meant for each other?" Edvard had felt this way since the first time their eyes met. And Birgit had read in her cards that he would meet a man who fit Bernhard's description exactly. Edvard had been so sure that Bernhard was the man of his life, so fucking sure—until yesterday.

"Then you've got to have good nerves."

"And if you find out that one of you is cheating on the other?"

"You've got to talk about things like that. But sometimes you just need a break, to take care of yourself." That was extremely untherapeutic advice, Edvard was sure of that. "There's an old proverb," the other man added to support his theory. "If you are thirsty, drink from the fountain yourself before you pass the ladle to the others."

That sounded seductive. The metaphor nestled comfortably in Edvard's chest. He raised the glass to his lips and let the fire run down through him, filling his mouth, numbing his thoughts.

Birgit was never wrong. That was why Edvard had been so affected when, two hours ago, she had confirmed what Edvard had feared for so long: "I see another man in Bernhard's life," she said. "He's young and blond, and he has blue eyes." The light emanating from the table lamp through the silk violet scarf had thrown a dark shadow on her face. "And he's wearing a ring, the ring you gave him."

The ring with a diamond and a ruby. Edvard thought about the man in the park, and found his worst suspicions confirmed, so he didn't listen as Birgit warned him from jumping to conclusions too quickly: "That could mean anything. Give it time, talk to him. Maybe there's a very simple explanation."

And then a sheer unquenchable thirst came over Edvard, as if that certainty had extracted every drop of liquid from his body at once. This thirst could only be stilled with alcohol, or...

Edvard peered at his acquaintance's large Adam's apple as it jumped up and down happily with each swallow. He seemed so full of life, as if he could quench the thirst of all of Africa with a single kiss.

"Where is the fountain?" asked Edvard. His throat was drier than before, his words floundered in the smoky air.

"Shall I show it to you?"

Edvard swiveled his refilled glass. He felt miserable.Where joy had once reigned, a sea of sadness stretched out. And he was drifting about it like a castaway. With every thought of Bernhard, his hope of ever reaching dry land again faded. If he didn't do something about it soon, he would drown, that much was clear.

"Do you have a ladle for me as well?"

"It's quite a ladle," he answered with a suggestive grin.

A beacon blazed up in the distance, and Edvard changed his course.

"What's your name actually?" he asked.

"Fred, quite simple: F-R-E-D, as in Frisky, Righteous, Excessive and…Discreet."

Edvard laughed. Yes, he could even laugh again. Then he set down fifty Marks on the bar and grabbed Fred by the arm: "Come on, let's go and…get frisky."

17.

Kim loved hotel bars. Bars in themselves felt somehow grown-up. They radiated maturity. They were full of everything that was forbidden to children: the magic of furtive contact, the blue-grey smoke of cigars, alcohol in long-stemmed glasses, secretive whispering, loud, uncontrollable laughter, winking eyes and the feeling of conspiracy.

Over the years, hotel bars had won Kim over. They were often filled with people just passing through, strangers who were more curious and open than the locals. It was easier to find contact, because everyone shared a similar fate: the loneliness of traveling. And she always felt as if she could catch a whiff of a distant world when she sat down there, sipping at a drink and looking into eyes that had seen so much more than her own.

The bar in her hotel in Miami, on the other hand, was not at all what she had expected. There was no sunset on the ocean, no washboard abs, not even good drinks. Here, near the airport, the ocean was nowhere to be seen. Even the eerie pool in front of her window seemed, in the dark, more like a landing strip for UFOs.

After her scolding from the head steward, she had lain down for a while. He had totally torn into her with his hysterical shrieking, as if the incident hadn't been horrible enough for her. He was probably just jealous. She had seen how he had stared at the doctor's open pants. He threatened to report the incident. That stupid fairy. She might as well accept that she'd get stuck flying to Siberia from now on. She hadn't been able to stand this Ritchie from the start.

Now she was sitting on a green couch covered in burn marks, drinking her second margarita, whose fruity lemon taste was not enough to mask a clear undertone of chlorine. She drank, hoping for her emotions to die down, hoping for her heart to grow calm, hoping for the doctor.

The Puerto-Rican bartender looked over at her again and again. "Another drink?" And his gap-tooth smile made her want to pull her orange mini-skirt tight around her knees.

The last few days had just been too much: her first time in America, her first flight abroad, her first death, Raimondo too far away, this sinister environment, too many contradictory memories of Fred, and then sex with a stranger to top it off.

It was this last thing that occupied her mind the most. Not the little intermezzo in itself; that hadn't been the first time she'd gotten into an adventure like that. What she really had a problem with was the fact that she hadn't wanted to do it.

After the passenger had died, after the pilot's impossible decision to leave the dead man in the aisle and act as if he were still alive, she had been totally overwhelmed. When the doctor came to her in the kitchen, she had really believed he had wanted to help her. That was why she had held onto him. She hadn't thought anything of it when he put his arms around her, she thought he was lifting her onto the drink cart for the sake of comfort. Then seconds later, when he was inside of her, she had only felt warmth and relaxation. She had been too weak to defend herself. He had exploited her helplessness shamefully! That was the reason she had slipped him a note as he got off the plane, asking him to talk with her.

"Is this seat free?" Kim followed the sonorous voice back to its source. In the dim light she recognized the doctor, Dr. Hohleben.

He slid over to her on the couch. There was something childlike about his appearance, the way he spoke and took her hand into his.

"I thought you were going to stand me up."

"How could I stand up such a delightful woman?" His hands exuded something calming. His teeth flashed white, as white as his pants, his shoes and his buttoned-up shirt.

"I'm glad you came. But please, let's go somewhere else. It's awful here."

"Gladly. The best thing to do would be to drive to the beach and sit down in a nice little restaurant. We can talk better there than in this gloomy hole in the wall."

He stood up and gave her his hand. She hesitated, then accepted and let him lead her out of the booth.

He was suave, she had to give him that. How old was he? Around fifty maybe, although he seemed young enough to be forty.

Kim asked for the check.

"I'll take care of it." He pulled a wad of bills from his pocket and went up to the bar.

Dr. Hohleben drove a lipstick-red convertible. With the sunroof down, they zoomed along the road, the wind rushing comfortably through Kim's T-shirt, cooling her down. The doctor's thin, silky hair shimmered in the evening air. There was lots of activity; colorful billboards gave the streets a magical veneer.

They sat for a while in halting traffic by the boardwalk before finding a place to park. The air smelled of salt and fish and sweet perfume. A cool breeze blew over their over-heated bodies.

He led her by the hand over wooden steps up to a small, romantic restaurant. It was full; lots of Germans and Dutch people were there. They stood out among the few Americans, being much paler, thinner, with flat faces and no toothpaste-smiles.

"Enchanting, isn't it?" asked the doctor, his eyes gleaming.

They found a small table by the street, above their heads an air conditioner spun away noiselessly into the night. The doctor flipped through the menu. Kim observed his movements. They were smooth, supple, always changing, like a dolphin or a snake on the desert sand.

Along the street, tanned models ambled past, with long hair dyed blond and artificially enlarged breasts. Hohleben ogled a woman who must have been a bodybuilder. Her skin smelled of pineapple and coconut. Her companion's leg muscles were so swollen that they rubbed against one another as he walked.

"What would you like me to order for you?" asked the doctor. He smiled at Kim, keeping his eyes locked with hers.

"Doesn't matter, I'm not very hungry," answered Kim.

"All right, then we'll have two tunas with sweet mango sauce." As he ordered, he seemed more like a fifty-year-old, so grown-up, so mature, so smooth, as if life's problems would slide off him like water from lotioned skin. His English was nearly accent-free.

"What did you say to your wife to explain why you're leaving her alone?"

"I told her that I needed to speak with you about the little incident on the airplane. It does need to be cleared up, after all."

He was charming, too charming—and Kim knew for sure he was lying.

"And she didn't object to that?"

"Please. We're grown-ups. The stress, the tension. Things like that can happen."

Kim looked out at the ocean. She had planned to say so much, and now nothing came to mind. She didn't even know what she was expecting from this conversation. She was sick of always running away, yes, she was sick of life always happening to her, she was sick of always drifting around in relationships instead of taking the steering wheel into her own hands. But what could she change about the incident in the airplane now?

"That was a strange thing in the airplane, wasn't it?" she asked, since nothing better occurred to her.

"Yeah, I'm very embarrassed about it. Things like that don't normally happen to me, you must believe me. I just don't know what came over me."

Kim was fascinated by his mouth. It was strong but not fleshy, it always stood slightly open, a large, dark hole. And the corners of his mouth pulled down on both sides, very erotic. How could a mouth like that tell such terrible lies?

"Although I'm not trying to say it wasn't fun. I hope you understand. It's very awkward for me, very awkward."

She heard the surf and a few seagulls squawking as they flapped against the wind or begged around the restaurant for a few crumbs.

A cat sprang onto the railing and crept along it, its wide eyes fixed on a fish-head lying on an abandoned plate. A muscular waiter with a Scandinavian accent chased after it with a towel, then cleared off the table. It seemed as if everyone was beautiful here—no admittance to the ugly.

Another waiter brought up big plates with thick slices of fish. Orange sauce flowed around it. On top of the fish, a thick slice of melted butter gleamed.

"Okay, two orders of the tuna. Can I bring you anything else, or are you all right?"

Another charming young waiter, tanned, muscular, but with long dark hair. He was Latino, his eyes glowed green like a cat's.

"Can I order anything else for you?" asked the doctor, again just a tad too friendly.

Kim shook her head. Something was happening to her. She looked up into his large eyes. When he breathed, his chest expanded into a puffed-out cushion. This feigned regret with a trace of awkwardness was getting under her skin.

He cut into the fish and set a piece of it on his broad tongue, which was stretched out wide. His eyes were fixed on Kim's all the while.

"You know, there's nothing more beautiful than an evening by the sea," he said after swallowing. "Are you sure we shouldn't get a glass of wine…?"

Kim lifted her hand in refusal. Then she directed her eyes downward, staring at her fingers as they played with the waistband of her skirt.

"These beautiful people, the fresh air, bright colors, every time I come here, I fall in love with this city all over again," he gushed. "But you're not eating at all."

Kim struggled with her emotions. She couldn't look at him anymore, or all would be lost.

"Is there something odd about the ocean? You keep looking over there." He turned, looking out into the dark, stretching out his hand for his glasses. "Am I missing something?"

She turned towards him. When it came to charm, even Raimondo couldn't beat him. He looked at her with puppy dog eyes. How was she supposed to react?

He leaned back in his chair again, his lips resting calmly on his glass of water. He had spilled his sperm inside her, and they hadn't even kissed once.

Kim felt herself dissolving into him. His composure was like a pillar she wanted to lean against. As if he could read her thoughts, he said: "Anyway, I don't think it's a good idea to talk here in the restaurant. What do you think about going back to your place and talking about this where it's quiet?" His voice was so calm and convincing.

This finally set off the alarm bells inside her head. Leaning in, the seductive words, that soft lulling gaze… Something familiar had slipped into the conversation, something much too comfortable.

Why my place? She asked herself. "Can't we talk about it here?"

"I don't think it's a subject for a public place." He laid his hand on her naked thigh, and slid it slowly upwards. It made here feel sick. She looked around desperately. Could no one see the danger she was in?

She grabbed his hand. She wanted to push him away, but he was too strong and determined. A cold shiver ran down her back. "Just a minute."

"What, my love?" His eyes transfixed her.

She didn't want to believe it had been about sex for him the whole time. The winks in the airplane, his embrace in the kitchen: sex. Would he have gotten in touch at all if she hadn't slipped him the note? He couldn't be such a pig.

Kim started trembling. She grew stiff, her chest tightened. "I think I'd rather just go."

"Gladly." He placed his hands on the arms of his chair.

"Alone!" she said quickly, and definitely too loud. She felt feverish, as if she were standing high up on a mountain. One false step and she would fall.

"But listen. You can't just leave me here."

She jumped up, her chair fell backwards, a few guests turned their heads. Then she saw how his face was filled with rage.

"First you flirt, then you leave me sitting here!" he hissed rancorously, his beautiful mouth distorting itself into a grimace. "What kind of slut are you?"

Kim was paralyzed by his anger, and grew frightened. Either fight or flight.

"You're...horrible!" she spat from her much too narrow throat. Then she ran down the steps toward the ocean.

"Slut!" she heard him shout after her furiously, and Kim kept running.

She wanted to scream back, but what could she say? "Was I the one with the hard-on, or were you?" came to mind. Yeah, that's what she could ask him. He wouldn't have any answer for that.

The thought made her breath hot, a delicate film of sweat made her back tremble. She ran more slowly. A force spread through her pelvis; she felt it grow and rise. She should really let him have it in public. She stopped for a moment, took a deep breath, and turned around slowly. She felt ready to go back and look him in the eyes: but he was already speeding away in his red sports car.

18.

Study for Portrait III, William Blake was what Francis Bacon had called his small artwork. Actually an unremarkable painting among the artist's works, hardly more than a small black canvas with a little oil paint. But Bernhard remembered it on the flight from Frankfurt to Miami because it was just like his father: viewed from a distance, one saw a coarse face rising from a dark background like a colorful cloud in the night sky. But when one studied it closer, it became clear that the image only grew more indistinct, until nothing more was left than a few unconnected splotches of paint.

In the last eighteen hours he had grappled with his father more than he ever had in his entire life. And now, after that marathon of emotions, he couldn't even remember his face anymore.

His sister's words kept running through his head: "Just imagine you tell him and he has a heart attack. You would never forgive yourself for that." It didn't help to reassure himself that the doctor had ordered his father not to fly a long time ago, nor the hours of discussion about his father's alcoholism and the endless packs of cigarettes he had smoked.

Suddenly, his siblings had acted as if they were on his side. Couldn't their parents have traveled to Italy? Flying? The air in airplanes was as thin as on a 10.000-foot mountain. Much too thin for a cardiac patient who constantly had to take pills—as if telling him that would take away his feelings of guilt. Bernhard would have preferred it if his sisters had told the truth. He knew they held him responsible for their father's death.

When they finally ventured to go to bed, Bernhard couldn't sleep. As soon as he was alone and the room sunk into darkness, his thoughts took fire. Hatred boiled over within him.

His father's reaction had been unfair. If he hated his son for being gay, why hadn't he said so? Why had he just stood up and left him alone with it?

Everything always had to be about him. And his silence was the best weapon. His father couldn't have drawn more attention to himself than if he had danced the tango on his head. The family's entire life had always revolved around him. And now he had even staged his own death. Control and power, that's what he had always been after.

Now, squeezed into his airplane seat, Bernhard was annoyed not to have left earlier, as he had planned. Then one of his other siblings would be flying to Miami in order to handle his father's return and to clean up the mess his father had left behind. He would be lying in Edvard's arms or pressing his stomach against the soft hollow of his back, feeling like a newborn baby. Edvard! Shit! He still hadn't called him. He had to do it as soon as he landed in Miami.

Bernhard felt caged in. He stood up, walked down the aisle past tired passengers and whiny children towards the bathroom. It was barely bigger than a cupboard. As soon as he shut the door, the neon light turned on; it made his face look green and pale. He filled the small sink with water and washed his hands, splashing his face. His father's face looked back at him from the mirror; Bernhard couldn't wash that off. Those were his eyes, full of terror at the sight of the world.

Bernhard's throat grew tight, his eyes burned. It was definitely the dry air in the airplane, he thought, returning to his seat.

The ground beneath his feet gave way. It must have happened somewhere here, on the grey, fireproof rug, fringed by rows of light, which would flash in emergencies, leading fleeing passengers to the exits. Theo had slipped away without them blinking.

Bernhard imagined how they must have laid him down on the ground to resuscitate him. His entire life, Theo had been dominant, always making other people feel inferior. And then he had to squirm helplessly on the ground in front of hundreds of spectators. In the last minutes of his life, he had finally paid his dues.

Bernhard's knees grew weak. This feeling of being at someone else's mercy, of helplessness, reminded him of his dream. The young man had been tortured and beaten, and no one could help him. He had stood by and watched as it all happened. He was complicit in that crime, because he hadn't done anything to stop it. He was complicit because he was human.

He sat down in his seat, sinking deep into the soft cushion, and buckled his seatbelt; it snapped loudly into its clasp. It's a shame, he thought, that there's no belt like this in life.

After the stewardess found out that Bernhard's father had died on that airline, she came by more often. She asked him if he would like anything to drink, if he needed any pills or a bottle of wine. She would even give it to him for free, she whispered in Bernhard's ear, although she wasn't supposed to in the tourist class. Was he supposed to be thirstier as a survivor? Did he have more of a right to a sip of alcohol? Would a pack of crispy roasted peanuts change the situation?

They should have been there when he was a child, to give him candy or chocolate bars and stroke his head whenever his father was being unapproachable again, when he shrugged off Bernhard's childish drawings with the same disinterest he regarded the declining stock of a company he had no shares in.

Lydia opened the door to him. Standing in the doorway, she appeared small and lost, but her face was rosy. She hugged him, quickly, warmly, carefully. "Come in," she said, leading him into the room.

Bernhard had expected his mother to be broken, helpless, distraught. She had always seemed so dependent to him and his siblings, so they had all assumed in the long conversations after her phone call that now, after her husband was dead, she would fall apart.

Bernhard had prepared himself for their meeting. He had thought of comforting words, words to defend himself, explanations of the unpredictability of death, its necessity, about the Kinsey Report and strictly homosexual indigenous peoples, whose men and women only performed mating ceremonies once a year. All of that seemed unnecessary now. No sobbing, no desperation, no hint of bitterness. Lydia went out onto the balcony, a bit unsteadily but still light on her feet. In the harsh sunbeams she seemed radiant.

She beckoned her son out to her. The sun had heated up the concrete, and it seemed to Bernhard as if hot air were blowing onto him from a vent.

"Did you have a good flight?"

He examined her face. It was lined and emaciated, her cheekbones were much more prominent since her last chemotherapy, her nose was pale and pointed. But no trace of tears. Where was she hiding her sorrow?

"It was all right."

She smiled, shut her eyes and laid her head on her neck. He saw movement behind her thin eyelids. He had been prepared for many things, but not for her silence.

"Where is he now?" His voice broke, and he had to rasp.

"In a refrigerator at the Center for Disease Control." She squinted at him. There was almost something mischievous in her eyes.

"The CDC?"

"They took some blood samples from him."

"Blood?"

"The stewardess explained to me that they always do that. They're required to make sure that he died a natural death."

Bernhard shook his head. In a refrigerator! Taking blood! The whole thing seemed macabre to him. Why couldn't they just leave him in peace—after everything he'd been through.

Bernhard was shocked by his own thoughts. The whole time he thought he would prefer not to have anything more to do with his father. But now he felt a sort of sympathy for this dead body.

He looked out over the rusty railing. A thick yellow haze lay over the city like gelatin on a fruitcake. An airplane flew by overhead, but Bernhard heard nothing over the noise of the street and the constant hum of the air conditioning.

"They left him on the ground until we landed and acted as if he were still alive, to keep the other passengers from getting upset," said Lydia, and Bernhard turned toward her in horror. For the first time he realized that he actually did want to know what had happened to his father in the last minutes of his life.

Lydia pulled a handkerchief from the sleeve of her dress. "He said he was afraid," she told him, then started crying. "He must have been in pain, he was holding his chest. Two very nice doctors tried to save him. But his heart just wouldn't cooperate. They resuscitated him, they gave him injections, but they couldn't save him."

Lydia looked up and saw her son's bewildered face. He hadn't thought about it before. Now that she was telling it to him, he saw it before him like a film. He could see his father trembling on the floor of the airplane, holding his painful chest. And that throbbing returned, no, a rattling. Bernhard could feel it in his own chest. That tightness, the pain in his arm, the boundless fear, the helplessness, the young man and all that blood.

Bernhard felt dizzy. He leaned back and shook his head, as if he could shake away those impressions like drops of water.

"His eyes were wide and peaceful," she said in order to calm her son down. Her face grew brighter. "Don't worry. When he died, I had the impression he was released."

Bernhard wondered if he should tell her about his dream. Should he comfort her? Or should he follow his inner urge and just walk away?

"'Forgive me' were his last words." Lydia's face relaxed. Yes, she looked peaceful.

"'Forgive me', he said again and again. And then he went to sleep."

Bernhard turned pale. He propped himself up, his arm gave way. Lydia saw the terror in her son's eyes. She stood up and pressed his head firmly against her belly as he began to sob.

19.

Bernhard felt a heavy weight fall away from him as he looked into the boy's light blue eyes. Peace and hope shone in them. His body tingled like a leg after falling asleep and waking up again, and warmth spread through him.

They reached their arms out towards each other, but instead of touching they merged into on another, first their hands, then their bodies and finally their hearts, until all that remained was a warm soft light.

Bernhard's pelvis thrust, hard and rhythmically, then softer and more slowly. The feeling was as familiar to him as the boy's face. It was comfortable, intense and breath-taking. Then he awoke.

Where was he? How late was it? The radio alarm clock on the nightstand said four thirty. The air conditioner droned. He was in a hotel in Miami, the young man was just a dream. Sex. No, it hadn't been sex. They had shared an emotion. Safety, hope, life. Their love was a secret, it was magical and dangerous at the same time. But it didn't matter. Better to die for love than to live as a coward.

Bernhard lifted his head from the pillow and went to the window. The sky was a dull, dark red, stars swum in it like clotted milk in a cup of tea. A few cars glided silently down the four-lane road, huge vehicles bouncing with every pothole.

He hadn't had an erotic dream in a long time. Why was he dreaming now—about a man he didn't even know? Why not dream about Edvard? Edvard! He should call him now. He must be worrying.

A small out-of-date instruction sheet lay next to the phone. The dialing code for Germany, then the area code without a zero; then the number. Bernhard dialed. It wasn't Edvard who answered, but a computer. He needed to type in the telephone company he used, or enter the number of his telephone card. Which telephone company? What kind of telephone card?

Bernhard hung up and called the hotel reception. A sleepy voice answered and explained that it was only possible to call from this hotel if you were affiliated with an American telephone company. Or you could call with a credit card. Bernhard had neither: discouraged, he hung up and fell back into bed.

It was wonderfully warm outside the hotel. A mild wind passed through the dried leaves of the tall yuccas and banana trees. Bernhard wandered past dilapidated houses. The grass in the yards, if there even was any, was thick and tall, sharp as little swords. This early in the morning, hardly anyone was on the street, yet he heard televisions and booming music. Here and there was someone asleep on the street, a few chickens clucking in a pen, a goat rubbing its beard against a barbed-wire fence. Lizards scampered up tree trunks as soon as they saw anyone approaching.

Between hibiscus and blood-red bougainvillea blooms, he stumbled across a small square flat-roofed building at the end of the street. A neon sign said *Waffle House* in yellow and orange letters, *24 hours a day, 365 days a year.*

He sat down at an orange and brown-grained Neoprene table. An elderly woman in a brown apron and orange baseball cap took his order. Her hearing was bad, and Bernhard had to talk over the rattling air conditioner. Even after the third time she asked him to repeat himself, she smiled unapologetically. She wrote his order in block letters on a long notepad, pulled a cup out of her apron along with a paper napkin and utensils. She nodded confidently to him, as if to assure him "we'll manage it somehow, darlin'," then she and her orange-polished fingernails disappeared behind the counter.

His parents had wanted to take a vacation here? Bernhard couldn't remember the last time they had gone on a trip. When he was little, they had gone camping in Austria. They had even gone to the Adriatic

Sea once. But since the children had left home? And then to Miami? What were they expecting here? Did his father even speak English? What were they planning to do during the day? In recent years, Bernhard had only seen his father as someone who sat in front of the TV. He had no idea what motivated him, what his interests were.

After breakfast, he took a taxi to the CDC building and took care of the necessary paperwork, confirmations, conveyance documents, bills, certifications. If his father could see the trouble he was going to now for his sake, thought Bernhard, he would be overjoyed.

Lydia was sitting on the balcony in a white plastic chair marked with black streaks from years of exhaust fumes. In the sun, her face looked twenty years younger. A deep, humble smile played at the corners of her mouth, as if she were watching a child play. She must have a more cheerful outlook than he did, thought Bernhard.

He walked out to her. She was looking at the light-green tiled, kidney-shaped pool and two guards in black uniforms talking excitedly to one another. All around them a sea of untended, half-dried out palm trees swayed, separating the grey flat-roofed bungalows he had walked past that morning.

"Packed?"

"All done."

"Do you want breakfast?"

Lydia lifted up a glass. Bernhard discovered a coffee machine in the niche by the bathroom. A telephone call was impossible, but brewing coffee in your own machine was fine.

"Can I get you anything?"

"No, I'm all right."

"We still have time," said Bernhard. His eyes scanned the horizon, looking for the ocean. They stopped at a row of tall buildings held together by a yellow-green pall of smog. "We could drive out to the beach."

"Why don't you go on your own. I'll stay here." Lydia squinted into the sun. Her voice was calm and relaxed. "This is just what I need."

Bernhard hesitated. He didn't want to leave her alone, but he was afraid she would talk about his father if he stayed.

"Then I'll go now."

Lydia nodded.

Through the doorframe, she looked like a Madonna in a Pre-Raphaelite painting. The door shut heavily behind him.

The houses in South Beach were painted in typical pastel colors: aquarium green, cloud blue, marshmallow pink. Convertibles stood on the beach. Music boomed from a toxic yellow Corvette with bright red flames along the side. The restaurants were still closed, but a few bars were already attracting young girls who were obviously models, or at least aspiring to be. Gorgeous young men stood alongside them, their torsos naked and beautifully tanned. Sweet muscles swelled under their tight, kiss-red nipples, blond hair nestled against their vulnerable temples, crying out to be touched, stroked and loved.

Bernhard wanted to sink into their lips, but he hardly dared to look at them. Underneath the ease with which they laughed and spoke to one another, he sensed danger. He must avoid being discovered, getting caught staring at them.

Crossing the street quickly, he walked under a field of palm trees to the ocean. Rollerbladers rushed past him, the worn concrete path grumbling beneath their wheels. It had grown humid, the sun burned on his face. Within minutes, his body was covered with a sticky layer of sweat.

This early in the morning, the beach was still empty. Here and there were traces of nighttime parties. The lifeguard towers were not yet occupied. He pulled off his winter boots and socks and laid his bare feet in the sand. It was hot, the sun's rays stung like needles. Slowly, he tiptoed along the fine line of salt the ocean had left on the sand. In some places, the beach was covered with mussels, in others with driftwood, faded coke cans and unidentifiable bits of plastic—as if the sea had sorted its treasures during the night.

The water was calm. It dug softly into the sand with long foamy talons, sifting through it and pulling the finer parts into the sea.

In their place it unloaded small blue capsules on the shore that looked like condoms filled with water, fragments of jellyfish.

Small, quick-footed birds raced against the water. When it rushed towards the shore, they ran away from the waves, but as soon as it pulled back they followed it and plucked its fruits from the sand.

Over Bernhard's head seagulls circled, a small family of herons flapped towards the horizon on snow-white wings, and a girl with short, vanilla-colored hair sat on a broken surfboard. She smiled at him, a gust of smoke escaping from her slim, fine-lipped mouth and disappearing quickly.

Bernhard turned his back to her and sat down in the sand. He rolled his pants up high and stretched his toes out in the sun. Then he watched the waves play.

He looked out on the horizon that curved like a soap bubble. What did his mother tell him? "Father liked you best of all his children." Why hadn't Bernhard ever been able to tell? His father had always seemed threatening to him. His penetrating glance was so sharp it could cut you. A network of rules had built up around him, shelves and little boxes where he stored value judgments, reprimands and every so-called misstep, which he would pull out at the appropriate moment and throw in your face.

Bernhard often felt that his childhood had been like hiking through a minefield. No matter how wonderful the landscape looked, Bernhard was always aware of the danger lurking there. His father could explode at any moment. Bitterness and rage had shaped his life.

Early on, Bernhard had learned to cut his father from his life. With a single word, a single glance, he could destroy everything. Even the most beautiful experiences—a friendship, a well-planned gift or tenderness between two people—became bad memories through his mere presence.

His power was so far-reaching that he made others see things through his eyes. Bernhard remembered how disgusted he had been by his own need to touch another man. If the last months with Edvard had not been lodged deeply in his heart, the way his father had left the dinner table would have ruined his relationship in one blow.

Bernhard let a handful of sand sift through his fingers. The wind carried away a fine dust of it. A few seagulls stalked around Bernhard, tapped around him and blinked with beady black eyes from their silver-brown plumage.

"You're lucky you're not humans," he said, picking up a polished mussel shell, grown pale with saltwater and sun, soft and slippery in his hand.

The sun blazed down on Kim's pale, sensitive skin. Nevertheless, it felt good. She wanted to stay like this for hours, stop time and soak up the warmth. For years she had felt tossed about by life. It came in waves, suddenly. And now it had gone far enough. She needed an anchor, a calm bay to moor in, but every time she felt close a storm raged up and pushed her onwards.

"Could you tell me what time it is?" Bernhard asked her in English. His question reeled in her scattered thoughts and brought her back to the beach. She leaned up, wiped the sand off her hands and squinted at him, holding a hand up against the sun.

"I don't know" she said into the breeze.

Her face was round and fresh, her eyes were large. Light make-up emphasized her cheekbones. She was pretty, and to Bernhard she seemed very young.

"I'm sorry," she added, shrugging her fragile shoulders, and he saw that she was truly sorry. He had no way of knowing what she saw in his eyes: stillness, depth, a wide peaceful bay.

20.

The alarm rang in his ears as if he had put his head right next to a church bell. He turned on the lamp on the nightstand: the light burned his eyes like fire. Edvard had a horrible taste in his mouth: whiskey, olives, nicotine and a clear note of spit, sweat and…he didn't even want to guess.

He lifted his throbbing head off the pillow and leaned on his elbows. Next to him a man was dreaming happily, a man with a boyish face, white skin and black wiry hair. Slowly the events of the last night crept back into Edvard's consciousness: the bar, the conversation, the feeling of unfamiliar skin in his hands, the feeling of unfamiliar hands on his skin. He had let the man handcuff him to the bed. His nipples still hurt from the bites, and wax peeled off his skin. A box of melted ice-cubes stood on the nightstand; the handkerchief he had used to blindfold Fred lay between socks, underwear and cowboy boots.

Fred was a real catch. But what struck Edvard that morning was something very different: he had hoped he would wake up with feelings of guilt. He had expected that he would look into the mirror and say to himself: I shouldn't have done that. I was drunk, it was a slip-up that won't happen again. But in the moment he felt much more as if he had fallen in love all over again.

Edvard struggled out of bed. His head throbbed as if someone were trying to break into it with a chisel. He swallowed an aspirin and climbed into the shower. Drops of water rushed down on him, breaking on his sore body.

His life was coming apart at the seams. It seemed as if he had taken a wrong turn somewhere, and was now straying further with every subsequent action.

He climbed out of the shower and stood in front of the mirror. How had he let all this happen? He couldn't think about it anymore. Thinking was toxic in this situation. "Don't think, just don't think," he forbade his image in the mirror.

He rubbed gel into his hair and smoothed it back. He needed to dye it, his black roots were peeking out again.

There were not enough excuses to put everything straight again: this resounded in his head.

"Don't think, just don't think," he said to himself hypnotically. He quickly rubbed his body dry, sprayed deodorant under his arms and plucked out a few stray eyebrows.

The more awake he became, the faster the mill in his head began to grind. "Don't think!" If only it were so simple. On the face of it, he had already written off Bernhard a while ago.

His thoughts spun quickly, but there were no more new ones. Each thought had been chewed over a thousand times, and they tasted correspondingly bland. Edvard began to tinker about more quickly, as if this would allow him to escape the nagging of his thoughts. He rubbed cream on his face, slapped on pre-shave lotion and began to shave, leaving just a thin black line above his lips that pulled down around the corners of his mouth towards his chin. It was like meditating.

And if it all had been a mistake? "Don't think!" He had already managed to cut himself. Edvard took a step back and rubbed his forehead. With a glance at the clock he saw he had to finish up. He shaved it all off and felt naked afterwards.

In the bedroom, he slipped on a pair of briefs and pulled on a white shirt from the hamper. Probably the best solution was to split up. His relationship with Bernhard had no future anyway. They clearly had very different expectations of one another.

Tarot cards lay on the dresser. Edvard pulled *The Lover*. Adam stood in front of the tree of life, Eve in front of the tree of knowledge, where the snake already lay coiled. Above it, a golden angel spread its wings. Edvard knew this card well. It had popped up often in his sessions with Birgit. Adam and Eve lived in paradise, in a state of harmony, oneness with god. But it was also a life without consciousness. Only by biting into the apple did they learn to differentiate good from evil: this was what made them consciously-acting beings who could experience things. They lost their innocence—and attained real life.

Briefcase, planner, watch. Edvard pulled open the top drawer and opened a box. The ring lay inside it. He looked over at Fred, who stretched out in bed, turned around, and went back to sleep. What a hot night. A new beginning, new happiness? He slipped it on, stretched out his hand and let its deep gleam wash over him. Then he took a business card from his planner and scribbled a few words on the back; his pen scratched on the inlaid paper: *In case you don't have any plans for tonight, I might have a few ideas.* There was still the reservation at the hotel in Vienna.

He left the note on Fred's underwear and left the house.

Before the onslaught of Christmas shoppers arrived, he placed another row of figurines on the Biedermeier dressers and Empire tables, decorating the displays with ribbons and colorful Christmas stars.

His sales assistants Andi, Florian and Schnecke arrived in short succession, shook the snow from their coats and wiped up after themselves with a floorcloth.

Something was different about Edvard, they noticed this right away. They looked at him questioningly, but didn't say a word. He had become even quieter than he had been the last few days—which was not a good sign.

Edvard asked Florian to set out flavored coffee and mugs for their customers. He sent Andi to the daily market to get a few fresh fir branches, letting Schnecke decorate the table with gold objects.

Since the party last Thursday and Bernhard's unexpected exit, their boss had changed a lot. An enormous sense of industriousness had come over him, there was constantly something new to be cleaned, arranged or reorganized. It felt like they were part of a job-creation program. His decisions didn't always make much sense, but they refrained from contradicting him. Today of all days: the twenty-fourth! A difficult day awaited them. The last thing they needed was a weeping boss. And he was near tears, that was plain to see.

The problem with last minute Christmas gift buyers wasn't that they hadn't had any time beforehand. They simply lacked ideas, which didn't change on Christmas Eve. That's why it was so difficult to help them. They studied silver hairpins inlaid with mother of pearl with the same dedication as cigarette cases or flasks from the last century. It made no difference if the gift's recipient drank alcohol, smoked, was a man or woman.

Although Edvard was dedicated to his customers, he wasn't quite on top of things today. He had a hard time hearing anything but the injured voice in his head. Repeatedly, he quoted incorrect prices, told the wrong stories about objects or made comments when he should have remained quiet. His customers looked at him skeptically until he retreated in defeat, letting one of his sales assistants save the situation.

"What is wrong with you?" He asked himself in the mirror. His glance was as sharp and piercing as the burning in his heart. "Don't think! Don't think!" It answered him, but his head wasn't paying attention.

Then an elderly woman came into the store. She was wearing a large hat on top of a wig, and she was dressed entirely in brilliant blue, holding a tiny dog in her arms.

"I'm looking for a teensy little gift for my son," she purred, letting her eyes wander over the display.

"What do you have in mind?" asked Edvard.

"I don't know, some kind of...well, how do you say, you know, something nice. Do you have anything?"

Edvard laid out a silver case for business cards in front of her, along with an ivory lapel pin. But she wasn't content with them, nor with the napkin rings, the tea set or the letter opener.

Shortly before twelve, Edvard apologized and passed the customer on to Florian. "I need to get out of here before I kill someone," he whispered in his ear.

Florian stared helplessly over at his colleague, then over the customers' heads around the tightly packed sales room.

"I'll be back in ten minutes."

Edvard threw his coat over his shoulders and disappeared out the service entrance. In a few steps, he was in the park. The air was cool and clear, he felt the blood rushing to his cheeks.

On Marienplatz, Christmas shoppers stumbled from one store to the next. It was complete chaos. Edvard stood still and looked around. He felt the gravel beneath his leather-soled shoes, his ears started burning in the cold. "Don't think! Don't think!" The most important thing was to find other things to think about.

He hurried around the market, ordering things at every stall: English crackers, expensive, strong-smelling cheese, chilled champagne, French chocolates, two large juicy salmon steaks, a few tomatoes, leeks, a handful of shallots and celery. A star fruit was added to the pile, a premium, sugar-sweet melon, lychees and strawberries from New Zealand. How often had he gone shopping here for Bernhard? How much effort had he made to give him the fine things in life? But statistics and mathematical formulas had always been more important to his boyfriend.

"Don't think! Don't think!"

Roswitha drove down Leopoldstrasse, studying the faces of every pedestrian. Fred was somewhere out there. She just had to find him. Sitting around drove her crazy.

Three days ago, she had still been making Christmas plans with Fred. They had driven into the city, walked through the pedestrian zone hand in hand, bought Christmas decorations. In the afternoon she baked Christmas cookies while Fred cracked walnuts. In the evenings, they lay content and happy in front of the TV. Then he had stood up without a word and left. She thought he just wanted to go to the bathroom or grab a beer, but then she heard the door to the apartment slam shut.

Roswitha waited, first in front of the TV, then at the kitchen window. After an hour she got dressed and walked along the street, but there was no trace of Fred. Then she went back up and sat down on the couch; the ashtray was still full of his cigarette butts. At midnight, she finally undressed and slipped into her nightshirt. She turned the light off, then on again. She listened for noises, and as soon as she heard the door to the building open, she pretended to be asleep—it was not her intention to make him feel guilty. But Fred hadn't turned up.

Now she drove through the city. She had to do something after all. On Ludwigstrasse, she turned towards the inner ring. The ticking of her turn signal calmed her down.

The next morning she called the hospitals, but no young man fitting his description had been admitted.

Only three possibilities were left: he had been kidnapped, and his kidnappers had yet to contact her. If they did, she could find the money to pay them. If she sold a few valuables, canceled her savings account with the building society and received an advance, she could certainly scrape up fifteen or twenty thousand Marks.

Or he just needed a little time for himself to think everything over. Maybe he had traveled to his mother's or needed to talk with a friend about the marriage. Maybe he had never been loved this way, and was just sitting in a bar somewhere feeling insecure. She had read about lots of similar reactions in novels.

Or he had left her: if that was the case, it was her fault alone. She should never have asked him to marry her.

At the Isartor she turned towards Im Tal. People thronged together on the smooth sidewalks passing by display windows, wrapped deep in their coats and scarves.

This was not the first time that Roswitha's life had changed so abruptly. Fred was like a gift from heaven. He had become like a physical constant for her, something as fundamental as temperature, force and gravity.

The worst thing about his disappearance was that she couldn't shut her eyes anymore. As soon as the world left her sight, her thoughts turned into a wild, turbulent chaos, her body seemed to fall into a thousand pieces and a fear came over her that she had never known in her life, the fear of going insane.

Beneath the arcades of the municipal savings bank she thought she could make out Fred, then she heard a dull thud. Strawberries smacked against her windshield, flowers rained down out of the white winter sky onto her. She gave a start, slammed on the brakes and skidded. Tearing open the door, she saw tangerines rolling around like orange beads in the snow; crushed tomatoes lay on the ground like bloodstains.

Edvard was kneeling five feet behind her car.

"Oh my God! Are you injured?"

He pushed himself up. "I'll be all right."

"It's terrible. I didn't see you. I...I..." Roswitha shrugged her shoulders. Chocolates and leeks lay sprawled around, lychees. She bent down for them. "I'm so sorry. I'm...I don't know what to do. Believe me. I've never been in an accident before."

Tears ran down her cheeks. A car honked its horn. It sounded mute, almost dogged.

People rushed up to them. Did he need help? Edvard waved them away.

Roswitha gathered up a few groceries. He took them from her hand and stuffed them in the bags.

"No harm done. I was lost in thought. I didn't pay attention to the traffic."

"I'm sorry. I don't know what to do with myself anymore."

"It's all right, really. It was my fault."

"No, it was my fault. Everything is my fault." Roswitha brushed snow of Edvard's coat, his elbow was very white, his hand had been scraped. Then she saw the ring. "That ring! It belongs to my...husband."

"That can't be. It's a unique piece."

"You saw him, didn't you? Tell me where he is. Tell me why he disappeared."

"I'm sorry, I don't know your husband."

"But you must have seen him. He's the only one who has a ring like that."

"No, I'm the only with a ring like this. It's my ring."

"Tell me where my husband is." Roswitha begged Edvard, holding tightly to him.

"He's the only person I have in my life. I just want to have him back again. Tell me what you want. I'll do anything. It doesn't matter."

Edvard tore himself away. "Are you crazy? Let me go!"

"But you must have seen him. He's short and young and has a birth mark behind his right ear," Roswitha sniveled. "He always wears a leather jacket and cowboy boots. And he has such a charming smile. Please, give him back to me." She sunk weakly onto her knees and begged him.

Edvard looked around. More pedestrians were stopping to watch. He pulled his arm from her grasp.

"He has my bank card and three thousand Marks in his inner jacket pocket. I gave them to him for the move. Take it all, just give him back to me."

Edvard pushed her away and ran off, past the old town hall, up onto Dienerstrasse, past Dallmayer, where she couldn't follow him with her car. Once he was certain he had lost her, he leaned against a building and breathed deeply. An extremely disquieting feeling had settled upon him. He needed to think. No, it couldn't be true. It was much too crazy to have actually happened. Jeans. Cowboy boots. A birthmark behind the right ear. He tried to deny the thought, but he soon became certain: Fred!

But what had happened with the ring? Fred hadn't been wearing anything on his hand. Edvard had taken it from the guy in the English garden, Bernhard's lover. Unfiltered cigarettes, sharp nose, that profile! Of course! Now he knew where he had seen Fred before. And the blue spot on his nose! It had come from Edvard's own fist. In spite of the cold, Edvard felt a warm shiver run down his spine. That meant that Bernhard's new lover…that he had been with him last night…

He ran down Maximilianstrasse into his shop, pushing past the clients. Florian looked at him, shocked. Blood flowed from the scratch on his temple, his coat was covered in snow and dirt, a crushed strawberry was stuck to his shoulder.

"My God! What happened to you?"

"I can't explain it to you right now. First, there is someone I need to kill."

21.

Edvard slammed the door to his apartment behind him; his heart was racing. First he went into the bedroom, but the bed was empty. Then he looked into the kitchen, the dining room, the bathroom; the shower was still wet, but Fred had disappeared.

Stay calm! Edvard stood in the entrance hall and thought. Hopefully he hadn't taken anything with him. He went around the apartment and looked to see if anything was missing. In the kitchen, he found the business card with his note. Fred had read it, so he would probably come back. He just needed to wait for him.

Edvard flopped himself down on the couch. The rubber giant they had gotten for their anniversary was propped up against the wall, reminding him of Bernhard. Tuesday afternoon, Christmas Eve. The last time he had seen Bernhard was last Thursday. Back then he had still loved him and wished for nothing more than to live with him forever. Within five days, his feelings had changed completely. Now he was furious; he never wanted anything to do with Bernhard again. He had misjudged him this whole time. "Don't think! Just don't think!"

Then he saw Fred's cigarette butts in the ashtray. Edvard was seized with rage. He chucked it at the rubber doll, hoping to break it. But the ashtray rebounded and flew at the bar. A few carafes shattered, alcohol flowed over the ground. Wonderful! His streak of bad luck just wouldn't end.

If he left the puddle of alcohol there, the floor would be ruined too. Edvard trudged into the kitchen, grabbed a broom and dustpan and a roll of paper towels. Then he knelt down next to the fragments and started picking them up, cutting his hand in the attempt. Now there was blood dripping on the floor as well. "Don't think! Just don't think!"

Edvard leaned back on his heels and shook his head. He felt as if he were under a malicious spell. When would this finally end?

The doorbell interrupted his thoughts. Fred! He wrapped his hand quickly in a towel and slipped into the corridor. Then he opened the door and lifted his arm, ready to throw a punch.

"Edvard Bornheimer?"

In the backlight it took him a minute to make out the faces of the two uniformed officers: "Yes." He lowered his fist, confused.

"Police. We're searching for a man named Fred Wolf. Do you know him?"

"No, I don't know him, and I'm not interested." Edvard was about to shut the door when one of the men snapped: "Would you please show us your hands."

Edvard stretched them out. One of them pointed to the ring, the other to the bloody towel. "And what happened there?" He pointed to his hand.

"I just cut myself there."

"May we come in?" The larger of the two pushed past Edvard into his apartment.

"Look, I'm not really in the mood for solving riddles right now. Could we do this another time?"

"The man we're looking for has been missing for a few days now," explained the other in a calm voice. "You are strongly suspected of having contact with him."

Not the crazy woman, thought Edvard.

Then one of them called to the other from the living room: "Rudolph, look what we have here."

"That's the man. That's him." Roswitha jumped up from the bench as they led Edvard into the station.

"Keep that woman away from me," whispered Edvard. "She almost ran me over at noon today."

The policemen brought Edvard into the interrogation room. Roswitha tried to push past the barrier. "Please wait outside, all right?"

They brought Edvard into a small square room. He looked around for a large two-way mirror like the ones he had seen in films, but there was none. Just a desk with a lamp and a window with rusty metal bars.

"Do you smoke?" asked the policeman who had introduced himself as Inspector Grill. He had a penetrating gaze and lips as thin as drawn lines.

"No, thank you."

"I wasn't going to offer you a cigarette. The question is rather, if you don't smoke, how did those cigarette butts end up in your apartment?" He shook a bag in front of his nose.

"I had a guest."

"And what is this guest's name?"

Edvard groaned. "Fred."

"Fred what?"

"I don't know."

"But he stayed the night with you." The policeman scrutinized Edvard over the desk.

"Am I not allowed to let men by the name of Fred stay the night with me?" he asked sharply, lifting his nose in the air.

"Careful. We're talking about a missing person here. You're our only witness. You deny knowing the missing man. We find blood in your apartment. Cigarette butts that likely come from him. We have to follow up on this."

"I denied it because I was annoyed enough already. I just wanted to be left in peace and quiet, don't you understand?"

"And then there's still the question of the ring." Grill lifted it onto the desk and let the light play with it. He seemed almost hypnotized.

"That belongs to me. I already told your colleague three times." Edvard was growing impatient.

"Then explain to me why Mrs. Wengenmayer was able to give us an exact description of the ring?"

"I can't explain that to you. She hit me with her car, and then saw it on my hand. She must have had enough time to study it."

"And where is your receipt for the ring?"

"I don't have one." He put his hand on his head and considered. "It's like this. I bought the ring some weeks ago from an old man who came into my store. As soon as I saw it I knew I wanted it for myself. That's why it's not on the books. It's completely legal."

"How did you know that this man was the real owner of the ring?"

"How? How? I'm an antique dealer. If I had to investigate where every piece came from, I might as well just close my store."

"So there's at least a possibility that the ring really belongs to this woman's partner."

"It's quite simple. She's been missing her husband since last Saturday. But I bought the ring in late September. Since then, it's been sitting in a secret drawer in my secretary's desk. Why this crazy woman thinks it's her ring, I have no idea."

Grill looked at him with large eyes. "Is there at least someone who can bear witness to the purchase, one of your colleagues or…"

Edvard shook his head desperately. "No, no, no. But I gave the ring to a friend of mine five days ago."

"Ah, a friend of yours."

"Yes, a friend."

The policeman leaned back and thought. His head bobbed back and forth as if he were carrying out an inner dialogue.

"If that's the case, this matter should be easy to check. What's your friend's name?"

"You won't be able to reach him."

"Ah, of course. He probably went on vacation with Santa Claus. Right?"

Edvard grew angry, but he restrained himself. Calmly he said: "He's with his family in Frankfurt. But I don't have his telephone number."

"Do you think I'm an idiot or something?" Grill slammed his fist on the table. Edvard flinched.

"I don't care what you think. I'm telling you the truth."

"Your problem is that you've got to prove it."

Edvard leaned far back in his chair and shook his head. This couldn't be happening. No matter what he did, every breath drew him closer to catastrophe.

"Maybe you just want to think it over a bit. My shift is over. Maybe by morning you'll have thought of something new."

"Finally." Edvard breathed a sigh of relief, stood up and grabbed for his coat.

"No, I'm going. You're staying here."

"Now wait a minute!"

"I can't just let you go. You have no explanation for the ring, nor for this missing man, though you were apparently the last person to have seen him."

"But I don't know where he is. I swear."

The inspector shrugged his shoulders: "Well, good night."

"No, don't go. Okay, okay. I'll give you his name. But when you call there, just ask for him. Please don't tell the story to his family. Under no circumstances are you to mention my name."

Grill looked at Edvard mistrustfully then called his colleague into the room, ordering him to find out the name of Bernhard Moll's married sister in Frankfurt, and to get in touch with her. Then he took the ring back. He turned it and held it up to the light, then weighed it in his hand for a long time. His eyes glowed, and with a trace of envy in his voice he finally said: "It's a beautiful piece. Lucky find, right?"

"I'm not so sure anymore," murmured Edvard, laying his hand on the tabletop.

"Sorry?"

"I said, you're right. It's the kind of thing you only find once in a lifetime."

A short time later the door opened again. "Her name is Gudrun Esslinger. And she has a brother who lives in Munich who's currently visiting. Technically."

"And non-technically?"

"He's currently in Miami, transporting his deceased father. He's arriving in Frankfurt tomorrow morning on the seven o'clock flight."

"Thank you." Grill took the note from his hand, and his colleague shut the door behind him.

And to Edvard: "You'll need to stay here overnight. We'll pick up your friend from the airport, by then we'll also have the lab results from the blood in your apartment."

A night in jail, thought Edvard. It was a nightmare, but he knew a few friends who would envy him for it.

22.

Bernhard entered the room and recoiled. His father's clothes lay on the bed, as if he had interrupted him while changing.

"I've just got to go to the bathroom, then we can go," said Lydia, disappearing into the bathroom.

A blazer lay there, one that Bernhard remembered from his childhood. Pants lay next to it, various shirts, shorts and underwear. Although Bernhard had grown up seeing these clothes, they seemed foreign to him, more foreign than the clothes in store displays. Maybe because they were so different from the clothes people wear today. "Old-men's fashion" was what Bernhard called the way his father dressed.

He pulled out a green knee-length velvet bathing suit from among the clothes. It lay smoothly in his hand. He tried to imagine his father wearing it. His belly, his perfectly round navel that had always looked to him like a football valve, and his short scrawny legs. A polyester shirt with an almost washed-out zebra pattern and a pointy, much too large collar. His father had worn it when Bernhard was awarded first prize in a science competition. He had developed a computer program that calculated prime numbers. That was almost twenty years ago, and yet it was one of the only times his father had shown an interest in his son's way of seeing the world.

Bernhard slipped his hand into the shirt and let the smooth, cool material slide over his fingers. He remembered: he was about five when he had stolen a pair of underwear from his father's dresser and put them on. They were so large that he could barely button his pants over them, but it made him feel proud, big and grown-up. He felt as if he had found a shortcut into the grown-up world. And yet at the same time, this piece of material forged a secret bond between him and his father.

Bernhard heard the toilet flush.

"Why did you lay everything out?" he asked Lydia.

"I'm going to leave it here. What would I do with it at home?" She shut the door to the balcony; the air conditioning began to hum automatically. "Or did you want any of it?"

She said that as if it were the most unimportant thing in the world. "I can still picture him in this shirt," Bernhard whispered, remembering the award ceremony, his father's look of pride. Bernhard pressed his face into the shirt; it smelled fresh, like detergent, no trace of his father.

Of course, Bernhard didn't want any of the clothing. But to leave it here? His mother couldn't just leave his belongings behind. Things that belonged together were being separated. His siblings in Frankfurt, Bernhard in Munich, his father's grave in Heidelberg, and now the clothing was supposed to stay in Florida? Or was this just the natural consequence of death?

Lydia picked up her purse from the table, laid her cardigan over her arm and put her small sunhat on over her wig. Her coat lay over the suitcase, which stood next to the door, ready to be picked up and transported four thousand miles on its way home.

"All right." His mother seemed almost cheerful.

"All right," he answered glumly. Lydia took the coat. Bernhard lifted her suitcase and turned around. Then he followed her to the door, turned around one last time, and looked Lydia in the eyes. She was already standing in the hallway when he turned back and snatched up the zebra-striped polyester shirt. Then he followed her to the elevator.

Bernhard was so deep in thought that he didn't see Kim at the entrance to the airplane. If she hadn't pulled on his sleeve and beamed at him, he would have walked right past her.

"Did you have a nice walk on the beach?"

When Bernhard answered her with a frown, she added with a smile full of gleaming white teeth: "I have a watch now. It's a quarter past five."

Then he realized: she was the girl from the beach. "Now that's a coincidence!"

"I thought right away you weren't an American," she said, then her face grew serious, and Bernhard noticed the sun-tanned steward glaring at Kim.

"We'll see each other later," she whispered. "Have a good take-off."

Lydia was already in her seat. Bernhard stowed away her cardigan, handbag and coat in the overhead compartment, then sat down next to her.

The plane was half empty, but it still took forever to put away all the bags and purses, as if they wanted to savor every last minute in this wonderful country.

Bernhard felt relieved all of a sudden. When Kim had asked him the time on the beach, he had noticed right away what a fresh and lively presence she had, how full of curiosity and life she was. With his father under his feet and his terminally ill mother by his side, it was good to know there was someone in the airplane bubbling with life. There was something exhilarating about her mere presence. Maybe because she reanimated the deathly stillness in his head by reminding him of the burning sun and the wide ocean. Or maybe just because she was someone outside all the turmoil of his life, someone unburdened; she was like a bridge into another world.

Lydia sat next to the window. She wanted to see Miami and the Atlantic, which she had never laid eyes on before and would probably never see again. She hadn't seen anything of the city. But she had left something behind that would connect her with it forever. She imagined the maid picking up Theo's clothing, taking it home with her and giving it to someone in her family, or to a neighbor, who would walk with them along the city's long, wide beaches.

But Lydia wasn't just leaving something behind, she was taking something with her as well. She had breathed the air, she had seen things up there on the hotel balcony: palms and pelicans and a sky as full of motion as the life she had always wished for. For her son it was a pitiful view of an ugly city, because he couldn't see what she felt: beyond the houses, far beyond the cities, somewhere out there on the ocean was the beginning of eternity. And all of a sudden eternity had not felt so far away anymore. Lydia had smelled freedom.

The airplane rolled out onto the runway, accelerated and lifted off into the sunny sky. Moments later the giant behemoth of Miami shrank to the size of the window, and the sea contracted into a light-blue, silken cloth.

Now and then, Lydia met Bernhard's glance, they smiled at one another and then looked quickly in the other direction. He thought about his father's end, she thought about the beginning of the rest of her life.

The sky remained clear and open, then it gradually grew dark, the sun sank into puffy clouds and dyed them deep blue. Bernhard and his mother sent their meals back uneaten. The air was too thick for salmon with broccoli, and after everything they had been through in the last few days, they had enough to digest. Soon after that, Lydia fell asleep.

Bernhard looked up the aisle, searching for Kim. Stewardesses collected the meal trays. Dishes clacked, plastic bags were held open, coffee served. He unbuckled his seat-belt and went to the back.

"Do you need anything?" Kim asked him from the kitchen. She was tying up a trash bag.

He was thirsty for life. "I don't think so," he answered.

"It's really funny that we've run into each other again here, don't you think?"

"Yeah, somehow it is." His hand was already holding the door handle to the bathroom.

"Look," she whispered, pulling him conspiratorially into the kitchen. "I put aside two bottles of champagne. If you feel like it, we can polish them off."

"Sounds great," he said.

Kim looked around for the steward; he was busy in first class. She whispered something to Margret, then indicated to Bernhard to sit in the last row, right in front of the kitchen. Then she poured roasted nuts into a cup and put small plastic champagne glasses on the table.

"Can you just take time off?"

"The flight is empty, I've done my job. And I'm going to get fired anyway."

"Fired?"

"Ah, I'd rather not talk about it. How about you tell me what you did in Florida? Isn't Miami an amazing city?" She poured out champagne, then continued chattering brightly. "When I was sitting down there on the beach, it stole my heart. I totally have to live there. Don't you find it unbelievably exciting? The city's really tingling with life."

Words bubbled right out of Kim. After everything Bernhard had experienced in the last few days, she was a respite. Her words washed over him, refreshing, animating, renewing. After less than five minutes, Bernhard had the impression he had known Kim for years.

"But tell me, are you all right? You're not saying anything."

He looked at her. She had open, curious eyes.

"It's all right. The last few days have just been horrible."

"Tell me! How can you have horrible days on the beach?"

"No, there's nothing to tell," he said. He didn't want to burden her with his story. Talking about it would bring back all the discomfort, all the disquieting feelings. Anyway, Kim would no longer be unburdened if she knew, she would no longer be a bridge to a foreign world.

"Tomorrow morning it will all be over." He would deliver his mother to Gudrun and set off on the next train. His siblings could take care of all the funeral arrangements. All he wanted was to get back to Edvard.

"You're right. It's not good to talk too much about problems. It often makes them seem bigger and more important than they actually are." She looked over at him.

"Anyway, it makes a bad impression on other people."

She lifted her glass to toast with him. "I'm speaking from experience. I tend to talk a bit more than I should, and because of that a lot of people assume I'm just a dumb blonde. But it's not true at all." She looked appraisingly at him and paused for a relatively long time.

"I find it flattering that you're telling me so much about yourself," said Bernhard, grinning sheepishly. He liked her style. There was a very loud, bright façade, but behind it sat a small, sweet and very caring girl.

"That's just what I wanted to hear." She giggled again. "But still, I won't bother you with my drama."

Bernhard didn't answer. He watched her eyes play. They were large and round; full of curiosity, they scanned her surroundings. A shy wariness lurked in the background.

"All right. I've just had a catastrophic couple of days," she said. Her voice became markedly softer, almost despondent. "And whenever I think it can't get any worse, something else happens."

Bernhard sat up.

"It all started last weekend," she said, and he thought of the beginning of his problems: the party on Thursday.

"I had an affair with a married man. He promised me he would split up with his wife. But instead of divorce papers, he showed up with a giant ring on his finger. From her, of course."

Ring? Bernhard felt for his. Hopefully he had just misplaced it; the thought made him nauseous.

"So I threw the guy out. I mean, I'm not going to be screwed around with."

Bernhard nodded in agreement.

"Then I had my first flight abroad—to Miami. I've been waiting two years for that, you understand. And what happens?" She looked at him, as if he would be able to guess.

Bernhard shrugged his shoulders. "Some old geezer kicks the bucket on the flight." She slid down in her seat and pressed her knees against the seat in front of her. "At first I thought the old man was just shitting his pants with fear, but then he really had a heart attack and checked out."

Kim dug a pack of cigarettes out of her waistband. "Do you smoke?" She looked into Bernhard's pale face. He shook his head.

"Just hearing about it makes you go pale? Imagine what it was like for me." She lit the cigarette. "I had never seen a dead man before. He was panting and shaking, it was a real struggle for life."

"That was my father."

"What?"

"I said that was my father."

Kim sat up straight and pulled her hair back. "Oh shit. I hope I didn't say anything wrong."

"It's all right."

"Yes, of course. His wife…your mother. I should have realized when you boarded. What is wrong with me? I'm telling you, it's one thing after another. My life is pure chaos. I'm really sorry. I didn't mean to…"

"Hey, no harm done."

Kim put out the half-smoked cigarette and looked at him.

"But that wasn't all, not by a long shot."

"What?"

"Your father. I was so upset that I felt sick. Then I went into the kitchen. And then as I was hanging over the trash bag, the doctor who tried to resuscitate your father came in, and…"

"And what?"

Kim pulled the cellophane lining off the cigarette package and played around with it. "He took me by the arm."

Bernhard gave her a puzzled look.

"Before I knew it, his thing was inside me."

"You mean…?"

"Yes, dammit. He raped me."

Kim lit a new cigarette. Bernhard saw that it was uncomfortable for her to talk about it.

She changed the subject. "It must be really awful to lose someone you love." Bernhard lowered his head. "Will you miss him?"

Bernhard thought of his father lying in the icy storage space just a few feet below him, his eyes shut, his hands folded over his chest.

He was probably still wearing the same clothes as the day he left: brown and gray things, his fur boots, red suspenders over his round belly.

He looked out of the window into the black night. Emptiness, stillness, cold, thirty thousand feet above the ground, but Bernhard felt nothing. "No. He never meant anything to me."

She looked at him skeptically. He was sad, she could see that. Why wouldn't he admit it? But then she remembered Fred and all the injuries of the past few years. Maybe it was actually better to ignore your feelings sometimes.

Lydia was sleeping deeply; her breath was slow and regular. There was a warm, contented smile on her face.

Bernhard buckled up again. In Germany, it was midnight now, people were returning home after the evening mass: Christmas. In a few days, a new year would begin. The Molls would celebrate without their father in the future: New Year's, Easter, birthdays, confirmations. In spite of that, he would be there as always, although much more attention would be on him now. Furthermore, they had gained a new anniversary: the day of his death.

Bernhard pushed his seat back, laid his head between the armrests and turned off the light. He wanted to sleep, to shut off for a few hours and not wake up until he came back home and knew: it's all over now!

At three in the morning, Lydia woke up.

"You can't sleep?" she asked her son.

He shook his head. She laid her hand on his. Hers was cold and dry, his was hot and sweaty. No matter how old a man is, whether he is successful, is married, or has children of his own, a single look from his mother, a particular tone in her voice or in her touch, can turn him back into a child.

Lydia sat up and looked out: soft, flat blackness. "I just keep asking myself," he heard her say, and in an instant he knew what was coming. He turned away, looked down the aisle; it wasn't long enough to escape. She turned towards him and pressed his hand, forcing him to look her in the eye, "Why didn't you ever tell me about it?"

Bernhard held his breath. The question was so direct, he couldn't avoid it. But what was he supposed to answer? Should he tell her about the vague fear that had tormented him from the start, the shame of being homosexual, the feeling of doing something dirty? She would ask him if he didn't trust her. But it had nothing to do with trust. It was more like a law, or like gravity. It was useless to talk about it. It just had to be accepted.

She stroked his hair lovingly. "Don't carry secrets around with you, my boy. Believe me, they just grow bigger and bigger, and at some point they become so heavy that you can't breathe."

Something was going through her head, a thought, a memory. Bernhard couldn't guess.

"Someday you'll understand."

Lydia saw the doubt in her son's eyes. As if answering him, she pulled her purse out from under the seat. "Before I forget. I wanted to give you something. Could you turn the light on!" Then she unfolded a handkerchief: in the middle lay a simple ring, a golden band, her husband's wedding ring.

"Here. I want you to wear it." There was a gleam of life in her eyes, something he hadn't seen for a long time.

Bernhard reached hesitantly for the ring. It was thin, light and gave off a motherly warmth, so different from the one Edvard had given him. But what was he supposed to do with it?

23.

In the morning, as the dark sky faded into a silky blue, the airplane touched down on the runway. The plane swerved a little, but quickly righted itself, then the landing flaps flipped up and the whole airplane began to shake. Lydia clung tightly to her purse, Bernhard to his father's ring, until the cheerful voice of a stewardess informed them that they had landed in Frankfurt.

All morning, Lydia had been talking about her husband. What a wonderful person he had been, how much he had sacrificed for the family. Just when Bernhard thought he couldn't take any more of it, she added a sentence that made him prick up his ears: "Have you ever wondered why babies cry when they get tired?"

Bernhard shook his head.

"They feel something happening to their bodies, but they can't determine what it is. Their breath gets slower, their sight blurs, the limbs of their little, fragile bodies grow heavy. Babies can't classify this experience; it makes them scared. And because they lack the ability to ask, they scream." She looked at Bernhard. "It's like a cry for help."

Bernhard looked at her questioningly.

"I think it was the same for your father; he often couldn't understand what was happening inside him. Instead of talking about it, he would get moody or ruin our day. That was his way of crying for help."

A bell sounded and the passengers undid their seat belts, opened the luggage compartments, and soon they were moving towards the exit. Bernhard and Lydia waited until the very end.

Kim said goodbye to both of them. "Maybe we'll see each other again."

Bernhard nodded, then he saw two policemen across from him.

"Mr. Moll?"

"Yes, what is it?"

"Our colleagues in Munich would like to ask you to continue your flight. They have a few questions for you over there."

Lydia recoiled. "My son, for God's sake!"

Bernhard remained unemotional. "What about?"

"Unfortunately, they didn't inform us. All we know is that our colleagues spoke with your sister yesterday, a Mrs. Gudrun Esslinger. She's already taken care of your connecting ticket." He handed it to Bernhard. Then he turned to Lydia: "I'm sure it's nothing bad, Mrs. Moll. No need to be concerned."

"Well, now what?" Lydia looked anxiously over at her son.

"Your daughter is waiting for you outside. We'll bring you to her."

Lydia grabbed Bernhard's hand, he was starting to feel uneasy. "It's all right, Mama. I'll fly home and call you right away. Don't worry."

She pulled him close and gave him a kiss on the forehead.

"Be careful, my boy."

Then she linked her arms with the policeman and let them lead her down the walkway into the airport; Bernhard watched her go, then went hesitantly back to his seat.

The stewardesses collected leftover newspapers and remnants of food, then the new passengers streamed on. Men in dark suits and elegant coats, with briefcases as carry-ons.

"You look pale." Kim bent down to him. Passengers pushed past her. "What did they want from you?"

"No idea." He rubbed his forehead, looking worried. "Maybe someone broke into my apartment? Or maybe it's about my father, but what would the police in Munich have to do with that?"

"Maybe something happened to somebody?" suggested Kim.

"I have no idea who…" Edvard! Bernhard went pale. "Oh God."

"What's wrong?"

Beads of sweat formed on Bernhard's forehead; his heart started pounding. Images from his dreams popped into his head. The young man, dead, slaughtered. Soldiers, skull insignia, filth and blood. Visions flashed like lightning; they hardly lasted a second, but it would have taken hours to interpret them, decades to understand.

"Tell me, what are you thinking of?"

"Edvard! I was thinking about Edvard."

"Edvard?"

"My…boyfriend."

She looked at him questioningly. Hundreds of thoughts shot through his head, but this time he sorted them quickly. It couldn't have anything to do with Edvard. For one thing, if Edvard was sick, the police would never get involved. If something more serious had happened to him, how would the police know Bernhard's name? And thirdly: nothing bad ever happened to people like Edvard. Or did it?

"Well, keep talking." Kim was insistent. Her colleague tapped her on the shoulder, since the airplane had already begun to move. The steward's voice rang out of the speakers.

"We'll see each other afterwards. Don't worry. I'll stay with you," said Kim, and went back.

Bernhard relaxed a little bit, but the feeling of nausea remained.

The noise of the motors droned in his ears; Bernhard was leaning against the wall of the kitchen. Kim poured him a cognac. He felt sick. He felt an unbelievable fear, an irrational, crazy fear linked to dreadful images. He needed to talk, he needed to tell everything to someone else, his dreams, the images, the horror.

"My head is swarming with images and thoughts I can't figure out. There are all these feelings that don't belong to me. I'm like a radio receiving every station at once."

Kim passed the cup over to him.

"And sometimes I feel like a baby. All I want to do is scream."

Bernhard still felt nauseous as he left the airplane. Sick to his stomach, he staggered down the hall. Going up the stairs to baggage claim, he could feel how wobbly his knees were.

He sat down on a bench until the conveyor belt started moving.

Fluorescent lights reflected mercilessly in the polished marble floor, only interrupted by the shadows of hectic passengers rushing by.

The automatic doors slid open and closed again and again, letting Bernhard hear cheerful voices welcoming their loved ones back home. Edvard would have picked him up, but he didn't even know Bernhard had flown away. He must have been waiting for days now, he must be terribly worried. Edvard. Oh Edvard. He missed him so much.

Of course he could call him now, then he'd know right away if this whole matter with the police had anything to do with him. On the other hand, if he reached the answering machine now, he'd worry even more.

If only he had given Gudrun's telephone number to Edvard, then he could have called and heard about everything.

Bernhard stood up and went over to the payphones. He dialed, and it went right to the answering machine: Bernhard cringed. Edvard should have been home at this time. Just don't get upset, the last thing he needed right now was more agitation.

"Hi, my darling, it's me, Bernhard. I hope you're not mad at me because it's been so long since I've gotten in touch with you, but the last few days have been pretty chaotic. All these horrible images have been floating around in my head, scaring me, like last Thursday at our party. I wanted to explain it to you, but I just couldn't.

Then there was a horrible scene with my parents at dinner. I can't even think about it now, and on top of that my father died.

I've tried to reach you at least ten times, but the line was either busy or I couldn't talk or I couldn't get through, like in Miami.

Now I'm in at the airport Munich, I need to go to the police station first but then I'm coming home. I'll call you soon; we need to see each other. I miss you. I don't know how I got through the past few days without you. I…I…love you."

Bernhard hung up and leaned his head against the wall. Soon he would be holding his boyfriend in his arms, and everything would be all right again.

After his suitcase had gone around the luggage belt twice, Bernhard picked it up by the handle and slipped out of the airport into his old world.

"Bernhard Moll?"

Bernhard made out two police officers in the crowd. "Yes?"

"Good morning," one of them said with a friendly, but very official voice. "We'll drive you into the city. If you would please follow us."

"Bernhard!" he heard Kim's shrill voice. She was running so fast that her suitcase hummed against the marble floor. "Wait for me!" She flung her arms around his neck, then linked arms with him. "Personal pick-up service, or what?"

"I'm sorry…" the policeman began.

Kim stood protectively in front of Bernhard. "He's my boyfriend. Surely it won't bother you if I come along?"

Bernhard's heart was pounding in his throat. He had never had to deal with the police, and in that moment he was very thankful for Kim.

As soon as they exited the building, the cold pounced on them with icy talons. Bernhard was nervous, overtired, and continually on the verge of vomiting.

"What is this about actually?" Kim asked pointedly against the background noise of running cars and planes taking off. "Could someone inform us?"

"It's about a ring," one of them answered in a strained voice, "and a man who's missing," the other one completed the sentence.

A man? Missing? Beads of sweat formed on Bernhard's forehead. Kim saw the terror in his eyes.

"Don't worry. They said it's nothing bad," she reminded him.

Nevertheless, he slipped palely into the car and went rigid.

"Can't you tell us anything more specific?" Kim pressed further. "You can see that my boyfriend is very worried."

"Unfortunately not. We're just supposed to pick up Mr. Moll."

Kim laid her delicate hand in Bernhard's, and her face, still pointing with stoic coldness towards the policemen, grew soft and motherly.

"We've got him," one of the policemen said into the car phone. "We should be there in about half an hour."

We've got him? That didn't sound good. Anxiously, he looked into Kim's in eyes, and for the first time he became aware of the unbelievable power that fragile being possessed.

Both of their hands gradually grew warmer. Bernhard leaned his head back and shut his eyes. A lost ring, panic attacks, coming out at dinner, a dead father, policemen, and Edvard missing. What else was in store for him?

They had brought Edvard back into the interrogation room. He was confused and exhausted, his feelings changing with every thought. At night, he had realized the possibility that he might have acted stupidly. If Bernhard had flown to Miami because of his father's death, he couldn't have been with another man. And the fact that he hadn't called was probably less a matter of bad intentions than a question of difficult circumstances.

On the other hand he was annoyed: if Bernhard had at least given him his sister's telephone number, he could have called her and been informed. The way it was, he had had to worry unnecessarily. And however the ring had ended up on a strange man's finger, Bernhard had better come up with a good reason for it.

Bernhard, oh Bernhard, he missed him so much. He would forgive him everything in the end, he already knew that. A warm feeling spread through his body, as if Bernhard were stroking him. They would have lots to tell one another in the next few days. It had certainly been the most eventful five days he had ever experienced: the nightly fight in the park, a married lover pretending to be a therapist, a woman who almost ran him over and a night in prison. And all of that because of that ring. It had been the cause of the whole drama.

But help was on its way. Bernhard would come and clarify everything. Then they'd embrace one another, and everything would be well again.

The policemen led Bernhard and Kim through the waiting room flickering with yellow neon light. A woman sat waiting on a bench. Kim felt her stomach twist. She had seen her on Fred's arm once; it was his wife, the one he wanted to split up with.

Kim pressed closer to Bernhard in order to avoid Roswitha's glance. The last thing she needed right now were complications with Fred. "That's my last lover's wife," she hissed between her teeth, after Bernhard gave her a puzzled look.

Inspector Grill shook Bernhard's hand: "I'm sorry, Mr. Moll, to have imposed ourselves on you like this. We heard of the tragedy in your family. Before we start I would like to express our condolences. This must be a difficult time for you. Nevertheless, we have allowed ourselves to make this demand on you, because we assume you would also like this little case resolved. And with your help, we will probably manage this very quickly."

The inspector opened the door to the interrogation room. Edvard was cowering on a wooden chair in front of a large desk. His coat was filthy, his temples bright red, crusted blood stuck to his face.

Bernhard should have been relieved, since he had been afraid Edvard had gone missing. Instead, he became dizzy, and felt very cold. Another panic attack. He leaned against the doorframe to keep from collapsing.

"It's a small world!" said Edvard; he hardly dared to look Bernhard in the eyes. His anger had fled, feelings of guilt took their place: how could he have trusted Bernhard so little? It served him right that he had gotten into trouble with the police because of that.

Kim observed how Bernhard got paler by the minute, and grabbed for his hand. Edvard winced. Who was this girl? Then he saw the wedding ring on Bernhard's finger, where his ring had been before. Edvard turned away. The thought that Bernhard had another lover was bad enough. But to see him with a woman was like being slapped in public. Edvard wondered what he had done to drive Bernhard into a woman's arms. Had he failed as a man?

He imagined Bernhard snuggling up to this woman's body. Edvard had never wanted to tie himself down, because he wouldn't have been able to bear to have someone outdoing him—and now with a woman, no less. In his whole life, he had never felt so humiliated.

"You men know each other?" asked the inspector.

Edvard nodded.

"Sit down, please, Herr Moll."

The inspector's voice droned in Bernhard's ears. His fear grew. The young, blond man, his desire for him, the secret, forbidden love, the threatening power of the uniforms, and then the blood on Edvard's temples. Bernhard heard dull thuds: boots kicking into stomachs, and hateful voices echoed within him: "Which one of the pigs did you have sex with?"

Kim tugged his hand; they sat down and Kim smiled warily at Edvard. Bernhard was alert to every noise. He needed to flee with Edvard. But how?

"Do you know this ring?" asked the inspector, holding it in front of Bernhard's face, and then laying it down on the table between him and Edvard.

Bernhard looked up. "Yes."

How could he give Edvard a sign so he would understand? He probably didn't know the danger they were in. They had to hurry before it was too late!

"Where do you know this ring from?" he asked further. Bernhard's panic grew. Did they already know about their relationship? What had they already beaten out of Edvard?

"It belongs to Ed…ummm…to this man here."

He doesn't even accept my gift, thought Edvard. He acts as if the ring wasn't his. Why did it have to be like this? Couldn't Bernhard just have said that he didn't want to be together with him any longer? The thought that he meant so little to Bernhard made Edvard bitter. "Why didn't you tell them I gave it to you. It's yours. Did you forget about that?" Edvard pushed it over to Bernhard.

The inspector observed them both attentively. Bernhard stared mutely at the ground; his breathing was shallow. Edvard's eyes gleamed with rage.

"When did you see the ring for the last time?"

"Thursday evening," answered Bernhard barely audibly. He figured he was lost. They'd broken Edvard already, he had turned against him.

"So the question still remains: how did Fred Wolf end up with this ring?" the inspector asked finally.

Fred Wolf? The name shot through Kim. The ring? She craned her neck to get a glimpse at it, then shrank back. She didn't want anyone to notice. Fred, the ring—what did they both have to with this man? She wondered, and with this thought of Fred the mill started churning again, at every turn increasing her desire to lie in his strong, hairy arms.

"Fred?" Bernhard felt feverish. Who was Fred? He didn't know anyone named Fred. Was it dangerous that there was a Fred involved?

"The man who's missing."

Missing? Now Kim became nervous. Had something happened to Fred?

"That's why you're here," the inspector continued. "A woman has accused your…friend of being responsible for the disappearance of her…life partner."

Bernhard couldn't concentrate. He saw the pistols at the policemen's hips. Where were they hiding the knife they'd stab him with?

"Maybe you can just ask the crazy woman herself," said Edvard irritably. "And we can get all this over with."

"Meilinger. Bring Mrs. Wengenmayer in."

Mrs. Wengenmayer? Kim wondered. His wife should be named Wolf. Her agitation grew. She hid her face behind her hand as they led Roswitha into the interrogation room.

"Mrs. Wengenmayer. When was the last time you saw the ring on your life partner?"

"On Saturday."

"So, on the day he disappeared."

Roswitha nodded and looked at him expectantly.

"And where did he get the ring from?"

"From me. I gave it to him."

"And where did you get the ring from?"

"That's irrelevant. We're talking about a man's disappearance."

"The problem is that, up until now, the ring has been the only evidence of a crime. Of course, under the assumption that the ring belonged to your partner, or to yourself. Now, Mr. Moll's statement contradicts this. If the ring was the property of Mr. Bornheimer, why would he harm your partner because of it?"

"I just want him back," pleaded Roswitha, sobbing and leaning against Grill. "Fred is all I have. I just want him back. You have evidence that he stayed overnight in this man's apartment," stammered Roswitha, pointing to Edvard. "You found blood and cigarette butts, broken furniture."

Bernhard stared at Edvard. Both of them were pale—Edvard with disappointment, Bernhard out of fear for his lover.

"It was his own blood, Mrs. Wengenmayer. The lab test left no doubt about that. We can't retain him because of some broken bottles or cigarette butts. There's no motive and no body. We can't do anything for you. I'm very sorry."

Roswitha howled: "But what am I supposed to do now? I don't know where else I'm supposed to look for him. He has to be somewhere. Please help me."

The inspector nodded to his colleague, who led Roswitha out.

Blood? A broken table? Cigarette butts? "A man in your apartment?" Bernhard let out, full of concern.

Edvard stared at him, rage spluttering from his eyes. "Oh, don't act so innocent!" he burst out, leaping up.

"But…"

"You can just go screw yourself!" Edvard shouted and ran from the room.

Bernhard watched him go, full of surprise. Then he looked into the inspector's quiet eyes and finally at the ring, which was still lying on the table. It radiated icy cold, enormous power. Bernhard took it into his hands; he was afraid of it.

"If I understand correctly, Mr. Bornheimer gave you this ring as a present."

Bernhard nodded imperceptibly.

"I would advise you to keep a closer eye on it in the future. It's a quality piece, seems to be very valuable. And besides...you see what unnecessary complications it can lead to." Then the inspector pulled a form out of his desk. "If you would just confirm that we've handed over the ring," he said, handing him the paper. "That will be all."

Roswitha was still sitting in the waiting room, sobbing. A policewoman was trying to talk to her. Kim pushed past her and pulled Bernhard along with her.

It was icy and wet outside, and although it was already after ten, it was still as dark as if someone had spilled a bottle of ink on the city.

They had barely left the door when Kim beset him with questions: "How do you know Fred? What do you know about him? Why did he stay overnight at Edvard's? What does that have to do with the ring? And what did I hear about blood? Why is he missing? Come on, tell me!" Then she looked at him and noticed that her friend's face was still white as chalk.

She exhaled deeply, then asked: "Are you okay?" and laid her delicate arm on his bent shoulder. Bernhard's whole body was shaking, the city swam before his eyes. He wanted to sit down, or lean somewhere, or ideally just die right then and there.

"Yes, everything's just fine."

24.

On Christmas Day, the weather gods were kind to Germany. The ice on Königssee advanced over the rocks that lined the shore, pushing towards the village. The Meissner porcelain chimes in the Green Zwinger in Dresden failed to ring because of the snow. On the Inner Alster Lake, ice-skaters and pedestrians snacked on sausages, chestnuts and mulled wine, while in Rothenburg the snow fell in sheets from the steep roofs, drawing loads of photographers hoping to catch this on film.

Leafless trees stretched their black claws against the low sky, blossoming into new beauty in the crisp, blue winter light. Ice formed strange, beautiful bouquets, and the entire country was covered with a sea of frozen breath that led some stray Christmas strollers to grasp dreamily at the ground, as if to make sure they weren't actually walking on diamonds. For on a morning like this, anything was possible.

Raimondo stood in the kitchen and let the sounds of the morning news wash over him as he kneaded roast almonds and honey-colored raisins into a dough. In his hands the various ingredients had come together: a mountain of golden butter, orange egg yolks, sugar, yeast, and more love than any vow would ever merit, all fused in a constantly quivering form, softer than a soothing mother's breast, but firmer than the ever-changing face of desire. He kneaded until the dough began to form threads, as long and rough as his romantic history.

The republic reveled in Christmas joy. From all around, cameramen sent romantic and beautiful images into the ether, even from the smallest cities: all except for Munich. Munich was omitted, with good reason. All nature's ugliness had gathered there in a cloud, causing fear and apprehension. It droned above the city, dark brown, sinking foot by foot down upon the inhabitant's heads, as if it wanted to squeeze out the very last glimmer of light. What little light penetrated through it cast eerie green shadows onto the walls of buildings, a broad brush casting a dirty veneer over everything that moved.

Butter, almonds, flour, yeast, sugar, eggs, raisins. When ingredients came together in the right proportions, something magical happened. Something that looked different, felt different, and smelled different than each of its ingredients alone—just like in a relationship. Maybe that was why Raimondo loved baking bread so much, because things had never worked out for him in relationships. At one point, he had still hoped his love would some day rise, but it had always collapsed in on itself like pastry dough in the cold air. Even though there had never been a lack of good ingredients. On the contrary. But maybe there had been somewhat too much.

Lots of men had promised him eternal love in his beefy arms, but most of them hadn't even glanced back at him as they left. Over time Raimondo had learned to let them go. But if he had to let them go, he wanted to at least tie a bond that could never be broken: with a Bundt cake. Just the sight of these little masterpieces was unforgettable. They melted on his lovers' tongues, slid down their dishonest throats, dissolved in their greedy, never-satisfied stomachs into small particles that their blood would carry through their bodies, turning into muscle and bone, eternally retaining the love of that night within pulsing cells. Even after years, the aroma of lemon and vanilla was enough to bring forth the memory of Raimondo's hands on their skin, causing them to tremble with desire—and feel regret.

Every time, something remained for Raimondo as well: a piercing, constant pain like a not-quite-healed war injury that flamed up in bad weather.

After setting the third pot of jam on the round Biedermeier table next to the glowing candles, he went to the window and was amazed to see that it was darker now than earlier in the morning, the light even greener and more poisonous. It almost was like staring out into an oversized aquarium.

A murmur came from the bedroom, and shortly afterwards he heard quick feet padding over the shiny fishbone floor. Adrian, small, sturdy and naked, shone like an elf in the pre-storm atmosphere. He stretched his strong arms into the morning air, slicked back his hair, which was prematurely grey for a thirty-five year old, and yawned.

Raimondo felt a warmth in his heart; he was glad the baker had slipped into his bed again, even though Raimondo had stood him up for Kim. But he wasn't lulling himself into security. Adrian was like a ray of sunlight in an endless polar winter. He promised warmth, a little happiness for some hours, maybe even only for minutes. But ignoring the fact that the sun would go back down at some point made it possible to enjoy it.

"I don't believe it. What a breakfast!" Adrian's eyes grew wide and he laid his hands on his chest, as if he were searching for a collar.

You could have this every day, Raimondo wanted to say. Just say the word and I'll cook for you your whole life.

Adrian went around the table and sunk his warm arms into Raimondo's aura of white flour and hot desire. "I could see myself falling in love with you."

Could? Raimondo asked himself. Do it! And even if you don't want to, at least say it. At least for a few hours, give me hope.

But no. Soon this man too would slip into his clothes and walk away as if he had only been checking the radiators. Raimondo felt it coming, he knew it. Maybe another hug, a kiss, that warm, cake-sweet tongue in his mouth again, and then Adrian would be history as well, another thread in the thick dough of his love life. Raimondo pressed against him, embracing his firm body.

A flash of lightning lit up the face of Raimondo's already-relinquished lover, turning it pale as death. Then thunder roared nearby, shaking the windowpanes. Adrian broke loose and looked outside. Snowflakes, yellow as lemon slices, floated down. Soon there were so many that it looked like a waterfall. The houses on the other side of the street shrank back behind the snow like frightened ghosts.

Adrian's hand was attempting to sneak under Raimondo's apron when the timer rang, and Raimondo left the room without a word, without even turning around.

When he came back with the steaming Bundt cake, Adrian was dancing, astonishingly light-footed, around the grand piano standing black in front of the overflowing bookshelf.

It's a good thing no one knows...thought Raimondo, pouring coffee into bulbous mugs. Then he put sugar and cream in Adrian's cup and cut the cake with a long knife. Baking had to be learned, of course, but so did cutting.

"I can't believe men aren't lining up to be with you," said Adrian, gaping at the cake. Before Raimondo could offer him a piece, he dug into it with vigor.

Serge had called the night before, the only man who had come back to Raimondo regularly in the past few years. After three weeks of silence, he suddenly wanted to see him again. Raimondo had stood up straight in front of the mirror and fixed his silk scarf. Tomorrow, Raimondo said, tomorrow, hoping it would stay today forever.

Outside, thunder rolled.

"You're just heavenly," said Adrian before reaching for another piece of cake, stroking Raimondo's unshaven cheek. "What an unforgettable evening."

The telephone rang.

"Kim, my little darling. Back home again? What, still confused? Fred! Missing? Not his ring? Don't cry, mousie, I can barely understand you. What? Raped? Good grief! Of course I'll make time. Right now?"

Raimondo turned around and looked at his lover's strong back. He didn't even want to imagine he could hold onto him forever. But at least as long as breakfast lasted, he wanted to enjoy him, and to make sure he ate as much cake as possible.

"But Kim, I just woke up."

Raimondo wanted to steal a few more glances at Adrian, close his eyes and melt into him. He wanted to watch him eat, observe his lips and remember what they had done the night before. And he wanted to feel his hands again, their heated desire, their soothing strokes.

"And it really can't wait?"

Raimondo lowered his eyes and turned away from Adrian. He no longer saw his tongue running along fingers sticky with marmalade, his nostrils flaring as he inhaled. For Raimondo, it was like a band-aid you had to tear off a wound: the more hesitantly you approached it, the more it hurt. It was best to do it in a single pull.

"I'm coming, dear. I just need to get dressed."

25.

"Sieglinde?"

"Ah, Gudrun, I'm glad you called. I've already tried to reach you a few times. Is the funeral arranged?"

"We've been running around all day. It wasn't easy to find someone who will make the effort the second day after Christmas. He's being transported to Heidelberg tomorrow. I'm staying with Mama. She absolutely refuses to come to us in Frankfurt."

"Maybe she prefers to be in familiar surroundings?"

"And I think that's exactly what's bad for her. Every breath here will remind her of Papa. In her place, I would rather be in an unfamiliar environment."

"Is she depressed?"

"No, that's the strange thing. I haven't seen her so lively in a long time. She's in an almost frighteningly good mood."

"Well. Maybe she's just relieved."

"I have no idea. But I think there's something else going on."

"Have you already talked with her about what to do next?"

"No, we really were running around all day. We were at the cemetery and in the church, we talked to the priest and the funeral company. I'm totally finished."

"It can also wait until after the funeral."

"The problem is just, I can't leave Karl and the girls alone for so long." There was a small pause.

"I can't get away at the moment. Eberhard showed up again this morning."

Eberhard? Gudrun almost dropped the receiver. Sieglinde couldn't be serious. But she kept her mouth shut.

"The funeral is on Saturday at four. I'll stay with Mama until then. Karl is taking the girls to his sister's for the holidays. But afterwards I need to get back home. That means by Saturday at the latest we need to have a solution for Mama. There's no way she can stay alone."

"We'll think of something. I'll call an old school friend of mine tomorrow, she works in social services. Maybe she would have an idea."

There was silence on the line again. The house felt cold and stale, and much too large. Even if Theo hadn't been pleasant company, something was missing all of a sudden. His grim expressions, those deafening silences, the tense atmosphere. Life without him was like a schoolyard full of silent children.

What weighed on them even more was this: a person had left them, someone as much a part of their lives as their first breath, their first tooth, their first love. Now they were only talking about him in relation to the burial preparations: coffins, priests and invitations to the wake.

"Have you heard anything from Bernhard?"

"No. Mother said he would call as soon as he got back home. But we were on the go all day."

"He didn't call me either, and no one answers at his place."

"Maybe he's with his…boyfriend," said Gudrun. She had to force the words from her lips. "Can you try to reach Ludwig again?" she offered quickly to change the subject.

"Of course."

"And if you could let Barbara know about Saturday."

"I will. Call if there's anything else I can do to help. And don't worry about mother. We'll find a solution."

26.

Lydia sat on her bed stroking Theo's pillow. The last time she had slept here, he had tossed and turned fitfully next to her. Now he was lying stiff in a freezer at the Frankfurt airport waiting to be transported.

Most of her life had been spent at that man's side. She had washed his laundry, borne his children and learned to cook his favorite meals. And she had experienced how a quiet, injured person can become a bitter, enraged old man over the course of decades.

Lydia knew what her children thought of their marriage. She saw it in their eyes, and she heard it in the way they talked. They believed Lydia was dependent on him, incapable of leading her own life. They still disapproved of the way she had stood by him, took care of him and never contradicted his unspoken demands. But they did not know the power of guilt; they had not yet learned how dearly one must sometimes pay for cheap arrangements, and that a single misstep, even a small dishonesty, can change many people's lives forever.

The children had concocted what they knew of their parents' love life from Lydia's stories and a wedding album: one of the snapshots showed Lydia with long, flowing hair. Behind her, the rusty railing of a ship, and waves. Another photo bore witness to the wedding cake: a nut cake with a mountain of cream on top. There was also one of a joyful Lydia carrying the bridal bouquet. One of those photos documented the only kiss the children had ever seen their parents share. When they looked at the wedding photo now they always said: it was clear even then how it would end up! A newlywed couple at the church door, the bride lowering her face, the groom with a shadow over his eyes, gazing somewhere off into the distance.

There was a story about how their parents had met: in her youth, Lydia was a beautiful girl. Thick, firm braids hung over her shoulders, her eyes were determined, her cheeks were red. Her mother sewed dresses for her to make her even more beautiful—pleated skirts and jumpers with big plaid checkers—which made her very sought after with boys. When she was fifteen years, she thought she had met the man of her life, but the Blessed Mary, Mother of God, had appeared to her and warned her. She needed to wait, she hadn't met the right one yet: Lydia trusted this. For three years, she averted her eyes whenever a boy looked in her direction, until she woke up one morning and knew the day had come. It was Mother's Day, and her family was taking a boat trip on the Bodensee. Lydia stood at the railing and looked out over the still, deep water towards the mountains. He was out there somewhere, she felt it deep in her soul. And then they had driven to Mainau Island—and Theo was standing on the pier.

Every time she told this story, tears came to Lydia's eyes. Listeners assumed she was crying from emotion. But actually, she was sad because she had taken the story from an issue of *Reader's Digest* and pretended it was her own. The real story was something quite different: when she was 16, an "unfortunate occurrence" drove Lydia out of her native city, Konstanz, to her aunt in Heidelberg. And this unfortunate occurrence was also the reason her aunt shut the door in her face—Lydia was pregnant. In the truest meaning of the words, she was out on the streets. In the biting cold, she asked around whether anyone needed a housemaid or temporary help. Out of desperation, she begged everyone she encountered on the street. When that was unsuccessful, she started going into stores, which was how she ended up in Theo's paint shop.

Back then he was still skinny, upright, almost stiff, with that noticeable kink in his neck and a pallor around his nose. His eyes reflected such fear and injury that Lydia wanted nothing but to protect him.

Theo took her in; almost wordlessly, he gave her a room. From then on she helped around the house, in the store and storeroom, day and night, even right after her child was born. Three years later, her child died of a heart defect; the loss tore such a deep hole in her life that she couldn't even cry.

But Theo, who had until then merely treated her respectfully as a housemaid, not giving her a second glance, suddenly began to pay attention to her. Furtively, he followed her footsteps. He no longer grew angry when something slipped from her hands, he doubled her salary and allotted her a larger room in his house.

They didn't marry out of love. It was certainly not erotic attraction or sexual desire. There was something else, a recognition of one another's sorrow, a sibling-like affinity.

Lydia was not disappointed when they spent their wedding night on opposite sides of the bed. She didn't even feel rejected. She believed he merely needed time: time, love, and tenderness.

They had conceived five children together; in fact, the sum of their physical contact wouldn't have been enough for many more. She had hoped the children's joyful cries would penetrate Theo's hard shell and strike brighter tones within him. But instead of becoming closer to Lydia, he slipped away from her more and more with each newborn baby. The truth was: he had never wanted children, and Lydia didn't bear the children for his sake—they were necessary to shield her from Theo's loneliness.

Last fall, after the doctor's visit, Theo became even more peculiar. He no longer answered when she asked him questions, he disappeared without telling her. And then he suddenly wanted to take that trip with her, to Florida, which to her imagination was an unreachable place.

He hadn't wasted a single word explaining why. It was important, very, very important, that was all he said, and Lydia had seen her chance. The honeymoon trip in exchange for celebrating Christmas with the family; but she had no way of knowing how things would turn out.

When he died, their whole history was played out before her eyes like a film. Meeting one another, the children's births, the few vacations. But in the end, all she saw was guilt.

She should have asked him for forgiveness. Cancer had shown her how dearly she had paid for her selfishness. From the moment of her diagnosis, she had sought atonement. She had prayed, begged for an answer how she could make everything right. But Theo died before she got her chance; guilt was all that had concerned her at that moment: guilt and expiation. Then he said the two words that would change her life: "Forgive me!" No, it wasn't the words, it was the way he said it: the relaxed smile on his face, the calm surrounding him, the peace he radiated, and the impression that the shadow which had hung over Theo his entire life was suddenly flooded with light.

At the moment of his death, Lydia's tears had dried. And when she thought back on it now, she no longer remembered his pain, the horror in the stewardess' face, the helplessness in the doctor's eyes; she only remembered those two words that lifted an unbelievable weight from her chest: "Forgive me!"

For years, she had hoped for help from the Virgin Mary. For years, she had hoped for a sign that would cure her. And now she had finally received an answer.

27.

It was dark and quiet; Bernhard heard nothing, not even his own breath. The experiences of the last few days had melted together into a new reality; he could no longer keep track of what was real and what wasn't. He no longer knew if he was blinded by the insignia of the SS officers or by reflections in the snow. This threatening cloak the ring had cast over his shoulders, was it fear of the next bomb or fear of being gay? Was his body burning from the Florida sun or out of hatred for his father, who had never made him feel loved, hatred for the people who cold-bloodedly murdered an innocent lover, for the people who had let all that happen back then?

First Bernhard tried to move his hands, then his head. It worked, so he probably wasn't dreaming. His eyelids rubbed against his eyeballs; he was able to open them, but it was dark. No. A face appeared. It was red, red and smooth as a mirror. His father's face, reflected off a shiny surface. A window perhaps—or a blade? No, a pool of blood.

Bernhard sat bolt upright to escape this image. What had happened? He tried to remember. He thought of the police station again, of Edvard, his eyes filled with hatred. And Kim. He laid his head back down; the wall was cool. He had gone home and taken a sleeping pill. So he was sitting in his living room and it was already nighttime.

His stomach was rumbling, and his skin burned, a cold burn as if he had been cut by a knife. His limbs were tight, as if a puppeteer were pulling at them. And then an image appeared again on the empty screen of darkness: that sweet face, the blank eyes, his slit throat, and blood all around it.

"Not again," whimpered Bernhard into the darkness, but it swallowed his words.

He needed light, he needed people, he wanted to enter life again, enter his familiar world. He jumped up, stumbled, felt his way ahead. Just get to the door, get to the door. Out, he urged himself, just get out—and he ran.

Bernhard ran to Rotkreuzplatz, past the wooden stalls of the Christmas market and a smiling Santa Claus; he ran until his lungs threatened to burst. His shoes slid on the slippery street, and he fell onto the bike path. The night air stung like a thousand needles, but there was something pursuing him that hurt much more. He didn't know what it was, had no idea, but he was sure it was going to catch up with him soon.

The blond soldier's sweet smile slipped into Bernhard's consciousness again. Horrified, he leaped up and kept running, fled until he saw the columns of Königsplatz towering above him. Totally out of breath, he plopped down on one of the big snow-covered steps. The wind whirled a handful of dust-dry flakes about the corners, sighing and whispering, though in Bernhard's ears it swelled to a menacing power. "Piece of shit!" he heard an echo of frosty voices scream. "Piece of shit!"

Startled, he turned around. He was alone, but a dangerous shadow lay over the square. Hitler had given speeches here, standing here he had incited the people to hatred and madness.

"Who has this piece of shit been messing around with?" Bernhard saw the soldiers beating him: they believed he would talk. But his lips were sealed—with love.

In spite of the cold, Bernhard felt sweat on his forehead. He was exhausted, but he needed to get away from here. He ran down Briennerstrasse past Karolinenplatz. A few cars crawled warily around the icy corners. The Field Marshals' Hall seemed like an enormous pair of jaws in the night, snarling at him with lions instead of teeth.

Light, lacy snow sank down over Bernhard; star-shaped flakes covered his coat. He shuddered, yet felt an enchanting attraction. Bernhard bent down and shoved his hands into the snow, which was dry and light as down. He had to warm it in his hands a long while before it would pack together. Bernhard pressed and squeezed a handful, shoving all his fear into the snowball. Again and again he kneaded it, turned it, melted it, added new snow, but his horror would not leave him. Instead, new images formed in his consciousness: at night, they put the young man naked in the yard and poured ice-cold water over him, cooling off the "hot pig." One time they painted his whole body pink, then while the rest were allowed to flee into the bunker during an air raid, they let him stand there as a target. They shoved the butt of a rifle so deep into his rectum that the rear sight was visible against his abdominal wall. But when they finally slit his throat, life kept glowing in his eyes—and something more conspiratorial than anything Bernhard had seen.

Many of the soldiers who were forced to watch kept fainting. They vomited or had fits of crying. And each one who fell down was questioned. Some of them admitted things just to end the torment. They were shot or locked up; some of them hanged themselves in their cells.

If only Bernhard's thoughts would return to daily life, his schoolbooks, classical music, something banal; he couldn't handle this anymore.

Desperately, he wandered about the abandoned streets. By now Bernhard was so frozen through that he couldn't even feel the cold any longer. The snowball in his hand had formed to an icicle with a sharp tip.

A harsh lantern shone down on him, a bay window stretched out in cold bluish light. He knew the building; Edvard lived here. But why was the light still on? Did he have visitors this late at night?

Fred Wolf! The name came back into Bernhard's mind. He had stayed the night with Edvard, the inspector said, and he had worn his ring, that unusual ring Edvard had given him. Bernhard imagined this stranger lying in his lover's arms. Desire overwhelmed him, desire and a sharp, endless sadness.

Bernhard had been preoccupied with sex since his childhood. He was curious about the drawings in encyclopedias and schoolbooks. He listened at his older sisters' bedroom door while they whispered about their experiences in love, and at night he often lay awake for hours, having noticed that Ludwig made strange noises in his sleep. It was really nothing more than curiosity, since Bernhard had never discovered a feeling in him that surpassed exploration, a pure desire for knowledge.

When he was seventeen, a girl kissed him for the first time; it didn't do anything for him. She groped around in his pants, and Bernhard let it happen, wanting to know what it was about. Nothing. Even when she led his shy hand to the place his school companions only referred to reverentially as paradise, and a warm moistness enveloped his fingers, nothing happened within him.

It wasn't until he was twenty-seven that a need to urinate would change his life abruptly. He had been drinking coffee, trawling through the new releases in the bookstores, feeling good because he had finally gotten a permanent appointment as a teacher, when he felt pressure in his bladder. He went to the public toilet at the end of Sendlingerstrasse, and just as he began to pee, a sturdy man stood next to him. Bernhard was bemused this man, having unzipped himself, looked over at him instead of peeing, his eyes growing wide. Then Bernhard saw his enormous erection. He was truly shocked when he felt his own urine stream grow narrow and his cock swell more than he had ever seen it. But before he had time to recover from this surprise, he already felt the other man's salty tongue, saw his greedy eyes so close he could feel their heat. A hand touched his, pulled it over to the other body, pulling Bernhard with it into a new world. He felt his nipples being fingered hectically, a tongue slipping over his face, over his ears and throat, soon there was a life pulsing in Bernhard so strongly that it frightened him.

Moments later, it was all over. Before he understood what had happened to him, he stood alone in the harsh daylight, surrounded by calcified tiles, smeared wooden doors, stenches, and the sweet smell of seduction on his lips. His knees gave way and he had to lean on the wall; his hand clenched, and his heart throbbed in his throat because he was aroused and afraid of himself, having just discovered himself for a moment.

Bernhard didn't want to be gay. Not because he was afraid of admitting it to other people. No, he was afraid of everything the media said about gay people: they wore woman's tights, they had wild sex parties, they took drugs and suffered from dangerous diseases, and he wanted none of that. Nevertheless, he couldn't forget his experience. It followed him at every step. He woke up with it, fell asleep with it, dreamt about it. Then he finally decided to find out what was going on inside him.

The first time he entered a sex shop, he hid immediately among the shelves full of photo books picturing beary man and young boys. He peeped around it to see how this world looked: dark, musty, lonely. When a customer came in, he would disappear determinedly behind a curtain. The word *MOVIES* was written on it, and strange noises came from behind it. They frightened him, but at the same time made his heart beat faster.

The felt was thick, worn at the edges and grimy. Behind the curtain, it smelled like fresh polish, old fish and danger. Porn made him even more afraid: gays did it in parks, they used tools for their love-making that could just as well be used for car repair, and they wore clothes that belonged in a carnival fun house. Saunas, circle jerks, orgies, darkness, fear, pain, that was a life Bernhard wanted nothing to do with—nevertheless, he kept coming back. Because there in the darkness there were no names, no words, at most brief orders. And it was safe. You could retreat without explaining yourself.

Soon he found that he learned more about people in that flickering darkness than he wanted to. The noises they made, the way their hands slid over his skin softly or frantically, the way their bodies reacted to his touch, whether he was allowed to kiss them, how long they held him, if they sat up straight in his arms out of arousal or collapsed afterwards, whether they whimpered or twitched during the act, if their foreheads grew moist, cold or hot, or if their eyes closed, filling with tears. All these things told him the story of their desires: some of them about the ease of being gay, others about their feelings of guilt for the wife waiting at home with their dinner; of the freedom to have sex whenever and with whomever one desired; of their disappointment with a life that had brought a fate upon them that they did not dare show in daylight. And if he saw them again, in the opera or surrounded by schoolchildren, or behind the desk of the district administrative department, they lowered their eyes.

These adventures were like delicate chocolates. They melted on his tongue, concealing sweet surprises beneath their black coating, but in the end a bitter aftertaste remained.

Bernhard wanted more than a fleeting adventure. But how could that happen if he was afraid to talk to these men of the night, if they would flee at the first word? Paper and letters, that was what Bernhard knew—books, that was the answer.

One Saturday, Bernhard went to the library on Gasteig. Hot-footedly, he made his way through the small beer garden in the courtyard overflowing with people, when suddenly he heard someone calling his name.

He jerked, turned around, and searched, but didn't find a single face he knew. Instead he heard a laugh, bright and clear. Disquieted, he looked around again. He hesitated, then slipped into the library, but the call echoed in his ears.

It was simple to search for the right department among the filing cards: but it was much more difficult to go over there and check out books in front of other people's eyes. Bernhard walked past the shelves first because someone was already standing there, he hid, browsed around. An hour later he wrapped three books in a paper bag and clamped them tightly under his arm.

In the courtyard, the bright laugh echoed again. It was so full of promise. Soothingly, it settled into his soul, as if puzzle pieces were fitting into the right place. Bernhard turned around and saw a young man's face appear out of the crowd: blond, handsome and full of life. It was bubbling right out of him. Friends hung onto every word from those wonderful lips, pressing close around him. Bernhard couldn't take his eyes off him, and when the other man saw him, Bernhard looked quickly to the ground.

Contrary to his desire, Bernhard turned to go, but his legs were heavy. In the distance, he heard the tram rushing past; it would take him away, take him home, into security—into the past. Should he turn around? If only he dared. Instead, he slid into the shadows of the corridor and leaned against the blood-red bricks. He was sweating; as he was struggling with himself, he heard a voice: "Everything all right?"

Bernhard recoiled as he saw that face, radiant even in the shadows.

Since the first time, Bernhard had never seen any of his sexual partners by daylight. He closed his eyes as the other man approached his face. And as soon as he laid his hand on his chest, it seemed to Bernhard as if the other man was directly touching his soul. They fit together like a painting and its beholder, fire and smoke, ring and finger.

If Bernhard had been convinced that every life, every fate, could be reduced to a mathematical formula, then this man was the unknown variable of his life. He just needed to apply it, and the formula would work out even.

Now, as Bernhard stood in front of Edvard's building, it became clear to him why he had fallen in love with him right away: it was his eyes, as loyal and full of hope as the eyes of the soldier in his dreams. He had believed in them, trusted them. Suddenly Bernhard was flooded with the warming pain of nostalgia—and then another detail added itself to his dreams.

He's lying in a trench on the edge of a battlefield. The night is black, snow surrounds them. His comrades huddle together, freezing. Fear of death carves ugliness into their faces. Fighter jets speed by overhead, and bombs come down again and again, destroying buildings and bunkers.

The cigarette. It's there again. Someone passes it around. It seems to be the only light, the last bit of flickering life in this world.

What does he have to lose now? In an age where comrades split up in the morning and never come back, who is thinking about the next day, the next hour even, when every second feels like the end of the world?

Everyone does what they can to soothe the pain in their souls, even for a moment. Just as he says this, he feels a hand on his chest. Then he feels lips on his own, and a warm sweet tongue breaks through the wall of fear. He embraces out of fear, holds tight to keep from sinking. This touch is like a band-aid: even if it doesn't hold, it will at least cover the wound.

There's nothing wrong with seeking help for a moment in a comrade's arms. He's aware that he's crossing a dangerous line if he falls in love—and then he feels how he's already losing his heart.

Bernhard sank to the ground. The ice in his hand melted and froze, hardened and peaked, as if it were a fragment of memory. The horror of those trenches washed over him, the taste of death; the desire and madness of that age thickened into dark, dangerously sharp icicles.

Then hope trickled into Bernhard's chest, cold, like a drop of melted ice. It was blond, radiating towards him through lake-blue tunnels, with delicate hands and the kiss of eternal love.

When Bernhard opened his eyes, his knees were frozen tight to the ground. "I was just afraid. I was afraid!" He heard a voice call, and looked around, knowing it was not his own. His head tilted back, his eyes searched the sky for his blond angel.

A shadow danced over the stuccoed ceiling of Edvard's apartment, and suddenly a refreshing coolness shot along Bernhard's left hand all the way to his heart. Blood dropped down into the snow, thick and heavy. It was as black as the fear of his own shadow. The icicle melted in his hand's soft, innocent flesh, together with his fear of the past.

In Edvard's apartment, the light went out. All that remained was the soft glow of a candle.

28.

Birgit pulled the silk tablecloth apart at its corners and flung it over the dining room table. The thick votive candles flickered with a golden light.

Edvard paced nervously around the room. He looked miserable. His hair was cut short, his thin knitted shirt stained with tomato sauce. Birgit had never seen him like this before.

"Please, would you just sit down. If you're going to drag me out of bed at three in the morning, at least make use of my time. I'm tired. If you're not going to let me help you, I'm going back home."

"I'm begging you. Stay here. I'm going crazy."

"Then turn off the light and formulate your questions."

He flipped the light switch and came over to her at the table. "Am I going to win Bernhard back?"

"That's a yes or no question," she said emphatically. "You know the oracle can't answer a question like that."

Edvard had walked home from the police station in a furious state, working out all the reasons he didn't want anything more to do with Bernhard on the way: all of these entanglements, his cowardice, and then this woman holding his hand. He intended to remove everything from the apartment that reminded him in the slightest of Bernhard. But then he had heard the message on the answering machine and realized that he had acted like a complete idiot again. Everything, even this woman, could probably be explained with a little time and patience. Why did he have to be so goddamn sensitive all the time?

"I called him to clear this up once and for all, but he didn't pick up. I even drove over to his place three times, but he didn't open the door. I sent him flowers and wrote him a long letter explaining everything." Edvard wrung his hands. "I just have to know if we're going to get back together."

Birgit leaned forward in the white swing chair. "Please. You're getting dramatic." She flashed her eyes at him darkly. Then she lay down a pack of cards and folded her hands beneath her fleshy chin.

There was something hesitant in Edvard's movements, a reservation Birgit watched with narrowed eyes. "You don't want answers, Edvard. You just want someone to confirm your wishful thinking."

Edvard flinched. "No, no," he said hastily, sitting down next to her at the table. "Really, I want...to learn the truth. I have to." And then he began shuffling.

Meanwhile, Birgit unscrewed a small jar and sprinkled a few granules on a glowing white coal. "Incense, black pepper, red dragon's blood, copiava balsam, and delicate ylang blossoms open the doors to deeper realization." There was a crackling, then a heavy cloud of smoke began to spread out slowly. And for a moment Edvard thought he saw an angel.

Birgit didn't let him out of her sight. "The crucial point is actually not at all whether you're going to be together with Bernhard in the future. The question is why you sought this relationship in the first place."

Edvard nodded warily, but avoided looking at her directly.

"Now we'll ask the oracle."

Edvard cut the deck twice, then Birgit spread the cards in front of him like a fan. "Draw six cards and place them on the table face down!"

Edvard did as she said, his eyes glued to the floor all the while, where the wood was buckled ever since the ashtray had smashed the bar: the first scar of their separation.

"Edvard," said Birgit with a calm voice, but he didn't hear her. He thought of the summer nights when Bernhard had explained the constellations to him. He remembered the weekend in Amsterdam when they had listened to the burbling town canal in each other's arms, the stillness that spread around Bernhard as if in slow-motion while he sat on the couch reading Nietzsche. He saw himself sitting at Bernhard's kitchen table, remembered the evening he had been invited over for the first time, when Bernhard had served him lettuce and scrambled eggs with carrot strips. And Edvard would never forget the Acropolis, in front of which his lover had recited Greek epics for him. The sun burning down on them at a hundred degrees, hundreds of tourists walking past them sweating and complaining. Back then, Edvard had known love, the cooling power of boundless love. What if Birgit told him he would never be able to experience that again? Edvard felt miserable.

"Edvard!"

He turned towards her, and she could see in his eyes that he was far away.

"Let's look at what kind of partner you chose for yourself." She turned the first card over and laid it in the middle: a young man hanging from a cross with his foot in a sling.

"Aha! A person who sacrifices himself, willingly does penance for something he didn't even do himself." She examined Edvard and saw he understood little. "I will explain more about that later. First let me see what the issue is with you."

He risked a look. A man stood there wrapped in a long cloak, withdrawn into himself, surrounded by three chalices whose contents had spilled. In the distance, he saw a bridge and a castle. It was a mirror image of his emotions: abandoned, alone, all lost.

"You see!" he burst out amid tears. "The chalices tipped over, everything spilled."

"The card only says that you're persisting in your suffering. All you need to do is turn around. There are still two full chalices there. Lovesickness, wrecked hopes, disappointment—that's just one aspect of this card. The other is a new beginning and self-examination. That belongs to this state as well."

Edvard wiped his cheeks and sniffled.

"And that's the reason for your confusion." She turned the next card over: a tower, with people falling from the battlements. A bolt of lightning above it, flashing down from dark clouds. "Aha. You see, upheaval, agitation, a sudden change."

She took Edvard's chin in her hands and forced him to look her in the eye. Then she said in a penetrating voice: "It's a positive change. You have the chance to rethink fixed ideas, to break open old hardened thoughts. If you can manage to put your drama aside, and to see what's really going on, brand new dimensions will open up for you."

"What kind of fixed ideas?" Edvard shook his head. "Our relationship is wrecked, that's it."

"Nothing's wrecked. You asked the oracle what you can learn from the relationship. And it's answering you that it's a matter of change."

He gave her a puzzled look.

Birgit took the next card and rubbed it between her fingers as if she were trying to read Braille. Then she leaned back in her chair.

"Why did you even choose Bernhard?"

Edvard stroked his head and thought. Choose? He thought back to that Saturday afternoon in the Gasteig. He was sitting with friends in the beer garden when he heard someone calling. "Edvard! Edvard!" Brightly, much too softly to determine where it came from amidst all that laughing and commotion. Then when he looked up and saw Bernhard standing in the gateway to the tram. Tall, with dark brown hair nestled around his innocent face. There was something childish in his eyes and a depth that made Edvard grow still.

In that moment something unusual, something inexplicable happened: Edvard felt connected to Bernhard, as if they were brothers, as if they had known each other for decades. Edvard had countless friends who were much better suited to him than Bernhard, and he could say for sure he had had better sex partners than Bernhard before, but there was something else, something indescribable about it. "I felt that we belonged together. Quite simply."

"Have you ever felt that way with another man?"

"No, never," he said, thinking back on all his affairs and lovers. In the heat of ecstasy, he had often made promises. They were part of the game of love, fencing strategies, nothing more. With some of them, romantic feelings remained after the first climax, but in the end all that counted was the one rule: each man lives his own life.

"So there was something special about Bernhard. In fact, you changed your life for him."

He nodded energetically. "I gave up a lot of things for him: parties, smoking, dancing until the early hours of the morning. I even wanted him to move in with me."

"And then this happened." She laid down the card she had been playing with: a young man with blindfolded eyes sat by the ocean crossing two swords over his chest. "Aha! At the first misunderstanding, you distrust your partner. You doubt decisions you've made, you doubt the solidity of the relationship. You fall back into old behavior patterns as if you hadn't learned anything."

Edvard slumped down.

"There's more to a relationship than an expensive ring and pretty words, Edvard."

He put his hand over his face. She was right. He had betrayed Bernhard. That was not only stupid, it was immature.

"The art of relationships is not about acquiring the people you imagine. The art lies in still wanting them after you've got them. Do you understand the difference?"

He nodded heavily, and she laid down the next card under *The Hanged Man.*

"This is what you need to do," she said, pointing to a young man happily walking towards a chasm with a bundle of food on a stick and a rose in his hand. Not even the howling dog could disrupt his happiness.

Edvard swallowed. It looked dangerous.

"You're lucky," she said. "If you learn to enter the relationship as open and clueless as this fool, problems will resolve themselves. Look!" She pointed out the connection to the tower. "This is just the extension of that. There, your behavior patterns are disrupted, you're forced to reflect. And here what you have to do is to maintain child-like wonder, spontaneity and wisdom.

Her sturdy fingers tapped from one card to the next. Edvard furrowed his brow.

"And now I'm sure you want to know how it all will end up."

He wasn't sure anymore; what he had heard so far seemed difficult enough to him already. Birgit turned over the next card, stroking it as if it were made of silk. Her face brightened: a couple holding tight to one another, pointing happily at ten chalices hovering above them in the sky.

The anxiety Edvard had been carrying around with him for days dissolved, and he exhaled.

A lavender bloom crackled on the coals. Edvard looked out towards the window. The panes were fogged. This mixture of smoke, confused emotions and puzzles had laid a thin film over it, casting a halo over the street lamps. Outside it was beginning to snow again.

He looked down at the cards: a few sentences echoed within him, and slowly he began to understand.

"You wanted to tell me more about Bernhard."

Birgit looked at him for a while before sitting up straight and considering *The Hanged Man* again.

"Look at it closely." She tapped on the image. "He wasn't nailed to the cross. He hanged himself, you see? His foot is hanging loosely in the sling, his arms are crossed behind his back, there's a halo glowing around his head. He set out on a task that he wants to accomplish at any price. Evidently, he's ready to sacrifice everything. So at the moment, he can't occupy himself with you; that means you need to wait. Give him time. Let him make his experiences. Most likely, he'll be a new person afterwards."

Edvard fidgeted in his chair. He tilted his head as if he wanted to look at the cards from a different perspective.

"You want to know everything, right?"

He looked at her. His pupils were wide, his lips stiff and determined. "Well now you've made me curious."

"Think it over well. Sometimes it's better not to know things."

He was still struggling with himself, but curiosity had conquered him long ago.

"Why Bernhard?" he asked; Birgit pointed mutely to the deck.

Edvard closed his eyes and glided his hand carefully over it, then drew the *Wheel of Fortune*. Mythical creatures, obscure symbols and signs wound about the wheel.

"You are connected by a karmic bond."

"A what?"

"A karmic bond. Each of you is the key to the other's fate. You searched and found one another because each of you is the partner with whom he will accomplish his mission in this world."

Edvard leaned back. This would take time to digest. In the last hours, he had received many answers, but it seemed to him that every answer had opened up ten more questions at the same time.

"I warned you," she said with a knowing smirk. "Sometimes we don't understand what's happening to us. But I can promise you, that's okay as well. Understanding creates boundaries. Think about the fool," she pointed to the card. "To strive for understanding, that's the true challenge, understanding itself is just the consolation prize."

The candle flickered, a heavy aroma of incense lay over the cards. How complicated could life get? How was he supposed to take control of all these missions he had apparently imposed on himself?

"Trust," he heard a voice whisper within him, "Trust!"

29.

His left hand throbbed dully where the icicle had torn a deep wound, and a pain ran up to his heart, as if an invisible hand stretched his arm like a bowstring. Bernhard wrapped gauze around it to stop the bleeding, but the wound wouldn't close. It kept seeping through, sometimes yellow-white, then deep red again. He never felt real pain, only when he shut his eyes and his scattered thoughts streamed like a throng of ants over the terrifying images of his visions, or now, as he stood in front of the mirror deciding what to wear to his father's funeral.

Just thinking about it made him queasy. At funerals, people testify to grief, send the deceased into the next world with their best thoughts, closing the chapter they lived with that person. Bernhard, on the other hand, felt wrath and condemnation for his father, at best indifference, but no glimpse of grief, let alone any best thoughts. And closing his father's chapter, that was something he wasn't ready for after all that had happened, after all that was still happening. Quite the opposite. He wanted to know the truth so badly, he would have dug it up with his hands. The last thing he wanted to do was shovel dirt over it.

The only black piece of clothing in his dresser was the suit he had worn for his confirmation. The rest was colorless, lots of gray and brown, clothing like shadows.

He had already tried lots of things on, setting down a pile next to the dresser, when he stumbled on a dark duffel bag. In it were black jeans, two T-shirts, underwear and socks. Edvard's "emergency outfit." Bernhard sat on the ground, leaned on his left arm and flinched—the wound.

It was strange to hold Edvard's clothes in his hands. Bernhard pressed his face into the T-shirt and breathed deeply in his smell. He had thought it would trigger something, but he felt nothing.

The jeans were a little too short and very tight, but they fit. He looked around and grabbed the suit jacket. It pinched under his arms, and his white wrists protruded from the sleeves. But with a little effort he managed to even button it up. He looked in the mirror; white skin shimmered against the black like a fish's belly.

But what should he wear under the jacket? His father's zebra-patterned polyester shirt caught his eye, spilling out of the suitcase. Hesitantly, he slid his hand over it. Soft and cool, it rubbed against his skin, falling down over his chest like a cold shower over a sunburn.

Train tickets, money, briefcase. His father's wedding ring lay next to Edvard's ring on the dresser. Quickly, he grabbed his father's ring and put it on. But Edvard's ring stopped him in mid-step. The diamond collected the yellow light from the ceiling lamp, spilling a millimeter-wide rainbow onto the dark oak furniture: a barrier in the present, a bridge to the past. His wound stung.

He hadn't been back to Heidelberg in a long time. In the past, while he was still studying, he had enjoyed coming back: walking through the city, sitting in the ice cream store, which had been the premiere locale of his childhood, or going to the public open air pool to remember those summers, the too-large gaps between school years.

But then he had uncovered those feelings: the desire to lie in a man's arms, the urge for stubbly skin against his stomach and the heat of a hard erection against his flesh. From then on, Bernhard had the feeling that his father's eyes would penetrate him like a grenade splinter, and he began avoiding his hometown.

Instead of taking the bus, he walked through the city. There were still two hours until the funeral, and Bernhard was in no hurry to confront his family's grieving faces.

Back then, there had been milliners here, bakeries and charming old cafés. They had given way to fast-food stands with names like *The Hot Number* serving soggy cheese sandwiches from micro-wave ovens. Cheap stores offered T-shirts from Malaysia printed with laughing Disney characters, designs of the Heidelberg Castle or names like Gertrude, Alfred, Emma and Willi.

In summer, busloads of gaping tourists would mill about here. But now, on the first weekend after Christmas, all he saw were grim faces.

He was glad to reach the end of the city and slowly climb to the top of Bergstrasse. Familiarity broadened his chest when he saw the glow-ing sign of the Mom-and-Pop grocery store. As a child, he had spent all his pocket money there on lollipops and jelly beans. He and Fritz, the owner's son, had often biked to the lake, where they dreamed up plans, like discovering new universes and becoming leading researchers in astronomy: now they had not even had contact for years.

Even though hardly anything had changed in the area, he felt as foreign here as he had passing the new stores in the pedestrian zone.

The wooden sign next to the garden gate said *Theo & Lydia Moll*; it used to read *The Moll Family*. The last time the fence was painted, they had updated it. Bernhard rang the bell. Sieglinde opened; her eyes were red. What was he supposed to say to her in this situation? He nodded at her, tears flowed from her eyes, then she turned away and went into the living room. Bernhard followed her.

Barbara was sitting on the couch. Her hair was tied into a solid ponytail, but her puffy eyes made her look as young as she had twenty-five years ago. Mausi had his arm around her, but she was visibly uncomfortable.

Biggy, Sissy and Manu sat stiffly on top of the end table next to Karl. Biggy held his hand in her lap. Eberhard's hand was on Manu's back. Apparently, Eberhard had managed to slip away from his sec-retary to come to the funeral. He nodded at Bernhard, then lowered his eyes again quickly to his coffee mug.

Ludwig stood on the balcony. The frost had turned his nose and hands a deep red. Cigarette butts were piled in the ashtray on the railing.

The family doctor was there with his wife, the owner of the grocery store stood in the corner, both of the neighboring couples had come together in their grief.

A whole bunch of people had come whom Bernhard didn't know at all. Maybe they were old customers of his father's, poker buddies, coffee friends or his mother's church acquaintances. He had no idea. They stood together in small groups, spoke in hushed tones, looked glumly around the room with red eyes, fell silent as soon as anyone caught their eye.

Bernhard shook everyone's hand; some of them held his grip for much too long. They pitied him because of his father's death, they showed sympathy. Bernhard felt plagued by remorse because he felt no grief. Not even when he imagined his father dead, in his coffin, his short, stubby fingers crossed over his heart. His thoughts of his father were more like the light from a long-extinguished star. It was still shining, but the planet had not existed for hundreds of thousands of years.

"You came alone?" There was a trace of surprise in Gudrun's voice. Or was it reproach?

"Of course!"

Gudrun embraced her brother. "You could have brought Edvard."

He looked at her skeptically.

"Did you make it through the last few days all right?"

What kind of question was that? He was probably just supposed to assure her that he had forgiven her for the scene at the dinner table. But how could he forgive her for something he himself couldn't cope with? Again and again, he saw his father's furious eyes, that look of hatred. And again and again he saw the empty chair. He felt guilty of his father's death, he felt guilty for being gay.

"I called a few times but you were never at home."

"I'm doing well. It's all right."

She looked relieved.

"What's wrong with your hand?" She turned his left hand around and examined the soaked gauze.

"Ah, nothing. Bread knife." Bernhard pulled back his hand. "Where's Mama, actually?"

"There." She pointed to the TV chair, and Bernhard noticed Lydia, sitting with her back turned to everyone.

Bernhard gave his sister a questioning look; she shrugged her shoulders. Then he looked over his mother's head at the TV screen, where a talk show was flickering.

Bernhard stepped between his mother and the television.

"Bernhard?" She lifted herself up out of the chair and hugged him.

"For a minute…I almost didn't recognize you. The shirt, you know?"

Her face was pink and soft. Black suited her. Even her wig looked more natural than usual.

"Hi Mama, how are you doing?"

"Well, very well. Have you already greeted our guests?"

Bernhard was surprised again by her light-heartedness. Her eyes were almost euphoric, her voice was cheerful.

"Yes, Mama. I saw them all."

"Have you met Ms. Jung? She's the nurse who's assisting me a bit."

A woman stood up from the chair next to Lydia. She was tall and thin, her hair short and white as snow. She wore a vibrant purple scarf that positively lit up her face. She looked youthfully pretty, but judging by the wrinkles on her hands she was well over fifty.

"Divya, this is my son Bernhard. Bernhard, this is Ms. Jung."

Divya? His mother took the nurse's hand and pulled it to her chest.

"Hi. How are you?" Bernhard looked into her eyes: they seemed peaceful.

"What do you think of Mama's nurse?" asked Gudrun.

Bernhard looked over and observed the way Divya helped his mother into her chair and then sat down again next to her.

"Seems to be a big help for her."

"Don't you find her a bit strange? Divya? What kind of name is that?"

He shrugged his shoulders.

"What's going to happen with her now?" asked Sieglinde.

"Well, we can't take her in," said Eberhard dismissively; Sieglinde looked away.

"But there's no way she can stay on her own," Barbara affirmed. "She can't even shop for herself. You saw how weak she was before Christmas. Can't she live with you?" Barbara asked Gudrun.

"I already talked with Karl about it. The house is big enough, we can afford it to, I would just need to cut back on my work."

"Have you actually asked Mama what she wants?" Bernard narrowed his eyes furiously.

Lydia stared at the screen, hearing neither what was discussed on the talk show nor the interviewee's tear-soaked cheeks. Her thoughts were focused on the future. She knew the children were racking their brains about her at the moment. She was supposed to go and live with one of them or move into an assisted living community. But for the first time in her life she felt free. After giving up so much, she wanted to at least retain her freedom.

"I hope we'll see Father again up there," Barbara said with a choked voice. This was a perfect opportunity for her to play herself up as the good daughter. Bernhard felt like vomiting.

"Imagine, if we get up there and he's not there," she sobbed loudly.

The idea of spending eternity with his father horrified Bernhard, but he didn't say that. Instead he turned towards the guests, observed the little groups that had formed to pay their last respects to Theo. He inspected each person individually. Did they know why Bernhard had been avoiding his hometown for so many years?

"We should go." Divya leaned her head into the circle of siblings.

"We should be the first ones," Lydia added as an explanation, grabbing Bernhard's hand and pulling him into the kitchen. "Your boots are so dirty. You're not coming to my church like that." She knelt down and polished his black boots. "Pull your pants a bit higher. Okay, that's good."

Then they set out.

Entering the mortuary chapel, they headed for the first row. Bernhard secured a seat on the edge, Gudrun sat next to him, then Sieglinde and Barbara. Ludwig remained standing at the entrance, which suddenly left a seat open next to their mother. Sieglinde pulled on

Bernhard's sleeve and directed him to sit next to Lydia, and before he knew it he found himself taking on his father's role, sitting, quiet and stiff, next to his mother.

The chapel filled with people. Bernhard heard their voices, their coughs, their heels clacking on the cold marble floor, the heavy creaking of the benches.

Then something moved behind the stained glass windows separating the chapel from the morgue. Coffins were being pushed between the cooling cells frantically, like pieces in a backgammon game. Then classical music welled up, as if Theo had ever been interested in that. The doors opened and the coffin was wheeled in. The funeral guests stood up, Bernhard felt his eyes burning.

The priest approached piously and splashed the coffin with holy water, then began his speech: "Theo Moll was a loving man. And he was an upright believer."

This mendacity annoyed Bernhard. Why should people suddenly become better after they died?

He decided not to listen anymore, concentrating instead on the plastic flower wreath and the flat tire under the cart carrying his father's coffin.

And in this emptiness he noticed a totally new emotion arising: compassion. What had his father gotten out of life? Years of fear and horror in the war, a family he clearly had not wanted, and a heart problem that robbed him of every opportunity to enjoy life?

"Theo Moll was a kind man," Bernhard heard the priest say. Those words had come out of his mother's mouth just days before. But what was kind about a man who punished his children with inattentiveness, who considered happy smiles a disturbance of the peace, who answered innocent questions with silence?

What had others thought about Theo? Bernhard would have given quite a bit to know what these people were thinking as they sat here, freezing, on the hard pews. Pain marked his siblings' eyes; only his mother's eyes were sparkling with clarity.

"His children now mourn their father…"

What was a father, actually? What made a person into a father? His sperm, a quick orgasm, a little sweat and desire? Was that all it took? No, Theo had never been a father to Bernhard. His progenitor at most. The connection between Bernhard and his father was no greater than the length of the sperm cell that had produced him.

Gravel crunched beneath their feet as the procession exited the chapel; the sun shone down harshly, making people squint. Thick beads of water clung to the coffin, turning white in the cold: drops of holy water.

Bernhard went first behind Theo with his mother on his arm, thinking: in death he's the same way he was in life: quiet, forcing everyone to march obediently behind him.

Next to the grave, the earth lay in large frozen piles. Memorial wreaths with printed ribbons were piled around the modest wooden cross. *Theo, we miss you*, he read, *For Papa. Mama and the Children. In Honor of our Faithful Brother, Theo Moll.*

For the first time, Bernhard became aware of the crowd of people that had followed the family. How many had known him? Where did they know him from? Some of them must be schoolmates, who had always stood close by him, and customers of course.

The coffin was lowered into the earth, accompanied by the priest's prayers. Now his life was at an end. Bernhard imagined his father: eyes closed, stiff, gray and cold. He felt the hairs on the back of his neck stand up, and a shudder colder than death ran down his back. But it was over again quickly, all that remained was a strange sensation behind his eyes, and his eyelids felt heavy.

Desire for the loving man in his dreams rose up in Bernhard like a well; and at the same time, he felt his wound burning. When he looked down at his hand, he saw blood dripping on his polished boots, running down and melting into the snow.

His mother shoveled a little dirt onto the coffin and threw a white silk handkerchief in after it. Ludwig came up to the grave behind her. Sieglinde and Gudrun prayed for an instant before making room for their little sister. Barbara threw a kiss down to her father and sobbed. Then they were finally allowed to escape out of the cold.

As soon as Lydia had returned to her seat, the requiem mass began. The organ tones were almost intoxicating, the scent of incense filled the incoming cold with magic, and then the priest drifted in, followed by his acolytes.

A smirk came to Bernhard's lips: this scene reminded him of how a friend of his had come out, a priest who had apparently not even suspected he was gay for many years. Then one day, during a Corpus Christi procession of all things, it had been revealed to him. Surrounded by young altar boys, he was prancing about in gold-embroidered material, swinging the incense thurible through the air, when a young man called out to him from crowd on the sidewalk: "That's a pretty dress you're wearing, young lady, but look out: your purse is on fire!"

During the resurrection mass, Lydia really blossomed. Bernhard watched as her skin grew rosier and a glow came to her eyes, burning brighter than the paschal candles.

Every time the priest said: "Let us pray," Lydia was on her feet quicker than anyone else, though she had hardly been able to get out of her chair a few days ago. She sang full-throatedly, her voice lifting above the heads of the family like a halo—and with each song, a little more weight seemed to fall off her shoulders.

Then the priest spoke the words for the transubstantiation: "This is my body, this is my blood." The congregation kneeled humbly, and the acolyte rang the altar bell; tears of joy sprang into Lydia's eyes.

It was almost possible to believe that her greatest wish had been fulfilled, and that she was encountering the Virgin Mary.

"Give him eternal rest, O Lord!"

The living room was crowded. Bernhard stayed standing at the door; it was simply too much for him. He heard the guests discussing varicose veins and successful cures with kombucha, which was making its rounds about the neighborhood. They were talking about the final matches of the soccer season, the city's construction plans, and the injustice of social reforms, which were making it increasingly more difficult for retirees to survive.

"Don't you want to go in?" Bernhard's mother asked him, grasping his arm.

"I…I have a headache. I'm just going to lie down a bit upstairs."

A soft, affectionate smile spread over her face. "All right, my boy. It's a bit too much for me too. But in an hour they'll all leave the house, then we'll have it to ourselves again."

He went upstairs: nothing had changed. The stairway was just as silent, just as dark. As a child he had often seen a shadow darting about here, a large, formless shape. A wanderer without a destination, he had thought back then, a soul in search of redemption. Bernhard smiled to think that he had dwelt on such nonsensical thoughts when he was a kid.

He had never felt fear near the shadow, only compassion. Bernhard could remember nights when he slipped out of his room and curled up in his blanket on the stair landing. He had hoped to get to the bottom of that appearance, to investigate it, discover what was driving it.

The first door led to the girls' room. It was still furnished the way it had been before: a double bed and a pull-out sofa for Barbara. Bright dressers, light-blue curtains and a trace of doll-like unreality. Sieglinde and Gudrun didn't belong in this atmosphere at all, though Barbara perhaps did. But the only person Bernhard saw in the room was his mother.

Then he walked into the room he had shared with Ludwig for fourteen years. He sat down on the bed and looked around. This is where his life had started, this is where he had dreamed of the future for the first time, here he had dealt with his first disappointments. He had struggled so much to earn his father's love.

Bernhard had never had a good relationship with his father; more precisely, he had never felt that he had a relationship with him at all. Whenever his schoolmates talked about their fathers, he was envious. It is not that he had ever expected an ideal father who would read Homer with him, solve tricky mathematical formulas or build the Parthenon out of Styrofoam. It would have been enough for him if his father had read him a ghost story every now and then, or at least given him a talking-to.

His parents had turned the room into a guest room. Nothing was left of his past, or his brother's. Ludwig's soccer trophies made way for a *Reader's Digest* novel collection, their childhood scribblings had been replaced by macramé objects. Bernhard tried to remember what he had drawn back then. Probably scenes from old Westerns. Or had he drawn soldiers?

The thought shot through him; he tried to concentrate. Was he already fascinated with the war as a child? Where had the drawings gone? He pulled open the dresser drawers and groped around. Were the visions somehow coming from his childhood?

He couldn't find anything. Of course. His mother had some things hanging up in her room. He rushed over into his parent's bedroom. He looked around: a Madonna, a crucifix above the bed, and two bathrobes. Not one child's painting.

Disappointed, sapped of strength, he fell back on the bed. Why did these horrible dreams keep overtaking him?

He turned on the lamp, which cast a dull glow over his father's bedside table. As children they were strictly forbidden to go into their parents' bedroom, let alone touch the nightstand. The thought alone made him tremble.

Bernhard opened the top drawer and felt around, as if touching were less forbidden than looking: ironed handkerchiefs, thick wool socks, earplugs and a spray bottle for angina attacks.

In the drawer below it, Bernhard found an oblong wooden box. He pushed back the lid: many compartments, each filled with unusual objects. A naked woman made of ivory, a few wooden screws, a baby tooth, a cigarette holder, a glass bottle of white snuff. *Menthol* was written on it in faded green letters. Bernhard pulled out the cork and sniffed; it smelled smoky. There was a key with a decorated handle, a few mussel shells. When they went to Italy as children, they had dragged them back home by the bag. Their father had thrown all of them away, no, clearly not all of them. And one compartment was empty. A small square compartment. Bernhard placed his finger in it as if he would be able to feel what had once been in there.

Underneath the insert compartment, there were papers: his passport, Gudrun's immunization certificate, a birth certificate: Theo Edgar Moll. Beneath it was a military insignia, a kind of medal with a red and black ribbon. Bernhard picked it up. It brought back all the images he so desperately wished to suppress: dying people, battlefields, explosions, broken hearts and so many tears.

"What are you doing here?" his mother asked suddenly.

Bernhard recoiled.

"You shouldn't do that, Bernhard. That drawer was always off limits for you children. And it still is, even after his death."

Lydia took the box from his hand and sat down next to him on the bed, holding it in her lap. Then she put the insert compartment back in and pulled the lid over it.

"What were you thinking?"

"I...I..." He didn't even know himself. Instead of answering her, he held out the insignia to his mother.

"Where did you get that?" she asked, taking it from him.

"From the box."

She looked at it from all sides.

"Did Papa wear that?"

"I can't imagine. But I don't know. He never talked about the war."

"Did you really even know him, Mom?"

She looked at her son with confused eyes. "What kind of silly question is that? Of course I knew your father. I spent almost fifty years of my life with him."

"Then tell me what was going through his head when he would sit with us and not talk to anyone. What are all these objects in the box? Why was he such a bitter man?"

Lydia slipped the insignia back, then placed the box in the drawer.

Sitting down again she said, "Your father was a very sensitive person, shy as a deer. No one was allowed to get too close to him." Her flat hand stroked the snow-white comforter. "For years, we each slept on our own side of the bed, and even later…," she looked at the Madonna, "even later, when were…together, I always had the impression he was about to jump away at any moment."

She brushed a strand of hair behind Bernhard's ear.

"All that wasn't so simple for him. The time after the war, the children, our family. He had to provide for us when there was almost nothing to eat. Life hardened him, but he wasn't a hard man, believe me. Lots of things affected him, he just didn't know how to show it."

"But other people lived through the war as well, and they didn't turn out like him."

He could see her shoulders sinking. "I don't know what happened to him, but it must have been terrible. You have to remember, he was a young man. He didn't know what was right and what was wrong. He saw his comrades in the trenches fall one by one. Where do you think his heart problems came from?"

Bernhard shrank back within himself. "Did he have them back then?"

"From the very first day we met." She looked out the window at the grey sky, which was slowly darkening. "Your father experienced things we can't even begin to imagine, my boy."

Little did she know that he could very well imagine … Even as his mother was speaking, he could feel the tremor of falling bombs again. B-17s zoomed by overhead, trailing thick black clouds. Defense artillery rattled, Messerschmitts fell like hailstones from the sky, spirals of black smoke followed burning bombs. Parachutes opened up, machine guns drilled holes through soldiers helpless with exhaustion, and somewhere Hitler's blind followers were torturing a soldier to death simply because he loved.

"Your bandage is all bloody," his mother commented. "Come downstairs, I'll change it for you. The food should be ready anyway."

"I can't eat anything right now," Bernhard said, out of breath. His heart was racing, he felt dizzy. The memories, again the memories. "I need to go home. Right away. I'll call you, okay?"

Bernhard hugged his mother, and before she could protest, he was out the door.

30.

"Could you maybe pick up the phone every once in a while?" Kim was standing in front of the door in a bomber jacket and skintight jeans. Her fur collar, covered in small melted beads of snow, framed her delicate face like a bird's nest around a newborn chick.

"For three straight days I have been dialing till my fingers were sore, and you never answer. I was worried."

He looked terrible: his washed-out zebra shirt was buttoned up wrong, one sleeve was rolled up while the other had a huge coffee stain on it. A tattered bandage protruded from his left sleeve, his hair stood on his head like a straw fire.

She hugged Bernhard quickly, then marched past him into the apartment. He closed the book in his hands and looked at the clock: it was nine. He hadn't slept for two days.

"So this is how live!" Kim did a little pirouette. Then she pointed skeptically to the pile of dirty laundry, the mountain of used paper, and the food remains lying scattered around. "What a catastrophe!"

"I was just clearing out some junk," he said defensively.

"Well maybe you should bring stuff down to the trash every now and then."

"I didn't have time to do that."

Kim went over to the bouquet of flowers wrapped in cellophane. "Why aren't they in water? If you leave them like this, they'll wilt soon."

Kim read the card, which was fastened to the bouquet with a light blue ribbon: *Let's talk. Please. Edvard.*

She held out the card to him. "You probably haven't even called him, have you?"

Bernhard took the card from her and put it on his pile of books without reading it.

"I just can't," he said, rubbing his eyes.

"Why? What's wrong with you?"

The telephone rang. Bernhard looked at it as he had never noticed it before. Kim grabbed the receiver: "Yes, hello, you've reached Moll. Just a moment, please."

"It's your mother," she whispered.

Bernhard rolled his eyes and took the receiver from her hand. "Hello, Mama."

"Bernhard, my boy. I've been trying to reach you for days. You promised to call."

"I haven't been well, Mama."

"Is it something serious? Should I be worried?"

Bernhard turned his back on Kim. "No, just a…cold."

Kim looked around. No snotty tissues, no bowl of chamomile vapor, not even any aspirin. A cold? She took of her jacket and hung it over the bookshelf.

"Ah, all right. Well that's a relief. The way you ran away after the funeral, I was worried. Are you sure you're all right?"

He shuffled from one leg to the other. "Yes, I am. I'll be in touch again, Mom."

"Bernhard." His mother's words were like a spider's threads, slowly weaving into a net. "Sieglinde isn't doing very well. Maybe you should give her a call."

"What?"

"You saw that Eberhard came to the funeral."

"Mom, I really can't talk right now." He appealed to her.

Kim spread open a trash bag and began to collect dried cheese sandwiches, orange peel and instant soup cups that were still half full of soup.

"It's a difficult time for all of us. We need to stick together. At least give her a call."

The trash bag filled up, but the chaos was barely straightened out at all.

"All right, I will. But now I need to hang up. There's something urgent I have to do."

"And Bernhard." Her voice grew softer. "Where Papa is now, he's doing well."

Bernhard didn't want to talk about his father anymore, and yet he heard himself ask, "What do you mean?"

"Death redeemed him, my son. He looked so relieved, as if there were nothing he wished for more deeply."

There was a pause.

"Are you still there?"

"Yes, Mama."

"I think he suffered a lot in this life." Oh God, now she was starting with her Catholic explanations, Bernhard feared. "Your father undertook a mission that was much too large for him. He didn't manage to master it. But that doesn't make him a bad soul by any means. Believe me, he did his best. You children always saw him as the culprit, but in truth he was just a victim."

Victim! Bernhard had read lots about the Third Reich in the last few days, he was convinced that everyone who had taken part was culpable. After all, his father hadn't done anything to stop Jews from being gassed or homosexuals from being slaughtered.

"Bernhard?"

"Yes."

"Don't jump to any conclusions. Don't judge before you know the whole truth!"

That was all very well, but how was he supposed to find out the whole truth?

Kim shoved a piled of old newspapers from the windowsill into the trash bag. It tore, and its contents plopped out onto the floor. Kim bit her lips, but Bernhard didn't even turn around.

After he hung up, he flung himself down on the couch.

"Everything all right?" asked Kim.

"She sounds strange."

"How so, strange?"

"Disconnected somehow, you know. I wonder if she's going to get over my father's death."

"Do you want to go to see her?"

He looked at her helplessly. "Oh God, no!"

She pushed a few books aside and sat on the small table.

"Are you sad because of your father?" Kim stared at him.

He shook his head.

"Not even a little bit?"

Bernhard tilted his head back far past the headrest, rubbing his face with both hands. "To be honest, there are other things going through my head right now."

"Like what?"

"You remember at the police station?"

Kim nodded.

"When I saw the uniforms, I totally panicked."

"Why?"

"I was afraid they were after us."

"Who was after whom?"

"The police, after...after Edvard and me."

"Why would you think something like that?"

"I've been trying to figure it out all this time." He pointed to a pile of books behind Kim. She took down the one on top and read: *Homosexuality in the Nazi Regime.* She looked at him quizzically. "I don't get it."

Bernhard stood up and paced around the room. "I don't know where to begin." He ran his fingers through his hair, then told her about his daydreams and visions, the boundless panic and horror that had been haunting him for days like a bad conscience.

"The images are all terrible," he closed his report. "But there's one I can't get out of my head. I see it day and night, everywhere, even in the mirror: it's a young man, blond and blue-eyed, the epitome of a soldier. He is strong-willed, courageous, bursting with strength. And I can't escape the feeling he's somehow my dearest friend."

"It sounds like you're describing Edvard!"

Bernhard gave a start.

"Is that not what you're doing?"

"No, for God's sake. Why would you think that?"

She shrugged her shoulders. "Who is he then?"

Bernhard leaned against the window frame and looked out. The sun had just lifted its heavy head over the tips of the tree branches, letting its rays fall on the glass.

"That's the crazy part, I don't have the slightest idea."

"Maybe the dreams are just wishful thinking. You shouldn't worry about it so much."

Bernhard turned towards her and looked at her uncomprehendingly. "He was murdered, Kim. In front of my eyes, he was sentenced to death by SS officers. That's not what a wish looks like, is it?" His voice broke.

Kim stood up, went over to him and laid a hand on his arm.

"I can't tell you all the things they did to him. It's so terrible, it's so terrible!"

Bernhard laid his head on her shoulder. He cried so softly that no one could hear it, not even he himself. His tears were hot and thick, and they seemed to wash the feeling of helplessness away from him. Then he wiped his nose and continued talking. "I need to figure out what all this has to do with me, you understand? That's why I've been reading all these books." He pointed to the table.

"And?"

He shrugged his shoulders. "It happened so often. Ten thousand homosexuals died in the concentration camps. But I still don't understand what that has to do with me."

Kim took a few steps back and leaned against the desk. "Don't you think," she said warily, "You might want to… see a doctor? You're making yourself crazy."

Bernhard let out a tormented laugh. "It sounds pretty crazy, doesn't it? But something about it makes sense, I can feel it. And there are a few pieces I've put together already. Look, people always bring up the Jewish topic. If you think about how much Jews still suffer from it, it must be similar for gays. But no one tackles the question. And then it's no wonder our parents' generation had guilt problems. They were there. They feel guilty, but they were never held accountable. How heavy must that weigh on them? Just because it's in the past doesn't mean it's forgotten."

His thoughts were foreign to Kim. While he was rooting around in the past, her questions centered on the future. She stirred a spoon around in an old, half-full mug. The cream had separated from the coffee, leaving white smears. Bernhard watched her doing this, and it became clear to him that no one could begin to understand his thoughts—no one but himself.

"What do you actually know about this Fred guy?" he asked so suddenly that she jumped up a little. Had she made it so obvious that she wasn't interested in his Nazi story?

She had had lots of time to think about Fred the past few days, and she had figured a few things out. "He was my last lover. But I think the only thing I really know about him is that he's a con man."

"A con man?"

"Or whatever. In any case, he promised the earth to me, but in the end he was just after my money. And it looks like he abandoned that old lady, and he went home with Edvard as well."

Bernhard flinched.

"He was probably just trying to rip him off too. Oh God, I honestly don't want to think about it anymore. I feel crappy enough as it is."

She was right. Bernhard didn't want to think about it anymore either. Edvard would get along all by himself. And after that scene with the police, he didn't want to have anything to do with him for now.

"Is it all right to smoke in your place?" asked Kim, and he nodded. She fished a squashed cigarette pack from her waistband and lit one up.

"I'm pregnant," she spoke into the blue fog.

"What?" Bernhard peered at her intently.

"I just got tested. I'm pregnant."

"You mean…"

"I'm sure of it. It could only be the doctor's. Until the flight I was on the pill."

This story was turning into a real hospital romance; it just kept getting more unbelievable.

"And? Are you going to keep it?"

Kim felt much too young for the task of being a mother. It was one thing to change a diaper now and then or to play with a baby, but to be responsible for it? She would have to be there when it cried, comfort it when its first teeth came in, stroke it when stomach pains tormented its little body, not to speak of school, drugs and the first disappointed love. And then there was the complete change of lifestyle. She would have to get a bigger apartment, find a regular job, and then she'd be tied down to it for at least twenty years.

"No, it's impossible." She pulled on the cigarette and blew the smoke out. It made a light arc, followed the draft through the gap in the window and was lost in nothingness.

"Anyway it would always remind me of that…sack of crap."

She felt nauseous at the thought that one of her eggs had been fertilized by that asshole's sperm, and was now growing into a small being inside her uterus. It needed to get out of there, and fast.

"Have you already talked to the doctor?"

She stood up and wiped a few tobacco crumbs off her pants.

"Yeah, in Miami. But not about the kid. I mean, I didn't know about it then yet. He's horrible. There's no way he would help me out."

"Surely you don't want to go through this alone? It's his kid as well."

With her ring finger, she stroked her quivering lower lip, lost in thought.

"You should at least go to the police and report him."

"Ha!" Her face twisted to a grimace. "No one would believe I was raped in an airplane."

Bernhard had to admit that she wasn't entirely wrong. Even he had a hard time believing it.

"Why does this kind of thing always happen to me?" she asked. "Why always me?"

Bernhard felt overwhelmed by her helplessness. "At least go for a consultation. The worst thing for you right now is to feel powerless."

She looked at him with some hope in her eyes.

"What are you going to do about your visions?" she asked.

"I'll keep looking. Something will turn up eventually. I'm not going to get discouraged."

She pulled on her cigarette again and blew a wide swath of smoke through the room. The ash on her cigarette kept getting longer, and her thoughts were amassing dangerously. Then she nodded silently. "You're right," she said softly, pursing her lips.

Then they both grew quiet.

"Oh my god! I need to go. I have to go shopping before the stores close."

Bernhard wrinkled his brow.

"It's New Year's Eve, Bernhard. Did you not realize that?" She turned on her heels, swung her jacket over her shoulder and headed for the door.

"I'm having a party. Lots of interesting people will be there. And you'll be one of them."

Bernhard laid his hand on his forehead. New Year's! He had completely forgotten about it. He looked around at the chaos in his apartment.

"Lie down and get some sleep so you don't nod off at my place." Kim pushed the door handle down.

"Thank you," she whispered in his ear and gave him a quick kiss. Then she sniffed. "And…take a bath."

Bernhard laughed.

31.

Edvard had been invited to at least twenty parties, but all he could think about was the hotel in Vienna he had booked for himself and Edvard. He had imagined their New Year's Eve so beautifully: a gala dinner by candlelight at Haas, high above the roofs of the city, endless champagne and all the fireworks just for them, for their relationship and their love.

He couldn't go to any other party. Tonight was Bernhard's night. How was he supposed to celebrate, to ring in a New Year of cheerless promise, without his beloved? No, he didn't want to see anyone, he didn't want to drink champagne, he didn't want fireworks. He just wanted Bernhard.

Edvard had pulled the heavy leather couch in front of the window and turned off all the lights in his apartment except for the neon yellow sign flickering behind him. He wanted to see the sky and the stars.

That day, he had already tried to call Bernhard ten times. He had already taken a taxi over to his place three times, but he had neither picked up the phone nor opened the door. What else could he do?

All day, the sun was shining, making the snow slippery as butter. Now tree branches bent low under its weight, and snow crunched beneath his shoes like dust-fine splinters of glass.

The town hall, bathed in bright orange light, stood out against the blue gray sky as if encased in beeswax. The figurines in the mechanical clock stood still; they had time before the clock made them spin again. They had no choice. Regardless of the weather they had to stay there, there was no escape.

Bernhard stared up at the sky and breathed in the darkness. Nothing moved.

The golden column of the Virgin Mary was shrouded in a bizarre sheen. When was the last time it had been renovated? What gold had they used? The teeth of Jews? Of gays? He thought about the Victory Column in Berlin, the monument of the gay movement. There was even a monthly magazine named after it. It was horrifying to think that the gold used to restore that icon might have been paid for with so much blood and pain.

Bernhard turned away and passed by the ugly mall on his way to Sendlingerstrasse, the soles of his boots rhythmically hacking black holes in his field of vision. Rows of post-war buildings lined next to one another, small shops with flashing Christmas decorations.

A trio of men in uniform approached Bernhard, frightening him. Then he saw they were gay. Where did the desire to dress up in uniform come from? Did they find it sexually arousing? Or did they just want to reverse the game, turning from prey to predator?

They were blond, wore their hair cut short, their blue eyes gleamed in the night. They were probably even wearing colored contact lenses. Like true Aryans, thought Bernhard. Did they even know they'd turned themselves into clones of what the Nazis had always desired? Was it like the pink triangle: elevating the mark of shame into an emblem in order to transform the negative image into something positive? Or was it an unconsciously perpetuated wish to be superior to others, to finally belong to the noble class of "superior people"?

Was that how the glorification of rape became part of the scene? All those bars with handcuffs, camouflage nets, prison grates? And darkrooms that seemed like gas chambers in a concentration camp?

Why didn't they understand what they were doing? Why didn't gay people have any consciousness of their past? They needed to fight back, to rise up and struggle against the injustice that had befallen those who thought and felt the same as them. Instead they were concerned with looking pretty. As long as you pulled the right strings, they would jump.

It wasn't until Bernhard reached the ornate Asam Church that he realized he had gone too far. He turned foot and walked through the threshold into the Asam yard.

Kim had said it was number 26. He searched for her name on the large nameplate at the door, then discovered a yellow post-it note held up with scotch tape. It said *Kim*. He rang the doorbell, the opener muttered wearily, the door snapped shut. He climbed up to the third floor. Considering all he knew about Kim, he was expecting chaos, clothes in every corner and loud heavy metal music. But this apartment was more suited to someone delicate and fragile, as frail as butterfly wings: two tidy rooms with large windows, clean, orderly, quiet.

Kim held out a glass of champagne to him. "Cheers!"

"It's a beautiful place you've got here."

"Yeah, it's quite nice. But don't worry, I'm not as stuffy as it looks. It's not my apartment. It belongs to a friend of mine, she's got a job in L.A. at the moment. I'm only here for a few weeks."

"Where do you live otherwise?"

"Here and there. I haven't liked anywhere well enough to stay." She let out an open, unrestrained laugh and took a sip from her glass.

"Well, what do you like?"

"Good question." She raised her eyebrows, shook her head and pinched his nose. "You'll have to excuse me. I've got to get some things ready."

Bernhard went onto the balcony and looked out over the city. All was dark, down to the small red roofs stretched out beneath the sky like a modern Persian rug.

There was a man standing in the courtyard, or was it just a shadow? Leather jacket, black hair: no, it wasn't Edvard. Anyway, how would Edvard have known where he was?

And how was he spending the night? With Heiner, or Gerhard? Maybe Birgit was reading him the prognosis for next year from her cards. Or was he with Fred, his new lover? Well then, the best of luck to them!

241

Bernhard looked at the night sky lit up here and there by individual beacons, remembering that night less than two weeks ago. The shooting stars, Edvard's soft embrace, his face grown pale in the moonlight, and the desire to stay with him forever. What remained of that feeling? A pressure in his chest, his throat tight with longing.

Behind Bernhard, the apartment filled with people, their eyes full of lust for life, fear for the future, doubts, love and contentment. Through the balcony door he saw a woman with dark curly hair and tiny eyes looking around as if she were entirely lost. The next to enter was a dark-skinned man with oval glasses, hair dyed red, and a body to die for. A thin blonde with a face like porcelain hung on his arm. A bald-headed man with a body like a gnarled tree paced the living room pensively, giving a much too curious look at a young boy wearing clothes that would probably suit his father better than himself.

Bernhard followed these events like a play, hearing only the murmur of the city, laughter from a nearby apartment, firecrackers, and the rustling of his coat whenever he lifted his glass to fill it up again. He didn't know any of these people kissing and hugging; he had never touched any of these hands that clinked glasses together and toasted one another. He was just a spectator to this play, completely superfluous.

"My little darling! Have you recovered from the shock?" asked Raimondo with a serious look, grasping Kim tightly by her fleshy arms.

"Oh, you're so sweet. I've really demanded a lot of you the last few days haven't I? What would I do without you?"

"You see, that's why the good Lord gave me the time to take care of you."

Kim pressed tight once more against his soft, cuddly belly. He laid his heavy, warm hand delicately on her head.

"So have you decided? About the baby, I mean?"

"It's impossible for me to keep it, Raimondo. How is that supposed to work?"

Kim was twenty-five. She barely knew how to handle herself.

What was she supposed to do with a child, on top of that the result of a rape?

Worry wrinkles formed on Raimondo's forehead. "I'll say it again. We'll find a solution."

"Let's talk about it some other time, okay?" she said. "Today, I want to celebrate."

She took off his coat and hung it on the coat rack.

"Did you come alone?"

"No, Serge's just getting cigarettes. He should be here any minute." Kim narrowed her eyes. "Serge?"

It was obvious to him that she was criticizing him about Serge.

She noticed this and quickly tried to soften her tone. "I was just looking forward to meeting a real baker sometime."

And Raimondo smiled. How was she supposed to know that he had sent Adrian home in order to hurry off to her.

The doorbell rang.

"Could you open the door for him," she asked him, "I need to go to the kitchen." And she stalked out of the room, disgruntled.

"Honey!" A shrill woman in her mid-forties fell upon Kim, tugging at her arm. Blood-red hair piled over her black eyebrows like a bundle of naturally-dyed sheep's wool, falling in long, dark strands over her bare shoulders. Her skin gleamed with expensive body lotion, and the apartment was already filled with the scent of her perfume.

"What is it, Mama?"

She looked around frantically, laid her tanned, bony fingers on her collar and fell into a whisper.

"I just wanted to say that Jürgen is a bit sensitive at the moment. Make sure to avoid any discussion of business. Unless you want to make him angry."

"Please."

"Also…" she looked deep into Kim's eyes, which was a signal for Kim, "there's another problem."

Kim laid her hand on her hips and straightened up a bit.

"What's the name of the problem this time?"

Her mother looked around again. "Christine, please…" Then her gloomy face brightened suddenly into a lily-white smile, and her hand moved like a feather duster through the air. "Hi, darling! I'm over here."

Kim pressed her fingertips against her temples; she could feel a migraine coming on.

"Kim, would you bring my dear Jürgen a glass of your wonderful punch?"

"But of course." Kim smiled at him in disgust and disappeared.

"Can I help at all?" her school friend asked when they were in the kitchen.

"Yeah, could you maybe exchange my mother for someone else?"

"Is she making your life difficult again?"

"She's not actually doing anything, which makes it worse. She's just being herself—and I can't stand it."

Kim ladled punch into two glasses, then lifted them both up in the air. "For the lovers," she cooed, making a disgusted face.

"Look, I'll take care of it before you spill it all over your shirt," her friend said, taking the glasses away from her.

Kim huffed. "No. Not unless you spill it onto his pants. Too bad he didn't ask for coffee, it would hurt more." Then her eyes gleamed. "Wait."

"What's that?"

Kim dug a piece of garlic out of the salad and hid it in one of the glasses under a slice of pineapple. "Give this to dear Jürgen."

They laughed.

Kim followed her friend out, then she noticed the bolted door to the balcony. She ran over and opened it. "Bernhard, for God's sake! You must be freezing! I didn't even notice."

Kim stretched out her hand to Bernhard. He laid his icy hand in her overheated one and stepped up into the apartment. She took his coat off his shoulders and asked him reproachfully why he hadn't knocked.

"It was so comfortable out there. So much air, so much room."

"And this is?" her mother asked, her eyes full of expectation.

"Bernhard, my…a dear, dear friend, whom I only met just recently."

"Ah, how romantic."

"Mama, you'll have to excuse me. I wanted to show Bernhard something."

Kim pulled him away to the one secure place: the kitchen.

"I'm sorry. She thinks every man around me is my lover." And when he looked puzzled, she added: "My mother."

"Ah, that's your mother? She seems nice."

Kim rolled her eyes, but didn't say anything. She took down a bottle of vodka from the cupboard and passed it to him.

"Here, this will warm you up again."

He took a sip from the bottle while Kim studied him. An aura of stillness surrounded him, radiating something calm and serene, like an ice floe bobbing on a lake or a phone booth at night in an abandoned street.

"And? Have you made a decision yet?"

"How like a man! As if this were the kind of thing you could just decide. It's not merely a baby. It was conceived under circumstances I don't want to be reminded of. I don't think I would be able to love it."

She grew quiet for a moment. Bernhard could see in her eyes that she was thinking about something. But then she added adamantly: "Plus it would turn my whole life upside-down," as if that closed the subject.

Bernhard looked at her for a moment with concern. Taking the bottle from his hand, Kim led him out of the kitchen.

"I'm going to introduce you to a few people, okay?" she said, her teeth gleaming. "So you can finally start thinking about something else."

There was a middle-aged director who had retired from the business, living off the interest from his savings, doing nothing but meditating when he wasn't traveling. That image of manhood he had seen before turned out to be a young model from Tobago who was currently doing photo sessions for a sunglasses commercial; and contrary to expectations, the blonde girl on his arm was neither Swedish nor dumb.

Kim introduced Bernhard to her masseur and his wife, her school friend and her lover from the Dominican Republic who worked as a reggae musician, and her co-worker Margret who had also been on the flight to Miami.

And then there was Gregor, an acquaintance of Kim's school friend. He looked like something out of a catalogue: tan, dark gelled hair, five-o'clock shadow and a smile as white and artificial as snow from a can.

"So my kitten. Already on the hunt for mice," the man said pressing up to Kim, but she pushed him away. She wasn't going to let any man slip under her radar so soon.

"Have you actually talked with your daughter today?"

"Kimmy? Of course. Isn't she a golden child? You know, she's really made something of herself. Her taste does leave a little something to be desired. This…Bernhard. He seems a little uptight to me. She's always had such charming young men."

"So she didn't talk to you?" Raimondo interrupted her flood of words.

"About Bernhard? She claims he's just an acquaintance, but I can see what's going on there."

"Not about Bernhard!" Raimondo was getting impatient. His discussions with Kim over the last few days were still lying heavily in his stomach. If she had actually been raped, she needed help from a woman. This was her mother's job.

"What would she tell me? A secret?" Her eyes lit up. "Which reminds me…"

Raimondo looked his childhood sweetheart in the eye, apprehending her entire soul in one look: sweet and beautiful, like a white nectarine. Her flesh was uncommonly beautiful, she smelled tantalizing: and all that just to protect her core.

"…I found this letter, and the latest thing is that he's flying away with her for the weekend. Of course he tries to hide it, but the travel agency where he booked the flights, the woman there, Astrid, she's a good friend of mine, she told me everything right away. He had barely left the store, the phone was already in her hand. I mean, in principle it doesn't bother me, I just find that…"

How could a mother like this be any help to Kim? Raimondo wondered.

"Kimmy!" Her mother called across the crowded room.

"Just a minute, Mama." Kim left Bernhard with a young man. He was tall with short blond hair. In spite of the cold, he wore a T-shirt, probably in order to show off the tattoo on his upper arm: a Celtic ornament wrapped in barbed wire.

"Hi. I'm Hans-Harry." He leaned coolly against the wall, twirling the last stub of his self-rolled cigarette between his thumb and middle finger. A little thread of tobacco spun like a propeller.

"Hi, Bernhard."

They shook hands.

"And how do you know Kim?"

"To say I know her would be an exaggeration. We just met each other on the flight from Miami to Munich."

"And now she's probably already your best friend. That's typical of Kim."

"What does that mean?"

"That's just the way she is. Doesn't mean anything else. Kim's a wonderful person. Once you've gotten to know the Kim behind the hyperactive façade, you can't get enough of her."

"You seem to have known her a long time."

"Years ago we had a…let's say, an affair."

"Oh!" said Bernhard with surprise.

"Don't worry. I haven't had anything to do with women for a long time," added Hans-Harry, laughing.

"Oh!" said Bernhard again.

"You need to take better care of Raimondo," Kim's mother said reproachfully. "He looks all gray. He's going to waste away on us." She stroked the back of her childhood friend's head, which was covered with sweat. He smiled and answered her with a kiss on the cheek.

"Ah, I'm sorry. I think I interrupted you," she said afterwards to Raimondo. "Didn't you want to tell me something?"

He shook his head. "Nothing important, my darling. Really nothing important."

"Well then I'll leave you two alone," she said, leaving the two of them standing there.

"She's the same as ever," said Raimondo.

"Yes, unfortunately," Kim assented.

"Go mingle among the guests. The two of us will have enough time to talk later," she suggested to him, and he knew that was just a code for the fact that Serge was hitting on another man behind his back. Raimondo focused on his punch and drank it up in one gulp. Since he hadn't reacted, Kim added: "Where did Serge get off to?" she asked disingenuously.

Raimondo shrugged his shoulders as if it didn't interest him. He had already noticed Serge a while ago hitting on the tall dark-haired man.

"Ah, he's over there. He's talking to Bernhard, my new friend. I wanted to introduce him to you in any case. He's in quite a crisis at the moment. He could use a bit of your special attention." Kim cast her eyes upward.

Bernhard was visibly relieved to be taken out of the conversation.

"Would you give me a hand," Kim said with a fiery gleam in her eyes, grabbing Serge and dragging him away.

Raimondo shook Bernhard's hand and held it for a long time, and a softness settled into the stillness around Bernhard.

"Don't you find it awful how people feel more and more lonely in our society?" Raimondo observed, suddenly feeling strangely exhilarated.

"You're totally right," Bernhard confirmed, nearly stuttering.

"You come to a party and can't help but notice how difficult it is to have a conversation with other people."

Bernhard sipped at his champagne. His eyes covertly sounded out his conversation partner. They assessed the fine hairs protruding from beneath his silk scarf, the strong, ungainly hands holding his punch glass.

"While it would be a lot more pleasant for everyone not to just stand around alone, right?" Raimondo asked.

"Right," Bernhard answered, and since he didn't want to express any of the thoughts that were tossing around in his head, he asked the standard New Year's questions: "So have you made any New Year's resolutions?"

"I don't think much of New Year's resolutions," Raimondo stated. "Why do people only think about their lives once a year? Why should it be easier to stop smoking at New Year's than any other time of the year?"

Bernhard nodded and sipped at his glass again. It was almost empty. Meanwhile, Raimondo's eyes were searching the room for Serge, but fortunately were unable to find him.

Bernhard felt lighter now that this man's soft, loving eyes were fixed on him. It seemed childish to him, but his heart started beating faster.

"Take for example the resolution to fall in love. Why should I waste a thought on that, let alone making a resolution about it?"

"Yeah, why?" Bernhard asked.

"Either it happens or it doesn't. 10:48 is just as good as midnight, right?"

"Of course, you're totally right," Bernhard affirmed, laughing. Then he looked at his watch as if by chance: it was actually twelve minutes before eleven. Bernhard grew quiet, and Raimondo turned red.

"Everyone listen up!" Kim had turned the music off and was beating a spoon against a champagne bottle. "Everyone take a lead figurine, and then we'll ask the oracle together."

Most of them grabbed into the bowl randomly to fish out an object, but Raimondo had a particular wish. "Do you have a lucky clover?" he asked.

"No, but here, this little pig suits you," she said with a grin, putting it in his hand.

Once everyone was outfitted with their lead figurine, Kim lit the candle solemnly and held up a big spoon. "Who's first?"

Hans-Harry stepped up to the table. His muscles rippled, and Bernhard observed each of his movements. Harry lowered a flower figurine into the spoon's hollow. It melted quickly over the flame, and Kim poured the liquid lead into the cold water.

"An anchor! A triangle! A fish!" people called over one another.

Harry went to the pot and looked inside. "No, it's a...dog shit," he said, and his teeth flashed white.

"Oh, what lyrical ideas you have," Kim teased, flipping through her little book. "Dog poop, dog shit. Here it is: dedication and perseverance will lead to your desired success," she read, patting him on the shoulders approvingly.

While the director melted his scale under Serge's watchful eye, Bernhard asked Kim who this Hans-Harry was.

"You mean Haha? He's a journalist, and he's just published his first novel: *Calamity Refutes*. Very romantic. A wonderful book. You should definitely read it."

"A bird!" the director said, eagerly awaiting Kim's interpretation.

"Good news," read Kim. "Sometimes even connected with prophecies."

Her colleague Margret's ball melted into a heart: "Enjoyment, friendship, love, marriage," announced Kim.

Her mother insisted that her melted hand bag had turned into a full moon.

"All right, if that's what you want." Kim read: "Full moon: sadness, breaking ties, a marriage for money."

And while Kim looked at her sadly, her mother seemed to positively blossom.

Kim threw her heart figurine boldly into the fire. It turned into a dagger, its point facing away from her.

"Revenge," she read in the book. "An act must be atoned for. It will be crowned with success." She hesitated. Her mother looked at her with curiosity. But Kim didn't have any time to think about it, since Raimondo's melted lead pig was already sinking to the bottom of the pot, finding a new shape. The others saw it as a crown, a tooth, or a nugget of gold. But for him it was clearly an iceberg.

"Disappointed hopes. Self-chosen injury," Kim read, her voice meek. Raimondo looked at her with narrowed eyes, and she held out the book to him. "Read it yourself if you don't believe me."

Meanwhile, Bernhard made his way to the candle. He didn't think anything of predictions, but he didn't want to ruin the fun for everyone else.

"A ring!" everyone called in chorus. And there truly wasn't any other way of seeing it.

"An old relationship will dissolve, a new one will form."

Bernhard swallowed. Saliva ran down his throat. Which was the old, which was the new? Raimondo raised his glass to him over Kim's head. Then a firecracker made the window shake, and the party guests all jumped back in shock.

"All right kids, it's five of twelve. To your places!" Kim's mother turned on the TV, Kim turned on a waltz. Champagne corks popped, and everyone pushed onto the small balcony.

Kim's school friend's boyfriend put rockets and all sorts of fireworks on the balustrade, and soon bright veins of light shot through the sky over Munich. There were cracks and bangs everywhere, Roman candles spewed small colorful cascades of light over the courtyard, and bells started ringing across the city.

"Happy New Year!" said Kim, passing around champagne glasses and kissing every pair of lips that puckered up for her.

Handsome Gregor closed his eyes as soon as she had arrived at him, forming a kiss with his lips. She tapped his lips with her finger, which was cold from the champagne, and gave him a kiss on the cheek. "I hope you find the woman of your dreams soon," she whispered in his ear and left him standing there.

Raimondo held out his glass to Bernhard. "Good luck with the ring!" he said, pointing to Bernhard's hand.

"Oh, that's just my father's ring. My mother wanted me to wear it. And now it's there."

"And here I was thinking you were in a relationship."

Relationship? Bernhard thought of Edvard. His sensitive temperament, his funny ideas, his loving embraces, and the party where he had asked for Bernhard's hand.

"No, no. I...I'm not in a relationship."

Raimondo exhaled. "Well then. I just have to wish you lots of happiness for what's to come."

"What?"

"Well, the oracle, did you already forget? A new one will form, it said. Lots of luck with the new relationship."

"Oh, yeah, thanks," Bernhard said, looking him in the eyes for just a tad too long. He was about to sink into them when Kim's mother screeched: "You're allowed to touch each other. Men are allowed to fall in love too. You don't have to be ashamed of it."

Bernhard would have liked nothing more than to jump off the balcony in embarrassment. Then he felt Raimondo's lips on his own. They were moist and smooth and very gentle, pulling his desire from him like a magnet.

Then Kim popped up between them. "Oh, I just wanted to..."

Raimondo was annoyed; he took Kim's cigarette from her fingers and said: "You're going to stop smoking now. Think of the baby."

"What baby?" Kim's mother cried out.

"Thanks," said Kim furiously, stomping off with tears streaming down her face.

Raimondo watched her go with an injured look on his face. Then he ran after her, leaving Bernhard standing there.

Edvard was standing on his balcony. In the past hour, he had opened another bottle of champagne and drank it to the bottom. And now he was using it as a launching pad for his fireworks. He wanted to shoot up a rocket, a comet with a long tail that exploded loudly. Maybe it would light the way for Bernhard to come back to him.

The match flickered in the wind, then the wick lit. The rocket zoomed off, climbing higher and higher. A glowing silver tail traced across the New Year's sky, gleaming brighter than all the other fireworks—then with a burst it rained down a thousand colorful stars.

Bernhard saw a comet whizz across the sky and thought of the night of the party. Three shooting stars had fallen from the sky that night, and he had only wished for one thing: to be with Edvard forever.

Bernhard picked up a rocket and put it in an empty champagne bottle. Before he lit it, he made a wish. Then he sent it flying up in a high arc. It disappeared into the night, soon showering the sky with its sparks.

And at the other end of the city, a young man wept thin tears of joy.

32.

Stupid New Year's resolutions! This was the third time she'd stood before this door, and still she didn't have the courage to ring the bell. Raimondo's words were coming to seem more and more plausible: why even make resolutions at all? And why specifically on New Year's Eve?

"Revenge!" the lead had called to her from the depths of the water—Kim had heard it without a doubt—forming into a knife, with a tip so sharp it hurt her eyes to look at it. Just thinking of it made her hand feel as if it were burning. It lay heavily in her consciousness, a massive weight, heavy with fate and responsibility. She was supposed to get revenge, but on whom? So many of them deserved it. All night long, they marched past her: Stefan, Markus, Richard, Helmut, Fred and all the rest.

Again and again, Kim paced about, breathing the gunpowder-tinged air, walking down the alley among burnt fireworks, only to end up standing in front of this door again.

Her body was shaking; she knew it couldn't go on like this. Spending New Year's with her mother had shown her that she didn't want to spend her later years being pushed around by men.

She shook with the pain of deceit, and with desperation, wondering why she was always denied respect and esteem.

Now she was looking for an answer to this question. Only someone who shared her pain could give it to her, someone who understood her deeply, every pore, every breath, every cell of her body.

There was only one person who came to mind, a single person suffering the way she was: Roswitha. At the police station, she had seen her crying, whimpering in pain, begging for love. Roswitha was a kindred spirit.

And there was something else that connected them. Kim had definitely contributed to Roswitha's suffering. Kim was filled with regret, she wanted to atone, to be able to forgive herself; New Year's Eve had made this clear to her. Damn resolutions!

Trembling, she pressed the doorbell.

"Yes, hello?"

"My name is Kim. You don't know me. But I need to talk to you." It was New Year's Day, nine o'clock in the morning. Who would open the door to a stranger at this time? "It's about Fred!" she added to make sure, and the opener buzzed.

Kim pushed the door open; warmth flooded up against her. A large radiator behind the door, dark gray marble steps, iron railings. She felt her way up the stairs. With every step her heart beat faster in her chest, and as she climbed higher she could hear the woman's panting breath more and more clearly.

Roswitha's delicate body was framed in the lime green doorway. Her perm was bushy in the middle, her black angora sweater embroidered with a bellowing moose; its silver bead eyes rolled rhythmically back and forth in time to Roswitha's breathing.

Kim's desire to run away grew. She had prepared lots of things to say, feeling courageous and strong enough to admit her wrongdoing and withstand this woman's anger. But the only thing she felt at the moment was the desire to throw herself into her arms and cry.

"Do you know where Fred is? Do you have a message for me? Talk to me!" Roswitha demanded excitedly, and it became clear to Kim that she had gotten into this adventure without thinking.

Roswitha was an only child, she told Kim in the kitchen while the coffee machine hissed steam, producing a seductive aroma.

Her parents had married early, but her mother had been unable to become pregnant for a long time, which had caused them both a great deal of suffering. As she grew up, Roswitha had discovered that her father had a fondness for the bottle, and that her mother was severely depressed. She would never forget her dark gray, stringy hair and her eyes, always swollen with tears; saying this, she sighed.

After eighth grade she had had to leave school in order to earn money. Her mother needed special treatments that weren't covered by their insurance, and her father had more and more problems because of his little secret.

When she was twenty-four her father fell from the roof at work and broke his neck; her mother went completely off at the deep end.

Roswitha had never had lovers, simply because it never crossed her mind to take anyone home with her. They would just run away if they saw the conditions she grew up in.

And yet there were a few times, she remembered, that she had contact with boys. A clandestine kiss behind the school yard, a love letter during vacations at the farm, the boy next door who had played with her in the sandbox, whose eyes still appeared to her now and then in her dreams. When she was thirteen a boy had dragged her behind the bike racks at school and tried to pull her panties down under her skirt. A hard piece of flesh protruded from his zipper; Roswitha ran away screaming.

She told Kim all this and more, surrounded by wool curtains, a yellow tablecloth, brown earthenware plates, a beige flower-patterned thermos and stainless steel cutlery dangling from pink grips in a stand.

The life Roswitha revealed to Kim was much different from her own. Different people appeared in it, different places, different occurrences, and yet all her experiences sounded so interchangeable. Kim could have pulled out the thread at any moment and continued weaving on her own.

"I knew Fred was living with another woman," Kim admitted. "He told me he was married, that he wanted to get divorced. But still, I shouldn't have had an affair with him."

Roswitha's face grew dark for a moment. Hatred flared up, then quickly died away. She knew all too well what she would have done for this man's affection. Both of them were victims of desire, easy prey for a predator like Fred.

"The awful thing is," Roswitha said, staring into her half-empty coffee mug, "I still can't forget him."

Kim nodded. Fred was certainly not the man of her dreams, but she couldn't forget him either. A gentle smile or a touch at the right moment had been enough at times to bring about sleepless nights.

"Even the way he looked into my eyes. And then I found that ring and believed it was something like destiny. Crazy, right? As if there was such a thing. But when you're in love, anything is possible. I held that piece of metal in my hand and saw my whole future in front of me. But they were just wishes from my past."

"Desires, even," Kim completed the thought. "Fantasies of how life should be, what love looks like when it's right."

"Exactly. I thought a ring could seal a connection. Or that a promise of marriage could set a relationship down in the book of love."

"Wrong!"

Roswitha took another sip from her mug. "Can I offer you anything else?"

Kim placed a hand over her mug. "No, thank you." She cleared her throat and slid back in the brown leather chair.

"Don't you think it would be better to forgot him?"

"Look. Memories are all that I have left of him, memories and an empty bank account. If I give them up, all that's left for me is my anger. Is that supposed to be any better?"

"What I mean is…well, how can I say it? My problem is that I always notice too late when I've fallen into a trap. And I'm afraid that if I romanticize my memories, I won't notice what's happening the next time around."

"Why is it romanticizing if I just like to remember the way he called me honey? That's something at least. No one can take that away from me."

Roswitha looked into her eyes. Kim had grown very quiet all of a sudden. She realized her next words would crush Roswitha's illusions to dust, carrying them away in a single breath. Knowing this, she spoke softly and slowly, and Roswitha grew more feverish with every syllable that left her lips: "Honey, sunshine, bunny, pumpkin, doll face, butterfly." Kim counted off the terms of endearment that had flown from his mouth like cold, clear spring water on a summer's day. And with every new word Roswitha winced as if Kim were shooting arrows at her.

"He told me he had never been with a woman who understood him so well, who was so good. He had never felt so close to anyone. He wanted to melt into me. Shall I go on?"

Roswitha shook her head. Bitterness flooded over her, rolling down her cheeks in thick drops. She grabbed her napkin and turned away. She was ashamed of her stupidity. How could she have been taken in by this cheap scam?

Reality rained blows upon her. But as much as it hurt, it also felt good, relieving, liberating, like iodine on an open wound or a fire devouring deceitful love letters.

Kim sat at the opposite end of the table. She couldn't have touched Roswitha even if she had stretched her arm as far as it would go, and yet she felt close to her. Not close like one lover to another, but close like veins and blood.

Her heart was heavy and her chest was tight. In her stomach, an insatiable hunger roared, and at the same time, nausea. She wanted to stand up and go over to her, kneel down before Roswitha and hug her. But she knew this pain well. No embrace, no words, not all the gold in the world could help. It was a pain that had to soothe itself. So instead she remained sitting, wrapping her arms around herself.

"What am I supposed to do now?" Roswitha asked desperately.

Kim was surprised by her question. There were thousands of possibilities, but which was the right one? She couldn't answer for Roswitha, but for herself it was clearer than ever: for once, she had to be stronger than the men who had done this to her. She had to find revenge. But who deserved it most, she wondered - and at that very moment it became clear.

33.

"Have you been able to reach Ludwig?"

"No, and I've tried at least twenty times. I even left him a message at the office, but he's just not calling back."

"Then we need to decide without him."

"Have you thought about it any more?"

"Eberhard absolutely doesn't want her to move in with us. And to be honest, with the way things are between us, I don't think it's a good idea. Besides, she doesn't want to leave Heidelberg."

"That's understandable. She would have to leave behind all her friends and acquaintances. But I think it's a total pipe dream for her to stay in that house."

"All of her memories are there. Not just of Papa, but of us kids. We were all born there. She saw us grow up there."

"But it's a crazy idea to have this Divya move in and live with her. I'm sure she's competent, but why should she spend day and night taking care of a woman she's not related to?"

"That's her job. Mama pays her for it."

"Well, it seems strange to me. It just doesn't feel right."

"What does Bernhard say about it?"

"I haven't gotten a sensible word out of him. He's still babbling stuff about the war. I think this whole thing has taken an unbelievable toll on him."

"He blames himself. Which is understandable. I mean, Papa did practically die right after that scene at dinner. You could actually assume it had something to do with Bernhard's…well, you know… but it must have been just a dumb coincidence. Don't you think?"

"Yeah, well, who knows?"

34.

"Don't think so much," Kim had advised him in parting, hugging him tightly to her chest. "Give your head a chance to recover."

But it was much too late for that. Bernhard already knew too much: the persecution of gays under the Nazis, the murder of innocent lovers, his father's heart attack after discovering his son was gay, the much too life-like dreams, the insignia in his father's night box. Too many things fit together for him to just push them aside. It was like a song that was stuck in his head, or a face he recognized without being able to think of the name. He could try to forget, he could try to distract himself, but the next moment the thoughts returned. And then he would pick at it like at a hangnail, knowing it would hurt to pull at it, that it might bleed or even get infected, but still he was not able to leave it alone: he had to rip it off.

Bernhard was looking for the key, the one piece of information that would illuminate everything. Meanwhile he had discovered many things: for example, that no one seemed to bother with this issue any more. Was the persecution of gays less a part of our history than the murder of the Jews, gypsies or preachers? Was no one interested anymore to learn that homosexuals were used back then as living targets for soldiers' shooting practice? Or what they did with the metal buckets? They pulled a bucket over a prisoner's head and drummed on it until he went crazy. Then there was the snow-clearing order: prisoners were forced to shovel snow from one end of the camp to the other, and then when they were done they would receive an order to carry everything back—with their hands!

As if it weren't sick enough that countless victims were tortured to death in clay quarries, it was quite common among concentration camp leaders and SS officers to have male partners. Himmler himself, the greatest anti-gay agitator, immortalized his own homoerotic fantasies in his diaries. But is was the gays who were called perverts?

From early on in school, he had learned about the Nazis, and continued learning about them at university. The horror of it had made him shudder, but it had also remained distant, like a film. He could look away or just turn off the television, and everything would go away. At every moment, the certainty remained that these images could only have arisen from the sick mind of a screenwriter. But this time it was different. This time, he lived the horror directly; looking away couldn't protect him any longer.

"Rather a hot pig than an ice-cold criminal," he murmured into his empty room.

Now, as he sat at his desk holding his head in his hands, he had to admit that he had come no closer to understanding what was going on inside him. What was he supposed to make of this pain, this grief over a person he didn't even know? Where was it supposed to go? What could he do against it?

There was nothing he could do, nothing at all. He could only find peace for himself: and he needed to start with it right now.

35.

The chair was hard and uncomfortable. The people seated in the rows in front of him were hanging on every word from the speaker's lips. The whole thing reminded him too much of the horrible boring hours he had spent as a child in church.

Edvard had arrived late. He didn't think they would be so exact about it. But why was someone actually giving a speech?

"…and today, I'm particularly glad to welcome a new face into our circle." All heads turned towards Edvard as if on command.

The man sitting next to him jabbed him in the ribs with his elbow. "Stand up and say your name," he whispered to Edvard.

He recoiled. Hesitantly, he got up from his chair.

"My name is…Edvard."

"And?" someone asked him compassionately.

Finally he deciphered the sign the speaker had been covering up until then.

"And…I think I'm in the wrong room." He turned around and ran out. Make sure you go through the door on the right, that's what Gerhard had said.

Edvard knocked hesitantly on the left door. Someone opened it, and he was greeted by a horde of flaming queens.

"Ah, my darling. I was afraid you were going to stand us up."

There were about fifteen men in the circle. The youngest was barely twenty, the oldest in his mid-fifties. There were three plates of Christmas cookies on the table, a pair of thermos flasks and fir branches covered with purple ribbons. The room was filled with an urgent ticking.

"No, I just ended up in the wrong room."

"No way! Alcoholics Anonymous? Because Gerhard always mixes up left and right. One of these days we'll have to tattoo it onto his hands!"

"Sit down."

Edvard joined the circle. The scent of cinnamon lay in the air, with a clear note of ylang tea.

"Won't you introduce your friend to us?" asked a young man with a shaved head and glasses that made his eyes bulge as if they were inside a goldfish bowl.

"This is Edvard. We've known each other for what…fifteen years?"

"Seventeen."

"Weren't you at the game night yesterday in the gay communication center? I think I saw you there."

"The last five nights I've been to every event that crossed my path. Tomorrow I'll become an alcoholic just so as to have a reason to sit over there with them."

"Edvard is lovesick," Gerhard explained to the other man, turning down the corners of his mouth.

"And I thought you were out looking for a wife," another man said, his eyes gleaming. He moved the knitting needles so quickly that stitches seemed to simply fall off them. Beneath his fingers, delicate blue rompers were growing.

"No, I just can't handle it at home."

"Poor thing. Shall I come and comfort you? Just give me your telephone number."

The circle laughed shrilly, and even Edvard himself couldn't contain a grin.

"Here. Here are the needles," his neighbor said, passing him a basket. "You should take the bamboo ones, you'll get rheumatism from the steel ones. Start with the thick ones, they fit better in your hand and it goes quicker…"

"Ooooooh!" the others howled.

"As it does with other things too," he added, fiddling with his T-shirt in embarrassment. *I'm not gay, but my lover is* it said in pink letters. He laid his long, slim fingers intimately on Edvard's knee and whispered: "I'll just do a few stitches for you, then you can try it."

Edvard rolled his eyes.

"Everything is permitted here, as long as you knit. Those are our club rules. It is a knitting group after all," Gerhard explained.

Edvard acted defeated, picked up the stitch-covered needles and tried his luck. With grim determination, he looped the woolen thread round twice; the third stitch slipped through the needles. He let the knitting things fall and turned towards Gerhard.

"I made a mistake," Edvard said in a whiny tone.

"Well that's what we're here for," his friend said calmly, taking the needle from his hand.

"No, I don't mean the stitching. I'm talking about Bernhard."

"Oh." Gerhard gave the needle back to him.

"I didn't trust him."

"That happens to the best of us. But should he be so impossible just because of that?"

"What are you referring to?"

"Well, if you want my opinion," explained Gerhard and went on without waiting for Edvard's answer. "After the scene at your party and the things that have happened since then…"

"What things?"

"That whole story with the police, the unanswered letters, the flowers, the phone calls, etcetera."

"How do you know about all that?"

Gerhard placed his fingertips defensively on his chest. "It's the talk of the city."

"Next thing I know you'll write it up on a bulletin board!"

"I think it's posted up there already," said the young man on Gerhard's other side; his smile was innocent and sweet.

Edvard huffed and threw his knitting things onto the table.

"Come on," said his neighbor. "You lose one little stitch and you're already close to tears. We'll have to dub you Our Lady of Impatience."

"Our Lady of Impatience!" the others called in chorus.

Gerhard poured out tea that smelled like Christmas and held a plate of cookies out to Edvard.

"Let's a drink a cup of tea to that!"

Edvard looked at him furiously, then grabbed for a cookie in a conciliatory gesture.

"Well, I would have sent him packing a long time ago."

"There are so many yummy men," another interspersed while concentrating doggedly on transferring the woolen thread from one needle to the next. "Look at us. On your first visit you can choose whomever you like."

"It's not about having sex," Edvard answered, annoyed.

"Shame," someone piped up.

"I want a man, I want love, I want a relationship. Too much importance is placed on sex."

"Someone's talking big!" a red-haired man butted in. "Gerhard? Isn't he *the* Edvard?"

"What do you mean, *the* Edvard?" he asked, regretting it instantly. The scene already seemed to know his whole life.

"I still remember how much you used to praise the advantages of the single life," said Gerhard. "Your debauchery made me feel like I ought to split up and emulate you."

"Wasn't he the one who even went cruising in the classical music department of *Ludwig Beck*?"

"Yeah, after they banned him from the *Four Seasons* hotel for hitting on men in the elevator." Gerhard laughed resoundingly, and Edvard wished the ground would swallow him up.

It was true. It had always been much more exciting for him to try something or somebody new. Every body was different, every mouth, every ass, every cock. Everyone kissed differently, and the things they did with their hands! There were the withdrawn, quiet types who blossomed into entirely different people in intimate settings. Edvard had seen cocky machos whimper; rough, hard men who made their money with a hammer and axe could melt into unexpected tenderness. But his favorite thing was to "crack" businessmen. It always had given him particular pleasure to peel these buttoned-up model citizens out of their dark suits, and to lead these CEOs, politicians, managers and God knows what else, twitching, to a 'little death'.

There had been nothing wrong about living that way. He had never lacked anything. He had enjoyed his freedom, and because he had so many friends, there was always someone there when he needed someone to listen.

"I've always wanted a man. It just took me a while to realize it," he said softly.

"Mir. Right, that's what we all want. But fidelity? Those are uptight heterosexual ideas," another interjected.

"Gays aren't made that way," one of the homos said. "You can see that in all the porn we have," another answered. "We're much more…" He searched for the right word. "Sexual!"

"Well, the breeders also have some porn on offer, that has nothing to do with being gay," another answered. "Homosexuality is just a cheap excuse for some people."

Edvard's neighbor clapped him on the shoulder. "Nice to have a new face among us. Kind of revitalizing having you here."

"Although it's not ever boring, is it?" a voice rang out from the other side of the table.

"A toast to the fresh meat!" They lifted their tea mugs.

"And you'll learn to knit eventually," his neighbor added.

Edvard let a sip of the lukewarm tea run down his dry throat.

"What are you going to do about Bernhard?" Gerhard asked.

"Nothing. I'll wait until he's ready."

Gerhard raised his eyebrows skeptically. "And in the meantime he'll have fun with other men."

"That's nonsense! Bernhard's not like that. He would never sleep with anyone else."

36.

What were you supposed to bring a sixty-five year old man who invites you to dinner? Music, maybe? But how was he supposed to know what Raimondo liked to listen to? Chocolates? That's what you brought your grandmother. A jar of caviar; since he was obviously a connoisseur?

Roses were a crazy idea; this became apparent to Bernhard when tears came to Raimondo's eyes at the mere sight of them. How could he have been so stupid? Bernhard lowered his head in embarrassment.

"On time, as befits a teacher," said Raimondo, taking the flowers from him. "Come in."

He led his guest into the apartment. Raimondo gave off the scent of fresh laundry, cologne and Healthy Heart Tonic. He wore brown corduroys, a light blue shirt and a silk vest with a cowboy on the back attempting to tame a wildly bucking horse. A dark-blue kerchief with red polka-dots covered his throat. Every hair seemed to be in place, the entire man ironed clean.

"I must warn you. My cleaning lady went home for the holidays. It looks awful."

Taking off his guest's coat, he steered him into the living room. The furniture there stood so far apart that Bernhard felt the indescribable urge to pull it together. A six-foot cherry wood dresser with dozens of drawers towered behind the door, and a bookshelf covered the entire wall. The grand piano stretched its gaping maw out towards him. Bernhard felt like an intruder. Only the leather sofa and chair stood close enough to one another, looking like an oasis, an island drifting on the fishbone parquet. Bernhard made his way towards them.

Raimondo placed the roses in a transparent Lalique vase adorned with a light-green faun.

"What would you like to drink? We can open a bottle of Barolo later, it goes fantastically with the food. Or would you rather have white wine? It's fine either way. I've got everything. Feel free to choose."

"No, no, I like red wine," said Bernhard, not wanting to complicate things.

"Should we toss back a Campari first?" the host asked conspiratorially, raising his hands as if justifying himself in front of the good Lord. "Gourmets would throw their hands in the air and run away screaming. Pure poison, you don't have to tell me, I know. But it's a touch of home for me, and I just can't do without it."

Raimondo disappeared; Bernhard looked for something to hold onto. He traced his open hand along the overflowing bookshelf. German classics rubbed shoulders with gay poets: Goethe, Stephen Spender, Oscar Wilde, Hermann Hesse, Hölderlin, Christopher Isherwood, Schiller. The collected works of Tennessee Williams waited there to be marveled at, and a whole row of Italian novelists: Tornabuoni, of course, he had been on Edvard's shelf as well; that was wartime pornography. Moravia, Antonio Tabucchi, Umberto Eco, Fruttero & Lucentini. L'amante senza fissa dimora, Bernhard loved that book. In front of them, between them, and all around them were small vases, old postcards and jewelry.

It was dusty, true, but nevertheless it gave an impression of cleanliness, of almost housewifely comfort. The life-size photograph of a naked young man hanging on the opposite side of the room did not contradict this at all.

"Satisfied?" Raimondo handed his guest a glass of red, bubbly liquid. Bernhard wrinkled his brow. "With my collection of books?"

"Yeah, yeah," he stuttered. "Seems decent, I think."

"I took the liberty of adding some champagne to the Campari. It opens the stomach." Then he looked at Bernhard appraisingly. "You don't mind my getting your phone number from Kim, do you?"

"No, no. I…I was very glad." Bernhard tried to smile.

"All right then. To our friendship."

"To our friendship."

Grey, shimmering satin flowed over the huge table. On the front corner, crystal glasses stood out from this snowy landscape, along with knife rests, silver cutlery and large polished plates. Curtains hung modestly in front of the three windows looking out on the garden; candles flickered expectantly on the walls.

They ate in silence. Not even the silverware dared clatter. There was something solemn in the air, something delicate that didn't want to be frightened off. Furtive glances were exchanged. A cough, an attempt to speak, then, again, silence in the flickering candlelight.

And then Raimondo embarked upon a lecture about his philosophy of food. Suddenly he set down his fork, rocked back in his chair as if he were about to jump up, wiped his bristly mustache with a linen napkin, and began before he had swallowed his last bite: "The rotten thing about our society is that people scarf down large portions of tasteless and over-spiced dishes, then wonder why they lose their appetites. Serve small portions, be modest, then neither the palate nor the spirit will tire."

Raimondo's small portions were so small that Bernhard sat in front of his first main dish, already amply satisfied after his second appetizer.

"They call themselves gourmets," he began to pitch with further conviction, "simply because they can tell an Italian chardonnay from a Californian one—as if that were a feat. And then they go and buy second-rate olive oil. But olives are like vines. Every location has a different taste, the soil, the fertilizer, the sunlight, even the farmers' hands—so many things influence its character. Good olive oil is just as much a work of art as good wine."

Raimondo served roasted porcini mushrooms—God knows where he had acquired them at this time of year—on arugula with a few drops of strong truffle oil. This was followed by jellied tomatoes in a sauce of whipped mascarpone and basil. Then he conjured up a little pigeon—tied up with cords—from the oven, surrounded by the thinnest Kenya beans and crowned with an earthy golden yellow potato, followed by a hint of grapefruit sorbet. The baby turbot had been baked in aluminum foil with olives, tomatoes, onions, fresh herbs and olive oil—Tuscan in this case, because it had a fuller taste, and only oil from that region could compete with this potpourri of vegetables—immersing the guest in the illusion of sitting in Portofino on a stone terrace carved out of the rocks, looking out as the fog crept over the ocean with the evening wind.

"As long as you are only eating to fill your stomach," Raimondo began another one of his ideas, "you will always remain hungry. As long as you are only cooking because you are afraid to starve, you are a servant at best. As long as eating doesn't give you anything beyond the feeling of fullness, you're a mere philistine. It's only when you let yourself be carried away by the fine character of a dish, only when you have in mind the body who will eat your food from the moment you begin shopping, only when you become aware that every bite is a part of your personal history, that you know what savoring really means."

Slowly, Bernhard was beginning to understand his host. His gestures, his words, his thoughts. There was nothing that simply took up time and space. Everything, down to the last breath, was bent on a goal: to seduce. Raimondo savored, and he would draw on unlimited resources until he sank drunkenly to his death.

Bernhard remembered Plato's words when he claimed that "beauty is in the eye of the beholder." Raimondo was proof of the opposite: Raimondo lived beauty itself, he offered it up for everyone to see.

The dishes seemed almost to cook themselves, but Raimondo still had to keep disappearing, leaving Bernhard alone with his thoughts.

Soon a feeling of comfort settled within him, greater than any he had experienced in a long time. Every moment, the tension of the past few weeks melted away a bit more. It was so beautiful here. Even by night, even by candlelight, these rooms seemed radiant.

"Some more wine?" Raimondo was already letting the dark, blood-red wine trickle into the glass. It was delicious, but Bernhard felt the urge to decline. He wanted at least to refuse something before he lost himself entirely. But the glass was already full, and Bernhard raised it to his lips.

"Go into the living room. I'll just clean up here, then I'll come and join you."

"Can I help?"

"No, no, no, no, no. This is my evening. Go, sit down, vamoose!" Raimondo pushed his guest gently through the double door. His grasp was firm and determined, but filled with desire. Bernhard turned and looked at him—for much too long.

Raimondo shut the door in his face. Bernhard went over to the grand piano and laid his fingers on the cool keys. He played individual notes, delicate ethereal melodies, then silence fell again.

Outside, snowflakes rushed by the windowpane. Bernhard leaned on the wide wooden windowsill, watching their traces in the dark blue of the night.

Desire arose in his breast. Not for sex, not for a new relationship, not even for love. That would have frightened him. He just wanted to be held, to feel another person's warmth for a moment, hear another person's blood rushing in his ears. He wanted to go into the kitchen, press his face into Raimondo's chest, and feel his hot breath in his hair.

He felt hands on his shoulder, and suddenly Bernhard's stomach pulled itself into a knot. The touch was so soft, so careful and shy.

Before Bernhard had accepted the invitation to dinner, he had understood: the New Year's kiss, the deep look, the farewell deep with meaning and the phone call the day after. Raimondo wanted him, and Bernhard needed a bit of security, a place of refuge from the horror of his inner world. But since he had known Edvard, he hadn't touched another man. Bernhard wanted to melt into these hands, but he was afraid.

A fat bluebottle between the double-glass windows caught Bernhard's eye. Covered in dust, its legs reached skywards. Last summer it had buzzed around sugar, from one salty skin to the next. Life was so short, much too short, Bernhard thought, laying his head on Raimondo's chest.

They were lying in bed. Raimondo couldn't take his eyes off him, Bernhard kept his closed. Each of them cautiously explored the other's body with their hands. Cuddling with Raimondo felt like putting a hand in a drawer of silk stockings while walking straight into a Rubens painting. Everything was present in abundance; it poured right out of him. Everything was soft and warm and gentle. Raimondo's skin was sweet as marshmallows. Bernhard, on the other hand, was firm, his muscles tight under a thin layer of skin, stretching over his ribs.

Bernhard climbed Raimondo's belly, let himself be embraced and rocked, drifting on his breath like a floe in the ocean. A small pink nipple swelled beneath his cheek and grew hard. Bernhard kissed it, licked it, sucked on it, then gradually his tongue made its way towards Raimondo's mouth. They grasped for one another like carp gasping for air. Their tongues beat against one another, circling in each other's mouths, as if to make sure that every inch was coated with saliva. Their bodies heated, glowed; cooling sweat formed on their skin, their foreheads, their backs, growing to large beads and rolling down onto the twisted sheets. They rubbed and slid until their erections were struggling against one another; Raimondo's was thick and soft, Bernhard's hard and long. A pillow slid off the bed; the blanket, startled by the flailing legs, soon followed.

Raimondo's tongue found its way to Bernhard's cheeks, up to his eyelids, back to his ears, his throat, his chest. Bernhard tilted his head far back, offering himself to the older man: a bite, followed by panting, then they spilled onto each other's bodies.

Raimondo grew pale, almost transparent. He gasped, gave one more twitch, then color returned slowly to his face. Bernhard sank down into the sweat-soaked sheets, exhausted. Hectic breathing was heard in the air, slowly calming.

Tenderly, their hands found one another, their eyes met and Bernhard climbed back up onto Raimondo's belly; their sperm dried and stuck them together.

Raimondo stroked a strand of hair out of Bernhard's sweaty face. "What are you thinking about?"

His eyes opened wide. He looked at Raimondo, then slid off him and curled up on his shoulder.

"Something is weighing you down."

After a while, Bernhard turned onto his back, pulled Raimondo's hand from underneath his head and laid it on his stomach. "I keep thinking about my father. I somehow never really connected with him."

"Did he know you're gay?"

Bernhard turned his head and looked at Raimondo.

"He…found out. My niece blurted it out at dinner."

"Ouch!" He bit his lips. "And how did he react?"

"He gave me a nasty look, stood up without saying a word and left. I never saw him again. Soon after that he had a heart attack and died."

"I hope you don't blame yourself?" Raimondo was indignant.

Bernhard shrugged his shoulders. "Maybe he just couldn't handle it."

"Bernhard, you're connecting things that don't belong together. *You* are gay, *he* had a heart attack. You're turning life into a game of chess. You have to live *your* life, you're the only one responsible for it. And even if—though I seriously doubt it—your father had such a big problem with you being gay that he suffered a heart attack, it's still his own choice."

Bernhard looked at him doubtfully, but there was a little hope in his eyes that Raimondo was telling the truth. "You think?"

Raimondo pulled him closer to him and held him tight against his chest. "How old was your father?"

"Seventy-one."

"Then he grew up in a time where being gay was still considered shameful, and gays were sent to concentration camps along with convicts."

"That's no excuse."

"No it isn't, you're right. I only wanted to point out that the older generation grew up with very different ideas. We were told that homosexuality was a disease, like cancer or AIDS today, you understand? Maybe he wasn't looking at you hatefully, but fearfully, because he knew someone who was taken away, a neighbor or a friend. Maybe he was just afraid for you."

Bernhard chewed his lower lip. He considered how probable Raimondo's ideas were.

"Was he a sick man?" Raimondo asked.

"What?"

"Because of the heart attack, I mean. Did it come out of nowhere?"

"No. He always had heart problems. Then a few years ago he had two attacks, one right after another. He was always at the doctor's. Every week it was something else. Hemorrhoids, then his prostate, then colon polyps. What do I know."

Raimondo laughed a deep, loud laugh that shook his large belly.

"What's so funny?"

"I'm sorry," Raimondo was still laughing. "But it sounds as if he let people play around with his things a lot?"

Play around with his things? He went to the doctor, that has nothing to do with sex! And then the images appeared again: the war, the shock in his father's eyes, the horrible words of the SS henchmen, the torture, the suffering, the brazen expression in the blond soldier's face.

Bernhard felt at the mercy of them; he needed protection. So he curled up and pulled Raimondo's arms over his chest. In Edvard's arms his thoughts always calmed down, no matter how much they had been raging beforehand. A kiss, a word, a touch, and he had relaxed—not so with Raimondo.

Raimondo had only ever gotten roses from women, friends or his family, never from anyone he had spent the night with. When Bernhard brought him the roses, an old hope awoke in him again. And he had been carrying it around with him all night. Before, as they clung to one another, he had even believed he might be able to keep this young man. But now that he had crawled into his armpit and shut his eyes tight, he felt his Bernhard slipping away from him.

"I would like to go on vacation with you," he whispered into the stillness. Bernhard didn't react. "Let's fly to Capri. My cousin owns a beautiful hotel there. You could swim, and I would watch you from the terrace."

Bernhard lay on his back. His eyes were dark, as if a shadow had come over them.

"You don't want to, do you? You'll never sleep with me again, will you?" Raimondo asked in a whisper. "No, don't answer." He laid a finger on his lips. "Sleep with me, sleep with me just one more time."

Bernhard's breath was peaceful and even. In sleep, his lips relaxed and swelled to small, soft hills.

In the morning, Raimondo wanted to bake a Pan d'Oro for him, the goddess of doughs. He wanted to hold onto Bernhard at all costs.

He would need almonds for that, lots of butter, vanilla and a bit of rum. Raimondo would bake before Bernhard even thought of getting up. Then the fine, seductive aroma would creep into his dreams and connect him with Raimondo's love. And when Bernhard woke up, he would already be lost in almonds, raisins, and candied orange peel, the threads of dough would have long since spun a thick net around him.

Bernhard would fall in love before he even brought the first piece of golden cake to his lips, and after the first bite he wouldn't want to leave Raimondo ever again.

Butter, vanilla, rum and eggs. Oh God, the eggs! Raimondo had forgotten to buy any. Now he couldn't even bake for him.

37.

Kim had intended to just burst in there and cry out: rapist! She wanted to throw it in his face right there, in the waiting room in front of all his female patients. He had groped her, he had exploited her weakness and even tried to bully her afterwards. They should know what kind of doctor was examining them, who they were exposing their most private parts to. She was carrying the evidence of his misdeed in her womb.

Kim had seen the lead dagger start to glow at the mere notion of this act. But then she had realized that such an act wouldn't prove her maturity or establish her as a believable person. In the end, she needed more than revenge; she needed a solution for the child. So she had chosen a different strategy for her revenge: the clueless, innocent tactic.

Ten o'clock seemed like a suitable time to show up at the practice. With her hips swinging, she walked in, filled in the registration form, entered her birth date, acknowledged that she suffered from hay fever in August, and gave Raimondo's name and address in case anyone needed to be notified. Pregnant? "Yes," indicated with a large checkmark. The receptionist's face remained expressionless. Silly cow, thought Kim. She could have at least congratulated her. Then she sat down and waited, along with seventeen other women, to be admitted through the white door.

The magazine rustled at every turn of the page, but she didn't even read the headlines, only perceiving the images as blurs of color; as soon as she reached the end, she started over from the beginning.

She would let herself be examined. Quite simple. She would act as if she had never encountered him before. No different from all these other women sitting here in these wicker chairs under posters of all the beaches in the world.

Kim looked around. Most of the patients were older than her. Some of them had pulled down books on cancer prevention from the unpolished wooden bookshelf and were studying them intently. No one had dared to pick up the AIDS pamphlets, it seemed.

Kim was actually prepared to let herself be examined. He would be sure to try and grope her again, and she could call for help while he stood there unable to hide his erection. But even if that didn't happen, she would still end up confronting him. And here, on this narrow playing field, he couldn't just hang up the phone or walk away.

In the corner, under the net-curtained window looking out on the historic city, there was a white shag rug and boxes around it with children's toys: wood building blocks, giant Legos in bright colors, some dolls and a wide assortment of picture books.

New patients kept coming in; others were called in and disappeared into the consulting room. Every time the door opened, Kim hid her face behind the magazine. She wanted to make sure he wouldn't be able to prepare for their conversation. She had thought of everything.

At quarter past twelve, it was finally her turn. And suddenly, it didn't seem so simple to her. She hadn't planned on her knees shaking the way they were. Then she sat in front of him and had to fight off tears. How was she supposed to speak when her heart kept beating so loudly?

Dr. Hohleben, on the other hand, smiled disarmingly and leaned back in his chair, relaxed.

"Not bad," he said, took off his gold-framed glasses, stretched his arm behind his head and crossed his right leg over the left. All in slow motion.

"You must have found me on the passenger list."

She nodded. One to nil for Kim.

"That is not allowed, is it? Because of customer confidentiality, I mean."

Kim swallowed, her legs prickled, the turbulence in her stomach grew. What now? Attack! "I came for an examination. I think I'm pregnant."

"Ah, really?"

He was so charming, a doctor you trusted unconditionally. It would be easy to fall for him, but Kim pulled herself together. She had something to accomplish.

He took her patient sheet and read: "So your last name is Davideit, born on March second, nineteen hundred seventy-one, which makes you twenty-five. Height, five foot two, weight one hundred pounds." He looked at her doubtfully. "And now you're pregnant. Had unprotected sex? That can be dangerous!"

Kim was fuming, but she wasn't going to let herself be intimidated that easily.

"All right, then get undressed. The dressing area is back there."

Kim stood up, her knees had grown weaker. Undress? When she imagined it, it had been very easy, but now, under the enemy's derisive glare? Just look at his fingers: well-manicured, clean, tan and white on the inner surface from so much washing. If she undressed now, she would be naked in the truest sense of the word.

"You don't need to examine me. I've already been to another doctor. I'm pregnant."

"Then what are you doing in my practice?" His lips narrowed smugly, defiance in his eyes. He was a pro at intimidating; she had to give him that. But she hadn't played all her trumps.

"It's your baby. If you won't admit to that, I will apply for a paternity test."

He fumed, and the charm disappeared from his face for a moment. Kim looked down at him entrenched behind his desk, sucking lewdly on his knobbly index finger. She'd gotten the better of him.

"You really think you could pin this on me? You're deluding yourself. It's not so simple. For one thing, you'd need to prove we had sex."

"No problem, the steward saw us," she blurted out, immediately gnawed by doubt whether that flaky fairy would stand by her.

"Then you'll have to put together a list of all your sexual partners, and they will all be invited to a blood test. It will be very, very embarrassing for you. What's more, the test is not at all conclusive, and I will challenge it."

Her courage fell. Don't give up, the dagger called for revenge; he would assist her, she could tell.

"And the third thing is, paternity can only be proven after the child is ten years old. Until then, you will pay the court and lawyer costs, and for the kid. And on top of that, I'll stick a libel suit on you. It will all be very expensive."

Kim felt her breath taken away. "What are you trying to say?" she said meekly.

"It's not my kid, and it will never be." He leaned back, and Kim went up to him as if he were pulling her by an invisible hook. "But… that's unbelievable!"

The doctor propped his head up and smiled at her expectantly. The ground grew hot beneath her feet, and she literally felt the soles of her platforms melting.

"But…" Kim's stomach cramped, and she could feel the dagger slowly turning.

"You swine!" she cried. "You swine! You swine!" and ran out. "This doctor! He's impossible!" she whispered barely audibly. The receptionist raised an eyebrow and then immersed herself again in patients' charts. In the background, a chair squeaked, someone appeared in the door to the staff room.

"He will pay," Kim swore. "He will pay, even if it's the last thing I accomplish in this lifetime." Then she stormed out.

"Next, please," said the doctor, grinning.

38.

"Mama!"

"Bernhard, my boy. Nice of you to call. You've been in my thoughts the past two days. How are you?"

"Everything's great, Mom. I'm just preparing for school, that's why I've been a bit incommunicado."

"Well I'm glad to hear it. I've been worrying enough about Sieglinde. I don't want to have to worry about you too."

"Mama?"

"Yes?"

"I wanted to ask you something. Do you know where Papa was stationed during the war?"

"I have no idea. He never talked about the war."

"Didn't he have any comrades?"

"Oh God, I'm sure he did, but he wanted nothing to do with them."

"Oh really? Why not?"

"For your father, the war was over and done with. I remember when one of them tried to call us. That must have been in the sixties, I think it was the twentieth anniversary or something like that. Papa was at the office, so I passed on the message, but he didn't call back. A few days later, his comrade called again, and I gave Papa the receiver; he just hung up—without a word. Afterwards he was grumpy for days."

"And he never mentioned anything?"

"What would he have mentioned?"

Bernhard was looking for more pieces of the puzzle, but he didn't want to explain that to her right now. "Oh, nothing."

"Bernhard, I'm worried. Since Papa died, you've changed completely. Something isn't right with you."

So many things were wrong. His whole life was a mass of chaos.

"It's all right. I…tell me something more about my grandparents, Dad's parents I mean."

"His mother took her own life in the war, and his father…" She moaned. "My boy, do you need to know all this? It's been over and done with for so long."

"What happened to his father?"

"Papa never talked about it, but I once heard that he apparently ended up in a concentration camp and died there."

"In a concentration camp? He never told us that."

"Well why would he? What would it have changed? It's bad enough that it happened, why do you want to burden yourself with it?"

"But why was he in a concentration camp?" Maybe this had something to do with his father's behavior.

"Bernhard, I don't know. Lots of people ended up in the concentration camps. It was a simple way of clearing undesirable people out of the way, even if it was just the neighbor who played his music too loud. Denunciation was the order of the day."

She was right. The reason would have had little significance, and yet he wanted to know what it was.

"Can you really not remember at all, Mom?"

"I never knew, Bernhard. Really. I don't think even Papa knew. Don't think about it so much."

That was quite a light way of putting it, considering his whole life had fallen into single, enigmatic pieces in a matter of days.

And there was one more thing he couldn't get out of his head, Raimondo's joke when he said: "…it sounds as if he let other people play around with his things."

"Papa went to the doctor a lot, right?"

"He always had to have his blood levels checked—because of the medication."

"No, I didn't mean because of his heart. I'm talking about…you know, his prostate and colon."

"Yes, he often had problems with his digestion. But the doctor explained to us that that's not unusual among heart patients."

Yes, but what did the prostate have to do with the heart? "Did he ever have…a friend?" he asked carefully.

"Of course we had friends. Our neighbors, he was in a bowling club, and he had his poker buddies. But as you know, Papa tended to be a more withdrawn person. If you mean a real friend…"

"I mean…" No, he couldn't ask her if his father had ever slept with a man. That would simply hurt her. "Forget it."

"Would you just spit it out? What are you struggling with?"

"I wanted to ask if he was ever truly close to another man."

There was a sudden emptiness on the other end of the line, then she answered in an unusually harsh tone of voice: "I have one thing to say to you: don't go looking to your father for the origins of your… feelings. That's not right of you."

"I was just hoping he wasn't as lonely as I always believed."

His mother didn't respond. The silence was broad, flowing like oil from the receiver, cleaving his mouth shut. He knew she knew he was lying.

"Don't you think it's about time we really talked?" she asked finally, and her words were motherly again.

He understood what she was referring to, but he wanted to avoid this conversation. For years he had dodged the subject, believing his private life didn't concern anybody. And now that his father had died knowing about him, that his father had perhaps even died because of that knowledge, he really didn't want to talk about it. On the other hand, he felt a yearning to finally express it. Then he heard himself say. "School starts up again tomorrow. I can't come until next weekend."

"Good. I have nothing planned. I'm looking forward to your visit."

"Mom, I didn't even ask you…how are you doing?" he added.

"I'm well, my son, very, very well. I've never been better."

Bernhard sat at the computer again. He had used the last few hours to summarize everything he had read in the statistics: various estimates of the number of homosexuals executed in the camps, the estimated number of unreported cases on top of that, the probable number of homosexuals in Germany based on Hirschfeld's research, all the executions that had taken place outside of the war zones, and many other things—somehow, he had to come closer to the source of his visions.

But it hadn't helped him at all. And since it was impossible for him to simply sit still with all his racing thoughts, he had attempted to translate his lack of emotion for his father, along with his inability to forgive him, into statistics. How long would it take? He wanted to know, leafing through psychological literature—books that discussed grief the way other texts discussed constructing high-rise buildings. They didn't make him sad, but they didn't free him from the pressure left by his father's death either.

And as if all these questions weren't enough of a torment, a very different question was torturing him even more: would he get back together with Edvard?

The doorbell broke his stream of thought, but Bernhard was immersed in an article by a professor who had written a study on the average length of homosexual relationships and the most common problems that caused couples to split up: promiscuity, social pressure, family pressure, lack of confidence and fear of coming out.

The doorbell rang again. Bernhard stood up, lost in thought; his limbs were stiff from sitting so long, his eyes blurry from concentrating on the screen for hours.

He opened the door, blinded by the ceiling light in the corridor.

"Mr. Moll?"

"Yes."

"I'm supposed to give this to you," said a young girl, handing a package to him. And before he could ask her anything, she had disappeared. He undid the cord, tore down the paper and opened the black box: a key. On the note tied to it was written *Here is the key to your life. Use it when you're ready. Edvard.*

Edvard, Edvard. He missed him so much! If only he could conquer his fear.

He put the key down next to the computer and sat down. Maybe he should go to therapy like Kim suggested. No matter what he read, no matter what he did, he got nowhere. True, the visions hadn't overwhelmed him lately the way they had a few days ago, but he could scarcely think of anything but the war.

And how were things supposed to go on with Edvard? At some point, he would have to pick up the phone, thank him for the flowers, the letters, and the key, and explain himself. He owed him that much at least.

He weighed the key to Edvard's apartment in his hand. The polished surface gleamed, a strange presence amidst this chaos. "I want to live with you," Edvard had told him at the party, finally expressing something Bernhard had dreamed of deep down for a long time: to have someone by his side. Not for nothing had he wished for just that every time a shooting star fell from the sky the night of the party.

He picked up the article about problems in same-sex relationships again. Therapy showed evidence of improvement and stabilization in twenty-three percent of cases. God only knew whether they would have improved without outside help.

What do these figures mean? He wondered. Statistics are the mean values of many people's behaviors and feelings. In hospitals, they're used to lull patients into a sense of security: "Every day, hundreds of appendixes are removed. At most, this leads to complications once a year." But what does that mean for the individual? That there was a probability of one in thirty thousand that he would leave there without complications? Or was it more like the lottery: one guy tries his luck for the first time and ends up with the jackpot; other people play all their lives and never win. In individual cases, it's always fifty-fifty. Either you win or you don't. Either you survive an operation or you don't. Either a relationship works or it doesn't. The probability of how something will work out is always fifty-fifty for an individual, and the only way of finding out how it's going to turn out, is to take a risk.

And Bernhard reached for the telephone.

39.

Edvard stood by the fountain in front of the university and waited. His nose was red with the cold, and his breath lay like a white helmet around his shaved head. When he saw Bernhard coming, he took two steps toward him, and then stopped.

"Hello."

"Hello."

They shook each other's hands, cold and stiff.

"How are you?"

"Okay."

"Did you make it through the funeral all right?"

"No problem." Bernhard lowered his head and dug into the snow with his boot. "And you? Recovered from the night at the police station?"

"It was pretty unsettling." Edvard stroked his black, undyed stubble. "Right afterwards, I shaved my head."

Bernhard nodded in understanding.

They were awkward, their words angular as the marble blocks of the surrounding buildings. Something hovered in their words that was much more uncomfortable than the cold.

"Shall we walk a bit?"

They trudged along between the buildings of the university, past student dorms and the veterinary clinic into the English Garden. The sky was gray, the air foggy and palpably thick.

For a long time, they hardly spoke, filling the silence with comments on architectural details, the menu on the park kiosk, or listening to the echo of their steps. It was as if they had to get used to one another all over again.

"I really tried to reach you a bunch of times, but it just never worked."

"Please don't apologize," Edvard interrupted him. "I…should have known you would have a good reason."

They wandered aimlessly through the white expanse. Hardly anybody was out walking; a cyclist zoomed past them, leaving a thin trail in the snow; a golden retriever panted after him, its long tongue hanging out.

"But I…just didn't know what to make of it all: you running away from the party, then I went after you and you weren't home. I waited out in the cold for hours. And then I saw the ring on someone else's finger. I was totally beside myself, you understand?"

Bernhard stopped. "I've just understood. Someone else was wearing the ring?"

"Yeah, a…" Edvard remembered his horny night with Fred, "…a nasty guy. I thought you were involved with him."

"That's ridiculous! I would never…," Raimondo passed through Bernhard's head, "never give your ring away."

"Then how did he get it?"

"I don't know. I think I must have lost it. In any case, it wasn't there the next morning." Bernhard shook his head. "But please explain to me what all that was about at the police station."

Edvard turned away. "Umm, what do you mean?"

"The whole thing with the missing person. Who's this Fred? And what was that hysterical woman's issue with you?"

"Oh God. Do we need to talk about it?" Edvard looked at him. There was an imploring look in his eyes, along with a plea for forgiveness stronger than words could ever have expressed.

"I made a big mistake, okay," Edvard said with a thin voice. "But that merely proves that I…that without you, I'm only half a person."

Shaved, Edvard's head was even smaller and more vulnerable. Bernhard's freezing hands twitched in his coat pockets. He wanted to reach out to Edvard, to pull him close and hold him tight. But he couldn't.

"I think we would have been spared a lot of this if I hadn't kept our relationship a secret," Bernhard admitted after some consideration. "I thought I could avoid so many problems, when in truth I was only creating them. I should have taken you with me to visit my family: then all this wouldn't have happened. At the very least I should have told them about you, and then a single phone call would have been enough to clear up most of the misunderstandings."

Edvard nodded. Now that so much had been said, he felt closer to him again. He took a step towards him, but it seemed as if Bernhard was surrounded by an invisible wall. "Something's still wrong, I can tell. You haven't explained to me why you ran away from the party."

Bernhard looked up. "When we were lying there on the bed…this incredible fear came over me."

"Yeah, you said that. But instead of explaining it to me, you turned and left."

"I can't explain it to you, Edvard. I don't understand it myself. There was a smell of mildew, and suddenly death was in the room. I thought something horrible would happen if I didn't run away. I know it sounds totally crazy."

"Has that ever happened to you before?"

Bernhard shook his head. "No, never before! But since then it's happened often. And every time it's gotten a bit clearer. They're images from the war: soldiers, tanks, trenches, and…a murder."

"Murder?

Bernhard nodded. His eyes were red. "These SS officers torturing a young soldier because he loves a man." Then Bernhard turned away and looked out over the wide park. Edvard wanted to hold him, but he was afraid to touch him. He stepped closer to him; their breath mixed into a large, bright sphere.

"Do you know who the man is?" he asked.

Bernhard shook his head and hid his face in his hands. A cry rose from his throat and was swallowed up in winter silence. Edvard threw his arms around him and held his loudly sobbing boyfriend tight.

There they were standing, two black figures, linked together, just as the Tarot card had said before. "You've searched and found one another," Birgit had interpreted the situation, the karmic bond.

Edvard pulled Bernhard closer. Then he tilted his head back and looked up at the silver-gray sky. But where were the ten chalices?

40.

Sometimes, life was like sailing on the ocean. One minute you're flying along, the wind full force at your back, and then a few moments later you're stranded in the doldrums wondering how long it will last. Kim was reeling between fierce headwinds, moderate tailwinds and a lull in the wind.

The next morning, her situation still seemed hopeless. Dr. Hohleben seemed to have the upper hand. But at noon she discovered from the pregnancy counselor that the doctor had been lying. It would be enough to report his name for the paternity test, then he would be obliged to take a blood test. In addition, the test results would be conclusive even a mere twelve months after birth.

Still, this was only a moderate glimpse of hope: all this assumed she was keeping the baby. Getting revenge on him was surely not enough reason to bring the little pipsqueak into the world.

But if she got an abortion, she would have to pay for it herself—and he would walk away unscathed. She still didn't have the courage to report him to the police. She had no proof, and she believed Dr. Hohleben when he said he would hit her with a libel suit.

At three in the afternoon, Kim had just opened her apartment door and was planning to curl up in a corner with Bon Jovi when the phone rang.

"Mrs. Davideit?"

"Yes, please?"

"My name is Dr. Gisela Hohleben. You were in our office yesterday."

Kim sank to the ground. Was this harpy going to give her trouble as well? She was about to just hang up when she heard: "I would like to help you. Maybe we could sit down together and talk about it, somewhere quiet."

Kim didn't know what to say.

"Would this afternoon work for you?"

How did his wife want to help her, and why, she wondered, making her way through the pedestrian zone. Maybe this apparent help was only a pretext, and she was planning on causing a scene in public. But that would be more embarrassing for her than for Kim. If she wanted to reproach Kim, she could have just showed up on Kim's doorstep.

Kim was cast adrift in life's vastness. Storms came crashing down on her from every direction; she would be able to withstand one more.

"How are you?" the doctor asked in a friendly tone, as if they were two neighbors meeting for a chat.

"Why do you ask?"

"Do you already have cravings for chocolate or sour pickles?"

"Yes, but..."

She laid her hand on Kim's. "Just so as to avoid any misunderstanding. I absolutely don't want a big stir about this."

What was she getting at? Kim furrowed her brow and looked questioningly at the woman.

"I would like to get rid of this matter painlessly. It is my practice as well, after all. I can't afford another scandal like this."

Another? What did that mean? Kim studied the doctor. She wore green pants and a white silk blouse. Her gold brooch matched the earrings she played with constantly. Her hair was white and very short. Perfectly styled, but a bit tomboyish and harsh.

Then Mrs. Hohleben pulled an envelope out of her pocket and set it on the table in front of Kim.

She looked inside it. There was a whole pack of fresh hundred and two hundred bills. There were at least five thousand Marks in it, Kim estimated.

"You'll also find an address inside where this business can be taken care of discreetly and unofficially."

At first, Kim didn't understand why she didn't feel any relief at all. Then, as soon as the surprise had worn off, she felt rage rising up inside her. An abortion wasn't a "business." And she didn't want this woman to buy her off. That piece of shit doctor should at least have the decency to give her the money himself. The whole thing was humiliating, an effrontery.

"You're not serious?" asked Kim. She had to restrain herself from throwing her cappuccino over this woman's far too white blouse.

"After all, it's my practice too," she explained bluntly. "If any of this goes public, I'll be implicated as well." She sounded so matter-of-fact, as if they were negotiating the selling price of a new car.

Kim jumped up. Her hand was on her mug, but she held back. "I can't understand why you, as a betrayed wife, would cover up for your husband. It's perverse." Her voice was loud, with a shrill undertone; some of the café patrons turned their heads.

Mrs. Hohleben's fingers began to tremble; her stoic face twitched, and slowly sank down into her slim gold-ringed hands. "Well, it wouldn't be the first time."

"Excuse me?" Dumbfounded, Kim sat back down. It was just getting more unbelievable.

"Do you think this is difficult only for you?"

"I don't understand."

"Just for a second, stop thinking about yourself. You can't really believe you're the only one. It's been going on like this for years."

"Then why do you protect him?"

"Because he's still…my husband." Then she started to cry.

Kim was stunned. It was pitiful to see that this swine seemed to have total control over this woman. Roswitha's behavior was pathetic enough; were there no women who would defend themselves?

Kim had to think of something, there was no way she wanted to be pushed around like those two women. She said, mostly to herself: "It can't end like this; this can't be how it turns out."

Then it was very quiet for a moment. They were stranded on a wide sea of helplessness—in a lull in the wind. But Kim felt, somewhere far outside herself, that a vicious storm was brewing.

Mrs. Hohleben raised her head, wiped the tears from her face with the back of her hand and rubbed them off. She pulled a handkerchief from her pocket and blew her nose soundlessly, then looked Kim in the eye and said: "I think I might have an idea."

Kim sniffed the air. Now she could smell it: the tailwinds were rising.

41.

When Bernhard was still at school, his classmates had often complained about their boring lessons, too much homework or their awful teachers. But school had always excited Bernhard. He had soaked up information about different forms of life, from the amoeba to the elephant. Chemical processes fascinated him as much as the almost dance-like dynamics of physical formulas, the logic of the Latin language, the links between various economic factors and the ambiguity of clearly formulated laws.

Bernhard was a man of knowledge. But he had never felt the need to pass it on. It had been enough to research, to integrate what he researched into his modes of thought and let it spread on its own, leading him to new questions and realizations.

His reasons for becoming a teacher had been quite different. He became a teacher because of that unique feeling of ten-to-eight-at-school. That was what he looked forward to the most when his alarm clock rang in the morning. He reveled in this bustle, not experienced in this form anywhere else: shrieking, frolicking children, paper airplanes sailing down the hallways, cards changing owners, followed by chewing gum, cigarettes and homework. It caused a tingling sensation when the aroma of hair gel mingled with peppermint, lipstick and Calvin Klein, hot kisses coupled with the fear of disappointment, puppy love and a reluctance to grow up.

Bernhard always compared it to a beehive. Not all the students were after honey, but each tried their best to buzz and beat their wings. Ten-to-eight–at-school was a concentrated charge of youthful drama, so full of innocence and life that it refreshed Bernhard every day anew.

But today, on the first day of school after Christmas, all this activity gave him stomach cramps. He felt like the bear who had stolen the honey, and now the entire school was after him. With his coat collar pulled high around his neck, he dashed into the teacher's lounge. The room grew still as soon as he walked in. A few colleagues lowered their heads, while others hid busily behind their papers.

It was all right with him that hardly anyone attempted to express sympathy. His father's death was like a protective shield he could withdraw behind.

"My condolences," the director said with a pained look, shaking Bernhard's hand paternally. "It's impossible to express in words what one feels at a moment like this."

Bernhard nodded. But how had they found out?

Ruth rushed up to him and pulled him aside. "I was starting to worry because I hadn't heard anything from you all vacation. Then my sister told me; she saw the notice in the paper. Did you make it through the funeral all right?"

"Ah, the funeral was the least of it."

"Are you very sad?"

He shook his head. "No, honestly, I'm not."

She looked at him inquisitively, and then he realized he would be forced to continue. He bit down on his tongue.

"Well, what is it?"

He had known Ruth for fourteen years now. He had always thought of her as his best friend, and now he couldn't even tell her what he had been through in the last few days. Nothing about Edvard, the ring, the horrible images in his visions. "I have the most horrible headache. I think it might turn into a migraine," he said and turned away.

Ruth breathed a sigh of relief. "And here I was thinking you wanted to tell me something really awful."

"No," he said and moved away. "Look, I still have to prepare a few things. We'll see each other later, right?"

"Of course. Have a good start to school."

"You too."

It was ten to eight. The noise level rose, life in the hallways reached its peak, which could only be outdone by a fight or a new attractive student. This was the time Bernhard would usually set out on his way, walking very slowly to his classroom in order to soak up every minute of it. Today, he sat in the most remote corner and pulled a few papers from his briefcase so it would look as if he was working.

Ten minutes. The clock ticked, and the question that had been tormenting him for days swelled up in his head: how could he teach Nazi history after all he had learned in the last few weeks without touching on the horrible things that had been done to gay people? And how could he talk about it without giving himself away?

Bernhard had the impression that other people were drilling into him with their eyes. How would he feel, red in the face, reciting details from books he had read, books everyone tried to suppress? What would the kids tell their parents? What would the parents say to the principal? What would the principal say to him? In the end, they would all see through him.

He remembered the student teacher from last year that hadn't even attempted to hide his sexual orientation. His colleague's comments ran through his head, their harsh observations made in secret and his surprising departure, with a farewell party no one attended, not even himself.

It would be just the same with him. But he wouldn't have the strength to smile the way his colleague had. He wouldn't have the courage, he would be ashamed. If Bernhard thought about it properly, he was still wearing the pink triangle, and it was right in the middle of his forehead.

He stroked his head. How childish, he thought. On the other hand: if he was already wearing the pink triangle on his forehead, did he really need to try so desperately to conceal it?

How did the proverb go? If you think there's a ghost living in your house, then set an extra place for dinner.

"Ruth!"

She was already standing at the door with an ironclad chest, ready to accept the first helping of school frustration from her students.

"Yes?"

Bernhard clasped his briefcase under his arm and walked towards her.

"I have to tell you something I've been meaning to say for years."

42.

She woke up feeling as if she had bathed in roses. Her skin was warm and silky, the air sweet, her soul felt freshly cleansed.

Kim sat up in bed, pulling aside the egg-yellow curtain of the canopy bed and looking around her. The world had changed overnight: the light blue velour rug suddenly seemed to smell of lavender, the heavy curtains were now as light as cotton balls. Amazed, she crawled from her nest and walked around the apartment. Sunlight streamed in through the balcony door, transforming the wooden floor into a runway, and everything gleamed in gentle pastel tones, daubed on like pollen. From the courtyard, the refreshing laughter of the first café visitors rang out like the voices of an angel's choir, making Kim feel as if she were in the womb: soft and warm, surrounded by concentrated femininity.

Her own rooms, her own furniture, her own address, she had left that all behind seven years ago when she left the foster home. Since then she had traveled around, setting up camp here and there, moving on again quickly, most of the time even before the last boxes had been unpacked. She had felt constrained, reduced to an address and regimented by the neighbor's friendly looks. But today, in her friend's apartment, was the first time she felt something close to "at home."

The shower streamed over her head, over her shoulder and breasts, her thin, delicate hips. This being was growing in her womb, a manifestation of rape, a constant reminder of this scumbag of a man. The thought disgusted her; squeezing extra shower gel into her hand, she foamed herself up. Away, away, it had to go away.

She leaned her face into the stream of clear water and let it sprinkle over her. Soon she would be clean again. The pregnancy counselor had already given her the certificate, and within three days she would be able to have the abortion.

The telephone rang. Kim turned off the water and threw her bathrobe on.

"Yes, please?"

"Gisela here. I have it. We could do it this morning, right before Ilona starts her consultation here. Then we would have more peace and quiet. Do you have time?"

Kim hesitated for a minute. The thought of what they were scheming still made her feel unwell. They were planning to be dishonest, sneaky, conniving even. It wasn't right, but it felt incredibly good.

"All right, I'll be there in twenty minutes."

"See you soon."

"See you soon."

Kim rubbed herself dry with a hand towel. "We can only combat him with his own weapons," Gisela had said. It just needed to be well prepared: the consultation with Ilona was just to make it look convincing that she herself had been groped by her boss. Gisela would enter Kim into the office's appointment calendar and gleefully hand her husband Kim's medical chart to sign; that way they could prove her apparent presence. From there, Ilona would take care of everything: the complaint of rape, and the proof. The rest would be done by the DA's office.

Kim was shaking so much that she put her jeans on the wrong way round. She dressed with lightning speed, and then ran out into a new life.

Her steps were still uncertain as she left the building. At first, she believed she was only concerned with revenge, but that wasn't all. There was more behind it. True, her actions would help Gisela, but that wasn't it either. And it didn't have to with the justification she had convinced herself of for a long time, that she was doing it for all the women the doctor had mistreated, and all the others who had ever been mistreated by men.

Arriving at the office before Gisela's college friend Ilona, Kim climbed the stairs and pulled back the heavy front door. There was something dreamlike about the rooms, they were filled with light and ease; a soft music lent them an ethereal quality.

Ilona greeted her warmly; her natural manner was comforting. She was a strong, full-busted woman, with thick black hair and a round, red-cheeked face. As soon as the three of them stood together, something conspiratorial spread between them, and their femininity combined made them indomitable.

"Are you still sure?" asked Ilona, and Gisela nodded.

"Do you still have any doubts?" she asked Kim, who shook her head.

"Let's get this over with," said Kim, and disappeared into the changing room and undressed.

The ultra-sound device caught her eye. "Take your time to think it over," the pregnancy counselor had said. "Of course, under the current circumstances, you don't want the child. But wait a few days'; you won't lose anything that way. Don't forget that this child is not just a result of rape—it's also a part of you."

"Could I see anything yet?" Kim asked.

"What do you mean?"

"The...baby." Kim pointed to the ultrasound.

"How long has it been?"

"Two and a half weeks."

"Hardly, probably, but we can give it a try. Lie back on the chair, it will be more comfortable that way."

Ilona pulled the paper roll over the chair, and Kim lay down. Then the doctor spread some gel on Kim's belly and turned on the device.

"No, nothing there yet...or is there? Just a minute. Gisela, look over there, what do you think?"

"You mean the black spot?"

"Yeah." Both of them leaned their heads over the screen and pointed to the black streaks. Then Kim saw it. A circular spot, hardly bigger than a coin. It didn't have any clear shape yet.

"In a few days, you will be able to recognize the shape of its body."

It was just a black spot, but Kim loved it. She couldn't describe it, but it was as if a new spectrum of emotion had opened up within her overnight.

"Do you want a photo of it?" Ilona asked.

A photo? "No thank you." No reminders. A shudder ran through her chest.

"How do you actually perform the abortion?" asked Kim.

Both gynecologists looked at each other, then Gisela said in a markedly quieter voice: "The...baby is sucked out."

The tube took shape vividly in front of Kim's inner eye; she could already feel it inside her. At the push of a button, that small being would be removed, washed out like...she couldn't think of it anymore.

Kim looked at the two women and said: "I think we should start now."

Then she stood up and climbed onto the chair.

Two glass tubes stood on the shelf. One of them was filled with thick white liquid, the other with frizzy hair. They would mix them with Kim's vaginal secretions and prepare her mucus membrane for the medical examiner so that there would be no doubts in court. They had thought of everything, they wouldn't give him a chance. It wouldn't merely give grounds for divorce; they intended to remove him from his office so he could never mistreat another patient again. He had to lose his medical license; they would make sure of that.

Kim lay back and tried to relax. She could hardly wait for the day when this was all over: then she would finally be able to concentrate on her future. With a bit of luck, her friend would stay in L.A. longer and Kim could take over her apartment. She would make herself comfortable and take on a regular job instead of her stewardess job.

Kim flinched, something cool was touching her inner thigh.

"Sorry," said Ilona, and all three giggled.

This was no longer her, thought Kim. These thoughts were no longer the thoughts of dazed, chaotic Kim. They were a mother's thoughts.

She felt a tension in her breasts, as if they were swelling, and something twitched in her stomach. Kim crossed her arms and suddenly felt as if she were holding a baby. In her thoughts, she rocked it, comforted it, and gave it soft kisses. She stroked its head, pushed aside its delicate, fluffy hair, and looked deep in its eyes. And then it became clear to her why she was doing all this. Yes, it was revenge on that awful doctor, but it was also revenge on her father, who had never cared for her, who had pushed her away and left her alone. It was compensation for the fact that in this regard, she herself was an aborted child.

A jolt ran through her belly. "Ouch!"

The two women's heads appeared between her legs. "What's wrong? We haven't even touched you!"

"No, no, it's all right."

Abortion. With this word, the world grew dark again, and the ethereal tones were reduced to banal classical music, the furniture like that in any other doctor's office, and Kim was certain that when she went home now she wouldn't feel at home, the apartment would again look the way it had in recent days: just like any other.

"Take a look at your life," the pregnancy counselor had encouraged her. "How have you handled crises in the past?"

Abortion. What she was about to do to this child was what she had suffered from her whole life: being pushed away, unwanted, abandoned, and forgotten.

And that woman had also asked her: "Would a child change you for the better?"

Perhaps, through all the small changes it triggered in Kim's body, it was this little innocent soul helping her attain something she had always lacked: a family. Together with her daughter—Kim knew it was a girl!—things would be better, she could set up a life independent of men. And maybe, just maybe, she would invite a man to join her every now and then.

43.

On a quiet Sunday afternoon, the tourists directed their gazes up at rthe castle towering majestically over the city. But the Heidelbergers were overjoyed by the sky, which was letting its glad blue belly hang out of its gray nightshirt for the first time in weeks. The river toyed around with ice floes, driving them here and there, pushing them to the shore when they grew tiresome, where they basked in the sun.

In a living room, children stood at a window, having just eaten half a marble cake with whipped cream at their grandmother's house, pointing out to the street, at a woman who was occupied with something very different from marveling, watching, eating or freezing. She was headed for the cemetery.

In sky-blue moon boots, she tramped through the city. She wore a white anorak decorated with jolly pink snowflakes as large as children's fists, and a jaunty pom-pom hung from her hat. She walked carefully and slowly, as if she had to deliberate at every step. Her back was slightly bent, as if she were pulling a heavy sled behind her, but relief radiated from her face.

Slowly, she threaded a path between the graves, past the fountain and the chapel, the compost heap full of old wreaths. In the second row on the left, at the fourth grave from the cemetery wall, she stopped. The grave was fresh, the brown mound of earth only covered with a thin layer of snow. There were no rows of boxwood saplings yet, no pines thrusting against cedars, and the flowers on the wreaths had long been frozen. There was still no stone to testify to the life of the man who lay buried there—just a small, simple wooden cross with the initials *T.M.*

The woman crossed herself, folded her hands over her chest, clutching her rosary; her lips moved noiselessly. She stayed standing like this for several minutes, then knelt down, pulled the gold wedding ring from her finger, swept the snow aside and pressed the ring deep into the hard earth. She laid a hand over it, as she often had over her children's cuts and bruises. Then she turned her face to the sun and went back to the street.

Her fingers played with a note in her pocket. She didn't have to look at what it said; she had already read it over a hundred times. By now, she knew the text by heart. Silently, she recited it to herself like a prayer. Her steps grew faster and lighter and a close observer might almost have been able to see her skip:

Oldies are Goldies
Dance School for the Older Generation
Beginners always welcome
Saturday, 2 pm.
Friedrich-Ebert-St. 33

Outside the cemetery stood a pretty woman: tall, with short, white hair. Her face broke into a smile when they caught each other's eyes. They stretched out their hands to one another, linked arms and quickly walked away.

44.

The train to Heidelberg was delayed because of the sudden snow-storm, so Bernhard went to the train station's restaurant, wanting to put the waiting time to good use by eating a proper lunch.

As soon he slid open the door, the aroma of chicken soup, brown sauce and cigarette smoke washed over him. Most of the tables were occupied, but there was a table in the middle where a man sat alone.

"Is this seat taken?"

The other man shrugged his shoulders weakly and went on staring into his already half-empty beer glass. He was small but very strong, his pants were tight; the spurs of his cowboy boots clanged as he moved his legs back so that Bernhard could sit down.

Nice man, Bernhard thought, studying the menu, if only he would take better care of himself. His fingers were yellow with nicotine, and a blue mark stood out above his nose. A shower wouldn't hurt.

He would order roast pork - roast pork and sparkling cider. Bernhard laid his menu aside.

The man opposite him washed the rest of his beer down his throat, then watched foam run down the side of the glass onto the table. A mass of white bubbles, thick as saliva, ran down and grew longer until they reached the bottom, spreading out evenly, pushing into a circle and finally forming a beautiful ring.

The drinker pressed his lips into a pout and nodded. "The problem is…," he began, grabbing the string tie holding together his wide-open denim shirt, "A ring is just a ring. But the desires, hopes, and the memories people connect to them are very diverse." With strenuous effort, his tongue formed the words: "Waiter, a beer!"

"I'm sorry, what did you just say?" asked Bernhard.

The guy tried hard to focus his eyes. "If she hadn't given me this ring, I would still be happy. But that damn ring! It turned everything upside down. Stupid cow!" He shook his head again. "Waiter, a beer!"

Bernhard looked around: there was no waiter to be seen far and wide.

"I never really hurt anyone, you understand. Never!" the man continued. "They always got what they wanted." He lifted a finger menacingly. "Then that dumb cow gives me a ring and ruins everything."

"You must be attached to this woman?"

The man nodded.

"Why can't you just tell her?"

"Because I left her."

"Left?"

"She would never forgive me," he whispered confidingly, propping his chin up on his short, thick thumbs.

It was obvious that he was horribly drunk. Bernhard didn't know if the man really felt regret, or if he was just raving.

"Well, have you tried?"

He shook his head.

"Then you should try, otherwise you will never find out. If she really loves you, she'll forgive everything, no matter what it is."

"Do you really think so?"

Bernhard nodded, then the waiter came and both of them ordered.

Arriving in Heidelberg, Bernhard walked straight across the city to the cemetery. Because of the delay, it was already almost dark, and he wanted to make it to the grave before it grew dark. Afterwards, he would go and see his mother.

Bernhard still couldn't forgive his father, though he conceded the possibility that he might not have been able to act any other way. Maybe a man who has experienced the horrors of war has to withdraw within himself in order to survive. To forgive him, Bernhard would have had to forget what his father had done to him, but that was very difficult.

"What are you holding to?" his mother asked him, but it didn't have anything to do with holding on, did it? It had actually happened. His father had treated him badly, he had always put him down, he had never hugged him.

"Happened, didn't happen," Lydia had answered him. "It doesn't matter what happened. What's important is what you remember. If we were to talk about the past, you would have very different memories than I would. Who knows what actually happened? Think up new memories; create a new past for yourself."

"But that's a lie."

"No, it's not a lie. It's just the other side of the coin of freedom. Your negative feelings hold you down. If your past was miserable, why should the future be that way as well?"

And then she had sent him a letter with a calendar sheet. *To feel compassion is one of the greatest gifts. That's why Tibetans say that a beggar asking for money or an old sick woman who touches your heart could be Buddhas in disguise. They come into contact with you to make your compassion grow and allow you to come closer to Buddhahood.*

The sun was about to sink below the cemetery wall when Bernhard reached his father's grave.

"There was so much I wanted to tell you, and now I can't think of anything." Bernhard pushed a bit of snow aside with his boots and built a little wall.

It was just as before. They had nothing to say to one another. But had his father ever thought as much about Bernhard as he had thought about his father in the past weeks?

An old woman slipped past behind him. Her face was serious, her back bent down by life.

"I always wished I could talk to you. Like father and son, or man to man. I wanted to tell you that I'm gay. But because I was afraid of you, you found out in a different way. That wasn't good. I'm sorry."

From over the wall, some of the traffic noise reached him. Bernhard looked around. The woman was gathering up fir boughs. She was at least fifty yards away and concentrated deeply immersed in her task, but Bernhard still lowered his voice before speaking further.

"And I'm sorry that I never fit in with your idea of what a son should be. I'm not sorry I'm homosexual, but I wish I could have spared you the shock you felt when you found out. I can imagine well what it was like for you, believe me; for a long time, I was ashamed of myself, I disgusted and rejected myself."

Bernhard looked over at the old woman again. She was lighting a candle.

"And maybe you wondered what you did wrong. Whether it was your fault that I turned out the way I did. Well, rest assured. If you had anything to do with it, I would thank you for it now."

Bernhard paused for a long time. He thought about whether he had said everything. His fingers found his father's wedding ring, which he had been wearing since the flight back from Miami. A piece of cold metal, a small band with a long history. More than forty years Theo had worn it on his hand. In his store, while eating, in bed. His heart attacks, the alcohol, his thoughts; this ring had experienced every second of his life along with him.

Bernhard kneeled down. "I'd like to give this back to you," he said. "It's yours, it doesn't belong to me."

There was already a circular spot where the soil was raised; Bernhard wanted to put the ring next to it on the grave, so he scraped a bit of snow aside.

Now it looked as if two large, brown eyes were looking up at him from the depths, full of secrets, calm and silence.

Bernhard pressed the ring deep into the soil. He didn't know how he would explain it to his mother, but he was doing the right thing, he was sure of that. And then the New Year's prophecy occurred to him again: "An old relationship will dissolve, a new one will form."

Bernhard pulled Edvard's ring from his pocket. For days he had carried it around with him, wanting to have it with him, but he had never dared put it on. It was much heavier than his parents' wedding ring, and despite the biting cold which became almost unbearable that evening, the ring radiated an incredible warmth.

"Now I think I know where I belong. For months, I lay next to this man in bed. I kissed him and caressed him, but my heart was never really open to him."

The image of the young soldier appeared to him again, his resolute eyes, the loyalty and fellowship they expressed.

"I think I'm ready," Bernhard said and put on the ring. A sense of well-being spread from his fingers up to his chest, and his field of vision suddenly grew narrower. Fear again? That panic and horror, those horrible images that wouldn't leave him alone? No, not at all. He was looking through a tunnel at a white, blazing light. He saw a soldier with dark hair. He was young, he looked happy and fresh, and he bore a great similarity to Bernhard. He was holding the blond soldier by the hand, whose temples were so thin they seemed to reveal his thoughts.

A sharp pain shot through Bernhard's wound and raced up to his heart. He lifted his hand up to the light and regarded it. The wound was healing slowly, but it was healing.

A scar would remain—and that was how it should be.

EPILOGUE

When one knows one will die soon, it makes one think about life differently.

On a Wednesday in September, Theo sat on the balcony, and suddenly it was no longer important to him whether his favorite soccer team would beat Hamburg's in the next match. He was no longer interested in the fact that property taxes would be raised in the next year, or that the falling leaves were clogging the gutters again. It all mattered so little to him that he had even taken up smoking again.

But what *was* still important now?

Lydia appeared in the door behind him, wanting to know what the doctor had said about the pain. How had he assessed his blood pressure, and had he prescribed new medicine? But Theo didn't answer. He let his cigarette burn down, the smoke swirling around in playful gusts until the ashes fell to the floor only a few inches from his beer bottle, scattering over the brown floorboards. In the end, it wasn't important what the doctor said, and medicines couldn't help him either.

Theo no longer wanted to be friendly to people who had never meant anything to him, not even to his wife, to whom he had been married for countless years. He wanted to think, he wanted to be alone, and he had to hurry. So he remained silent until Lydia left again.

In recent years, he had often been afraid of dying. But now, sitting on his balcony among autumn leaves dancing in a capricious breeze, he even felt a bit relieved. No more cold, no more winter, no more snow. No more of the revulsion that came over him when he felt that white moisture on his skin. He only hoped that death would come for him soon; if not, he would have to escape. To Mallorca perhaps, Tenerife, or somewhere warmer, somewhere farther away from winter.

And then he thought of something else he had to do. Theo flicked his cigarette butt down onto the rosebush, which he had arduously freed of withered leaves just that morning, and went into the bedroom. Opening his nightstand, he pulled out a long, hand-carved box and opened it.

All his life, Theo had felt as if someone was watching him. By day, his customers swarmed around him like flies; in his little free time his family had clung to him. There had never been a place for him, a moment that belonged to him alone. This box was all the privacy he had ever had.

He took the naked ivory woman in his hand. She lay cool and smooth in his hand, and within seconds she reminded him of one of the most difficult moments of his life: 1953. Theo had taken in the young, pregnant Lydia. For three years now, she had been looking after the household; he had shared many days with her. He had noticed her furtive glances, and several times she had undressed when she knew Theo was nearby. But it hadn't sparked anything in him, no desire, no arousal, no need to touch her face or even her breasts. This "not-feeling" tormented him. He should have at least felt something.

Back then, Maria lived at the end of Bergstrasse. The whole village talked badly of her, because she was apparently an "easy woman." Nevertheless, lots of men could be seen 'taking walks' around her house every evening. When the garden light was on, you could visit her—though it only stayed lit for minutes at a time.

Out of desperation, Theo had gone to her. He thought he could learn arousal, learn to love a woman. Maybe it was all just a question of experience. But when she had pressed him to her large, soft bosom, he had only cried. As a farewell, she gave him a kiss on the forehead and the ivory woman.

Theo put it back in place next to Ludwig's baby tooth. He didn't know why he had kept it. Now it was as irrelevant as the memory of his Bavarian friend Gustl who had bequeathed him the pack of snuff or the mussels his children had collected by the bagful when they were on vacation. The only thing that still interested him was the ring.

It lay there, brightly polished, as if no one had ever worn it. Theo held it up in the pale autumn light. Not much remained of what had persecuted him his whole life long: a slight pulling in his throat, a pressure in his neck and this tightness in his chest.

Theo put on the ring. Back then, back then there had been more. A shadow, heavy and black though it was only morning, when he crawled out of bed. It followed him into the store, clung to him when he chatted with the regulars about their health, approached him in his TV chair and sat among his children while the family sat at the dinner table in the evening scarfing down roast pork. At one point in time, the shadow was so much a part of him that it had felt like a Siamese twin.

In the beginning, he had tried desperately to escape. He had actually taken in the young Lydia and her infant because he hoped the cry of a child would chase the shadow away. But even one's own children couldn't help drive death away.

"How can you undo what has happened?" he had asked a priest, back when he still hoped the church could free him from his past. "How can you make good what you've done, what you didn't do?" But all his Ave Marias faded away in the hollow space between fear and guilt.

Theo went back out onto the balcony. Over the years, his persecutor had gotten thinner, lighter and paler, but had never left him. Even though he had been invisible for years now, Theo could still feel his presence. And now that the doctor had warned him that any little thing, a tiny shock, even a harmless cough could cause his dangerously widened aorta to burst, he intended to face this shadow again.

Theo drank another sip of his beer, fished another cigarette from the box and lit it. He sat back, looked into the distance, over the meadow, the river, the houses on the other side of the city, past the horizon, deep into his past.

December 1944. Snow blinds the world with its insidious beauty. Theo and his comrades lie surrounded by the enemy in a trench in Alsace. For days there has been nothing to eat but brown bread and snow; it still tastes sweet.

They cower together, pressing close to one another to stay warm. Lots of shaking, but not because of the cold. Most of them have already resigned themselves to death the evening before. They were certain the enemy would take them out in one strike. All night long they have been waiting for death, smoking and waiting, passing around one cigarette after the other. It was like a counting rhyme, but no one knew if the one who took the last drag would be the first one to die or the only one to survive.

Theo's eyes keep wandering over to Philipp, the beautiful private. He wants to reach out his hand, like last night. He would like to pull him close to his chest, feel his warmth, melt into him, but that was not allowed. No one may know of their love.

Their eyes keep meeting, weaving a bond of desire as delicate as a spider web, yet enduring as steel. They feel their way along it to each other, crawling through each other's eyes into their souls, cradled in the memory of last night when, instead of keeping watch, they made love. Carefully, their hands explored each other's bodies, caressing each other softly. They lost themselves in each other's touch, escaped the madness, covered up their fear of death. At first they thought it was the enemy driving them to this act, that it was war. But now, as they look over their comrades' heads into each other's eyes, they understand it can only be love that brought them together.

Then they hear shots. Tanks are scraping towards their unit. Bombs explode, and cries of victory fill the clearing.

"We've been saved!" some of them cry. "They're here, they've finally arrived."

Philipp takes advantage of this moment of confusion to draw close to Theo. "Here, take this," he whispers, putting a beautiful ring on his finger. "It's the ring of lovers. Take it and wear it, no matter what happens."

One kiss and their love was sealed.

They had driven the enemy far back and decided set up a new base. Tents were pitched around the trenches, a kitchen and an arms store; SS officers came to visit to praise their bravery, congratulate them and boost morale.

But someone had seen them and betrayed them, Philipp had been identified. Theo stands there as he is pulled from the lines and denounced for apparently besmirching the honor of the troop and leading his comrades astray.

They pillory him right there in the clearing, beat and torture him in front of the company, making an example of him and attempting to beat his lover's name out of him. But his eyes only speak words of love, which no one can understand—no one but Theo.

Again and again they are forced to line up and endure this tribunal until Philipp is sent to a place where he has been waiting for Theo ever since.

Until that day, snow had always been something holy for Theo. It came from the sky, it was light and innocent, it laid a white, smooth covering over the earth. As a child he had played at catching large flakes and collecting them on his scarf. Packing the dust-fine crystals into heavy balls was an art to him, throwing them at windowpanes, and he loved to slide down snowy hills until the seat of his pants was frozen solid.

But ever since he saw Philipp's blood seep into the snow, freezing into dark hard lumps he had to trample for days, until it melted mercifully in spring, ever since then snow had filled him with horror and disgust.

Theo shook himself. The coldness of that memory had settled over him again. His chest had grown tighter, his throat so constricted that he could barely breathe.

The cigarette in his hand had burned down to the filter. The glowing red sun sank down into the canopy of a maple tree, and the wind snatched at his warmth. Theo let the butt fall into his empty beer bottle.

He felt that love again, the entirely innocent blameless love he had felt back then. He still remembered exactly what paths his hands had taken. He still remembered the way Philipp's breath had smelled of apples, the sweet smell of his skin, and he had never forgotten the blue of his eyes.

Theo turned the ring around. By now, the sky had grown dark, but the ring was glowing. This piece of metal harbored a beautiful, terrible secret. Everything that had happened back then was connected to the ring. He couldn't leave it behind. When he died, no one must inherit it. He was afraid that if it fell into his family's hands, the same fate would be repeated. At all costs, he had to avoid that.

But he couldn't destroy it. Throw it away? Submerge it in the river? His heart flinched at the thought of betraying his one love. All he could do was pass it on, but to whom? Or he could sell it, but not in Heidelberg. Too many people knew him here. Then he thought of the antique store behind Maximilianstrasse, the one he had passed on a walk through Munich after his examination at the heart clinic. None of his children cared about antiques. The ring would be safe there.

An angelically bright bell rang as Theo entered. A young man stood behind the store counter, much too young and beautiful to be an antique seller. He had such a trustworthy, charming smile that Theo's last fears dissolved.

"You must be careful," he said to the young man, looking deep into his eyes. "This is the Ring of Lovers. Think hard before you give it away."

Pale memories all that remain;
a life
blurred and near forgotten,
hardly more than a dream.

You wished
it would last forever,
and Death, which you could already smell,
could seek another.

"One more adieu," you begged, "one see-you-later."
There's so much you'll never see again.
"Once more the sun, one more tomorrow,"
as if life were something you could borrow.

"If I could do it all again," you said,
"I'd do it better;
and the days I rapidly forgot,
I'd hold, cling to, and fetter,
I'd do everything to persuade
them never ever more to fade."

Memories like
pale and distant lights.
A life
blurred and near forgotten
and love – which transmutes
and like yearning
breaks at your lips –
calamity refutes.

Acknowledgements

Thank you, thank you, thank you. There are many people I need to thank for their help with this book. You know who you are. But most of all I must thank my family, because that which my grandparents, parents, my brother and my sisters lived through forms the core of this novel. I would like to thank Jim Baker, my first editor and publisher, for believing in this book, so much that he worked with me on it until it became a best-selling novel in Germany. And I would like to thank my husband Michael—for life is just so much more fun with you by my side.